"*The Winter Loon* is a compelling ⌇⌇⌇⌇ ⌇⌇ ⌇⌇⌇⌇⌇⌇⌇ ⌇⌇⌇⌇⌇⌇⌇ choices and courage. Both tender and wise, Henriksen is a fine story teller and her characters are skillfully drawn and memorable."

—*Sandra Butler*
Award-winning writer, group facilitator and activist
www.sandrabutler.net and www.motheringdaughters.net.

"This is an ambitious, gripping, often painful story with a lot of drama and emotion, ups and downs and an ending that leaves the reader in satisfying tears."

—*Alan Rinzler*
Consulting Editor,
www.alanrinzler.com

"What a beautiful, thoughtful book. *The Winter Loon* offers up complex characters and issues, a multi-textured plot and lots of heart. I have felt wrapped in the cocoon of this beautiful love story."

—*Alissa Lukara*
Writing Mentor, Editor,
Author of Riding Grace: A Triumph of the Soul.
www.transformationalwriters.com

"*The Winter Loon* is the literary equivalent of the long slow opening of the loveliest of corollas in harsh environs. It is the quintessential love story of our times."

—*Stephen Victor*
Coach: Cultivating Human Promise
www.stephenvictor.com.

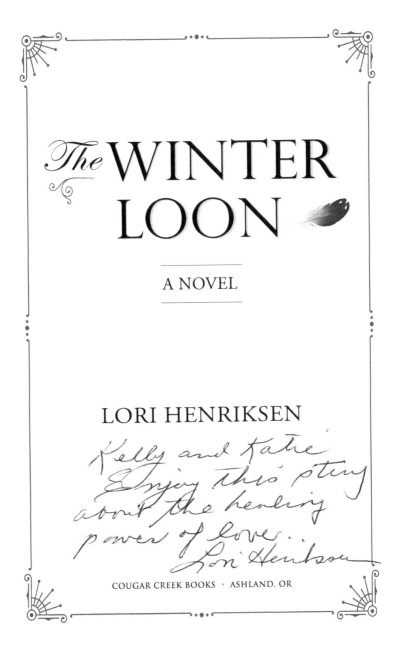

The WINTER LOON

A NOVEL

LORI HENRIKSEN

Kelly and Katie
Enjoy this story
about the healing
power of love.
Lori Henriksen

COUGAR CREEK BOOKS · ASHLAND, OR

The Winter Loon
Copyright © 2017 Lori Henriksen

Library of Congress Control Number: 2017908332
ISBN 978-0-9977406-0-8 (pbk) 978-0-9977406-1-5 (ebook)

The characters and events in this book are fictitious. Any similarity to real
persons, living or dead, is coincidental and not intended by the author.

Printed in the United States of America
Set in Palatino with Bodoni ornaments

Cover by Chris Molé, Book Savvy Studio
Book design by Maggie McLaughlin

 COUGAR CREEK BOOKS
cougarcreekbooks.com

In memory of Anna-Kajs Johnson
Activist and Friend

March 21, 1926 – April 3, 2016

Being deeply loved by someone gives you strength,
while loving someone deeply gives you courage.

– Lao Tzu

ONE

On a chilly spring day in 1931 my cousin Chloe and I, along with a cowboy called Mac, headed to our first host ranch on a rodeo circuit. At the Billings, Montana train station the conductor's shrill whistle and shout of "All aboard!" reverberated over the commotion of the crowd. Steam spewed from the pistons of the waiting engine. Bits of coal dust caught in my throat as Chloe and I hurried to keep up with Mac.

I brushed a few cinders off my clothes and climbed the three steps onto the train. We settled into our seats, Chloe and Mac facing me as the train rolled out of the station toward Wyoming.

No turning back now.

Shortly after the train gathered speed, Chloe started to complain.

"It's too stuffy in here and too many people," she said. She pushed out her lower lip in a pout. "Let's move. I'm dying here."

"You're not dying, darlin'," Mac rolled his eyes and crossed his arms over his chest.

"Oh yeah. I just might, and then where would you be?" She slugged him in his bicep. I doubted he even felt it.

Chloe and I had been friends from the first time we met at age six. We were cousins, but couldn't have been more different. I had light hazel eyes and auburn hair, chestnut like my horse Satin Dancer's flanks. I guessed that with her black hair and dark eyes, Chloe resembled her mother, who had died of consumption shortly after she was born. Chloe's dad had raised her to be tough and bold, while I tended to be more cautious and circumspect.

Chloe had been sweet on Mac since the two of us worked alongside the ranch hands on several cattle drives with her father Michael, my mother's brother, so Mac knew we were strong riders. He'd made all the arrangements for our transportation, competition, and lodging. His daddy owned a big ranch south of Billings and was fronting the money for all three of us.

I silently agreed with Chloe. The windows were closed against the outside chill, and we had ended up in the first car behind the engine. It could have been the heat from the coal burner making it so warm inside that they collected their belongings and left to find a less crowded car. *So what?* I didn't mind a bit, having tired of their boring banter.

With a whole seat to myself, I preferred staring out the window at the sagebrush that had been buffeted into odd shapes, unable to escape the prairie winds. The click of metal wheels on the tracks repeated: *Free. I'm free. Free. I'm free. Free. I'm free.*

I'd stepped off the edge of my world without knowing where I would end up. Me, Ruth Thompson, age eighteen, a chambermaid turned gypsy cowgirl.

The Great Depression had pushed us all to our limits, closing things down, including hearts and minds. Everyone was scrambling to earn money any way they could to stay out of soup kitchen lines, and for me the rodeo circuit meant no more weary shifts cleaning rooms at the Nicolet Hotel in Minneapolis. No more paltry paychecks, dashing my dream of saving enough money for college tuition. And the bonus, no more feeling trapped by the expectation of my family that I marry my sweetheart, Duke. Sure I missed and loved him, but I didn't want to get married. I had never pictured myself wearing the white dress, ending up a wife and mother.

Duke and I hadn't discussed marriage—a logical step into our future—although we'd been inseparable since age thirteen. He was sensitive, smart, and an accomplished artist with a goal of becoming an engineer. When I asked why he chose engineering, he'd pushed his reddish blond hair off his forehead in a familiar gesture and with an intense look in his clear green eyes answered, "I want to build bridges."

Later in the day, I subdued my hunger gnawing on strips of beef jerky and chunks of hard cheese, pungent and oily, cut with my penknife. My buttocks, sore from relentless practice directed by Mac for the last few months, chafed on the wooden seat. I recalled the day he had explained his plan to teach us the basics of barrel racing and said, "Let's just say you gals are going to be a hobby of mine." Chloe had laughed and declared, "You're a lucky cowboy."

I'd pushed away my discomfort and laughed along with the two of them. The grueling practice sessions didn't bother me. All I cared about was spending my time with Satin Dancer, and the harmony of the two of us together all day, every day.

For the time being I ignored my aches, folded my jacket to use as a pillow, and soon fell asleep to the train's rocking cadence.

We stopped in Casper, Wyoming to pick up more riders. Rodeo folk milled around, securing their horses in the stock cars before boarding the train. I got off to check on Satin Dancer, who greeted me with a whinny and nuzzled her thanks for the fresh oats I added to the feedbag in her makeshift stall. Satisfied with her comfort, I left to search for Chloe and Mac.

I found them asleep in a car near the rear of the train. Mac's chin rested on his chest and his hat was pulled down to cover his eyes. His feet, still in his boots, were propped up on the seat facing them. Chloe, her petite body curled like a snail, rested her head on his shoulder. The noisy shuffle of people boarding the train and throwing bags into the overhead rack didn't seem to disturb them.

The smell of food lured me outside to the throng of vendors selling fresh meat sandwiches and hot soup. I bought a hunk of crusty bread from an old woman who filled my tin cup with strong black coffee and charged me a nickel.

I drank the coffee and climbed aboard the train, taking a different seat in order to leave our old ones for a foursome of new passengers. Without Chloe and Mac to keep me company, I pulled a book out of my bag and settled in next to the window, but the noisy greetings of rodeo folk filling the train car had a festive air that distracted my attention, and I closed the book after reading the same couple of sentences several times. As I looked up, a woman wearing a black cowboy hat and loose pants tucked into red boots walked down the aisle. She waved and called hello to a few people, then stopped next to me.

"This taken?" she asked in a gravelly voice.

I shifted my body closer to the window. A loon feather hooked in the band of her hat tickled my arm when she reached down to push a small bag underneath the seat in front of us.

"I'm Rollie Denton. Been on this rodeo circuit more times than I care to admit." She took off her hat and placed it in the overhead rack.

The black and white feather reminded me of home. The loons would be mating now, soon gliding across the water with chicks on their backs. I pictured Mother out on the lake in her rowboat, fishing for walleye. The image of her at the stove, fish sizzling in the pan, made my mouth water and I resolved not to be homesick.

I introduced myself and said, "This is my first rodeo."

"I thought so. Welcome." She reached out to shake my hand.

"How can you tell?"

"Sometimes you know things." The leathery skin around her eyes crinkled when she smiled. "Besides, everyone else is either playing cards or having fun, talking and laughing, catching up on things. You're sitting here all by your lonesome, reading a book."

"I'm here with my cousin and her fella. He's our sponsor. They moved to another car."

She grimaced. I could swear she rolled her eyes, and I wondered why my comment had bothered her. She excused herself and left to chat with a few people I guessed she knew. She returned when the train began to labor, chugging and grinding as the terrain grew more mountainous.

"We're climbing into the alpine desert. It'll be colder soon, especially at night. What're you reading?"

"*Anna Karenina.*" Happy for her interest in my favorite book, I wanted to talk with her about it.

"Never heard of it. Sure is thick."

A little later I heard a snort and saw she had fallen asleep. I held still, not wanting to disturb her. Her face looked as if it had been sculpted by the wind and sun, its many lines giving her the wise appearance of someone who could take care of herself.

After a while the train slowed to a crawl, and the change in pace woke Rollie.

"We're getting close to our stop." She stretched her neck

from side to side. "It always seems that old engine won't make the climb."

I wanted to learn more about her. "You must know a lot of people on this train."

"I do. Every year I get tired of listening to the same old stories, lies, and bull." She let out a hearty laugh.

I struggled to keep the conversation going. "Where're you from?"

"Here, there, and everywhere. I don't call anywhere home."

"I'm from Minnesota, near Minneapolis."

"Been out to Minnesota. Rode a bronc at the Fort Snelling rodeo a few years ago, before they pushed us gals out from competing on the bucking stock at the big rodeos."

"You mean because of Bonnie McCarroll?" I knew from reading Chloe's rodeo magazines that she had been fatally trampled, and rodeo rules had changed for women because of it.

"Yeah. Now we're mostly confined to barrel racing, trick riding, and relays. She had nerves of steel."

"You miss riding broncos?"

"My body doesn't miss the wear and tear, but I do miss the thrill." She closed her eyes and thought for a second, as if deciding to say more. "We're cheap entertainment on this small circuit. We bend the rules from time to time."

"Come on. I'm going to get my stuff together. We'll be there in about ten minutes. All hell breaks loose soon as we arrive, so it's best to get off first."

Rollie walked down the aisle, reached into the overhead rack without needing to stretch, and swung her bag down. She gestured for me to join her.

With my book tucked under my arm I grabbed my duffel and hastened to where Rollie steadied herself against the seat next to the exit.

The train lurched, brakes squealing, and came to a stop.

"Where are we?" I asked her.

"Middle of nowhere. Closest town is Douglas, Wyoming."

A powerful, cold wind almost knocked me down as I stepped off the train. Pinpricks of sand stung my cheeks and stuck in my hair. I trotted along the length of the train searching for Chloe and Mac, but didn't see them. Nervous sweat dampened my underarms. I lost sight of Rollie as people pushed past without seeming to notice me, and had to watch my step to avoid patches of snow that had been trampled to mud.

Then someone grabbed my arm, and I whirled around as Rollie pulled me aside. "Something wrong?"

"No. Well, I don't know, I can't find my cousin or my sponsor."

"Don't fret. We'll all end up in the same place. You can find them at the ranch. There's no way to get anywhere else." She nodded at my book. "Maybe you should put that in your duffel."

Cowboys on horseback rounded up cattle, making their way down ramps from the animal cars. Black and white dogs, their noses close to the ground, wove in and out, yipping and nipping the livestock into paddocks set up near the tracks. The crowd swarmed around us. Wind and the stench from the livestock made me dizzy. I stumbled and Rollie caught my arm to steady me.

"Toss your gear in the trucks," a cowboy shouted. "We'll sort it out when we get to the ranch."

"Damn, it's the same every year," Rollie said from behind me. "They treat us like them cows out there. Come on. Let's get our horses."

She led the way and pointed out a line of Ford flatbed trucks, many of them hitched to horse trailers.

"The ranch hands from our host, the Settle R, leave those trucks over there for us to load up. I claim one so I can keep track of my stuff. They'll either catch a ride with one of us or herd the stock from the train to the ranch on horseback."

By then the wind carrying the sweet dusty fragrance of sage stung my nose and had whipped my curly hair into a tangled mess. Rollie hung on to her hat with her free hand, I'd left mine tied to my saddle in the tack car.

As Rollie headed toward the rear of the train where the horses were unloading I hurried to keep up with her long stride, then spotted Satin Dancer in one of the paddocks.

"Give me your bag. We'll take the truck third in line. The only way to claim it is to grab the key they leave in the ignition." Rollie dashed away toward the trucks, leaving me alone. I attached a short leather strap to Satin D's bridle and zigzagged through the crowd, doing my best to keep up.

Rollie stopped and spun around. "Hey, Sue Ann," she yelled above the commotion to a woman heading toward the vehicles. "Good to see ya, girl. Come on." She waved toward the truck. "Ride with us."

They shook hands and exchanged greetings. "Stay with the rig," Rollie told Sue Ann.

"She's been through this as many times as I have," Rollie declared as she turned toward me. "Let her hang on to your horse. We need to get our saddles and the rest of our stuff and load the flatbed."

Hating to leave Satin Dancer, but having no choice, I handed the strap to Sue Ann and followed Rollie.

I found my saddle and relieved to see my hat, crammed it on my head, securing the tie under my chin. Carrying our gear, we wended our way through the crowd to the truck Rollie had selected where we retrieved Satin D and Rollie's horse, a sorrel gelding named Hornet. I led the horses into the open-air trailer while Rollie grabbed the rest of our belongings.

The two of us waited in the truck while Sue Ann got her things and led her horse into the trailer in front of us. When she squeezed into the small cab, her ample body barely left enough room for me.

With Rollie driving we headed west, squinting into the setting sun. The gravel road ran along a creek lined with cottonwoods, their branches bending in the wind.

"Does it always blow this hard?" I shouted over the roar of the engine.

"It does most days." Rollie shifted gears on an incline. "Some folks have a real hard time with it."

Sue Ann pulled a pouch of tobacco and a tin holding rolling papers out of her pocket. With expert fingers, she placed a pinch of tobacco in the crease of the paper, rolled it, lit it, and passed it over me to Rollie. She started another. "Want it?"

"No thanks." I shook my head.

"How old are you?"

"Nineteen" I answered, fudging more than a year to impress her. "I'll be twenty in July." I had trouble catching my breath and coughed. It could have been from the cigarette smoke filling the cab of the truck, the dust in the wind, or maybe it was due to my lie.

"It's the altitude, honey. We're above five thousand feet. The air's thinner." Sue Ann handed me her canteen. "Here, drink some of this. You'll get used to it if you remember to drink enough water."

What would my family think if they could see me bouncing along in a beat up old truck between these two seasoned cowgirls? When my brother Hal, six years older than me, learned I'd joined a rodeo he had bitterly objected. "My sister running all over the country on a horse playing cowboys and Indians, how do you think that's going to reflect on our family?"

But it sure didn't seem fair that he had everything *he* wanted—a college degree, a fiancée, and a job in Dad's office that had paid his college tuition.

"I need to earn enough money so I can go to university like you and Duke."

I'd squirmed under the gaze of his dark hazel eyes, always so curious and probing behind his thick glasses. "I want to study psychology. Times have changed. I can't earn enough as a chambermaid, and there's not enough money for Dad to help me." I'd thought that for sure he'd approve of me earning my own money to go to school, especially since he'd met his fiancée, Dorothy, at college.

"What about Duke? You two are always together. We thought . . ."

"We're not engaged. I need to get away for a while."

He ignored what I wanted and said, "I've always known that horse was a mistake, and Mother taking you out to Montana every summer. You should stay home. Help her run the house."

The memory of our conversation still annoyed me.

I downed a slug of water from Sue Ann's canteen and passed it back to her.

Within an hour we arrived at the entrance to our host ranch, where whitewashed letters spelling "Settle R" formed an arch over open gates. The ranch sprawled in several directions and was dotted with two bunkhouses, a couple of barns, and several corrals and pastures. A large white farmhouse surrounded by oaks sat off by itself. We piled out of the truck in a bare area not far from the horse barn.

I clucked to Satin Dancer and Hornet, encouraging them to back out of the trailer. The horses shook out their manes and stomped the ground with their hooves, testing their freedom. I left them side by side, necks stretched to the ground as they sampled the grass.

Sue Ann also corralled her horse, and then headed in the direction of the bunkhouse.

Rollie waved to her. "We won't see much of Sue Ann," she said to me. "She'll find herself a cowboy in no time."

Rollie and I carried our saddles to the barn. "I stay away from the cowboys, and if you're smart, you will, too. If you let 'em, they'll be all over you like ants on a honeypot." She laughed and gave my arm a gentle punch as if we were old friends.

"I've got a beau at home. I'm here to ride." I took the shovel she handed me and tackled the horse trailer. I shoveled and swept the straw into the wheelbarrow and she dumped it behind the barn.

"I like the way you handle horses and can't believe you're a sponsor girl." She shook her head and walked ahead of me toward the bunkhouse.

Wondering what she meant, I grabbed my bag and followed. What could be wrong with having a sponsor? She made it sound irritating or shameful.

Two

A musty odor oozed from the wooden floorboards and bare walls inside the dimly lit interior of the bunkhouse. Tiny particles of dust sparkled in the waning sunlight filtering in from a few small windows and the open door. Kerosene lanterns waited to brighten the room after dark. I chose a bed across from Rollie as a couple of other cowgirls tossed their bags onto nearby beds, and left right away. Chloe still hadn't shown up, and Rollie hadn't said anything to me since we'd unloaded the horses and cleaned the trailer.

I had nothing to lose, so I thought I'd try to explain. "I wouldn't even be here if Mac, my sponsor, hadn't put up the money."

"You mean he's paying your way?"

"Well, sort of. He pays the fees for the contests and rodeos and will take part of my winnings. Chloe's, too."

"How's he know how much to take?"

"He's going to hold onto the money for us. We'll split it up at the end of the circuit."

"Keep the money for you?" She sounded incredulous. She shook out the thin blanket folded at the foot of her bed. "I hope he's honest."

"He's also arranged for us to work in the kitchen for our room and board at all the host ranches." I followed her lead and made up my bed with the rough sheets and hard pillow.

"That so? I should of known. Sponsor girls don't ride the rails, they're too rich to mingle with us cowgirls, and way more glamorous than qualified in their fancy riding clothes."

My face burned. The misunderstanding had almost cost me my first friendship on the circuit.

"Come on, let's clean up for supper," Rollie said.

The washroom had a crude wooden floor and walls dank with the smell of sweaty ranch hands and rancid tallow soap. I dipped a ladle into the barrel of water provided and filled a tin basin. The rough conditions were actually a step up from my time on the roundups where Chloe and I slept on the ground and had sometimes gone a week without bathing.

I splashed cool water on my face and scrubbed the grime off my hands. Even though I prided myself much more on my riding ability than my appearance, I enjoyed being mistaken for someone who could be thought of as glamorous. I ran my finger down my long nose, my worst feature, so prominent no one could miss it. My hair went rogue without constant taming, but now that I was a real cowgirl I could squash it down with my hat.

"Let's go before the food's all gone," Rollie called from the main room.

"I'm famished." I grabbed my jacket and followed her.

We headed up a gravel road toward the farmhouse. The wind had almost completely stopped, and I asked Rollie about it.

"This whole ranch is tucked in its own valley and somewhat more protected than the plains."

I noticed a couple walking ahead of us. "There's my cousin and Mac," I said to Rollie. "Let me introduce you."

Mac had his arm around Chloe's shoulders and she leaned into him while they sauntered toward the dining area set up outside the ranch house. She'd braided her black hair into two plaits, and even with the heels on her boots the top of her head barely brushed Mac's armpits.

"She sure looks tiny tucked up under his arm. How're her riding skills?"

"She's been riding since before she could walk. She's fearless. Been doing it forever."

Relieved to see them both, I shouted "Hey Chloe."

She turned, but Mac kept walking and shoved his hands in his pockets.

"You go on. I'll get us a place at one of the tables," Rollie said, ignoring the invitation to be introduced. Disappointed that she didn't seem interested in meeting Chloe, I just nodded.

"You okay?" Chloe asked when I caught up to her. "We lost track of you."

"I'm fine. I met a cowgirl who's been showing me the ropes."

"Yeah. Mac and I noticed. You'd be better off finding yourself a handsome cowboy like Mac."

I didn't say anything. Mac's arrogant manner, handlebar mustache, and long stringy hair didn't appeal to me.

"I'm joking. I know you've got Duke. See you in the kitchen tomorrow afternoon."

She left me standing alone, so I found the mess tent and rejoined Rollie.

☙

The next day, Rollie woke me at five a.m. She wanted to get out early and miss the breakfast crowd. After eating, we saddled our horses in the soft glow of morning while the sun hiked up the far side of the Laramie Range. We rode toward the practice arena set up in a pasture beyond the barn, taking a roundabout route to let Hornet and Satin D stretch their legs after the long train ride. Mac had scheduled me in a barrel race for my first performance, and Rollie wanted to see me practice.

At the time Mac had first explained this kind of race to Chloe and me he'd made it sound simple, and after setting up three oil barrels on a triangular course said all we had to do was run a cloverleaf pattern around them. But the last few months of practice in Montana had taught me how difficult it really could be—and how much speed and skill were necessary to maneuver as close to the barrels as possible without knocking them over. As we raced against the clock, our goal of completing the run in less than fifteen seconds turned out to be much more challenging than we'd initially thought.

Rollie and I found a spot where someone had already set up barrels inside a large paddock.

After my first run she shouted, "You're too slow."

Discouraged, I dismounted.

"I'm going to show you a thing or two about the barrels." She rode Hornet into the corral to demonstrate. "Get your feet behind you, toward her flanks. That way when she leans into the barrels and you circle around, you won't fall forward and lose control."

I followed her instructions. The more upright I rode, the easier time Satin D had, and I felt more confident the third time around. Mac had never tried to help us perfect our technique. Instead, he'd yelled and bullied us to improve our time.

"Hey. Now you're pulling the reins and slowing her down. You're messing up the turns."

By my fourth time I had improved, although not enough for Rollie. As more people and horses arrived, she raised her voice to a shout over the increased activity.

"Start slower. Sit up high in the saddle, girl."

I straightened.

"Now start by loping and then increase your speed." She gave me a wave when I passed her.

After the fifth run, I needed a break.

"You're good. I'm going to have a hard time teaching you much more about the barrels."

"I'm so clumsy."

"You're just nervous. It takes an inner focus to size up the competition and trust you can win. We can do a bit of adjusting here and there the rest of the week."

※

On opening day, all the performers who'd traveled with us, plus ranch workers from the region, showed up to compete. We gathered in the town of Douglas on Center Street, which was lined with onlookers, and paraded to the large arena outside of town. Three young ladies with powder rouge and bright red lipstick led the parade. Each wore a light blue outfit with a split skirt and hand-tooled boots. Braided ribbons in all colors of the rainbow adorned the manes and tails of their horses.

The trick riders followed next, headed by Chloe, who rode Sultan, a palomino with an ivory mane and tail. He radiated elegance and knew it; she carried a large American flag that flowed over her shoulder. The rest of us cowgirls were next, then the cowboys, and finally the clowns rollicking around the horses and mugging for the spectators, tossing hard candies to the kids.

Still on our horses, while we waited to enter the arena Rollie reached over and nudged me. "Those are the sponsor girls I told you about." She pointed to the girls who had led the parade.

I nodded, twisting Satin Dancer's rein around my left hand as if I could hang on tight enough to hide my jitters. I smiled and waved with my right hand, hoping I looked more relaxed than I felt as we circled inside the arena with the whole parade and then exited. A roar rose from the crowd as the first bareback rider entered the ring. He bounced and jolted in a wild dance on the bronco, with nothing to grasp except a handhold strapped around the horse's belly.

We rode around behind the bleachers and got off our horses.

"We've got plenty of time before we're up," Rollie said. "Let's watch that cousin of yours. Trick riders are up next."

I let Satin D loose to graze in a holding corral and found Rollie in the bleachers. We waited for Chloe's performance.

Second up, she started her routine on Sultan in a crouch stand at his withers. Then, with her feet pointing downward in the straps attached to her trick riding saddle, she popped up from a jockey position, legs straight, leaning forward over Sultan's mane as he took off in a gallop. The crowd roared as she stood and spread her arms wide in a perfect hippodrome stand while her horse charged around the arena. She finished, rolling under Sultan's belly maneuvering into the saddle, facing his rump. She exited the arena hands-free, waving to the crowd from this position. She took first place.

"Damn. You're right. Your cousin sure can ride and is daring as any trick rider I ever saw," Rollie said, clapping hard when Chloe and Sultan rode into the ring and took a bow.

I'd seen enough for a while. I found Chloe with Mac and congratulated her. He beamed from ear to ear. "Expect the same from you," he said to me.

Rollie found me later, sitting on the ground waiting while Satin Dancer munched grass. "Come on. We're up next," she said. "We're going to line up according to our appearance. You're riding last."

My heart sank. "How'd that happen?"

"Luck of the draw. You'll be fine. You're the best rider we've got."

I glanced over at the three young ladies still wearing their satin blue split skirts, now waiting to compete in the barrel race, and wondered why they hadn't changed the fancy outfits they wore during the opening parade.

"Don't worry," Rollie said, passing me on Hornet to take her place. "They don't stand a chance even if there's bias from the judges. Don't forget the audience's got eyes to see the truth."

The announcer's voice boomed over the arena. He introduced the young ladies, and then the rest of us. We all waved and tipped our hats to the cheering crowd.

The applause thundered. I sat up straighter, committed to riding hard and fast. I could feel the ripple of Satin D's muscles, her nervous energy fueled by the stink of fear sweating out of the bulls crowded in their chutes next to us, her impatience held in check only by my touch. The sweet smell of perfume as the sponsor girls passed me mingled with the fresh manure and tobacco smoke. Satin Dancer's hooves scraped the dirt.

Finally hearing my name called over the loudspeaker, Satin D and I shot into the arena at full speed. With my feet behind me resting on her flanks, all it took was a light touch with the locked rowels of my spurs to push her round the cloverleaf pattern at full speed, spewing a cloud of dust behind us. The rousing cheer of the crowd energized me. Everything else faded—the dusty air, the sharp odors from the holding pens, and my jittery nerves. Satin Dancer and I were one, racing the clock.

At the end of the competition, despite any favoritism for the sponsor girls, the judge awarded Satin D and me second place. Rollie had ranked third. She and several other cowgirls excitedly surrounded me as they offered their congratulations.

"You did real good, Ruth. Even beat an old pro like me." I could hear the pride in her voice.

Mac sauntered toward us, hands in his pockets, head down with his hat covering his eyes. Chloe followed close behind.

"Nice ride" Mac said, shaking my hand. Rollie had moved away, so she didn't hear him add with a chill in his voice, "Don't forget who brought you to this party."

THREE

Mac never stopped pushing us. In addition to the barrel racing and trick riding we were doing, he would enter us in relay races when we competed in rodeos that had a racetrack. The need to change horses at the end of the first and second lap were part of the reason these three-lap relays were considered one of the most dangerous of all the competitions.

Pushed to their physical limit, this type of event was hard on the horses too, and required that they stand steady while we touched the ground with both of our feet during the changeovers. Satin Dancer and Sultan weren't trained for this, so we rode relay horses Mac provided to compete in the races.

We'd been at the Settle R for three weeks and were scheduled to move soon to a ranch near Colorado Springs. Chloe and I had finished a particularly grueling practice run, over and over, around a relay track. We sat on the fence, tired and bored with the repetition. Mac had stood around most of the day, keeping an eye on us while he chatted with other cowboys.

Our practice over, Chloe and I relaxed while Satin D and Sultan nibbled grass alongside Mac's relay horses. I liked it with just the two of us. I missed the closeness we'd had over the years.

Chloe wound and unwound the lariat she'd used earlier in the day for practice. "I think Mac is going to ask me to marry him." She concentrated on twirling the lariat in a wide circle above the grass.

It took me a few seconds to comprehend what she'd said. Mac's swift mood changes were hard on both of us. Marriage in general didn't interest me, and with someone as unpredictable as Mac it didn't make sense.

"You want him to ask?"

"Of course. Why wouldn't I?"

"He makes you so mad." Although I sensed her irritation, I added, "He can be so surly and mean to both of us."

Chloe jumped down from the fence, tossing the lariat aside. "That's because he wants us to do well. If we look good, he looks good."

"His rudeness doesn't always work with me. Sometimes he reminds me of my brother. Nice one minute and dreadful the next. I don't like it."

"I thought you would be happy for me. It's what I want," she said. "You'll understand when you fall in love."

"Maybe." I thought about Duke, the tallest boy in our class. We fit together so well—I wasn't tall or short, but betwixt and between, always out of sync it seemed with everyone except Duke. He usually wore denim overalls and an old plaid shirt that had shrunk from its many washings. The cuffs barely reaching his wrists drew attention to his long, artistic, almost delicate hands. So different than Mac and his coarse manners, Duke's good humor and sensitive nature made him fun to be around. I'd left him, and the loyalty and stability he stood for, behind. He'd always treated me with respect, and in my own way I loved him, but was there a difference between loving someone and being in love?

I should have kept my mouth shut, because following that conversation I saw even less of Chloe. She hardly spoke to me anymore. Even when we worked in the kitchen together, she ignored me if she could. But it didn't really matter, most of the time I was out of bed and rehearsing my skills with Rollie at least an hour before she got up.

Rollie and I spent so much time together that I'd relented and taken up smoking to fit in. One night after supper, as we would often do, the two of us relaxed with our cigarettes. She took a long drag and exhaled toward the sky. Lanterns hanging on the branches of the oaks that shaded the outdoor dining area had been lit and were dancing in a cool breeze. We sipped tepid tea sweetened with lots of sugar, a rare treat in such lean times.

In an offhand way, as if we'd been discussing it, she said, "You're too damn good to give that cowboy a cut. Rumor has it he comes from money." She ground out her finished cigarette with the heel of her boot. "That's why he can afford those extra horses you two ride in the relays."

I loosened my collar.

"One of these days you'll have to tell Mac that you're through with him. It doesn't make sense, you only getting room and board for your kitchen work. A person willing to work hard can earn good money doing outdoor chores in addition to competing. You could pay your own way and still keep something in your pocket."

"I think I've proved I know how to work hard."

"If you want, when we get to Oklahoma I can arrange for you to pair up with me doing outdoor ranch chores. I need some extra cash myself and know who to ask to get the work. I might even be able to call in a favor and get you paid for kitchen duty from now on."

"I'd like to go out on my own, it's just that Mac and I have an agreement. I'll think about it."

"You've got a spot softer 'n butter, Ruth. It hides your backbone and can cloud your vision."

☙

By May we'd moved to a new host ranch near Guymon in the Oklahoma panhandle. As usual, from there we moved around on trains and trucks, performing in small venues nearby. Sometimes we slept in tents and other times in bunkhouses. I figured new people joined us, and others left, depending on their own life circumstances. Rollie's offer of arranging for odd jobs to earn extra cash made sense, and I had accepted.

On a day the sun lazed high above in a cloudless sky, we worked side by side, mucking out an old paddock with a run down fence and broken gate. Our work woke up old manure, chaw spit, and I didn't want to know what else. We shoveled and pulled weeds with neckerchiefs tied over our noses to keep out the swirling dust kicked up by a dry wind.

Rollie took a break after a couple of hours and lay down in the shade of the barn.

"I've got to rest. You finish the clean up. We'll start on the fence later."

"These chores make my kitchen duty seem easy. I'm going to end up an old prune working all day in this kind of weather." I flopped down beside her and rolled a smoke.

"You mean like me," Rollie said with a smile.

Ashamed by my remark, I kept my head down, searching for a reply.

"I should be so lucky."

She punched my arm and pointed to my shovel. "Get out there and let this old prune rest." Sheltered by the barn from the stiff afternoon breeze that rolled tumbleweeds on the open plain, Rollie stretched out in the dry grass and closed her eyes. I retied my neckerchief over my nose and went to work.

An hour later, I collapsed next to Rollie after dumping the last wheelbarrow of debris on the pile we'd made.

"We better get at that fence," I said. "If we hurry we might finish the south side before supper."

"You're too much, gal. I can't keep up with your pace." She stretched and offered me her hand. "Help me up. Let's take a ride and relax the rest of the day. This here work's not going anywhere."

On the way to get our horses, we met Sue Ann at the corral, talking with a cowboy. Rollie had been right, I'd hardly seen her since the day we met. She introduced the cowboy as Bobby Smith. He had a banged-up face, a patch covered his left eye, and a scar resembling a scythe cut across his cheek from lip to eye socket.

"Pleased to meet you gals, but I've got to get going," Bobby said as he winked at me with his good eye.

"What happened to him?" I asked.

"Got kicked in the face by a bucking bronc that dumped him," Sue Ann said. "Among other things, Bobby's also been assisting the big fellas who wrestle steers, keeping the steers running straight. He can't do either one now with only one eye." She sighed. "He's still a good looking cowboy, polite, treats everybody the same. What's he, about twenty-five?"

"I don't know, Sue Ann. But I do know he's too young for you. Come on. Let's go for a ride." Rollie gestured for her to follow us.

"I've seen him watching me practice. Seems to always be hanging on the fence. Mac said he asks all kinds of questions about me," I said.

"Don't forget what I've said about falling for one of these cowboys," Rollie chided me. "One day you could find your-self taking care of a ranch house, surrounded by scrappy land, waiting for your old man to bring home money for you and the kids."

"I'm not interested."

"I hope not," Sue Ann said. "Bobby's polite. But he's got the same randy equipment the other boys' got."

We rode single file along the creek. After a while, we tethered our horses beside the bubbling water in the shade of a cottonwood and reclined on the soft grass.

"You having any fun? Rollie seems to keep you pretty busy working chores on our days off," Sue Ann said to me.

"She's got a beau she left behind," Rollie said in a teasing voice.

Fluffy cottonwood seedpods floated down on us like warm snow. I pushed my hat over my eyes to hide my warm cheeks, which I knew had turned pink. "We're more friends than anything," I managed to say.

"You got his photograph in that stash of letters in your saddlebag?" Rollie grinned at the surprised look on my face. "It's hard to have secrets in the close quarters we keep."

Her kidding made me feel like I belonged. Brushing the cottonwood fuzz off my chaps, I stood and rummaged in my saddlebag to find the packet of letters that had recently arrived—the one from Duke had included a photo of the golf team at the university with him kneeling in the front row.

As I handed the picture to Rollie and pointed him out, admitting to myself that he looked handsome in his golf knickers and sweater, I realized his enthusiasm for engineering classes and his fraternity seemed like a long ago dream I'd forgotten.

Rollie passed the photo to Sue Ann.

"Nice," Sue Ann said. "Kind of a waste, you bein' only friends and him so smooth." She read the inscription on the back of the photo out loud: "Miss you, Ruthie. Can't wait till you get home. Golf is a pastime until I can hold you in my arms. Love, Duke."

"Sounds like he feels he's more than just your friend," Rollie said.

"I guess so. Sometimes. He's probably lonely since we spent all our time together and he's used to having me around." I wondered what Duke would think if he saw me looking so rugged, covered with dust, caked with sweat, and smoking with cowgirls. "He wouldn't fit in here. He's afraid of horses."

I felt a surge of guilt for not being keener on Duke. It made me anxious to think about not being able to stand up to my family's wishes that we spend the rest of our lives together. I wanted to leave all that behind and put away the letters.

Rollie passed me a smoke. "Honey, we've been talking. You've got to untangle from Mac." No longer teasing, she had turned serious.

"We can help you. Rollie and I know how these cowboys think."

No more joking around. They talked. I listened. Later, by myself, I practiced in my mind. "Mac, I'm going out on my own without you and Chloe." No accusation. "I can earn my own way now and want my cut of my winnings." But I dreaded having to confront him, and kept putting it off.

FOUR

T wo nights later, I lounged on my bed, rereading *Anna Karenina*, still the only book I had with me.

I read the first line: "Happy families are all alike; every unhappy family is unhappy in its own way." It got me to thinking about how my family enfolded me in loving security. Even though Mother rarely left our home on Lake Minnetonka, she had said to me many times, "Education, Ruthie. It's your key to independence. Without it you limit your choices."

But sometimes the security felt like confinement.

What would it actually mean to be an independent woman able to take care of myself? Even though women had been able to vote since 1920, it didn't seem much had changed for my mother.

What would it take to let myself feel a passion so intense that it would make me willing to give up everything, as Anna Karenina had done for her lover, Count Vronsky?

I doubted I would have the courage to survive such an intense tragedy—giving up a child, family, and a place in society—to change the course of my life.

Rollie's voice startled me from my thoughts.

"Come on, Ruth, you can't sit in this old bunkhouse by yourself. Let's go have some fun."

She had pulled her hair—dark as a raven's feather and streaked with silver—into a bun, and had applied red lipstick and a touch of rouge high on her cheekbones.

The lantern flame flickered over my book. "You remind me of the stories about Abe Lincoln," she said. "Always reading the same book by firelight."

The low lamp light softened the crevasses that crisscrossed her cheeks and the creases that crinkled at the corners of her eyes when she smiled or belted out her hearty laugh. She wore her best western-styled shirt with pearl buttons and had tucked her black trousers into her fancy red boots.

"Where are you going?" I asked.

"We're off tomorrow. Remember?"

"Oh, right."

I welcomed a day off, even though a pesky loneliness crept in on the times I saddled up Satin Dancer and explored the area around the ranch by myself.

"We're going for a ride." She insisted I get up and get dressed. "Wear your best shirt. That bright blue one."

We saddled up and rode down a gentle hill and across an almost dry creek. The wind had quieted. Heat, hoarded all day by the earth, warmed the night air. A full moon illuminated everything. Even the shortest blades of prairie grass threw shadows.

"Where are we headed?" I asked, excited to be out on such an exquisite night.

"Never mind. You'll find out soon enough," Rollie answered. "It's a surprise."

In the distance, coyotes bantered with the moon. We rode to the edge of a ridge where the lights of the Four Bar Ranch, our closest neighbors, lit the ravine below us.

"There it is, over to the right." Rollie pointed to a building that looked like a barn. "Come on! I'll race you down," she shouted over her shoulder, taking off before I could answer.

I nudged Satin D into a gallop and easily caught up with her. We reached the barn and hitched our horses. I noticed a few automobiles—Chevrolets, old jalopies, even a new Dodge—were parked along the road nearby.

A woman sitting outside the door welcomed us with a smile and said, "Go on in." When Rollie opened the door, we were greeted by music echoing off the windowless walls of a square, smoke-filled room. As I hesitated behind her, Rollie stepped aside to allow me to enter, then closed the door.

There were several women gathered in a semicircle around a piano, a fiddle player was off to one side. Other women mingled in small groups. Some were dancing.

I didn't see any cowboys. A party with only women? I'd never heard of such a thing, and wondered where the men were. Isn't that what every cowgirl wanted, to meet the right guy and get off the circuit? I thought of Sue Ann, Chloe, and a few others I'd met who rarely seemed to think of anything else.

"Come on in, Ruth," Rollie raised her voice over the din. "Let's get some punch." We walked over to a table that held cups and a large glass bowl filled with red liquid.

I wavered. "Do you think it's spiked?"

"It's fruit punch. You have to bring your own flask if you want liquor." Rollie handed me a cup, said hello to a couple of the women nearby, and then motioned me to follow her.

Just as we found a couple of seats at an empty table, one of the musicians shouted "Hey Rollie, get over here. We need two more hands."

"Will you be okay by yourself?" Rollie asked. "I'll introduce you around after we play a few songs."

"Go ahead. I'll be fine." Rollie scooted in next to the piano player. They pounded out a honky-tonk piece I didn't recognize. It got the place hopping.

As women whirled around the wooden floor, my feet tapped to the music without permission. Rollie finished playing and returned to our table. "Come on," she teased, "Let's get those feet out on the dance floor."

The music had changed to a western song I knew, "Keep on the Sunny Side." A third woman who had joined the piano player and fiddler belted out the words made popular by the Carter Sisters.

Rollie held out her hand and pulled me up. I followed her lead while we whirled around the room with the others in a lively two-step.

It felt good to let go and have fun for a change.

The music stopped and Rollie introduced me to a few of the women she'd said hello to earlier, then left me with them and again headed toward the piano.

"Come on, Ruth. You know how to line dance?" one of the women asked.

I shook my head.

"Stand beside me," she said and demonstrated. "It's easy: cross, step, cross."

I followed the best I could, laughing at my clumsy mistakes. The whole building vibrated with boots stomping on the wood floor. When we took a break I didn't see Rollie anywhere, and started to feel uncomfortable by myself when a short, plump woman in a plaid dress joined the musicians.

"Let's see if we can get all you buffalo gals going," she hollered in a big voice that didn't fit her appearance. Right away the floor got crowded.

My line dance partner came over and grabbed my hand. "Come on, we need one more for our square."

I tried to protest.

"It's easy," the woman said, dragging me into position.

"Here we go," cried the caller. The fiddle started us out and I quickly picked up the steps. We switched partners with each new dance until I thought I'd drop. Overheated and thirsty, but excited and happy, I was both relieved and sorry when the musicians announced a break. I noticed Rollie alone at our table, so I poured us each a glass of punch and joined her.

"Well, what do you think?" she asked.

The hum of conservations had grown louder, and were laced with laughter. I leaned toward her and said, "You weren't kidding. This absolutely is a surprise."

I couldn't decide what shocked me most, how well Rollie could play the piano, how much fun I'd had dancing with a whole bunch of women, or how right it all felt.

"This is the best time I've had since I left home," I said.

"I meant about all women, no cowboys allowed."

"It's different." I struggled to think of something else to say.

"That's true. The Four Bar's owned by those two women over there." She nodded toward two women standing at the punch bowl. "Once a year, when the rodeo's in town, we get together to dance and renew our acquaintances. There's lots of new faces every year."

She glanced around and continued, "These are my friends." The lights dimmed and the music started up, playing a waltz. "Some folks say it's wrong . . ."

A woman cut in before Rollie finished her thought and started talking about people I didn't know. Women filled the floor once again. *What does she mean by wrong?* At school socials the boys usually lined a wall and the girls paired up to dance. We didn't need the boys to have fun.

I heard Rollie decline the woman's invitation to dance. "It's almost midnight," she said to me. "We've got to get our horses home and bedded down. I'm going to make my goodbyes. I'll meet you outside."

"You sure you want to leave?"

"It's time. As the saying goes, the party's over."

I gulped my punch and walked outside. The air had cooled. I untied my jacket from my saddle—glad to have it on by the time Rollie came out.

She had trouble untying Hornet's rope from the post. "Are you all right?" She always seemed so in control.

"I thought I might see an old friend here," she said, giving the rope a final yank. "It didn't happen."

We rode home in silence, our horses picking their way in the faded promise of the moon.

I slept late on Sunday and didn't see Rollie again until Monday morning.

FIVE

Rollie and I hurried through breakfast on Monday morning. Neither of us brought up the dance. She seemed preoccupied while we ate, and I hesitated to interrupt her thoughts. Afterward, we headed out to start repairing the old paddock fence.

Unyielding heat bore down on us. I hauled heavy boards from the truck while Rollie built the fence. Sweat ran down my neck. I paused to wipe my face and take a drink from my canteen. A few crows cawed and fought over something in the field beyond the fence. Other than the crows and the hammer hitting the nails, it was a quiet Monday morning. But then our bubble of time apart from the rest of the world burst with a bone-rattling scream and uproar of voices that scattered the crows. It sounded like it came from the other side of the barn. I dropped my canteen.

"What the—" Rollie threw down her hammer. Without saying any more, we ran toward the noise.

"Somebody got launched off that new bronc brought in a couple days ago," Sue Ann shouted when she spotted us.

"I can't see who it is," her latest cowboy friend added.

Mac was on his knees bending over someone who lay motionless in the dust. A bronco he'd bought at auction a week ago pawed the ground nearby, shaking its head and snorting, agitated by the growing crowd.

"Someone get that damn animal out of here," Mac's voice roared over the chaos of the crowd gathering nearby.

A ranch hand raced through the gate with his lariat twirling over his head. With one expert toss, he lassoed the bronc and coaxed it out of the gate and into a nearby paddock. The agitated mare snorted and charged around in circles, still halfheartedly bucking until she seemed to tire, at which point she walked to the far fence away from all the commotion.

Rollie grabbed my arm. "Ruth, it's bad. There's blood, and her arm's broke in a couple of places." The intensity in her voice made my legs weak.

"It's Chloe!" I yelled the moment I recognized her. My cousin lay in a heap in the dirt as Mac knelt beside her and held her head.

"Make room," he yelled at the circle closing in on them. "Make room for the doctor." His voice was tense with fear.

I pushed through the crowd and knelt on the other side of Chloe, covered in dirt and blood. She lay still. Mac pressed a handkerchief to a cut on her forehead. Her arm was bent at a grotesque angle. I could see her chest barely moving as she took shallow breaths. Two men with a stretcher and the doctor, carrying a black bag, came toward us in what seemed like slow motion.

"You're going to be all right, hon, the doc's here," Mac spoke to Chloe in a soft voice that seemed out of character for him.

She moaned in pain and the doctor gave her a dose of medicine from his bag. We both looked on helplessly as he carefully bent her arm back into position and fashioned a makeshift splint to keep it in place. I cringed. My stomach churned and I went queasy with dread. She seemed to be unconscious while he worked slowly and methodically, securing her arm with tape to the splint, then assisting the men who lifted her onto the stretcher to keep her arm from moving.

Mac barely acknowledged me until after Chloe had been attended to by the doctor, then he said "She's tough, Ruth. She's going to be okay." He stared somewhere over my shoulder and sounded out of focus. His hands shook when he looked down at the bloody handkerchief he held. He stuffed it in his pocket and spoke to Chloe as the men lifted her for the walk to the ranch house.

"You're tough, baby. You're going to be all right," he murmured while I walked silently behind. Reaching the house, we tried to follow the doctor into the bedroom, but he shooed us away, closing the door as he ignored Mac's protests.

The two of us waited on the porch. "What happened?" I finally asked.

"She's good enough. She could've ridden that bronc, could've held on for the eight seconds to win," Mac said.

"You pushed her. You know she didn't want to ride a bronco."

"No. She got cocky, showing off for the boys. She let go with one hand, grabbed her hat to wave at us. I told her to hold on with both hands."

My temper almost got the best of me as I held my clenched fists at my sides. If I'd been a man, I would have slugged him, punched him until he bled, but I knew better than to hit him. Instead, I struck out with words.

"Damn it, Mac. Don't you ever think of anything except making more money, pushing us beyond our limits? Now you're blaming Chloe for what's happened?"

It worked. He flinched as if I'd hit him. I started to soften until he astonished me, returning to his arrogant self. "Careful, Ruth, you've been spending too much time with those rough

gals you pal around with." His tone warned me I'd better
shut my mouth. "We'll finish this later."

I sat with Chloe in the ranch house guest room, and missed
supper that night. The doctor had given her something for
the pain and left the rest of the syrup with directions on
how often to administer it. Mac arrived a little later, and I
left them alone, returning shortly with a bowl of chili the
cook had saved for me. Mac and I were quiet in our own
thoughts, uncomfortable with each other as we watched
Chloe drifting in and out of a fitful sleep. I didn't have the
energy to chat with him, and settled for sitting with the
tension between us until I finally left him alone with Chloe
and walked to the bunkhouse.

"How's she doing?" Rollie asked when she saw me.

"I don't know. She's in a lot of pain—stitched up and
bruised. Her arm is in a plaster cast."

"Well, she's lucky. She could have been killed."

"I know. I've been so mad at her for ignoring me that I forgot how much she means to me. Now it's Mac I'm furious
at—him and his greed."

I blew out the lantern and got in bed.

"You're wakin' up, Ruth; that's good. He's been taking
advantage of both of you for too long. You're the one who's
better off."

I hadn't thought of it that way.

The night seemed endless. I woke often worrying about
Chloe. In the morning I pulled myself out of bed, dressed
quickly, and went out to the barn. I put Satin Dancer out to
pasture, mucked out her stall, and headed for the kitchen
to report for duty after making a quick visit to Chloe, who
still slept. I couldn't stay, since we did most of the prep
cooking in the morning. Being late would not endear me
to the rest of the crew. Even though we all planned to
pull out in the next week for Texas, I didn't want to let
the cook down.

The summer heat peaked around three thirty in the afternoon while we prepared for the evening meal. In that blistering time of day, we took a break. The other two workers scattered, but I relaxed at the kitchen table, sipping a glass of water and listening to the faucet drip. The ruffled chintz curtains had trapped a fat black bumblebee that did combat with the window screen. A current of hot air flirted with the soft fabric, offering false hope of relief from the heat and false hope for a getaway to the bumblebee. My disappointment and anger with Chloe dissolved while I listened to the desperate struggle of the bee. Chloe lay so helpless and fragile, trapped in her bed. I decided I had to stay with her while the others went on to Abilene—we'd been so close over the years, until Mac came between us.

⚜

Rollie found me after my shift slumped, limp as a Raggedy Ann doll, in an old stuffed chair on the porch. I had untied the damp bandanna that covered my head and pulled back my hair with a leather tie in a futile attempt to discipline it. I took out a pouch of Bull Durham tobacco, rolled us each a cigarette, and handed one to her.

She lit hers and passed me a match.

"I don't know, Rollie, maybe the heat got to me. I'm not moving on to Texas with the rest of you. I'm going to stay with Chloe."

She lounged against the porch rail. "You're giving up," she said, her voice so flat I couldn't tell if it was a question or a statement, and I saw her disappointment as she looked away from me. "I didn't take you for a quitter." Her jaw was clamped tight as if to avoid saying any more.

"No," I protested. "It's only for a couple of weeks. She's family, Rollie. I'll catch up with you." I didn't want to lose her friendship.

"What made you decide?"

"It's what you said last night. I wonder how happy Chloe's been with Mac. Sometimes he seems to really care about her, and other times he's plain mean."

"There's that soft spot of yours showing up. Your cousin's mighty fortunate."

The dinner bell rang. We lined up to get a plate of food and ate in the outside dining area, the songs of evening birds calling in the dusk. The sun slipped behind the hills, and the first star twinkled as Rollie stood and put out a hand to help me up from my chair.

"Let's bed down our horses," she said. "I've been thinking. If you really do plan to catch up with us, I better take Satin Dancer. You won't be able to pay to transport her. She'll ride for free on the circuit's pass in the animal car."

Her offer made sense, and I finally managed to agree. When I tried to thank her, the words got stuck in my throat—the thought of being separated from Satin D hadn't occurred to me.

"You know I'll treat her like my own," Rollie assured me. "And this way I know you won't change your mind about showing up in Abilene."

That last week flew by, and as I watched the train roll down the tracks toward Texas I began missing them both right away. The ranch seemed empty with everyone gone except the hired hands, the owners, and Chloe, Mac, and me.

I didn't know I could feel so lonely.

The next day Mac decided we needed to call Chloe's dad and tell him what had happened. He asked me to make the call and arranged a ride for me into Guymon with a cowboy to use the telephone in the telegraph office while he stayed with Chloe. I let him treat me like a hired nurse and didn't argue.

"You've met him. Bobby Smith. He'll pick you up around one," Mac said.

I recognized Bobby, couldn't mistake his good-looking beat-up face. He arrived in a truck with an empty flat bed.

"Hi, Ruth. Hop in." He reached across the seat and pushed open the door for me without getting out. "We've got to load this old rattle trap with hay bales a little south of town."

He caught me sneaking a peek at his face. "Guess you heard I got hurt dancing with a bucking bronco. I'm healing up real fast," he said, touching the scar. "It's all right. I can drive with one eye."

"How long have you been riding the rodeo?"

"About all my life. Followed my old man on the circuit from a young age and learned everything from the ground up. Funny thing is I'd planned to quit right before I got hurt. I had myself a sweet deal riding hazer for the bulldoggers, in addition to riding the broncs."

I knew that the steer wrestlers were called bulldoggers and that the hazer rode alongside the steer, keeping him in line until the bulldogger caught up and wrangled the animal to the ground. Bobby sounded kind of sad. His whole life had been the rodeo and now he had to give it up.

"Guess you miss it," I said as the truck bumped and creaked over the ruts in the dirt road.

"I do. No more glory inside the arena."

He was quiet for a while. "Don't plan on disappearing, though. Going to change directions. Some guys get bitter, eat themselves up with whiskey, sitting around. I'm making other plans. You might fit right in." He turned toward me and gave me a big grin.

"Me?"

His good eye smiled along with his lips, sweetening his face.

"How?"

"I've seen you ride. Seen you win the barrel races and take first place in a couple of relays outside Laramie.

It's my opinion that you are wasting a lot of time working in the kitchen and nursing your cousin."

I accepted the cigarette he offered from a pack of Camels, and he continued. "I do feel bad for Chloe. Kind of know what she's going through, the pain and all, maybe losing her riding ability. But I've been talking to Mac about you. Asking a lot of questions. He says you been riding the roundup on your uncle's ranch since you were real young. That true?"

I nodded, and he got animated. "I got several cowboys waiting in Abilene. They need someone with the riding skills to keep a steer that's running for its life in line. All I have to do is convince them you're good enough, and I think you will be."

Bobby's enthusiasm stunned me, and I caught his excitement. Everything could change. I'd be independent of Mac and earn even more money. I knew hazing took both riding skill and good timing. And I knew I could do it. All I'd have to do is hang on.

But I couldn't understand why he'd choose me, so I asked.

"You've got talent. I can teach you to take my place in the next few weeks while you help out with Chloe. No use in you getting stiff, and losing your riding edge, while you nurse her."

Later, while we loaded the hay bales, I strained to keep up with Bobby wanting to impress him.

After we finished, I left Bobby with the truck and went inside the telegraph office to call Uncle Michael. I dreaded telling him the news, knowing he'd be heartbroken and worried sick. He'd raised Chloe by himself after her mother died, and he had treated me the same as a daughter every summer Mother and I visited.

I'd only called home once, to let Mother and Dad know Satin Dancer and I had arrived safely. As usual, as if I hadn't left, Duke had been there at Sunday dinner and he and the whole family had to say hello to me. The call was expensive, so to save money from then on I only sent postcards and an occasional letter.

The woman behind the counter dialed the number and handed me the receiver. I listened to the phone ring, but froze upon hearing Uncle Michael's voice. I hadn't realized how hard it would be to tell him about Chloe. "Who is this?" he asked, his voice sounding far away.

"It's me. Ruth," I finally managed to say. Right away he knew something bad had happened and demanded to know what. I told him how Chloe had been hurt and answered all his questions. At first he blamed himself. "I wish I hadn't let you gals go out there with him. I hated to say no."

I told him that I planned to move on without Chloe and Mac. "Your mother will kill me if something happens to you" he said, and tried to talk me out of continuing on my own.

I did my best to convince him I'd be fine. Then I couldn't help myself. He felt so bad, and I wanted to hurt Mac. I blurted out that I worried Mac might not give us a fair share of our winnings. That's when his temper flared.

"I've known him since he was a boy. He promised to watch out for both of you, and I promised your parents he would do just that." Uncle Michael took a deep breath and exhaled. "Don't you worry, you'll get your money."

His parting words were, "Tell that damned Mac to have Chloe home as soon as she can travel or I'll have his hide." I started to say goodbye, but he interrupted me. "And tell him he better call me and give me an update every few days. Not you, him."

After making the call, my enthusiasm about learning to haze started to wane. On the way home I said to Bobby, "I don't know. What are those cowboys going to think about riding with a woman in the arena?" I didn't want to tell him that I couldn't help worrying about getting hurt.

"Don't you fret about the boys. Your job will be to ride. Mine is to get you ready to show them what you can do."

"What about my horse? She's not trained to be in the arena with the steer wrestlers. And I've already sent her ahead to Abilene."

"I've got a horse you can ride. Bred and trained him myself."

"I don't know. It's pretty dangerous."

"Relay's a lot more dangerous, getting off one horse at full speed and back on another. All you have to do as a hazer is stay in a straight line and on your horse. Long as you don't fall off and get trampled, it's easy. It's good money. When the boys win, they share the purse with their hazer." He slowed the truck down and grinned at me. "Deal?"

I couldn't say no. I wanted the extra money and it did sound easy enough. I started spending most of my time with Bobby right away. He boosted my confidence with his quiet, patient teaching. And I bonded right away with his horse, a roan named Hobo Joe.

"Hobo knows what to do if you give him the right signals," Bobby told me the first day. "It's my job to teach you those signals."

❦

During the next few weeks, in between working in the kitchen and practicing with Bobby, I spent as much time as I could with Chloe.

"Mac's been so sweet since I got hurt," she said one evening while I helped her into bed.

"He's going to get me home, and we'll get married as soon as I'm able to walk down the aisle with Daddy. Mac's been going into town and calling him every few days. I don't know what they talk about, but Mac has changed."

"I'm so happy for you." This time I meant it. I'd also noticed the change in Mac, more than likely due at least in part to Uncle Michael's influence.

Mac and I said good night outside on the wide porch later that evening. "I'll be taking Chloe home soon. She's a trooper and healing fast."

I took a breath and let it out slowly. "Chloe says you're getting married."

"We are. This whole experience has changed me." Darkness fell while he continued. "I didn't realize how much I love her until I almost lost her."

He showed me his heart, a side I didn't know he had.

In the end, Mac gave me the money he owed me. "Keep it in your boot. It'll be safer that way," he said and handed me another hundred for my help with Chloe.

I couldn't take all the credit for standing up to him. I knew my childish tattling to Uncle Michael had gotten the job done and decided I would keep it to myself.

SIX

Rollie met me at the train in Abilene driving an old buckboard drawn by two workhorses. Before heading out to the ranch where everyone was staying we stopped at the general store to pick up some supplies. I loaded the bags of flour and sugar she bought without much effort.

Rollie let out an admiring whistle as she watched me carry a heavy bag of Mexican coffee beans over my shoulder. "You're stronger. You own the ground you walk on. What have you been doing the last three weeks?"

"Bobby Smith's been teaching me to haze. We rode down here on the train together from Oklahoma. He'll ride in later with the ranch hands." I paused. "You remember him, a hazer for the bulldoggers."

"I do remember him. He's the one who got hurt." She raised an eyebrow. "Bulldoggers?"

"Yeah, that's what Bobby calls the steer wrestlers."

"I know what a bulldogger is. My point is you even talk different."

"Things changed when I got to working with Bobby."

Rollie dropped me off at the bunkhouse. "I'll get this rig put away for the night and meet you up at the kitchen.

We'll put on a pot of coffee, and you can tell me all about it." She pointed in the direction of the house and drove off.

I went right away to check on Satin Dancer. As soon as she recognized me, she whinnied and nuzzled my cheek. I offered her apple pieces and told her that I'd also be riding Hobo, a horse experienced with bucking bulls in the arena, but we'd still be running the barrels together.

I waited for Rollie at a kitchen table covered with a red and white checkered oilcloth. A pot percolated on a wood stove, filling the room with the comfortable aroma of strong coffee and alder wood smoke.

Rollie arrived and filled our cups. I put in enough cream until mine resembled dark ivory, then added three teaspoons of sugar. I fiddled with the salt and pepper shakers while I told her the story of Bobby's proposal the day he drove me into town to call Uncle Michael.

"He's been teaching me ever since."

"Slow down. You're telling me you've been riding in the arena with a feisty steer, itching to gore you, between you and the bulldogger?"

Her surprise made me laugh.

"If I didn't know you better, I wouldn't believe it." She let out a whoop, and we both laughed out loud.

"Well, it's true. He says he's got it all arranged. I'll take his place, and just between us, I'm scared to death."

"I'd be worried if you weren't," Rollie said, sounding serious. "Not many cowgirls would ride with a castrated bull whose trying to save his own life by getting the hell out of the arena." She poured more coffee.

"I can do it. Bobby says now it's up to him to convince the bulldoggers to trust a cowgirl." We finished our coffee and tidied up before shutting down the lantern and leaving.

Nighttime in Texas seemed about the same as in Oklahoma, dry and warm. The Milky Way slashed across the sky, an ethereal river flowing noiselessly overhead. It felt good to be talking with Rollie again, and she had saved the bunk over her own for me.

"Guess what?" I said, unpacking my duffel. "I'm not signing up for kitchen duty. I'm going to make it on my own earnings."

Rollie shook her head, pounded the air with her fist, and sang out, "Hallelujah! You wasted your time cooking and cleaning up."

A voice called out, "Hey. Simmer down. We're trying to sleep."

"Sorry," we said in softer voices.

My bunk reeked of stale air desperate to escape. "Damn it's hot up here. I thought it might be cooler in Abilene," I whispered, leaning over the side as Rollie got in her bunk.

"Don't count on it. It's always hot. Every place we go it's the same—bull sweat and dust, whether we're in Wyoming, Oklahoma, or Texas."

❧

The next morning I rode Satin Dancer over to the arena to meet Bobby. The empty bleachers wore a fresh coat of white paint and had an overhang to protect the spectators from the sun. My stomach clenched, thinking about the cheering crowd that would occupy every seat on Saturday.

Bobby waved me over to where he stood with four other cowboys. I tethered Satin D and walked over, stamping my feet down into my boots, checking my spurs.

I wanted to look like one of the boys. I'd tucked my hair up under my wide-brimmed hat and tied a black bandanna at my neck, dressed to ride hard without the hindrance of fringe or loose clothing.

Bobby introduced me to the group. "You've all probably seen each other in Wyoming or Oklahoma." With their large thighs and muscular arms, each man must have weighed over two hundred pounds. Steer wrestlers were called the big boys of the rodeo, and meeting these four, I could see why.

Paco, who spoke with a Mexican accent, greeted me. *"Con mucho gusto,"* he said. "Happy to meet you."

The cowboy next to Paco pumped my arm and held my hand tightly in his large meaty paw without saying his name. "So, you're the little lady that's going to protect us from the mean old steer."

He took in every inch of me from head to toe, smooth as water over bedrock without meeting my eyes.

I stood my ground.

"Hobo and I'll do our best," I said.

"Hobo's a good horse. I trust him not to spook. If you can handle him, we might do all right. We'll have to wait and see."

"Ruth's not going to have any problem with Hobo. Been training her for the last few weeks." Bobby winked at me. "Come on, Ruth. Let's show 'em."

I buckled on thick leather chaps and checked to make sure the rowels on my spurs were locked. With the sun barely above the horizon, I could already feel the heat.

"Hey, Hobo," I greeted the horse. "We're going to show these boys we can ride almost as good as Bobby." Then I lowered my voice. "Maybe better."

I checked his blanket and saddle, adjusted the stirrups to fit me, all the while speaking softly to him. Hobo stood still while I anchored my left leg in the stirrup and used momentum to effortlessly lift myself into the saddle. We waited next to the chute that held a steer who was snorting his impatience to be let loose.

I faced straight ahead and nodded, ready to start.

Bobby yelled, "Go!" and released the steer from the chute.

At the same moment, one of the boys perched on the fence shouted, "I'm rooting for you, cowgirl!" Instinctively I rotated my head and shoulders to see who had shouted at me. Hobo blew forward, a tornado chewing up the plain.

In a split second, my left shoulder wrenched beyond its normal range. I ignored the sharp pain, and we trailed the steer by seconds.

In a flash the rope tied to the steer's neck went taut and easily broke the barrier restraining Paco, who simultaneously shot from the other side of the chute into the arena and in an instant caught up to the steer. Hobo and I nudged the animal to the left toward Paco, who dove from his saddle and landed on the steer's giant neck, grabbing his horns for the wrestle to the ground. He went airborne for a second, holding on tight, and then landed full force on his backside without letting go.

Paco's boots scraped the dirt, slowing both of them. Still sitting on the ground, he twisted the steer's head to throw it off balance and pulled the animal down. With all four legs pointing to the sky, Paco let him go. The befuddled animal trotted off toward the exit without interference from Hobo and me, who were already safely out of the arena. The whole thing took about twenty seconds, too long in Bobby's opinion.

"Good!" shouted Bobby to me, "Next time we need to shave seconds off your time. You were a bit slow taking off."

"Hobo saved my fanny," I told Rollie later as she rubbed liniment oil on my shoulder. "I almost lost my first steer."

"You're lucky it's not worse," she said, rubbing below my shoulder blade. "Guess you learned a lesson, though."

"Do you think someone wanted me to fail?"

"I don't know. I hope none of them would deliberately do anything to distract you," she answered, digging her fingers in deeper. "I'd be careful, though. Those boys won't get in the arena with anyone who can't take the heat they dish out."

"Ouch," I protested. "Not so rough. You just hit the sorest spot."

SEVEN

All week, the bulldoggers and I rode hard and fast in the blazing heat. We learned about each other's riding style and worked to improve our time. Trying to be one of the boys, I followed their ritual of cooling down by dunking my head often in the horse trough and jamming my hat over my sopping hair. I laughed at their jokes and endured their rowdy cowboy ribbing, even when they teased me about trusting their life to a little girl.

"You're keeping up with the bulldoggers and impressing them," Bobby said, catching up with me outside the barn a couple of days before our first competition. "You've been taking some hard knocks, kiddo."

I liked the way he said it—affectionately, without sounding condescending. Bobby's attention strengthened my self-assurance, and I wanted to make him proud of me.

"Hey," he said. "What would you say to taking a ride up Cedar Creek? It'll be cooler there."

"What about supper?"

"Saddle up Satin Dancer. I'll use my charm to wheedle the cook into making a couple of sandwiches and some tea for us."

I headed for the bunkhouse, humming under my breath.

A short time later I followed Bobby through cottonwoods and red willows that shaded the trail. He broke the peaceful end-of-day chatter of birds with a simple "We're here."

We tethered our horses near a bank with easy access to the slow moving stream that gurgled and swirled into a natural pool. All I wanted was to stretch out on the soft grass and bask in the serenity.

"Hey, come on, take off your boots" Bobby called, and I noticed he'd rolled up his pant legs and waded in up to his knees. "Feels good. You're wasting time."

I took off my boots and socks, dipped my feet in the cold water, then sloshed my way toward Bobby. "Step here" he suggested, pointing to a large stone close to him.

I held each leg of my split skirt and curled my toes over the edge of the rock. It looked solid enough, but suddenly I slipped and fell.

Bobby was at my side in an instant, asking if I was okay as he offered me his hand.

"I'm fine. A little clumsy though, don't you think?" We both laughed.

Kneeling on the sandy bottom I said, "Since I'm already soaking wet, I think I'll rinse the scum out of my hair from our earlier cool off in the horse trough."

I stood, dripping from head to toe, and moved to a wide boulder still warm from the heat of the day. I averted my eyes when Bobby took off his wet shirt and hung it on a branch before rummaging around in his saddlebag.

Feeling uncomfortable, I stood up and said, "I think I'll go behind those bushes and wring out my skirt."

"Here, you can wrap this around yourself." He handed me a yellow cotton tablecloth.

A cowboy with a tablecloth?

"It was for our picnic. We'll use my saddle blanket instead." He gestured toward the riverbank. "Put your skirt on one of those rocks in the sun. It'll be dry in no time."

I came out from behind the bushes dressed in my damp shirt and the colorful tablecloth tied at my waist. Bobby grinned.

"Very elegant." He invited me to sit with a flourish of his arm.

He'd laid out sandwiches made with thickly sliced bread, ham, and mustard. We ate to the evening song of a mockingbird and shared sweet tea out of a mason jar.

I'd never had supper with a bare-chested man. I couldn't help noticing the tufts of hair growing across his chest and in a thin line leading toward his navel, and tried to keep my eyes on his face—anywhere except his naked torso.

"How're you feeling now, kiddo?" We'd finished our sandwiches.

"Full." I glanced over my shoulder at the horses grazing nearby and winced.

"What's wrong?"

"I hurt my shoulder a couple of days ago. Pulled a muscle. It hurts a little now. I might have stretched it falling into the water."

"How'd you hurt it?" he asked.

"Someone distracted me on my first run when the steer cleared the chute."

"The boys were a little nervous. They never had a cowgirl hazer, but they're learning to trust you. Turn around. I'll work on it for you."

I hesitated.

"It's a fairly common injury. Massaging helps." I turned around as he suggested and was modestly rearranging the tablecloth over my legs when I was startled by his touch.

"You're too tense. Try to relax into my hands." He began to gently knead my neck, then slowly moved to my shoulders with a firmer touch.

Doing my best to go limp I leaned into him, sighing as tension released from my body.

"Thanks, that felt good" I said when he stopped.

"You've been riding too hard, pushing yourself."

"I don't want to let you down."

He gently rotated me toward him, his firm hands guiding my shoulders until I faced him. He reached up and brushed an unruly strand of hair off my forehead.

"You need to let go. You're doing great."

I'd been trying hard to fit in with the hazers and their banter, laughing at their jokes, telling a few of my own.

"It's so much responsibility."

"Don't stew over it. Relax." He brushed his finger across my lips, pulled me gently toward him, and kissed me. With his lips slightly parted, I could taste the salt from the ham and the sweetness of the tea. Holding my breath until he released me, I heard the mockingbird finish his song and a couple of frogs call to each other across the creek.

"It's okay to breathe." Bobby laughed as he let me go and lay down on the grass with his hands behind his head. "You're quite the woman, strong on a horse and cheeky with the boys. Why so shy with me?"

My inexperience made me nervous. He pulled me toward him again, and this time I responded, opening my lips. I also remembered to breathe. His mouth brushed my eyes and my neck while he held me lightly. His fingers got caught in my tangled hair as his lips found my mouth. My confused body tingled with new sensations, suddenly I sat up.

"The horses," I blurted.

"They're fine," he said, his voice sounding husky.

Satin Dancer and his horse stood together ignoring us, chewing on grass. "You're right, they're fine."

"What's wrong?"

"I'm not sure."

I wanted and didn't want to kiss him again. It felt good, sort of, and not quite right, either. Duke's kisses didn't confuse me like this. I couldn't let myself think about what Duke would feel if he could see me.

"I have a treat for you." Bobby stood up and fumbled around in his saddlebag.

With a flourish he waved something lumpy. "The cook packed us dessert," he said as he handed me a package wrapped in waxed paper.

The chocolate layer cake had gotten squashed, its rich creamy icing melting all over the wrapping. We ate it all, licking the last bits off our fingers.

"Luscious" he declared.

I stood, disoriented by my response to his kisses. I needed to get my bearings.

"We better get going," I said. "It'll be dark soon."

We rode home without speaking much in the hush of dusk.

The next morning I slipped onto the bench beside Rollie at breakfast. Sue Ann sat down across from us. Most of the ranch hands and rodeo people had already eaten and had started the day's work.

"A little late this morning," Sue Ann greeted me.

"We missed you at supper," Rollie said. "Where'd you go?"

"Bobby and I rode up Cedar Creek, cooled off, ate a sandwich." I hoped I sounded casual.

"You went up to the swimming hole?" Sue Ann asked. I caught a faintly amused look pass between her and Rollie. "Been up there many times myself."

I gulped my coffee.

"It's notorious, hon," Rollie said. "Most everyone's been up there."

"Oh," I said. I'd felt special to be asked out by Bobby. *How could I have been so naive?*

They weren't exactly making fun of me, and I left knowing the ride with Bobby hadn't been special at all. It had been common, like necking in the backseat of a roadster on a dead end road.

EIGHT

All day I tried to shake my agitated feelings about kissing Bobby, managing to avoid being alone with him until he caught up with me after supper.

"Great practice today. You're looking real good out there," he greeted me. "Come on. Let's walk over to the arena together."

I flinched and tried to make an excuse. He cut me off.

"My daddy taught me to always watch myself win the night before a competition. If you anticipate what's going to happen, you won't be so nervous."

"You mean imagine it?" Intrigued, I let my curiosity take over and agreed to walk with him. What harm could it do?

At the arena, a few people milled around and some sat in the bleachers. We walked to the far side, away from everyone, as tangerine clouds faded into dusk.

"Sit on the fence and keep your eyes closed," he said. "You'll get closer to the feel."

He climbed up beside me. "Listen to the bleachers full of the cheering crowd. Hear them roar." He waited a few minutes. "Do you hear them?"

I nodded. I heard the crowd. I smelled the dust and my own sweat. I could see my body upright in the saddle, my feet in the stirrups, waiting for the call to release the steer.

"Now watch yourself and Hobo out there, shadowing a steer, one of the boys catching up to you and wrestling it to the ground." His voice, low and smooth, egged me on.

I pictured each cowboy wrestling a steer in his own way while Hobo and I didn't miss a beat. By the time I opened my eyes, the sky had deepened to lavender and we were cloaked in semidarkness.

"As far as I'm concerned, you're ready for Saturday. Tomorrow's practice will be icing on the cake." He took my hand to help me down from the fence. Only a few people were mingling around in the almost empty ring as Bobby wrapped both arms around me and drew me close. My legs turned wobbly, and I tried to push him away.

Don't kiss me here.

"I'm real proud of you," he said close to my ear before letting me go.

☙

I arrived early for practice the next morning and saw Paco leaning against the fence by the chutes. He pushed himself upright as I approached.

"Where is everyone?" I asked, surprised to see him alone.

"Don't know. Guess they're here and there."

I rolled a cigarette. He seemed kind of agitated. The hair on my neck tingled.

"Saw you riding out with Bobby a couple days ago, and last night." He turned his head to spit in the dirt.

"It—" I wanted to tell him to mind his own business.

He didn't give me a chance. Instead, he talked over me.

"I appreciate you, Ruth. You ride smart, hold those steer in line. I'm real willing, all of us are, to share our purse with you, should one of us win tomorrow."

"Thank you. That means a lot to me," I said, more puzzled than nervous.

"I'm not used to riding equal with a woman, especially a young one like you." He gazed off to the distance over my shoulder. His brow furrowed. "It took a while watching you and riding alongside. Now I'm convinced—I don't want to lose you."

"I'm not going anywhere."

We were no longer alone. People, horses, and stock moved around us. I didn't see any familiar faces. Paco didn't seem to notice.

"Bobby's a good man. Keeps a lot to himself." He stood up straight. "He and his wife are good folks. Been out to his place outside Cody. They got two little ones. Not much of a ranch. Raises sheep, not cattle."

I wanted to fade away. The heat of embarrassment flushed up my neck to my cheeks. The toe of Paco's boot pushed around the dust.

"He'd be mad as hell at me for telling you. I thought you should know."

"I won't say anything."

He nodded. We joined the others.

I didn't have time to think about what Paco had said until after practice. I hurried off as soon as we finished. Bobby followed me to the barn.

"Want to go for a walk, kiddo?"

"No thanks." I didn't stop.

"What's wrong? You sound annoyed." He touched my arm.

I pulled away and walked faster.

"Come on, kiddo. You're cutting me up."

"I'm tired. It's been a long day."

He softened his voice. "Yeah. You get some rest. I'm counting on you. Run the picture in your mind over and over as many times as you can."

"Okay," I said over my shoulder and kept walking.

I felt restless and wanted to sort things out. Satin D and I headed away from the ranch across empty land. In the spring it would be littered with cattle. We ambled along, leaving the ranch and arena behind us.

"We're going home, D, soon as we win enough money." I rubbed her neck as she perked up her ears. The tension in her body told me she wanted to stretch out and run, so I touched her flank with my spur and flicked the reins.

"Let's go!" I shouted.

We galloped, dust kicking up behind us until Satin Dancer slowed down and found a watering hole in a thicket of low brush. I dismounted, soaked my bandanna, wiping my face then retying the damp cloth around my neck.

Welcoming the stillness, as Satin D slurped water I flopped down on the bare ground and gazed up at the pale blue sky. I closed my eyes and pictured Bobby with his wife and two children. Sue Ann and Rollie had warned me about ending up with a cowboy on a ramshackle ranch with tumbleweeds blowing across the plain.

"It's almost time to go home," I said to Satin Dancer's rump, but she seemed content to sample the weeds and sparse grasses struggling to survive in the dry wash.

❧

Saturday arrived, the air thick and still. Clouds scudded over the mountains, bristling with electricity.

"How's it going, Ruth?" Rollie asked.

"I'm nervous." The thought of my first time in the arena as a hazer gave me the big time jitters. I'd dressed in straight-legged black breeches and a black shirt buttoned to my neck.

I wore a string tie with a turquoise stone Bobby had given to me. He insisted I wear it, saying, "It's lucky. Belonged to my daddy."

I put on my vest and hat. "What do you think?" I asked Rollie. "I want the crowd to think I'm a cowboy."

"No one's going to believe it."

"Bobby said they would—from the bleachers anyway. And the boys thought it would be better if the spectators think so too."

"You're too good looking to be mistaken for one of them."

I headed to the barn where the even breathing of the horses calmed me. Their snorts and muffled whinnies, along with the tangy odor of sweet hay and manure, helped ease my tension.

I busied myself grooming Satin D and Hobo, hoping the mundane task would clear my mind.

Why did Paco tell me about Bobby? I took out my frustration brushing Hobo's flanks a little too vigorously, which caused him to stop munching his oats and look back at me. "Sorry. These cowboys make me so mad!"

I didn't want any of it to be my fault. I turned the whole incident with Bobby over in my mind until I felt satisfied I had sorted out all the snarls. I wanted to pretend the whole thing hadn't happened.

I saddled Hobo and rode to the arena. Paco stood off to Bobby's left, watching us. Lightning cracked the sky. The storm looming in the distance was moving closer.

Paco sauntered toward me, his large frame stuffed into an ironed white shirt and black trousers. He was wearing his own good luck charm, a silver belt buckle tooled like the head of a bull.

"How's it going?" he asked.

"Ready to win."

"Glad to hear it." He wiped his forehead with a bright red bandanna and tied it around his neck. "Even though we need it bad, hope the rain yonder holds off till the day's over."

The trick riders had finished, and the first steer wrestling team waited their turn. The crowd went wild when the announcer introduced the first bulldogger.

We were up next. A monster of a steer waited for us in the chute. I could smell his fear. The second team exited, and Paco said, "Let's go."

The microphone screeched, startling everyone, and then we heard "Next up Paco Garcia from Cody, Wyoming. He rides a spirited Pinto called Shotgun. Let's give a big hand for this veteran cowboy." I nodded to Paco and took my place. My pulse raced, every nerve ending poised to react.

Behind the gate, terror floated in the steer's liquid eyes. He looked to be close to eight hundred pounds of pent-up adrenaline straining to be let loose. The second Paco gave the signal, another cowboy opened the chute and the steer shot out on fire, the barrier rope loose around its neck. Hobo and I—one being with the goal of keeping the steer in line—caught up with him in a flash.

Paco stayed put. One false move, breaking the restraining rope before the steer had his chance for a head start, would add ten seconds to his time and disqualify him from any prize money.

Halfway across the arena, with Hobo galloping close enough to nudge him, the steer broke the rope that released Paco from the holding box. In mere seconds, Paco caught up to us, cutting off the steer's attempt to get away. The confused animal turned toward Hobo, who dodged the sharp horn headed for his foreleg then hesitated a split second to let the steer get far enough ahead to avoid contact. I nudged Hobo's flank, together we encouraged the steer into a straight line until Paco pulled up even on the other side and leaned over to grab its horns. Our job over, Hobo and I headed out of the way toward the exit.

Paco twisted the steer's neck until all four hooves pointed skyward. In a few seconds, the announcer rang the bell to signal Paco's success and the clowns chased the dazed animal toward the exit.

"Record time. You're the man to beat," Bobby greeted him, sounding thrilled. "Well done, Ruth. The steer had no chance to maneuver. You had him right where you wanted him."

Paco won first place, $150, and another of our boys came in third for a $50 purse. Since they all had agreed to give me the customary amount earned by a good hazer—a quarter of their winnings—I pocketed $50 and hurried to the barn to get Satin Dancer saddled for the barrel races.

Rollie and Sue Ann waited for me at the holding corral.

"You were great this morning," Sue Ann said.

"Thanks. I got real lucky."

"You showed 'em. I overheard several guys talking about your riding, wondering where you came from," Rollie said.

Both of them were dressed ready to ride. No frills except Rollie's red boots.

Satin D and I waited behind the gate until the announcer's voice reverberated across the arena.

"Let's put our hands together for Ruth Thompson, all the way out here from Minneapolis, Minnesota, riding her beautiful mare, Satin Dancer. Keep your eye on Miss Thompson, who rode hazer for first-place steer wrestler Paco Garcia. Yes folks, you heard right, she rode hazer."

The crowd gasped underneath the applause. I caught the energy as I charged into the arena, careening around the barrels, leaning out for balance as we circled around the cloverleaf pattern. We bolted for the finish line with the whole race against the clock over in seconds. I spotted Rollie standing with the women who had already raced.

"You were fabulous, Ruth. No one's come even close to your time," she said as I walked up to the group.

For the second time that day, congratulations and accolades surrounded me. I could hear Mother warning, "Don't let it go to your head."

The three of us cooled down our horses and turned them loose in the pasture. Then, instead of watching the rest of the rodeo, we sat in the shade of the barn, drinking cool water and smoking. Sue Ann took a flask out of her pocket. "Anyone for a pull of hooch?" She held it out to me. The stuff smelled vile. To be polite, I took a swig. I could feel the warmth surge through my veins and passed it on to Rollie.

"You'll toughen up in a year or so." Sue Ann laughed, watching my face, which was contorted in a grimace. "You'll be begging for my homemade moonshine. Got the recipe from my pappy."

"Bobby has set you up for some opportunities." Rollie leaned into the rough wood of the barn, passing the flask back to Sue Ann. "What do you think?"

"I'm going home after I finish my agreement with his cowboys," I said.

"Going home?" they said in unison.

All I could do was nod. I took a long drag on my smoke. "I can ride. But I'm not sure I'm cut out for this life."

"Why not?" Sue Ann said, looking concerned.

"I'm not sure I'm tough enough to keep going."

"Bull. What's really going on?" Rollie reached for the flask.

"It's Bobby Smith, ain't it?" Sue Ann said. "Damn. I knew it."

I avoided their eyes, shifting my position while I waited for Rollie to say something.

"Bound to happen," she finally said. "But I didn't take you for falling for him."

"I didn't exactly fall for him." I thought for a few seconds and decided to confide in them. "He's married."

"I'll be damned," Sue Ann said under her breath. "He sure held that card close to his chest."

Rollie shook her head. "You'd think he'd a let it slip sometime."

"He was so sensitive while Chloe was recovering . . ." my voice trailed off.

"It's okay. We've all been there one way or another," Rollie said.

NINE

The ranch owners put on a big spread for all of us that night. I stood in line, waiting to fill my plate with a thick steak and baked beans. The cowgirls, still lacing their apple cider with homemade liquor, were having a great time. Bobby scooted in line beside me.

"Why aren't you celebrating with your friends?"

"I'm hungry and tired and not fond of whiskey."

I accepted when he asked me to sit down with him. My mood wasn't a good fit for the fun at Rollie's table, and it didn't seem right to go off and sit by myself. Bobby and I still had a couple of months to work together before everyone, except me, left for the next destination on the circuit. He chose an empty table, and I joined him there. The two of us ate as if we were starved, but both relaxed once we had finished.

He offered me one of his Camels. "Winning makes me ravenous. We made good money today. Still there's room for improvement before we move on."

The air went still, and for a moment all the background sounds faded for me.

"I've decided to go home," I said. I must have sounded more determined than I felt because he challenged me right away.

"What do you mean go home?" Bobby shook his head as if he couldn't believe what he'd heard. We both flinched when a bolt of lightning fractured the sky and was followed in a few seconds by a deafening thunderclap. In the quiet that followed he sounded angry when he said, "Don't forget. We've got an agreement."

"You assumed I'd go north with you. I only agreed to Abilene."

Bobby softened his voice. "What's wrong? You're doing a great job, and we're getting along fine." His grin made my skin crawl.

I picked up my plate. He grabbed my free hand. "Come on. Sit down. Your cold shoulder's chillin' me."

I'd promised Paco I wouldn't tell. What choice did I have? Run away like a scared dog? Or face up to Bobby? My heart thumped while I gathered my courage.

I put down my plate. Adrenaline coursed through my veins like Sue Ann's hooch, giving me a burst of grit. "I hear you're married." Grateful for the evening light, my face scalded with a mixture of fear and embarrassment.

"Oh, who told you that?"

"It's no secret."

"I just got a little lonely, sugar, that's all. Besides, I thought you liked it," he said with a sly smile.

A hoot followed by raucous laughter sounded from the table where Rollie and Sue Ann sat. He waited until the laughter quieted.

"Why don't we sit on the front porch away from all this noise? It's going to rain any minute." He leaned across the table and whispered, "Come on. We'll be alone."

"No. I'm heading to the bunkhouse."

"We had a good time upriver."

I felt slimy and turned to leave, but he grabbed me lightly by the arm.

"Sit down. There's no reason to be unfriendly."

I hesitated.

"You're a pal of Rollie's, aren't you?"

I nodded.

Why would he ask me such an obvious question?

"I hear she doesn't like cowboys either."

"I'm sure she has her reasons." Still standing, I remembered that she'd told me the first day I met her that she didn't get mixed up with the cowboys like Sue Ann did. "That's her business."

"I'm telling you because I don't want you getting a reputation. She only likes the women." Thunder rumbled in the distance. The sky had darkened. "I didn't take you for being one of her kind."

"What do you mean?"

"Women together. It's not natural," he said, averting his eyes.

Confused, I hesitated, and then thought about the dance Rollie had taken me to in Oklahoma, regretting we still hadn't talked about it. It had gotten lost with Chloe getting hurt the next day and me staying behind.

I wanted to defend Rollie. We'd had such fun at the dance. It had felt good to relax in the company of women, away from the cowboys. It didn't make sense to think of Rollie as perverse. Without her kindness and wisdom, I'd have been lost from my first day on the circuit. She'd welcomed me to the rodeo and had become my best friend.

At that point, realizing Bobby had insulted both Rollie and me, I wanted to slap his face like in the movies, but didn't have the nerve, and instead I simply turned and walked away.

He caught up to me and held his hands up in a gesture of surrender.

"Hey. I'm just trying to protect you."

I stared at him without speaking.

Turning to leave he warned, "Just don't let this spoil your riding. We've got a few more contests before the rest of us move on."

The sky opened at last, drenching us.

"I keep my word" I said, walking away from him.

☙

I listened to the downpour pounding the bunkhouse roof. Ranchers, watching their thin and dehydrated range cattle raise their faces to the sky to quench their thirst, could dare to hope the recent drought would ease. By morning the rain had stopped and left low-lying areas flooded. The water just rolled across the arid land, leaving puddles instead of soaking in.

Rollie and I turned up for early breakfast with an un-usually large crowd. Bronc riders and steer wrestlers sat together and filled a couple of tables. Promoters and ranch owners gathered under an oak tree away from the rest of us. In line, talk buzzed with rumors about the riding conditions. Horses and mud don't mix. Should we or shouldn't we ride?

Rollie and I heaped our plates with scrambled eggs, fried potatoes and bacon, then sat at the table with the other cowgirls.

"Haven't been out to the arena. Hear it's a sloppy mess," Sue Ann said. She nursed a cup of coffee, no food.

"You haven't been up this early in ten years," one of the other cowgirls kidded her.

I tuned out the conversation. My uneasiness after my clash with Bobby had magnified during the night. Had I overreacted? More than anything, I'd wanted to sit alone with Rollie this morning. I finally understood the reason she'd said some people thought the dance was wrong.

Damn Bobby. Damn the rain. Everything is spoiled for me. I'd been stupid to think the rodeo was only about risk taking in the arena.

"If you're not going to eat, let's go see the muddy mess everyone's talking about," Rollie said. I'd just been pushing my food around on my plate, and finally shoved it away as I downed the last of my coffee.

We joined a few others who were heading toward the stadium, our boots squishing through gunk. Several large pools of water shimmered in the center of the arena, reflecting a flawless sky. Rollie carried a long stick that she poked into the largest puddle.

"Might dry out round the edges in this heat. This here'll be churned up in no time. I'm bowing out of the barrels," she said. "I got to protect Hornet and myself. You should, too."

"That's up last. Maybe it'll all be dried out by then," I said.

One of the other cowgirls said, "This ain't gonna dry out. Our horses could end up with a pulled tendon or worse if one of them slips in the mud."

"She's right," someone else said. "Maybe we should all pull out of today's competition."

"I agree," Rollie said.

It could be an easy win. I'd need the money if I left the circuit early as I planned.

Rollie turned to me. "Come on, let's go. That gal is right. It'll be too dangerous to run the barrels. I've been riding rodeo most of my life and never seen a field in muddier condition."

She tossed her stick aside. "What's worse, the crowd loves to watch a mud fight. The more splashing and slipping, the more excitement. I'll bet all my winnings so far that the promoters plan to put the barrels smack in the middle of that pool of water just to entertain the crowd."

"Guess I'm still green around the edges. I had no idea they'd do that. I would never put Satin Dancer in danger."

After I canceled out of the race I went to find Bobby. Hazing had to be even more dangerous than the barrels.

I found him in the barn and said, "I've been out to the arena. It's too risky, especially in the center where the steers run."

"We're not quitting," he said. "If we don't ride, we don't win."

I tried to argue with him. "I hear they threw up these grounds without proper drainage. It's going to be slippery out there."

"So what. You can handle it."

"I'm canceled out of the barrels. I'm not risking Satin D, and I'm worried about Hobo."

"Don't go soft on me now. You can't leave the boys without a hazer." His smirk mocked me. "You gave me your word. Remember?"

"Anything could happen. It—"

He interrupted me. "Hobo is sure footed and, with the right directions from you, won't slip."

He beat me down until I ran out of steam. He had a comeback for all my concerns, then dismissed me with a terse "Don't lose your nerve. A little muck won't hurt you."

I headed for the barn carrying a heavy stone of dread. Rollie found me there saddling up Hobo.

"So you are riding," she said. "Didn't you talk to Bobby?"

I couldn't admit that I'd caved in, shamed by Bobby and unable to stand up for myself.

"I've been lucky so far. And Bobby thinks we can win."

Rollie took a deep breath and exhaled.

"Typical," she said.

No use in trying to fool her.

"Actually, he dismissed me like a panicky schoolgirl."

"You're smarter than that. If you're going to ride, get over there and watch what's going on," she said.

I rode Hobo over to the holding corral and spent the rest of the morning planning my strategy. The bucking broncos and Brahman bulls tore up the ring, tossing riders all over the place. The crowd bellowed its enthusiasm for every cowboy who left the ring covered head to toe in a sticky mess.

The clowns did their best to help by covering the ruts with sawdust and smoothing the surface between events, taking deep bows and dancing with their rakes.

The steer wrestlers were up last in the competition. All but the middle of the arena had mostly dried, and with only seconds to anticipate the path of the steer it would take all my strength and finesse to encourage Hobo to veer a whisker more away from the steer than usual to avoid the soggy center.

Avoid the soggy condition in the center. Keep the steer in line. Exit with dignity.

I began to believe in myself. During our first three runs, each of the bulldoggers had managed to wrestle his steer to the ground. I used the reins to keep Hobo pointing straight ahead, my spurs and thighs providing cues through his body. So far, none of my wrestlers had a winning time, but at least Hobo and I had managed to maintain sure enough footing to keep the steer in line.

I waited with Paco, my last cowboy to ride. We watched a couple of boys from town lose their steer and disqualify.

"It's up to you," I said to Paco. "I heard Bobby say earlier you're our only hope today."

Paco shook his head and said, "It's brutal out there, that hole's getting deeper and sloppier. Even an old veteran like me can't stand the stench all the way up here at the fence."

That made me laugh.

"I thought it was just me about to faint from the smell of bull piss and wet manure."

"You're okay," he said. "We're a good team."

We were next up. Paco waited to the left of the chute with me on the right. I checked out the steer and judged his agility level to be high.

As soon as the chute opened, Hobo and I shadowed the steer. He rampaged toward our path, bucking like a bronco, spewing mud behind him. With his head low to the ground, he didn't notice Hobo and me catch up to him. I could hear his violent snorts over the roar of the crowd. In a split second, I touched Hobo's right flank. We changed course a millimeter toward the steer's left shoulder, surprising him into a straight line.

In that instant, the holding rope broke. Shotgun and Paco exploded toward the center of the arena and caught up even with the steer. Out of the corner of my eye I saw the steer stumble, and as the crowd erupted I knew Paco was in trouble because a bulldogger must wait for an animal that falls on its own to rise up on all four legs—only then can it be wrestled to the ground again.

I focused all my attention on getting Hobo safely to the exit and didn't grasp that Paco had been disqualified until after I had dismounted.

As soon as they were out of the arena Paco, covered in mud, ambled toward me leading Shotgun by his reins. He clapped his huge meaty hand on my shoulder and sighed. "Tough luck that SOB slipped and fell. The fat bastard couldn't get himself up out of the mud and ate up all my time." Then he turned and headed toward the barn.

Bobby rushed toward me.

"What happened out there?" he shouted.

"Maybe Shotgun spooked. Paco said the steer slipped in the mud."

Bobby lowered his voice. "No. You miscalculated. You let the steer move too far to the right," he said.

"I didn't lose my concentration or let the steer pull toward me." Bobby's accusation infuriated me. "And I know my place."

"That's not how I see it," he said and turned on his heel to walk away from me.

I joined Rollie for dinner. We had the mostly empty dining area to ourselves with the sun still relaxing behind the hills.

"Today is one of the worst I've seen," she said. "Thought that rain would ease things up. It just hurt us all."

I didn't answer; my thoughts were on what had happened earlier. I must have looked upset because Rollie said, "Rodeo isn't an easy life. Maybe it's best you're going home."

"Bobby chewed me out today. Said I caused Paco to lose."

She slammed down her fork.

"That damn cowboy makes me so mad. I saw the whole thing. Paco veered right instead of straight ahead. Spooked that massive beast into a panic, and it slipped."

"Why would he blame me?"

Rollie shrugged her shoulders. "He's one of the boys. They stick together."

We'd finished eating. I took our plates to the washing post and returned with two cups of coffee.

Rollie continued as if I hadn't been gone, "Or maybe he didn't like that you rejected him. I watched you two last night, and he seemed mighty peeved at the end of your conversation."

"He got mad at me and made a big deal of you not liking the cowboys."

"Me?" she said. Her brow furrowed.

I wanted to clear up my confusion about what Bobby had said without hurting her.

She sat waiting for me to answer. "He said the reason I don't like him is because you and I are too close."

She let out a sigh.

"That so?" She took a deep breath and exhaled. "It's not that simple. I tried liking the cowboys, even married one. I have a daughter about your age . . . somewhere. Haven't seen her in a long time."

Her hand shook when she held a match to her cigarette.

"It's been a long day," she said. "Let's get out of here before it gets crowded, put our horses to bed, and find a quiet place to talk."

We took care of our horses, and Rollie slipped into the bunkhouse to pick up her ukulele. We climbed a ridge, and lounged under an ancient oak, leaning against its massive trunk. The sun had dropped below the horizon, leaving a golden glow across the pasture where cattle grazed. Rollie strummed until the sky changed to indigo silk decorated with stars.

It was a warm evening, and I dozed as a choir of crickets accompanied Rollie's ukulele.

"You remember the dance?"

I nodded and sat up, totally alert.

She set aside her ukulele.

"I took a chance that night. Saw something in you I could trust. I keep trying to figure you out, always reading that thick book like you're a scholar but able to handle and ride a horse like the toughest cowboy. You've got a beau who declares his love for you, and you say he's just a pal."

I moved around a bit to get comfortable, and waited for her to go on.

"I didn't make a mistake taking you to the dance. Something tells me you've got more ahead of you than the rodeo . . . and a lot to learn. The world is full of people like Bobby Smith with all sorts of opinions."

"I had more fun at that dance than I've had in a long time."

"I noticed that," she answered. "Like I said that night, some folks say it's wrong for women to be together. They read their Bibles and find a way to quote the Lord against love. Makes me shake my head in disbelief every time."

I listened without saying anything.

"The man I married was nice enough," Rollie continued. "We worked the land together and raised cattle. But it never felt right."

She shifted her position.

"All along I had feelings for women, but I surprised myself when I fell in love with a gal married to one of our ranch hands."

I took out my pouch of tobacco and rolled each of us a smoke.

"The stakes were high. We tried to be discreet." Rollie picked up her ukulele and played a few chords. "But my husband found out and sent my three-year-old daughter away to his mama out in California."

I felt the rough bark of the tree through the fabric of my shirt. A sharp sadness started behind my heart and widened throughout my chest. I'd never been in the presence of such deep pain. It was one thing to read about it in *Anna Karenina*, but another to hear it said in person.

The thick canopy of oak leaves blocked the stars above us.

"He took your daughter from you?" I handed her a cigarette.

"Yes. I had no idea he would do such a thing. Her name is Angela." Her voice trailed off. "My angel." She took out a match and struck it on a stone. I bent toward her cupped hand so she could light my cigarette, then she lit her own, and slowly exhaled before going on.

"I loved Diane. She was both sweet and tough. We left our husbands, ran off, and joined a rodeo. We only lasted a few years. The hiding and pretending to just be friends took its toll. Every year, I hope she'll turn up at the Four Bar dance. She never does."

Her story lay heavy between us like an invisible fog.

Rollie picked up her ukulele and said, "I like that song we danced to that night, 'Keep on the Sunny Side of Life.' Kind of cheers me up when I feel blue, reminds me there's more than one way to see things."

She improvised a few bars and sang the first verse quietly in her raspy voice.

I joined her. We sang the rest of the song together.

Our voices faded, and I relaxed against the oak tree.

Rollie put her hand on my knee.

"Like I said, I didn't make a mistake taking you to that dance. You'll understand when the time comes. For now, don't let Bobby Smith pull you down. He's the man you work for. That's all."

We took our time walking to the bunkhouse.

Exhausted by the long day, I climbed into bed. As Rollie blew out the lantern she declared, "It's not gonna rain again. I can feel it. My bones don't hurt like they did a few days ago."

In the next few weeks, if anyone mentioned the weather it was about the drought.

As for me, I looked away toward home.

TEN

My rodeo days ended in October 1931. Sue Ann, Rollie, and I crowded into the cab of a borrowed truck, pulling a trailer with Satin Dancer behind us on the way to the Texas and Pacific Railway station in Abilene. I'd been inexperienced the first time we'd ridden together like this. This time I rolled the cigarettes and passed one to each of them.

"It's been quite a ride, gal," Sue Ann said to me. "I feel like I've watched you grow up."

I swelled with pride. I'd been a greenhorn eight months ago, now my boots bulged with the prize money I'd earned on the circuit. I had accomplished the goal of making enough for my college tuition and was heading home a prizewinning rodeo performer.

At the train station, I knew it would probably be the last time I'd see either of them. My heart wavered between Rollie and home. I pressed a piece of paper with my address into her hand. "Send me a postcard and let me know how you are."

"I'll be just fine, hon. I'm hardier and more stubborn than an old bull." She stuffed the paper with my address into her pocket. "Stay on the sunny side, girl, and you'll be all right."

Her face with all its lines of wisdom and heartache told the real story. "Don't forget there's more to life than the rodeo."

The conductor yelled, "All aboard! Last call!"

"You've both been great," I said, turning to run for the stairs. I found my seat and opened the window. *No tears. Tough cowgirls don't cry.*

"Send me a Christmas card!" I shouted, my voice lost in the clatter and hiss of the engine.

Three days later, the train approached the Mississippi River and moved slowly across the Short Line Bridge from St. Paul to Minneapolis. The river greeted me with reflected flames of red, orange, and yellow. The fall foliage flickering on the water mimicked my feelings, obscuring everything beneath the surface.

✢

I stepped across the threshold of home greeted by the aroma of cinnamon and apples.

"Mother!" I shouted and fell into her open arms, not caring that her hands were covered with flour and left prints all over my jacket. Duke grabbed me next and startled me with a kiss full on the mouth in front of my family. All eyes were watching us. For a moment I thought they might applaud.

He acted as if we were alone. "I missed you." He held me at arm's length and looked into my eyes. "Seems like you've been gone forever."

I'd expected a more reserved greeting from him. It astonished me that he wore a tweed suit like my brother Hal. And now they both smoked a briar pipe similar to Dad's.

"You look so different. I've never seen you in a suit and smoking a pipe."

"I'm not so different. Maybe it's you. I'm a frat man now, thanks to your brother." Hal had gotten married while I was away, and now seemed even more controlling than ever. I'd noticed his grimace when Duke kissed me earlier—which caused me to hope that Duke hadn't picked up any more of Hal's conventional traits.

Mother called us all to the festive dinner that she and Aunt Margaret had created for my homecoming. As I looked around the table at my family, the loneliness I'd carried vanished. For that moment, I belonged and reveled in the security and love surrounding me.

After the meal, Duke and I sat in the living room. He won me over and made me laugh with his new talent of blowing perfect smoke rings that passed through each other. At that point, I realized the *real* Duke lived inside that suit—my best friend, not a carbon copy of my brother.

For the next few days Hal's wife, Dorothy, gushed over me. She and Hal had been engaged before I'd left for the rodeo, but since they couldn't afford a lavish wedding the two of them had eloped to save money. They were living in Minneapolis, where Hal still worked in Dad's accounting office.

Dorothy did her best to restore my calloused hands and chipped nails, all the while chatting about the newest trends in hair and clothes. I appreciated that she donated dresses that were now one size too small for her to my cause. This generous act of charity allowed me to bank most of my winnings. If I watched my pennies, I'd be able to pay my tuition for the next four years.

She brushed off my thanks. "It's being in love. Puts on the pounds," she said, patting her hips. "Anyway, I'll never need this size dress again. Hal and I are so excited, we're hoping to start a family soon."

I hugged her. "I'm so happy for you."

"Truth is that all I've ever really wanted is to be married and have a family," she said, tossing me another dress. "You and Duke are next."

Even though her boldness and teasing made me uncomfortable, I was grateful that she didn't criticize me as Hal did in his older brother fashion. He'd welcomed me home, but I knew he still thought joining a rodeo had tainted my reputation.

My life seemed to move along without my permission. Dorothy and Hal introduced me to Kappa Rho, her sorority, and when I'd been accepted Dorothy said, "You'll adore all the girls. I had such fun." Then, with a dreamy look in her eyes, she continued in her breezy voice "Mrs. Sullivan, the housemother, is the best."

She soon decided I needed coaching on etiquette, and made sure I learned the finer points of dining. "No, Ruthie dear, the spoon on the right is the correct utensil to use to sip bullion."

❦

I joined the sorority on Twenty-Sixth Avenue in December 1931, and moved in before classes started in the spring semester that began in January. Duke escorted me to my first social event with my new sorority sisters—the annual Christmas dinner and dancing party with Kappa Rho alumnae and their escorts.

The Yule tree, ten feet high and decorated all in white, adorned the large social room. Pine logs blazed in the marble fireplace, and candles scattered throughout gave off a soft glow. I introduced Duke to my roommate Elena. They chatted while Mrs. Sullivan whisked me away to meet a few of the alumna girls.

"Ruth's our newest pledge. Quite the horsewoman, I hear." She introduced me and left me alone with the group while she flitted off to attend to her hostess duties.

"Dressage?" asked a woman wearing a bright red dress and lipstick to match. "I just love it. A ballet between horse and rider."

Duke arrived at my elbow. "Ruth is a prizewinning rodeo performer." I could hear the pride in his voice.

"Oh my," the woman said. She cocked her head toward me and folded her hands in front of her chest as if she might say a prayer for me. "All that dust, and all those cows. How could you bear it?"

Thankful I'd worn a dress with pockets, I hid my hands, which Dorothy had failed to completely repair, and managed to say, "You can get used to most anything if necessary."

Another woman in the circle waved at someone on the other side of the room. They all turned at once like a small school of fish and disappeared into the crowd.

"That's enough of that," I said to Duke. "Keep the rodeo to yourself from now on."

"Why? You earned your tuition in an exciting way. You should be proud. I only did drudge work in the cornfields with my father and milked your uncle's cows. Most of these girls probably had their tuition paid by their daddies." He put his arm around my waist and led me out to the sun porch away from the crowd.

"You don't get it. They think I'm a freak. They ask questions like I'm some kind of lowlife that jumped off a boxcar. Don't bring it up again."

"I surrender. My lips are sealed." He took me by the hand and led me inside, introduced me to a couple he knew, then barely left my side for the rest of the night.

Hal and Dorothy along with two other couples who were sitting at our table, were chatting about university social life. Feeling stifled by the conversation, I made several trips to the ladies room just to get away.

University life swallowed me up, and I threw myself into my classes while doing my best to adjust to rules at the sorority. It didn't take long to lose my quasi-celebrity status as quite the horsewoman. I hid my tough cowgirl rodeo persona behind the polite dinner conversation of an almost engaged young woman who failed to go anywhere near controversy. I conformed as if I were waiting for the white gown and the big day. No more rolled smokes. Like a clever chameleon, I exploited my talent for pretending to be someone other than myself and joined the Masquers Drama Club, performing in plays on and off campus.

Duke and I went through the motions of being a couple, a carbon copy of Hal and Dorothy. Duke's kisses were sweet, with none of the dangerous excitement I'd experienced with Bobby Smith—me all wet from my dunk in the river and him with a bare chest. I'd never seen Duke without a shirt. Even with swim trunks, he wore a tank top.

I took comfort from the soothing balm of my time with Satin Dancer, who I boarded at the stables near Bryn Mawr Meadows not far from campus, where I'd managed to secure a job mucking out stables and caring for the horses. My busy life fell into place like a child's wooden puzzle with a missing piece.

※

On an unusually warm Saturday in September 1932, early in the fall semester, I sat alone in the almost empty campus library. Too restless to study, I indulged in nostalgia for the rodeo.

My mind wandered back to the stink of dust laced with tobacco spit and manure, muscles strained sinew to bone. I could hear the pounding of Satin Dancer's hooves on the hard dirt, my buckskin skirt slapping against her sweaty flanks, the roar from the grandstand—followed by blue ribbons, congratulations from the other cowgirls, and the bills from winning purses tucked safely in my boot. I stared out the window at the empty quad and the steps leading to the library entrance.

Was it a fair exchange—glory for books?

Some movement on the grass caught my attention, and a woman appeared out of nowhere. With a long stride, she ascended the library steps two at a time, seeming to float toward the entrance. The fabric of her taupe trousers, draping from deep pleats at the waist, rippled as she moved.

At the top of the stairs the woman paused, her white silk blouse catching the sun filtering through the nearby trees. Then she disappeared.

Had she been a mirage?

No. There she was, standing at the entrance to the study room. Most of the dark mahogany tables were empty, but to my surprise she walked toward mine and settled in across from me, two chairs down. She nodded a quick acknowledgment, almost as if she knew I was trying not to watch her. I inhaled a subtle scent of wildflowers.

All business, she spread a yellow picket fence of sharpened pencils above her notebook and opened her text. Sitting up straight, she went to work. Her handwriting marched across the unlined page, tiny soldiers on a secret mission. My own notebook remained blank while I skimmed the pages of Freud's *The Interpretation of Dreams*, comprehending nothing.

Once in a while I sneaked a glance at the intriguing woman on the other side of the table, gathering small details. Smooth skin, high cheekbones, and an almost beautiful face. When she pursed her lips, maybe disagreeing with something on the page, I glimpsed deep dimples in both cheeks. Thick, honey-colored braids crisscrossed neatly over her head, every strand in place. I pushed my own short curls, frizzed out of control from the humidity, away from my forehead—Harpo Marx to her cool Garbo.

With much effort, I glued myself to my studies and didn't look up again until I heard a soft thud. She'd closed her book and was looking straight at me, her gaze captivating. I couldn't turn away. She spoke in a quiet voice with the hint of a foreign accent, "Weren't you in the Easter play put on by that Catholic group last April?"

My library whisper caught in my dry throat. "Yes. I played Mary Magdalene." I'd worn a long blonde wig and flowing robes, yet she recognized me.

"I thought you looked familiar. I've barely been able to concentrate, trying to decide where I'd seen you."

Unable to concentrate?

She continued, "I covered the play for the campus newspaper. Although not much to my taste, you almost made a believer out of me, bringing news of the Resurrection."

Was she toying with me?

"You wrote that article? It caused quite a stir at the Newman Center."

"You mean that Catholic club? I confess. I'm the guilty one. You must admit it could be rather uneventful to review a play based on the Gospel, so I added a bit of my own drama."

"You certainly did. Questioning whether or not the Bible is based on fact opened up a heated debate."

She had a look of amusement on her face. "Why shouldn't we question everything, even what's considered sacred truth?"

I knew she was referring to the sacred truth of the Bible. The way she said it made my heart leap. Her words touched me in a place I fiercely protected, and something in her demeanor tickled the lie I'd been living since returning from the rodeo.

She introduced herself. "I'm Gisela. Want to grab a cup of coffee? It's too warm in here to study."

Her name rolled over in my mind, GEEZ-el-uh. It sounded as exotic as her accent. I accepted her invitation without hesitating and followed her outside, feeling strangely excited.

There is no logic in such things. Standing together out on the steps her face, lit by the afternoon sun, charmed me.

Even though she'd been blunt in our brief conversation, I remained oblivious to whether or not she had offended me.

I smiled. My nervousness caused my upper lip to get caught on my front teeth. Gisela gave no hint that she noticed and offered to shake my hand, a gesture more common among men than young ladies. She reminded me of a sunny spring day with a gentle breeze, the kind where it's hard to decide whether or not you need a sweater. Ashamed of what my palms must feel like, now calloused from my stable work, I licked my lips and swallowed.

I introduced myself and tried to meet her eyes without flinching.

"I have a favorite diner down toward the river," she said. "We can walk. It's not far, and I like to get away from the campus hoopla."

We walked side by side. My brown V-neck blouse and white pleated skirt seemed ordinary. I had not seen another woman on campus wearing trousers.

On the way to the diner, I learned that she too studied psychology and that we were both enrolled in the same Thursday vocational class for the fall term. I laughed as I told her I'd been dreading what I thought would be a dull requirement.

"We can compare notes. I hear the prof is an old fogey," she said, holding open the door to the diner, which was almost empty in the lull between lunch and dinner.

We took seats in a booth by the window. A lone waitress glanced at us from behind the counter and waved at Gisela in recognition. Sun filtered in the grimy front window and reflected off the chrome trim around the tables. The waitress, who appeared tired enough to fall in her tracks, served us coffee. From behind the counter, she squeaked a piece of chalk across a blackboard: "Meat loaf with mashed potatoes and gravy 25 cents. Chili 10 cents." Smells from the kitchen mimicked the menu.

Gisela took out a pack of Pall Malls. Even though I'd given up smoking to save money for school, when she offered me a cigarette I took it. Leaning toward her for a light, I felt dizzy for a moment after the first inhale surprised my lungs.

"Let me guess" she said, shaking out the match and dropping it in an ashtray, "You're a sorority girl."

Was I that obvious?

I'd been doing my best to fit in with my sorority sisters and follow the house rules, but the way she asked the question made me suddenly want to distance myself from that part of my life.

"It's almost a family tradition—my brother's wife convinced me I should join her house, Kappa Rho."

"And you're Catholic, of course?"

"Sort of. I was raised in the church. What about you?"

"I live off campus in a rented room with kitchen privileges, across from the Marcy School. I'm agnostic. That's why I had such fun with your play. I find it impossible to know if there's a God."

"To say the Bible is based on myth . . ."

She didn't let me finish. "I only hinted that some people consider the story to be mythological. If we don't question where our beliefs come from, and why we have them, we're like lemmings."

"I never thought of it that way."

I hoped I didn't sound foolish.

"The idea of blindly following someone's ideas of what we should be . . ." She stopped herself and said, "I mean believe. Anyway, being a follower gets me riled up." Her smile softened her words. "I hope you don't mind my soapbox."

"No. Of course not." I paused to gather my thoughts. "I don't think of it so much like lemmings falling to their death in ignorance, more like a swarm of bees forming a colony with their queen. Like-minded people sticking together."

"Sticking together, you mean like what's happening in

Europe? No one over here seems to care, but my father lives in Paris and writes that despite street violence in Germany against the SA Storm Troopers, newspapers sympathetic to Nazi influence continue to wage a propaganda campaign blaming Jews for Germany's economic and social problems. It's unbelievable how the general public there often turns a blind eye to the SA thugs trying to intimidate customers from entering Jewish shops."

"It's so complicated."

"And in this country so many folks who can't find work, living in hobo villages. Why? Where are all the good Christians who claim to be their brother's keeper? It doesn't matter what problems we're talking about. People are too afraid of consequences, of losing what they have. Jesus said, 'Turn the other cheek,' not 'Look the other way.'"

"Fear can paralyze people."

"True," she said. "But so can ignorance."

I wondered what to say next. She had stirred something inside me I couldn't name.

"I do tend to go on" she said, fiddling with the red and white pack of cigarettes.

"Not at all." I admired her intensity. I lifted the heavy ceramic coffee mug with both hands and looked at her over its thick lip. I wanted to know more about her.

She smiled as if she might be reading my mind. The room seemed suddenly warmer. I again noticed the deep blue of her eyes and felt suspended—in what? Where? For a moment, it didn't matter.

"You can't be from Minneapolis with your accent. It sounds French," I said.

"It is. I attended boarding schools in Europe." She looked nostalgic. "It's a long story." She took a sip of her coffee and paused for a moment. "I lived in Minneapolis until about age seven. But enough about me, tell me something else about you besides your acting ability."

I could feel my face flush while my mind raced around for something that could hold her interest.

"Well, I started university in January of 1932, a month after moving into the sorority, and . . ."

I paused while deciding whether or not to tell her about my rodeo experience, but she had sounded so sincere that I didn't want to hide behind my usual socially acceptable politeness, so I continued. "Before that I spent eight months on a rodeo circuit."

"You make it sound like jail." She burst out in exuberant laughter.

I joined her amusement. "No, I actually enjoyed it."

"You must have been the Rodeo Queen. Or should I say Queen Bee?" She laughed again, as naturally as if we'd known each other forever. "I can just see you riding a white stallion, dressed in flashy western gear, carrying the American flag."

"No, never queen."

"Seriously?"

"I earned most of my tuition as a hazer, tracking a terrified steer, keeping him in line so a cowboy could wrestle him to the ground. I also competed in barrel races and relays."

"No kidding? I'd like to know more about all of it."

I felt an unfamiliar surge of pride. The rodeo had been the means to an end, something I could do because I knew how to ride. I hadn't meant for it to define me. With Gisela, I wanted to seem special, even courageous.

"Now I work over at the stables at Bryn Mawr Meadows. I grew up around horses with my Uncle Edward. He gave me my horse Satin Dancer when she was a foal and taught me everything about riding."

"Having an uncle like that is pretty keen."

Then she glanced at her watch.

"Oh no. It's late. I've got to fly. A story about those hobo camps around Minneapolis for the Sunday *Tribune*. I've got a deadline."

"You write for the *Tribune?*"

"I freelance to earn a little cash whenever I can. I learned from my father. He's a journalist. That's why I'm so passionate about what's going on in Europe." She took out her share of the money for our coffee.

Our hands brushed as we each put down a dime.

"I'm glad we met," she said, leaving her hand on the table next to mine. "Not many people are willing to listen to my diatribe."

A warm shiver pulsed through my body. I could have listened to her recite a recipe for potato soup without getting bored.

We arranged to meet again the following Saturday in the library.

"Let's have tea at my place after we study," she said over her shoulder as we parted.

We stood across from each other on opposite sides of the street, each of us waiting for our trolley. The pavement shook as hers, heading toward Eleventh Avenue, rumbled to a stop. She waved just as it cut off our ability to see each other.

ELEVEN

On the way home, I could still feel the moment our hands met on the table.

What if I'm a lemming? Or even worse, what if she thinks I'm boring?

From the trolley stop, I walked quickly with my head down as if I could outrun the thoughts that pursued me like footsteps approaching from behind on a dark street. Although relieved to have made it home in time for dinner at six, I stopped short in front of the sorority when I saw Duke's familiar roadster.

Why so early? Not expecting to see him until seven thirty for our usual Saturday night date, I rushed in through the side door only to be greeted by loud chatter from the dining room, so I sprinted up the back stairs, bumping into Elena in the hallway leading to our room.

"Hey, roomie, you're late," she greeted me.

"What's going on down there?"

"The fellows are here from Sigma Phi. Remember? It's the last Saturday of the month, our first exchange dinner of the term with a lucky fraternity. You missed the social hour."

Sigma Phi, Duke's fraternity. *How could I have forgotten?*

"Duke's been asking about you," Elena said with a smug look on her face. "I kept him entertained while he waited. He's saving a place at the table for both of us."

I walked down the hall and took a look over the stair rail. Duke sat alone at the dining table.

In the bathroom I tried to smooth my frisky hair with a damp comb. Personal appearance at the dinner table ranked right up there with promptness and manners.

I dropped the wrinkled white skirt I'd worn all day on the floor and rummaged through the closet, looking for a fresh dress. How could I have let Duke down like this? I knew how uncomfortable he could be in social situations.

By the time I finished dressing and glanced in the mirror, my hair had already bolted out of control. I searched for bobby pins to at least hold it behind my ears.

Elena returned.

"I'll go down and let Duke know you're home." I suspected she couldn't figure out what he saw in me—maybe she even had a crush on him.

I hurried downstairs and slipped into the chair Duke held out for me.

"Do you think anyone noticed?" I whispered to Elena across Duke.

"You mean Mrs. S? I don't think so. She was busy discussing politics with the Sigma Phi chaperone," Elena answered.

Mrs. Sullivan made it her personal mission to mold us into proper young ladies whose charms and manners would benefit our future husbands. She had a habit of consulting her gold wristwatch, clocking our comings and goings.

"I missed you at the social hour." Duke brushed his thick hair off his forehead and straightened the silverware next to his plate. "I thought you'd be home early today."

"I'm so sorry, I forgot all about this."

Mrs. Sullivan saved me from further explanation by tapping a sterling teaspoon against her water glass.

"Grace, ladies and gentlemen." Her trilling voice stopped all chatter.

We bowed our heads and waited while she thanked the Lord for our bounty, then served herself from the first dish and passed it to her right.

"Where have you been all day?" Elena asked while the food made its way around the table.

"Studying at the library. Statistics. It gives me fits."

I touched Duke's hand that rested on his thigh. "I'm sorry," I said again and hoped he would understand.

Duke appeared to relax as we made small talk with each other and with the couple across the table. The conversation turned to the upcoming masquerade ball sponsored by the drama club. Since I belonged to the club, Duke and I would go to the ball together, although we had not yet discussed it.

"Yes," Duke answered his frat brother across the table, "Ruth and I are coming. We're cooking up great costumes."

I nodded in agreement as if I knew the details. Duke and I always seemed to assume we knew what the other of us wanted, but it annoyed me that night that we took each other for granted.

Following the dinner we all adjourned to the parlor for a songfest. Mrs. Sullivan accompanied us on the piano, and one of the fellows had brought a guitar.

The men treated us to a comic rendition of "The Sheik of Araby" accompanied by the guitar. Then Duke took the floor. In his pure tenor voice, he performed an a cappella solo for Gershwin's jazzy "Slap That Bass." He got us all tapping our feet and received a sound round of applause. It never ceased to amaze me how he forgot his shyness when he performed.

One of the other boys replaced Mrs. Sullivan at the piano, and we pushed the chairs out of the way to make room for dancing. Duke and I connected best on the dance floor, both of us losing our inhibitions. As we danced the Charleston to "Sweet Georgia Brown," the other dancers made a circle and egged us on.

The party ended promptly at ten o'clock, and I walked Duke out to his car. "Hop in," he said. "We have plenty of time for a ride. The door isn't locked until eleven o'clock."

"You better, I don't want to have to knock! You know how mad Mrs. Sullivan gets if she has to answer the door after curfew."

Always a gentleman, he opened the door for me and waited until I'd settled in before sprinting around the front of the car to the driver's seat. We headed toward Cedar Lake with the canvas top rolled down and my hair blowing wild in the warm air of the Indian summer night.

At the lake we parked and held hands, watching the moon rising dreamlike above the trees. He put his arm around my shoulders and bent in to kiss me softly on the lips. I felt comfortable and safe, but something in me wanted more, even though I still loved the tough and tender kid I'd met seven years ago when we were thirteen—his long frame and kind face so familiar that I couldn't imagine dating anyone else. I tried to relax, unable to describe what the more might be and cuddled closer, kissing him again, but couldn't shake the uneasy feeling that lapped at me like the gentle waves swishing against the lakeshore below us.

☙

The next Saturday following our study session at the library we arrived at Gisela's.

"You're my first guest" she said, unlocking her door and standing aside to let me in. "Get comfortable. I'll make us a pot of tea."

I sat on a cushioned seat in a bay window that looked out to the street. An open album and loose photos littered a coffee table that held a vase with three stems of red gladiolus, vivid in the brilliant sun streaming through the window.

"The bathroom's down the hall on the right if you need it," she said, bustling around a table in a corner of the room as she poured water from a pitcher into a kettle on a hot plate.

I tried to imagine her life and what it must feel like to live alone in her very own room. On the rodeo circuit I'd slept in a room with more or less ten other women and no one telling me what to do. At the sorority I had only one roommate with what seemed like tons of dos and don'ts.

An oak desk took up most of the space along one wall, the Remington typewriter on top of it adrift in a clutter of papers and books. A steamer trunk with clothes spilling out of a couple of open drawers sat in the opposite corner from where Gisela made the tea. I noticed the outline of a Murphy bed on the wall across from where I sat.

"I know everything is topsy-turvy," she said, catching me looking around the room.

"It must be hard getting organized after a move."

"I've been here a few months. I'm kind of messy. I thrive on the chaos of deadlines."

Messy was not a word I would use to describe Gisela. I remembered her handwriting, so neat and precise while taking notes in the library last Saturday. I'd also admired her carefully woven braids that day, and again there wasn't a hair out of place. Her sense of fashion was impeccable—she wore a simple print dress in a shade of blue that accentuated her eyes.

"Looking at you, I don't think of messy. It's hard to believe from your appearance."

"I'm just vain. That's all. And thank you for the compliment." She set a pot of tea on the table in front of the window seat. "Well, what do you think?"

"It smells divine." I inhaled the comfortable aroma of the tea.

"It's Earl Grey, all the way from England. My father sent it last week along with that lamp." She pointed to a lamp sitting on the steamer trunk with an Art Deco base and a flapper with a perpetual smile who waved her hands and kicked up her heels in what looked like the Charleston.

"But I meant my home, Miss First Guest. Do you like it?"

Of course that's what she meant. *How could I be so clumsy?* She'd lived in Switzerland and France; I felt like a country bumpkin and answered her question like an overexcited child.

"I love it. My room at the sorority has two single beds, and I share a closet with my roommate. There's one window that looks out on the backyard. No visitors allowed. Curfew is eleven on Saturday nights with lights out at eleven thirty on weekends, ten o'clock on weekdays."

"Sounds like boarding school to me."

"I'm playing out a part of my mother's dream. My brother and I are the first to attend university."

"That's special," she said, and then went silent as if she were far away.

A lazy overhead fan clicked, barely moving the warm air. I looked down at the snapshots, unsure of what to say next. Gisela picked up a photo.

"I'm almost finished pasting my family pictures in the book. This is me at about age three with my mother and father."

In the photo, she was sitting on her father's lap, her mother standing behind them at a highly polished dining table with ornate pedestal legs.

"It looks so formal," I said. "Your father must have had a professional photographer." Her parents wore elegant clothes. Gisela wore a white lace dress.

"The picture was taken about three years before my mother died. We lived near Lake of the Isles in a beautiful old house with dark wood paneling and Oriental rugs." Gisela looked out the window. "I don't remember ever being happy as a child after my mother died."

"How could you?"

A sense of melancholy filled me. I couldn't imagine life without my mother.

"What happened after your mother died?" We had finished our tea and sat facing each other. Gisela handed me a couple of pillows, and I settled in to listen to her.

"I crossed the ocean," she said with a faraway look in her eyes. "Minnesota lakes had always been in my life—there's something about how lakes are contained that made me feel safe."

"What do you mean?"

"Have you ever seen the ocean?"

"No. But I'd like to someday."

"The ocean was so vast and turbulent. I hadn't seen it until I boarded ship with my father in New York. There seemed to be no end to the water. As a child I thought it might swallow the ship and all the people on board. But my memories of lakes are warm and gentle like my mother. On Sundays in Minneapolis in the summer my mother would pack a basket, and the three of us would picnic at one of the local lakes. My father rented a canoe and paddled us to a perfect spot to stop and eat. I'd splash in the water and we'd all nap after lunch."

I folded my legs under myself on the cushioned seat.

"In winter my father and I walked through the snow on the path to Lake of the Isles with our skates slung over our shoulders. Mother would refuse to join us, saying it was too cold to have fun. My father laughed at her. He claimed that he and I were of hearty Nordic stock, and she a fragile Irish lass. He liked to tease her and sang Irish ballads to her in his rich baritone."

I waited while she seemed lost in the memory.

"On our voyage across the Atlantic, I missed the lakes the most. I was too frozen inside to miss my mother."

She took in a big breath, closing her eyes, resting her head on the pillows for a few moments. She stood abruptly and stretched her arms overhead. "Let's go out, get some fresh air, do something else." She placed our teacups on the tray with the empty pot and carried it to the table in the corner.

I looked at my watch. "I can't. Dinner is at six."

"Oh yeah, the rules. Too bad for me."

I didn't want to disappoint her. "What about tomorrow? It's Sunday, so I'm working at the stables. We could take a horseback ride when I'm finished. Do you ride?" Not usually so self-assured, I held my breath.

"I haven't for years. You'll have to show me the ropes," she said. "But I'll be an avid student, teacher's pet."

※

The next day, as I led Satin Dancer out to the corral, my boots crunched on the path, releasing the fresh smell of cedar chips mingled with damp fallen leaves. Gisela walked toward me. Her dungarees looked new and her cotton shirt was ironed. She'd tied a patterned kerchief around her neck—a cowgirl right out of a magazine photo.

"Is that your horse?" Gisela called out. Satin D's flanks shone auburn in the sunlight, and she pranced right on cue. A breeze rustled through the leaves of the birch and aspens, not yet in their prime of fall splendor.

"She's a beauty."

"She's my joy." I could barely contain my pleasure at Gisela's admiration.

Gisela reached out to rub Satin Dancer's muzzle. I could tell she had some familiarity with horses.

I held out a piece of apple. "Want to try it?"

She took the apple and hesitated.

"Open your hand. Her lips are soft. She knows what to do."

As Satin D waited patiently, eyeing Gisela while we talked, I held out my hand. My sweet mare snorted as she bent to wrap her mouth around the apple in my open palm.

Then Gisela held out her open hand, and Satin Dancer leaned her long neck toward her. Watching them brought back the memory of helping Duke overcome his fear of horses. I usually spent Sunday with him, and felt a pang of remorse over putting him off today to meet with Gisela.

"Just hold steady, relax," I said and watched while Satin D gently took the apple.

"Her mouth feels like velvet," Gisela laughed. "Like a kiss."

Satin D showed her large teeth in appreciation and pushed her muzzle against Gisela.

"I think she wants more," Gisela said.

"Here, you two get acquainted." I handed her the rest of the apple pieces and left them alone.

I returned in a few minutes leading a tall gelding.

"This is Lonnie. Try giving him some of the apple."

"Hello, handsome," Gisela greeted Lonnie, looking more confident this time. She cooed, telling him they would be good friends.

"You're doing fine. Lonnie knows how to handle riders who feel a little rusty."

"That's me."

I tethered both horses to the rail of the corral. Old friends, Lonnie and Satin Dancer touched noses and snorted. Lonnie's golden body contrasted with Satin D's chestnut coat. Both horses bent to nibble the grass growing alongside the fence and ignored us.

We walked to the stable where I handed Gisela the blankets and grabbed a saddle.

"Here, put this blanket on Lonnie. Make sure it's smooth so the saddle won't chafe."

We worked well together. Gisela placed the blanket on Lonnie with care, smoothing it over several times. I finished saddling both horses.

"You sure look like you know what you're doing."

"I should. I've been caring for horses forever."

With both horses saddled up, I showed her how to check the girth strap, measuring with two fingers to make sure it fit properly so the saddle wouldn't shift.

"That's the easy part," Gisela joked. "Now show me how to throw myself up and over. It's been a long time."

We practiced inside the paddock. She watched while I stepped into the stirrup with my left foot, swinging my right leg high enough to clear Lonnie's rear, then slowly lowered myself into the saddle.

Gisela caught on quickly. "Oh yeah, I remember now, like riding a bike. I'm ready to try it."

"Don't forget to steady yourself by holding his mane in your left hand and the cantle in your right."

I counterbalanced the stirrups from the other side while she followed my instructions. Lonnie stood perfectly still. He knew the routine from years of inexperienced riders learning to mount.

I liked the way Gisela didn't try to cover up her inexperience and trusted my instructions. I walked beside them and we took a few turns around the paddock while she got a feel for the reins. Then Satin Dancer and I joined them, the horses side by side circling the fence, starting, stopping, and turning.

"You're a natural," I declared as we headed for the trail. I couldn't have been more impressed. I could tell that she had learned to ride from an expert and hadn't lost her touch with horses.

We ambled along in the open wetlands, away from the wooded areas. The horses led us down a wide trail that meandered alongside Basset Creek, flowing toward downtown Minneapolis. With the early fall breeze at our backs we let the horses lead us through the low brush.

Laughing at her own inability, Gisela tried to get Lonnie moving forward when he stopped to sample some grass on the side of the trail and refused to budge.

"You're doing great" I said, pleased that Gisela seemed to be enjoying herself. "Loosen the reins and lightly touch his flank with your foot. He'll move. He wants to make sure he can trust you."

That worked well, and as the morning passed Gisela visibly relaxed. Lonnie ignored her miscues and followed Satin D's lead and pace. We stopped to eat the lunch I'd packed, and I noticed Gisela had a little mustache of sweat.

"Whew. I thought the horse did all the work." She flopped down on the grass without seeming to worry about her clothes.

I'd tucked an old red sweater, cinched with a black leather belt, into my usual khaki riding breeches with knee-high black boots.

"You're really slim in the waist," Gisela observed. "Wish I had that kind of figure."

"It's hard work mucking out the stables, hauling tack; keeps me strong and lean."

I handed her a sandwich. I wanted to tell her she looked stylish in her riding clothes, but didn't say anything, concerned that I might sound awkward. Her compliment had been so natural.

But my thoughts were interrupted when Gisela asked, "Have you noticed the trash out in the wetlands?"

"I have. There's an effort to clean up this whole area."

"Maybe I'll write an article about it. I can probably sell it to the *Tribune*. Someone needs to take responsibility for the mess. I'd like to investigate and see who should be held accountable."

I admired her serious side.

As we finished our sandwiches Gisela said, "I think I'm ready to step up the pace. Lonnie and I are getting along great."

"Let's not overdo it, or you'll end up with a sore rump."

She made a face like a disappointed child and stuck out her lower lip. "But I'm having so much fun."

Her enthusiasm delighted me and made me laugh.

"You know what they say, 'too much time on a horse and you'll end up bowlegged and in pain,'" I said, my hands on my hips.

"Come on. Don't be a killjoy. Please. Pretty *pleeeease*."

"Okay. Don't say I didn't warn you. You're going to get acquainted with a whole bunch of new muscles you didn't know existed."

We followed the creek for the next hour, even stepping up the pace to a trot a few times before I insisted we turn back.

"I haven't spent this much time outdoors in years," Gisela said as we led the horses to the stable. "And I also haven't had this much fun in years. Thank you, Ruth."

I could feel my face redden at her comment, grateful for the cool dimness of the barn as we settled our horses in their stalls.

☙

I didn't see Gisela again until Thursday, when she sat down next to me in class. Struggling to get comfortable on the hard lecture chair, she finally folded her sweater and sat on it like a pillow.

"There, that's a little better," she whispered as the professor turned to write on the chalkboard. "I guess you noticed I'm kind of stubborn. My rump's sore as a boil."

I had noticed her stubbornness, yet also found it endearing when she hadn't wanted to stop having a good time.

She handed me a note that suggested we meet later. I nodded.

We rode the trolley to her neighborhood, and sat on a bench in a park near her house. Gisela tossed leftovers from her sack lunch to the pigeons clustering around us.

"So tell me about your rodeo experience," she said.

I thought for a moment.

"In the rodeo I hid my plans to attend college; now I'm uncomfortable talking to most people about the rodeo."

"You can talk to me."

She waited for me to begin.

"I loved it, and I hated it," I said. "I earned my tuition, but rodeo is a man's world. Used to be that women had equal status with the cowboys. It changed recently. The Rodeo Association drew a line, excluding women from the more dangerous competitions after a famous cowgirl named Bonnie McCarroll got trampled to death by a bronco in 1929. They'd already soured on letting women compete for the big prize money. Her death gave them an excuse to push women aside."

The antics of the pigeons amused us as they pranced and preened while vying for the best crumbs.

"I masqueraded as a cowboy in the arena and got away with it because we performed on a small circuit. The big arenas in Calgary and Madison Square Garden would have eaten me alive. It's not the kind of life I want."

"Sounds rough," she said.

"A veteran cowgirl took me under her wing, otherwise I wouldn't have lasted a month. I'm not sure what I expected. More glamour maybe. I didn't bargain on the hard work."

"Do you know what you want now?"

I didn't answer right away. My thoughts had strayed to Rollie. I missed her company and savvy insight. More than a year had passed with no word, and without an address, I was afraid that I'd lost her for good.

Gisela tapped my knee, "I asked if you know what you want now."

"I wish," I said feeling embarrassed I hadn't answered her question. "I love the psychology classes, learning what makes us tick and reading Freud and Jung, all that's happening with psychoanalysis in Europe."

"My father writes that even the famous Jewish psycho-analysts are in danger of persecution. In May of this year Berlin students, urged by Nazi propaganda, burned books considered un-German. Freud's books were thrown onto the fire."

I remembered seeing a short article on an inside page of the *Tribune* about a book burning in Berlin, and wished I'd read it more carefully.

She chucked the last of the breadcrumbs to the birds and crumpled the paper sack. "I wanted to continue my studies abroad after I finish here, but now I'm not so sure. There's too much uncertainty everywhere."

A group of children scattered the pigeons, chasing each other in a game of tag. I listened to their shouts of "You're it!" and "Can't catch me!" and admired their exuberance and lack of self-consciousness.

"Why can't we carry that innocence with us as we get older?" I said.

"Maybe it has to do with breaking the rules of life, the ones that teach us to conform."

"Could be. I'm always trying to fit in, guess I haven't found my niche."

As the children moved away from us, I gathered my thoughts in the quiet they left behind. "I feel different no matter where I am. I thought leaving home for the rodeo would change everything for me, that I'd figure out where I belong. I'm still not sure."

"It sounds like you think you have to learn to play a game to survive."

"Sort of. You have to learn the rules or you'll end up with an empty boot."

Gisela wrinkled her brow.

"It's where I kept my winnings—in my boot."

She touched my hand on the bench between us. Our shoulders brushed. "Sometimes you just have to take your chances."

"You're right. Learning to break the rules filled my boot faster than if I had followed the rules."

"It makes sense to me," she said.

We chatted for a while longer until I absolutely had to leave in order to be sure I'd make it back to the sorority in time for dinner.

TWELVE

That weekend, Duke and I spent Saturday night relaxing to the music at Carla's, a jazz club on Ontario Street near the edge of the East River flats. We sipped Coca-Colas while I did my best to get Gisela out of my mind. I couldn't stop thinking about how much fun we'd had on our horseback ride and in our conversation.

"Have you heard of the trash along the banks of Basset Creek?" I asked Duke during the musicians' break.

"I've heard something. Why?"

"I was out riding with someone a few days ago who is going to write an article about the cleanup efforts for the *Tribune*."

Duke didn't seem at all interested in the creek. He wanted to know about the person I'd been riding with since neither of us had any close friends aside from each other.

"It's someone I just met. Born here in Minneapolis, but went to school in Europe. A psych major."

"Oh?" His voice cracked like it used to when we were in eighth grade. It held a question he didn't ask.

"She's not like the sorority girls. She rents a room over by the Marcy School."

The musicians returned so we got up to dance. Duke held me tightly while they played "Smoke Gets in Your Eyes." The lyrics were for someone else, not us.

The music stopped and Duke confessed, "I'm glad your new friend is a girl. For a minute there something in your voice made me think it might be a fella."

❧

Gisela arrived at class on Thursday and sat down next to me. As the professor cleared his throat to quiet us down, she handed me a note containing just two words: "After class?"

Outside the lecture hall she asked, "What do you say? Want to come over to my place and finish the rodeo story?"

"I can't. I have to work today through Sunday. I work a half day on Saturday."

"Darn. Why don't you come on Saturday and stay for dinner? You could spend the night."

I couldn't just stay over on Saturday. I would have to get a pass and explain why I wanted to stay out overnight.

"Do you want to come?"

"Of course." I could feel a blush creep over my cheeks. "It's complicated. Home by eleven Friday and Saturday nights, and an overnight usually has to be a home emergency or something related to a college activity."

"Come by around one o'clock on Saturday and let me know if you've figured it out."

"Okay, I've got to run." I dashed out, not wanting to embarrass myself further as I realized she'd asked me over casually and had no concerns about curfews or having to ask permission to go out. No one told her how to dress, or when to eat.

She must think I'm a dope.

I arrived at the barn and discussed the whole situation with Satin Dancer, coming to the conclusion that I would somehow get to spend the night with Gisela. On our ride, we galloped full speed to let her stretch her legs, both of us letting off steam.

My head cleared as we slowed to a canter. I made a fail-proof plan—an ill mother. I knew how to play a role onstage. Mrs. Sullivan would be my audience of one, easy to convince.

⁂

As with all true desire, my eagerness to be with Gisela took on a life of its own, and I forgot to consider Duke's feelings.

I met him the next morning for our usual Friday morning bicycle ride and we headed for Cedar Lake. Pedaling around like an old married couple, neither of us spoke and seemed to be lost in our own thoughts.

All I could think about was how I craved Gisela's attention more than anything else in my life. It affected me like being one with Satin Dancer in a full out gallop, all heart and muscle. Bliss.

With Indian summer over, September had turned chilly. The brisk air pinched my cheeks and I called to Duke, suggesting we stop. We propped our bikes against a tree, then sat on a blanket he had carried in his knapsack. Feathery clouds still held a hint of dawn's pink light that reflected in the quiet water.

"Boy, your hair sure has the wilds this morning." Duke broke into a big smile as if he had just made a great joke.

I patted my hair. "Forgot my hat."

"You seem to be forgetting a lot these days." He tried to make a gruff face and ended up laughing.

"You mean the fraternity social? I still feel terrible."

He put on his fake face again. "Don't make that mistake again or you'll end up in the hoosegow, little lady."

"I'm glad you're not mad. I want to ask you something important."

"Shoot," he said, pointing his index finger across the lake and making a clicking sound.

"This is serious," I said, waiting for him to give me his full attention.

He poured us both a cup of coffee from his thermos. "Okay. I'm listening."

"I'm going to ask for an overnight pass for Saturday night. I'm going to tell Mrs. Sullivan that Mother is ill." I sucked in my breath. I needed Duke's support to carry out my plan and counted on him to understand.

"Why would you do that?" His eyes narrowed, and the crease between his eyebrows deepened.

"I want to spend time with my new friend. She might write a story about me and the rodeo, try to get it published in the *Tribune*." I thought he would buy this idea and agree right away.

"That would be great," he said. "But I thought you wanted to drop that subject."

"This is different. She wants to know about my experience."

"So do I. I'm interested."

"I've told you everything already. Besides, you don't write for the *Tribune*."

We sipped our coffee. The pale sun fought the chilled air and lost. Duke stood up and stretched. "I don't understand. Why do you have to say Rosie is ill?" He'd called my mother by name for years—ever since she'd adopted him into our family the first time I brought him home.

"I told you. It's important to me. I can't get an overnight pass if I don't have a valid reason."

"Why do you have to stay overnight? It seems kind of risky to lie to Mrs. Sullivan."

I steadied myself, clenching my teeth to keep from shouting "It's none of your business." I hadn't thought of why. I'd only thought of what I wanted. I waited until my breath evened out, and my thoughts were collected.

"I need you to trust me that it's important enough to lie to Mrs. Sullivan. I've never had a close friend other than you. I want her to like me." I let that sink in while he stared off across the lake. "I also need you to know what I'm doing. What if one of the sorority girls tells you that Mother is ill? You'd rush over to Mother and Dad's. They'd get riled up. I'd never live it down."

"She must be special," he said under his breath.

His questions made me realize that I hadn't worked out the details of my plan. Had I really thought he would say, "Sure, no problem?" I mulled this over and wondered what to do about his doubt.

We sat without talking. Then an idea came to me. "The story of the rodeo will take a while to tell. Since I have to work on Sunday, our plan is to get up early so we'll have more time."

"I don't understand the lying. It's not like you."

"The sorority smothers me. Sometimes I feel like I'm a prisoner." My voice felt tight. "I have to lie. I can't just say I want to stay overnight with a friend. I don't know what I'd do if Mrs. Sullivan told me I couldn't have a pass." I ran out of breath and out of ideas to use to persuade him.

"I still don't understand it. Go ahead if you want it that badly." He put his hand on my shoulder, giving me reassurance.

As relief flooded through me, I kissed his cheek and whispered "Thanks."

We rode our bikes to campus, arriving in time for our first classes. As Duke turned and headed toward the engineering building, he said "Guess I won't see you for a whole week," but didn't look over his shoulder for our ritual see-ya-soon wave.

❧

Early Saturday morning I could feel Elena's inquisitive eyes following my every move as I packed a small bag. I had dressed in my stable clothes, since I would spend the morning at work. I folded a clean blouse and skirt to wear later.

"How'd you get an overnight pass so soon in the term?"

"I need to check on my mother. She's not well."

Elena sulked. She stopped midway in her daily routine of brushing her shoulder-length blonde hair one hundred strokes.

"It's not fair. I'm stuck here all weekend having to come home by eleven o'clock."

"It's not like I'm going to a party."

Finished with my packing I sat down on the white chenille spread that covered my bed, the sun streaming through the window. A combination of excitement and nervousness made me impatient to get going.

Elena looked at herself in the mirror, adjusting the lace collar on her blouse.

"What's wrong with your mother? It must be serious."

"That's what I'm going to find out. She won't get out of bed. Dad's concerned."

It astonished me how easily I could come up with plausible, yet untrue answers to her innocent questions.

"Has she been ill lately?" Elena checked the smoothness of her hair combed to the side and falling just above her right eyebrow.

"Not that I know of."

I needed to change the subject. If I dug the hole much deeper, I might fall in. I stood and clicked my bag shut.

"What are you up to this weekend?"

"A study fest with a bunch of the other girls, then we'll go to the sock hop on campus and meet some new fellas."

She added, as if it were an afterthought, "What's Duke going to do without you?"

"I'm not sure. He has a big exam on Monday, and may spend his time studying. All I can think of is my mother," I called over my shoulder as I left our room.

I went downstairs to sign out with Mrs. Sullivan. She seemed sympathetic and reminded me to try to be home by five o'clock for an early Sunday dinner. She patted my arm, saying "I hope everything will be all right, dear." Lucky for me, she had a visitor and could not give me any more attention.

It didn't take long for that little rascal, guilt, to creep in. On the streetcar ride to the stables, I prayed for Mother's good health and crossed my heart.

❧

I rushed through my work and hurried to the boarding-house without taking Satin Dancer out for a ride. Gisela was waiting for me downstairs in the parlor, and answered my ring at the door.

"Swell" she said, eyeing my duffel. "I'm so glad you broke away from the wicked witch. I've already arranged to have you as my guest at dinner. Tonight we're having pot roast, mashed potatoes, and peas. Shortcake for dessert."

She looked comfortable, wearing the same trousers I had admired a few weeks ago. Instead of the silk blouse, she wore a light sweater the color of emeralds.

In her room, we relaxed on the window seat. The red gladiolus had been replaced with a mixed bouquet of fall flowers.

"I love fresh flowers. They make me feel alive. An extravagance, I know."

I stuck my nose in the new bouquet. A sweet, musky fragrance resembling honey and cloves tickled my nostrils.

"Heavenly," I said. "I smell horsey. I brought a change of clothes."

"Oh don't bother. It'll make your rodeo story more authentic to catch a whiff now and then."

"Very funny."

"Seriously, I really want to know how a girl from Minnesota ended up an award-winning rodeo cowgirl. And from the beginning please."

As I sat there thinking about what to say, I realized an explanation of why I'd decided to followed Chloe and Mac on the circuit should be included, and by the time I got to the part about the two of them leaving prior to my hazing experience a couple of hours had passed.

Gisela had listened with intensity until I finished and then she said, "You are a natural at telling a story. I feel like I know Chloe, almost like I'd been there. What a shame she had to leave the rodeo."

"Chloe is doing okay. She and Mac got married and they've taken over his father's ranch. I think it's what she wanted, even more than the rodeo."

Gisela put her hand over mine and caressed it. I didn't pull away, enjoying her gentle touch. "Thank you for coming," she said.

"I feel like I've been talking for hours," I said, basking in her praise and forgetting all about Duke and the sorority.

Daylight had faded to dusk, throwing the room into shadow. Gisela lit a candle, a tall taper in a brass holder.

"A relic from my childhood." She crooked her finger through the handle and held it up. "My mother would lead me up the stairs at night, carrying it just like this. She would set it on the table next to my bed and promise to let me blow it out if I didn't fall asleep before we finished my prayers and a story."

She set the candle next to the flowers. "I never got to blow it out. Her stories always lulled me into dreamland."

"I hope my story hasn't done that."

"No, just the opposite. It's funny that you started your story talking about your cousin. I told everyone this morning at breakfast that you're *my* cousin."

"Why? Who'd you tell?" I asked.

"The other boarders here. I don't want them peppering us with questions. They're always so interested in me, and my business. Probably because I'm much younger than they are. Mr. Ehlers, he's the worst, made some remark about me wearing trousers."

We both looked down at my riding breeches and laughed. Then I hurried down the hall to wash away the barn smells and change into my skirt and blouse.

By the time I returned Gisela had opened the Murphy bed. It dominated the far wall that had been bare the other times I'd visited. Louis Armstrong's "It Don't Mean a Thing (If It Ain't Got That Swing)" played on the radio.

Gisela turned on the Art Deco lamp her father had sent. Pointing at the lamp with a flourish of her hand she said, "I've named her Madge. She's the perfect roommate, always smiling, always dancing." Then she arranged a red scarf over the shade, spreading a rosy glow over the bed.

❧

After dinner we tore up the stairs, bursting through Gisela's door barely able to contain our laughter at our fellow diners. In the privacy of her room, we gave each of them buffoon names and made up stories about what we imagined as their dreary lives, laughing like giddy teenagers at a slumber party.

Gisela tuned the radio to a big band station. She grabbed my hands and we danced the swing, careful not to bump into the Murphy bed. The room filled with the staccato notes of a trumpet, egged on by the deep voice of trombones and the slither of a clarinet. She led while I followed, twirling under her outstretched arm and behind her back.

We jived together, heads bobbing, until out of breath we fell down on the bed. We lay close together, and I could feel the heat of her body next to mine.

The music faded. The room whirled. Gisela turned to me and said, "I'm glad I found you."

What happened next changed my life like the sweep hand on a clock whose small jerky movement, as it marks each passing second, erases the moment that came before. And in an instant, I unexpectedly clicked over to the "knowing" that Rollie had predicted.

Gisela kissed me full on the lips, gentle and sweet as the fragrance of her scent. It took my breath away. No kiss ever had been so soft and so thrilling. It made me dizzy and glad we were lying down.

We didn't speak. The clarinet took over, its sound floating sweetly over us, fading out as the announcer's deep voice touted the virtues of Ivory soap: "It's the pure complexion soap recommended by doctors that will make all you ladies out there irresistible." Gisela turned down the radio volume, holding out her hand to me.

We danced again. This time Gisela held me close as Fred Astaire's silky voice crooned the lyrics to "Night and Day."

With her sweater soft against my cheek, the words echoed in my head.

When the song ended she said, "Tell me more of your story."

"Now?"

"Yes, now." She took my hand and led me to the window seat. Her eyes were midnight blue in the soft light of the candle. "We have a lot to learn about each other. I want to know all about you."

We lit cigarettes. The smoke meandered toward the ceiling, disappearing into the darkness above the flickering candle as

Madge waved from her rosy pool of light atop the steamer trunk. My cheek still tingled where it had rested in the emerald green of Gisela's sweater.

"Give me a minute to figure out where I left off." I leaned against the pillows. "My mind's all jumbled up."

"We have lots of time for everything. I don't want either of us to be sorry for moving too fast." She turned off the radio.

I told her about Bobby Smith and why he had chosen me to replace him as hazer, about how the adrenaline pulsed through my veins in the seconds it took to guide the charging steer in a straight line so the bulldogger could drop down on it, and about the importance of timing. I left out the part about riding upriver with Bobby, and how confused I'd been with my physical attraction to him. An hour later I stopped.

"I'm out of steam," I said.

Gisela blew out the candle, and we stood close in the semi-darkness. My mind reeled, trying to decide what to do. I wanted her to kiss me again, and she did, lightly on the lips, taking both of my hands in hers and pulling me closer until our bodies touched.

"Me too," I managed to say. My mouth had gone dry. My voice strained.

Gisela put her finger to my lips, "Remember, we don't have to rush anything. We've got plenty of time." She sat on the bed and removed the hairpins that held her braids in place, then unwound them slowly, letting her hair hang loose.

I'd never seen such a beautiful cascade of hair. "Can I brush it?" I asked. She handed me her brush and I gently separated and stroked the strands until her hair rippled smoothly below her shoulders.

We put on our pajamas by the light of the street lamp shining in the window and got under the covers. She turned to me. "Good night," she said and held my hand until she fell asleep.

A few hours later, I woke from a deep slumber, sweaty and confused. The dark pressed against me. My heart pounded until I remembered Gisela next to me. Fragments of a dream floated to my consciousness: Hal and Dorothy pulling me from a burning house, holding me down to prevent me from running back inside, embers shooting high into the sky—beautiful bursts of passion fraught with danger.

Gisela slept soundly beside me. Her gentle breathing pushed away my angst.

The next time I awoke sunlight filtered through gauze curtains. Breathing quietly, I studied the dust motes swirling like glitter in the sunbeam touching Gisela beside me.

We kissed. We danced. I liked it.

She reached for my hand. I turned onto my stomach, facing her with my eyes closed. Her fingers explored my back with a light touch through my pajama top. My dream had disappeared into the ethers.

A church bell chimed somewhere in the distance.

"I've been lonely a long time," Gisela said.

She didn't say lonely in a needy way. The way she said it told me I fulfilled something she had wanted.

She moved her hand underneath the fabric of my pajama top. I trembled at her touch on my skin and exhaled with pleasure as her fingers made an airy journey up and down my spine.

Opening my eyes when she stopped, I thought her face glowed with the luminosity of a sunrise. Her look was open, hopeful.

"Come," Gisela said, pulling me closer.

The quiet of early morning shielded us from the outside world. Nothing existed for me except my flesh, burning with an intense need to be held.

I folded into her embrace while she hummed the melody of "Night and Day." My head fit perfectly on her shoulder. With my eyes closed, I thought I could stay like this forever.

Letting me go, she reached over and smoothed my hair that had gone berserk overnight. A sigh of yearning escaped my lips as she traced and caressed each of my ears.

I shifted slightly and turned over. This time I anticipated her touch on my abdomen and my body shuddered when she touched my bare breasts, her fingers light as feathers. "Your body feels so beautiful," she said and kissed me. Our tongues danced with each other. I moaned and leaned into her.

Her lips found my ear. "Are you okay?" she whispered.

"Yes," I murmured. We looked into each other's eyes.

"I want to make love to you," she said, her voice thick with emotion. "But I don't want to frighten you."

We lay still without talking, her arms wrapped around me. "Like I said last night. There is no hurry. No reason to rush."

I waited. Lost in my longing for her, not knowing what to do next, what to say, where to put my hands. I didn't want her to let me go.

"How are you doing?" she asked in a soft voice.

I searched for words to describe my feelings. "I'm resting on the shore of a primordial sea. No future. No past."

"Beautiful, my sweet," she purred. I watched her finger trace an imaginary pattern on the white sheet. "We can take things slowly, but there is reality beyond the shore."

I didn't respond, wanting to savor the feel of her electrifying touch. We rested in silence.

My thoughts wandered. Rollie had told me she hadn't expected to fall in love with a woman. Now, as I was beginning to understand what she meant, her story of loss made me shiver. My dream images returned and I found my voice.

"I had a dream last night about my brother and his wife pulling me out of a burning building. They represent everything my parents and society want for me—church wedding, children. That's my reality. What would they think of us?"

"Some people think it's better to be a free spirit with no obligations to family. Sometimes I'm not so sure," she said.

"I don't understand."

"I've often wished I had people who were concerned about me like you have. I know my father loves me, but he has always been too busy with his own life to give much thought to what I do."

I took love and family concern for granted. I couldn't comprehend not having someone to worry over me. Mother often wrote me notes, checking in with me. Even Hal and Dorothy's meddling and annoying criticisms showed that they cared.

We rested without talking until Gisela said, "Come on, my sweet sleepyhead. Let's get dressed and go out for breakfast."

Before reaching for her robe and heading down the hall to bathe, Gisela kissed me with a fervid tenderness that left me limp with longing. When she returned, she lent me her robe so I could freshen up too.

While sponging my body with warm water, I realized the missing puzzle piece of my life—passion—had fallen into place. I would never be the same again. I knew all about chastity, but lust for a lover's body was like learning a foreign language.

By the time I returned, Gisela had straightened the room and closed the Murphy bed. We sat on the window seat and drank the tea she had brewed.

On our way out, I used the phone in the parlor to call the stables and say I couldn't come to work because my mother was ill.

We strolled to the same diner where we had coffee the first day we met, ordering fried eggs over easy with toast and jam. Gazing across the table at Gisela, I shoved my doubts deep in the place where I kept stuff I didn't want to think about. I vowed that no matter what, my feelings for her would be more powerful than any threat, more powerful than stigma and more powerful than fear.

Across the street, church bells were ringing again. I looked out through the diner's front window. Parents and children walked hand in hand out of the church. Many milled around, chatting with a pastor dressed in red robes.

"We're doomed," I said, watching the crowd. "Half of them are headed this way."

Gisela added, "We better get going. They'll be descending on us soon with all those kids, and we don't want to waste our time together distracted by so many people." She paid our bill, and we left.

On the way home, a street vendor selling flowers caught Gisela's eye and she stopped to buy a fragrant red rose.

In her room, we sat together nestled in the pillows under the bay window. She handed me the flower and said, "I want to finish what I started to tell you earlier about family and caring."

I inhaled the delicate perfume of the rose, holding it while she talked.

"I had a romantic girlfriend during my junior year at boarding school when I was sixteen. Even though my father knew, it didn't bother him. She started out as what was called my "big sister," assigned to help me adjust. Soon she started sneaking into my bed after lights out and filled my emptiness. I missed my mother so much—and my father too. Her presence eased my loneliness and grief."

"You were so young," I said.

"I wasn't too young to understand that what I was doing was part of me, who I had been all my life. My 'older sister' lit the flame of my desire."

And now you've lit mine.

She continued, "I've always longed for a family who accepts and loves me for who I am. Being rejected would be horrible. But being invisible as I am to my father is just as bad."

Still holding the rose, I sat up and reached over to put it in the vase with the other flowers on the coffee table. Gisela encircled me in her arms and my body relaxed as I leaned in closer, finding the place where we were a perfect fit. We dozed, snuggling together while the sun moved west. The light in the room had changed to shadow when I next opened my eyes.

I stirred and sat up. "I have to leave soon," I said, glancing at my watch.

Gisela stood and walked to her desk. She rummaged through the chaos spread across the surface, and then through a stack of books on the floor.

"I found it," she said, handing me a book.

I looked at the title: *The Well of Loneliness,* by Radclyffe Hall.

"It's about a woman named Stephen. I'm not saying I'm like her, but I have a lot of the same feelings she has. She falls in love with a woman named Mary."

I took it.

Maybe I need instructions on what to do next.

"I want you to see what you're getting into if we keep seeing each other," she said.

But I already knew I didn't want to think about anyone, or anything, else.

"Your brother and his wife were in bed with us last night, trying to pull you to safety," she said. "You are part of them. They're part of you. Forever linked."

I had imagined a different ending to our time together.

"I have to go." I felt burned down to the nubbin, like the candle Gisela had placed in her mother's candleholder. Our tea mugs were empty and the ashtray full, dinner was being prepared at the sorority house, and I was expected home at five o'clock.

With the sorority curfews and my busy schedule, I knew I would not be able to spend the night in Gisela's room again any time soon. Reluctant to leave, I packed my duffel with my stable clothes and pajamas.

Gisela walked downstairs with me. I used the phone in the parlor to call a taxi. The cab fare would be a luxury. I didn't want to be late and didn't like riding home in the dark on the streetcar.

The taxi pulled up in only a few moments. The driver tooted the horn, not bothering to get out. Gisela followed me to the sidewalk, carrying my bag. She opened the door for me and set it on the seat. She grasped my shoulders and planted a quick kiss on each of my cheeks.

"A French farewell," she said loud enough for the driver to hear.

I got in and rolled down the window.

"Read the book," she called as we pulled away. "Save me a place in class."

It would be a long wait until Thursday. I waved and settled in for the ride back to my reality.

THIRTEEN

On Monday, I skipped dinner with Mrs. Sullivan's permission and worked late to make up some of the time I'd missed on Sunday. I came home exhausted and found Elena lounging on her bed.

"Where'd you get this book?" She held *The Well of Loneliness* and seemed to have already read about half of it. "And who's Gisela?"

How could Elena possibly know about Gisela?

I wasn't sure which question to answer first. I couldn't say I'd checked it out of the library, since it clearly was not a library book.

"What do you mean?" I asked.

"It's kind of strange, interesting in a yucky sort of way. It's about a girl who is a bit odd. Her father, who wanted a boy, named her Stephen. At seven, she's infatuated with a housemaid, wants to kiss her and everything. By the time she's grown up, she falls in love with her neighbor's wife."

I wanted to grab the book and run.

"Why did you ransack the things on my desk?"

"Hey, don't get mad. The book caught my eye. I figured it was for a class. You know how curious I am."

"It's none of your business."

"So you don't know who Gisela is?" She handed me the book. "Look inside the cover."

"Dear Gisela, Enjoy! All my love, Annabelle" was written in a bold script on the first page, with the exclamation point drawn as a heart that looked like a hot air balloon, waiting to take off.

"Mind if I finish it?" She held out her hand as if I would simply hand it to her.

"I do mind. I don't want you taking things off my desk without asking." I'd collected my wits and concluded, "I borrowed it from a classmate and need it for a paper I'm writing."

"Geez, you'd think I'd committed a crime," she said as she walked out the door.

Obviously Gisela wanted to share more than the book with me. The inscription, innocent enough on its own, wiggled under my skin. I stared at the heart-shaped exclamation point. *Why would she flaunt this Annabelle without telling me about her?*

That night I read *The Well of Loneliness* in bed under the covers with a flashlight.

This was the first time I'd read anything about love between women, and I thought Stephen's life seemed touching and full of heartbreak—not "yucky," as Elena had said.

I closed the book thinking about how the protagonist had grown up in Victorian England, conflicted about her own truth. How she hadn't realized how society would react when she finally followed her heart, and the pain she had experienced from the persecution and prejudice of others—especially her mother, who disowned her. Rollie had suffered a loss of similar proportion.

I switched off the flashlight and fell asleep, the book clutched to my chest like an old friend teddy bear. I dreamed of England, Stephen's home, and rolling hills. In my dream, that world existed as a perfect place with no sorrows.

The next morning, I wandered down the hall to the bathroom still basking in the tranquility of my dream.

"Good morning, you were reading late last night," Elena greeted me.

"I'm so far behind," I answered, not yet awake enough to have a conversation.

"I thought maybe you were in the world of Gisela and Annabelle." She smiled over her shoulder on the way down the hall.

She couldn't possibly know.

Her words poked at a place that warned me to be more cautious.

※

The following Thursday, Gisela and I both showed up fifteen minutes early for class without having arranged to meet in advance, which surprised me since she usually slipped into her chair at the last minute.

"Hi," she said. "I couldn't wait to see you. It's been four days."

"Me too." Students bustled past us in the dreary corridor. The dim light and faded green walls didn't suit us. We needed space, fresh air, and daylight.

"Let's skip class, go for a walk," Gisela suggested. I followed her outside. She didn't look ordinary, even from behind. She carried herself with dignity, like a fashion model. That day she wore a belted dress with a full skirt, brown and white oxfords, and white ankle socks.

I wore my unstylish riding jacket whose worn comfort topped a black skirt that I would later exchange for trousers at the stables. Outside, the air smelled of wet leaves and clean earth.

We decided to leave campus, heading toward the stop where I would catch the streetcar to work.

"I'll ride out with you. We can sit in the barn where it's quiet. We can talk, and soak up the ambiance."

That made me laugh.

"No, that won't work. You're not dressed for sitting on a hay bale, and it's not quiet there this time of day. Besides, I'll be soaking up the ambiance soon enough with a shovel and wheelbarrow."

We settled on a corner café, where the smell of bacon grease and coffee greeted us as we sat down in a vacant booth near the door. The patrons were all men dressed in boots and coveralls, and I realized the two of us must have looked out of place since most young women were home tending to children, or working any job they could find to keep their family afloat. We were privileged to have the luxury of time to sit in a café during the afternoon.

"What'll it be?" the waitress asked without looking at us, chewing gum with her mouth open. I wrinkled my nose at the smell of stale mint when she bent to fill my coffee mug.

I ordered a grilled cheese sandwich. Gisela ordered spinach with scrambled eggs.

"I read the book," I said as soon as the waitress walked away.

Gisela waited.

"I'm glad I read it. It was so sad that she sacrificed herself in the end, pretending she had fallen for someone else and sending the woman she loved into the arms of a man who could marry her."

"I see it differently," Gisela interrupted. "She betrayed herself for the woman she loved, cut her free to live in a world where she could marry, be provided for, have children. Or, I suppose you could say it was both a betrayal and a sacrifice."

The waitress brought our food.

Gisela waited until after she walked away. "Either way, she definitely fell into the *Well of Loneliness*," she said, drawing out the title of the book like a radio announcer.

"Indeed. I couldn't agree more," I said, entertained by her drama.

"Now that you've read the book, do you want us to go on?" Gisela asked, reaching for the salt and pepper.

"I want us to go on. I just don't know how."

"We'll figure it out."

Annabelle chose that moment to float into my head in her heart-shaped hot air balloon. I felt unsure of how to ask Gisela about her. I could be nonchalant. *So who's Annabelle?* Or confrontational. *Why didn't you tell me about Annabelle when you gave me the book?* Or I could be curious. *I'm wondering about Annabelle.* None fit the extent of my anxiety.

I opened the book to the page with Annabelle's inscription.

"She gave it to me," Gisela said. "A different kind of French farewell. She didn't believe I was committed to her. In a way she was right. She wanted me to read the book at the end of our relationship as a lesson to me about what she called my 'internalized oppression' because I wouldn't go to the all-night clubs she frequented.

"I was too young then to grasp the meaning of the grandiose words she used to chastise me. She assumed I hated myself, or felt ashamed, because I shunned her friends. She didn't want to understand that her life—staying out to the wee hours, sex, and drinking—was not for me. I wanted to learn more about the world, not spend my days sleeping it off after partying all night."

"I wanted to know who she was the minute I saw her name," I said. "I didn't think of her as someone who might have hurt you."

"It was impulsive of me to give you the book without an explanation. I wanted you to know more than I did in the beginning." She leaned forward and scanned the room. The other customers sat at the counter facing the open kitchen. She brushed my fingertips with hers across the table. "I know this is new for you, to have feelings you haven't been able or dared to acknowledge," she said, her voice soft.

The waitress returned to refill our cups, so Gisela sat back until we were alone again before continuing. "I want everything to be easier for you, and now I'm off to a clumsy start."

"How did you know you were right about my feelings?" What I really wanted to know was more about Annabelle.

"Annabelle taught me all about feelings. Remember? I told you about my 'big sister' at boarding school."

So that was Annabelle, assigned to watch over her, the one who helped her ease the pain of missing her family.

"Nothing was clear then. Annabelle swallowed me. I was so tender at sixteen, not yet ready for all that she taught me. She was eighteen and the most popular, beautiful girl in the school, fierce as a lioness. She baffled the headmistress and teachers, being sweet one minute and doing as she pleased the next. She kept me under her wing, and her thumb, for two years, even after she left school.

"Annabelle and I moved to Paris after I graduated, where I reunited with my father and met his new wife, Monique." She said new wife rather snidely. "I could tell Monique wanted me out of their life as soon as possible. She's only five years older than me.

"I spent most of my time with Annabelle. Yes, I loved her. We were lovers, but I soon found out in Paris that I was not the only one. I learned from Annabelle never to give myself again to someone who wants complete control over my thoughts and actions. She didn't see I was ready to leave the nest."

My sandwich tasted greasy. First Rollie, then the book, and now Gisela's story—were there any happy endings? I couldn't swallow another bite or speak over the heaviness of my heart.

Gisela stopped talking about Annabelle. "What's wrong?"

"It sounds terrible what she did to you, and it makes me sad to know you were so hurt by someone you cared for," I said.

"I fueled her self-absorption. She turned on me because I wanted our relationship to be more than just a convenience for her."

Gisela's expression bore the scars of rejection and heartache.

"What happened to Annabelle?"

"She's history. I've said all I want to say about her."

The waitress was chatting with the men at the counter until the cook, who was standing at the sizzling grill, bellowed "Order up!" to get her attention.

I nibbled at my sandwich while waiting for Gisela to go on.

"I haven't yet made any peace with Monique. I'm convinced she wants my father's money. He is well off. The joke's on her though, there is a trust set up for me that she can't touch. I'm not rich, but I'm comfortable."

Why was she telling me about her money? Was she implying she could provide for me financially, the way Stephen was able to for Mary in the book?

"I have my own money. I've always worked," I said. "My father still has his accounting job even though he took a big cut in pay after the Crash in 1929."

"I just did something I hate about myself," Gisela said. "I felt vulnerable and started talking about money. I didn't mean to make you uncomfortable. It was rude of me to bring it up."

"I did wonder about school in Switzerland, your beautiful clothes, your own room," I said, feeling more relaxed and hungry.

We finished lunch and walked outside into the crisp air. I buttoned my jacket. Gisela stood in front of me and straightened my collar.

"It's different for me this time," she said as we faced each other. "I want this relationship to work. That is, if you still want to go on in spite of what I just told you."

"I can't imagine not going on."

"We'll take our time to get to know each other, be open about what we each need," she said before leaving me alone at the trolley stop.

I watched as she slipped into the distance, and missed her even before she completely disappeared.

❧

Mrs. Sullivan greeted me the next morning with a terse "You're up early," when I met her in the kitchen.

"I'm meeting Duke for a bicycle ride" was my only reply.

"He's a nice boy, so smart and talented. Good looking, too, and you're such good friends." She looked at me as if she might ask a question and continued talking even though I had turned around to the stove to pour a cup of coffee.

"While you were seeing to your mother last weekend, I invited him to Saturday dinner along with three others from Zeta Phi. Elena sat next to him, made him feel welcome."

That little fink. Why didn't she tell me?

I took my time stirring the coffee, waiting for her to go on.

"Just between you and me, I think she's a little sweet on your fella," Mrs. Sullivan said, in a stage whisper.

"What do you mean?"

"She hung on every word he said." Mrs. Sullivan rubbed her thumb and forefinger over her chin as if she were deciding whether or not to say more.

"I wish she'd find a nice college boy of her own. That's all."

I shrugged off her comment. Sometimes she said things totally out of the blue. Even so, a small patch of unease lodged in my stomach. I pushed it down to the place inside me that was getting crowded with the all stuff I didn't want to think about.

I lied and said, "Duke told me all about the dinner." I hoped I sounded indifferent, and wondered if he would mention it on our bike ride.

Mrs. Sullivan looked skeptical. "What did he say about it?"

I paused, feeling trapped. I knew Duke would be polite and said, "He was grateful for your invitation. He missed me. He hates staying home alone on Saturday night. He asked me to thank you."

"Well that's sweet," she said. "We all enjoyed his company, not just Elena."

I couldn't take any more. "I've got to go." I left my half-empty cup of coffee on the table and grabbed my jacket.

The steely sky waited for the sunrise with tinges of coral off to the east during my short ride to Luxton Park where Duke waited for me.

"I missed you. It seems ages since I've seen you," Duke said.

"It's only been a week."

"I had dinner with the girls. Mrs. Sullivan invited me. Elena wouldn't leave me alone the whole night. It was lonely without you."

That settled the dilemma of whether or not to confront him. I looked at him and shook my head. His eyes were like the windows of home—a fire in the hearth, the aroma of soup simmering on the stove, comfort.

"Come on" he said, turning and getting on his bike. "Let's ride over to see how Old Miss is flowing." After riding for a while we rested on a flat gray stone softened with lichen and moss. Duke opened his familiar thermos and poured a cup of coffee, offering me the first sip. We sat quietly and listened to the river rushing below us.

"Looking forward to the costume ball?" Duke asked.

"It's under control." We'd decided to dress in fancy western garb. "Mother has turned an old pair of red velvet curtains into a skirt and bolero. She's still working on it. I've got the silver scarf and just need a blouse. I'm going home for real on Saturday to try it on," I said.

I didn't want to talk about the costume party. It annoyed me that Duke had turned our conversation to our social life. He was so predictable I wanted to scream.

"What do you think of Elena?" I asked to change the subject.

"She's a nice enough girl, I guess. Kind of ditsy, always asking questions. It's a good thing you gave me the right answers about the weekend, or I would have gotten you in trouble."

"What kinds of questions?"

"What's wrong with Ruth's mother?" he mimicked Elena in his best girly voice. "Should we call her? Why'd she take her best blouse?"

Then he said, in his own voice, full of concern, "I don't think Elena really believed your mother was sick."

"Mrs. Sullivan says she's sweet on you."

"Mrs. Sullivan's sweet on me?" he teased. "She's old enough to be my mother's mother. That is if I had a mother."

"Oh stop it, you big goof. I mean Elena."

"Elena is jealous of Mrs. Sullivan and me?"

This time I pushed him off the rock onto the damp grass and pummeled him with my fists until he yelled, "Stop. Stop. You're hurting me."

"Poor baby" I said, and let him go.

I brushed the loose grass and twigs off his sweater when he stood up, and as he rode away he yelled over his shoulder "Besides, Elena knows I'm taken."

I felt slightly dizzy; my stomach did a flip as I rode behind him. No need to panic.

Of course he thinks of me as his girl.

I wondered who he dated while I was away at the rodeo. I now realized I'd expected he'd be there for me when I returned; and hadn't bothered to ask. I peddled faster and caught up beside him.

"Who'd you take to dances your first year at university?" I asked.

"No one in particular. Mostly I stayed home and studied. The first year of engineering is pretty tough. Why?"

"Just wondering." We rode toward the campus. "Who would you date if I wasn't available?"

He put on his brakes and stood with one foot on the ground, straddling his bicycle. "Wait a minute," he called as I kept going. I turned around and stopped in front of him. "What are you trying to say?" he asked.

"Nothing. I was just wondering what you would do if I wasn't around."

Rolling his eyes, he said "Well you are around, so I don't have to lose sleep over it, do I?"

I didn't answer.

✦

That evening, Mrs. Sullivan asked to see me in the window-less room that served as her office. Her desk, piled high with papers, faced the door. Shelves with books shoved every which way and stacked on top of each other covered the walls. The room gave me a feeling of claustrophobia.

I sat down in the wooden chair that we all knew as the hot seat, doing my best to get comfortable. It had been a long day, starting early with Duke, plus I had attended three classes then worked at the stables. I wanted to eat dinner and get to bed as early as possible.

"Sorry to keep you waiting," Mrs. Sullivan said as she entered the room and closed the door. "Let's finish our conversation from this morning."

We were both dressed for dinner. I waited while she cleared a place on her desk and folded her hands.

"As you know, it's my business to make sure all is right

with my girls." Her voice dripped with concern. "Has anything gone wrong between you and Duke?"

"No. Why?" *Stay calm.*

"I thought you might get upset when I mentioned Elena was sweet on him." She took a breath. "You didn't seem to care."

She'd tried to trick me. Her question about Elena this morning started to make sense.

I shifted in my chair. "Now it's you that I'm concerned about," she said.

I waited to see what she would say next.

"I gave your mother a courtesy call today to see how she is doing. What do you think she said?"

Oh my god. Duke had been right. Elena suspected mother wasn't really sick, and had caused Mrs. Sullivan to question my story.

"I don't know." My voice sounded small, like that of a child caught in a lie.

"I think you do know. She's perfectly well. Thank the Lord for that." She crossed herself. "You have some explaining to do." She sat still, waiting.

The room closed in on me. My chest felt tight. It seemed unhealthy to breathe deeply in a room with no fresh air.

"I needed time away." My voice wavered. I forced myself to look her in the eye. "Away from rules and time constraints. "I remembered Rollie's admiration for me when I told her how I finally stood up to Mac and Bobby Smith, and my voice got stronger. "I spent the weekend with a friend who lives off campus. I met her at the library." I told the truth since I couldn't think of anything else at the moment.

"Her? You weren't with a man?" she wrinkled her brow, narrowed her eyes, and stared at me.

"No!" Now my voice sounded incredulous. Of course, that would be what she would think—in her mind the worst sin a young woman could commit.

I suppressed a nervous laugh.

"Don't lie to me, Ruth. You know my job is to protect you girls from bad choices." She looked weary, disappointed. "I trusted you, believed your mother was ill. Then I overheard Elena telling one of the other girls that she had a funny feeling your mother was really fine. That's why I invited Duke to dinner. I wanted to see if he was also spending the weekend away."

Even though caught in a lie, I was amused. She'd been worried about my virtue in the only way she knew how. What would she think of Gisela and me together? It was too scary to think about. I pinched my lips and tightened my stomach muscles to stifle the urge to laugh hysterically.

"I don't understand why you would lie about your mother to spend the weekend with a girlfriend."

I turned contrite.

"I'm sorry. It was impulsive of me. I've had trouble adjusting to curfews and rules. All the while I traveled with the rodeo, I didn't answer to anyone, and now I have to account for all my free time. It's so confining. Sometimes, I can't think."

"It's a privilege and an honor to belong to this sorority. You must take responsibility for your actions."

My thoughts wandered as she droned on with one of her familiar speeches, and I must have had a faraway look because she raised her voice to get my attention.

". . . There will be consequences. First, I will have to meet this friend of yours. Then I will make a decision." She looked at me and shook her head as if she was sad I had put her in such an awkward position. "I'll check my schedule for next week and let you know when to invite her here. Right now, it's time to get to the table." Mrs. Sullivan dismissed me by standing up and walking to the door.

At dinner I pushed the canned peas around on my plate, and barely tasted the meal. The conversations around the table hammered at my head, so I excused myself without eating any dessert.

Elena was out for the evening. In the quiet of our room I fidgeted, straightening the books on my desk, finally choosing one. I tried to read, but the words jumped around on the page. I set the book down, picked up my journal, and entered the date: October 20, 1932.

I stared at the empty page, wanting to put down my thoughts. What was I thinking, to have been so impulsive as to spend the weekend with Gisela? I didn't dare put her name on the page. Someone might snoop, find my journal, and learn my secret.

We'd known each other such a short time. What was I doing risking my security? I didn't care and missed Gisela. Mother must be frantic. My anxiety rebounded between the two. I couldn't just sit around brooding, and decided to call both of them right away.

I remembered the telephone number of Gisela's boardinghouse, Excelsior 897, and decided I would surprise her with an invitation to come with me to visit my parents the next day. I didn't need special permission to go home, as long as I returned by the Saturday curfew.

It would be fun. She would love it out on the lake this time of year with the fall colors in their prime, the loons gathering to migrate. Mother and Dad would welcome her. I would explain what happened with Mrs. Sullivan. Everything would be fine.

The hallway where the telephone hung on the wall was quiet. Most of the girls were out. I picked up the receiver, and the operator said, "Number, please."

The woman who answered at the boardinghouse gave a huge sigh when I asked for Gisela. "Just a minute" she said, setting the receiver down with a loud clunk.

I stood on one foot and then the other listening to the muffled voices of people in the parlor where only a few days ago the two of us had waited for the taxi.

It seemed to take forever, until finally I heard a concerned voice say, "Hello?"

"Gisela? It's me, Ruth."

"Is everything all right?"

"Yes. I didn't mean to alarm you." I tried to keep my voice light. "I wanted to ask if you could take the train with me tomorrow to visit my mother and dad. Dad will pick us up in Wayzata and take us out to our home on Lake Minnetonka."

"You sure everything is okay? You sound funny," she said.

"It's probably the telephone connection. I want to talk to you. Ask you a favor."

"What can I do?"

"Come with me tomorrow so we can talk." I tried to sound natural.

"I will." She hesitated. "Are you sure you want me to meet your family?"

"Of course," I said. Then I rattled on, talking too fast, avoiding the real meaning her question held. "They'll love you. Dad will know your house on Sheridan. He's a lumber broker and will want to tell you all about the construction. Mother will want to know about your experiences abroad. She dreams of faraway places she'll never see."

We made arrangements to take the early train the next morning.

I hung up and called home. After hearing it was me Mother said, "I was going to call you. Come home for Saturday dinner."

"Can I bring a friend with me?"

"Of course, and Duke too if you want." She paused for a moment then added, "Mrs. Sullivan called this morning, checking on my health. Poor thing, she sounded so confused when I told her I was fine. Guess she had me mixed up with someone else."

"I know. I can explain. I spent the night with my new friend last Saturday and told Mrs. Sullivan a big fat lie. I'm sorry. I hope you're not too worried."

"You just come home. We'd love to meet your new friend."
Mother always seemed to know what I needed.

❧

Gisela had arrived at the train station before me. She was
dressed warmly with a suede jacket over a white sweater,
trousers, and her two-toned oxfords.

She jumped up when she noticed me. "What's this adventure we're having today?" she asked as we sat down to wait
for the train.

I told her about Mrs. Sullivan, leaving out the part about
Duke and Elena. I would have to come clean about Duke
soon enough.

"I don't mind meeting her," Gisela said when I'd finished.
"If it were me, I'd just move out."

"It's more complicated than that," I said. "My life is tangled
up in the sorority—scripted. I attend classes, dances, and
other social events, act in plays, and . . ." I needed a few
breaths to go on. "That is, until I met you. It's going to take
some time to figure out how to change my whole life."

"I didn't think about how being a sorority girl is a whole
package."

"One more thing. I have an escort for the social events.
My best friend, Duke."

"I guess you don't mean a dog, as in man's best friend."

We both laughed, which relieved some of the tension I felt.

"No, Duke is a fella. I've known him since we were both
thirteen. Most people, my family included, think of us as
a couple."

Her eyes clouded over. She looked serious.

The arrival of the train gave me a brief respite.

Once we had settled in our seats, Gisela said "Go on."

I told her about befriending Duke, growing up together,
attending social events during high school, and now college.

"We picked up where we left off after my rodeo experience. It seemed natural he would be my escort for sorority social events and dances."

"What about your feelings for each other?"

I stared out the window to compose myself. "The truth is we love each other. He is considerate and caring. He doesn't push me. For anything." I paused. "When I say I love Duke, it's more like a brother. We've never been lovers like you and Annabelle. Now that I've met you, my life can't go on as it has in the past."

"Do you remember what I said last Saturday night?" she asked.

"What?"

"I said we have time for everything. I don't want either of us to be sorry for moving too fast. I'll meet Mrs. Sullivan. She'll welcome me as a friend of yours. Then we'll take the next step."

As the train neared the Wayzata station, I decided to tell Gisela one more thing about Duke. "Just so you know, another reason for this visit is that I'm picking up a costume Mother has sewn for me to wear to the Masquers Ball with Duke next weekend. It's been planned for months."

She rolled her eyes, turning away from me to look out the window. A loud hiss of steam signaled our arrival at the station.

Fourteen

D ad was waiting for us on the platform. When I introduced Gisela, he greeted her warmly, then on the way to the parking lot gave me one of his smiles implying something was up as he said, "We're going to be quite a crowd today. Hal and Dot are already home, and Uncle Edward and Aunt Margaret are coming. Mother has been cooking all morning."

I'd visualized a quiet day on the lake with Gisela, walking the paths of my childhood. I hadn't prepared myself for a crowd of the whole family.

"What's the occasion?" I asked when we were in the car.

"A couple of things. Mother and Uncle Edward shot three pheasants a week ago. And since you'll be home, Mother and I have an announcement to make." He kept his attention on his driving and sped up to almost thirty-five miles an hour. Dust billowed behind us. I rolled up my window.

Gisela leaned forward and asked, "Am I going to be the fifth wheel at this party?"

"No, of course not," Dad said. "Mother loves to cook. There will be plenty of food."

"What is it . . . what's the announcement, Dad?" I'd had enough surprises since my weekend with Gisela and my talk with Mrs. Sullivan.

"Now, Ruthie, you'll have to wait, like everyone else."

"Hint, pretty please," I tried a childhood tactic in a sing-song voice. "Will it make me happy or sad?"

Dad played along, "Maybe both."

"Is it bigger than a bread box?" Gisela chimed in from the backseat.

"Come on, you two. Don't gang up on me. Mother would sink my boat if she knew I gave it away."

I looked at Gisela and winked. "We won't tell," we said at the same time. I could see Gisela enjoyed the banter and that Dad liked it too.

"If I tell you, it won't be a surprise," Dad said with his sense of logic.

"We're getting close to home," I said to Gisela, giving up on getting Dad to tell us his news. "My grandfather built the house with trees he cut and milled himself. My mother has never lived anywhere else."

Dad turned his head briefly to glance over at me, patting my knee. "Everything will be just fine," he said. I wondered why he felt the need to reassure me, but decided it was just Dad being Dad.

When we arrived, Gisela and I stood for a moment looking down at the lake. Mother's weathered wooden rowboat, tied to the dock, bobbed in the sapphire water. During my childhood, at least one day every week—weather permitting—Mother would row on the lake alone, staying out all day to fish.

"It's so peaceful here," Gisela said.

Mother greeted us at the door, wiping her hands on her apron. She hugged me, holding me tight in her strong arms. The smell of warm biscuits and country gravy drifted from the kitchen.

I let go of Mother and introduced Gisela.

"Come in." Mother turned to open the door. "Are you hungry?" We followed her into the kitchen while she continued talking, "We won't sit down to eat until late afternoon. Did you have breakfast? It's so early."

Gisela sat down at the kitchen table where Mother indicated.

"Hal and Dorothy are on the porch," Mother said.

"Is there anything I can do to help?" Gisela asked.

"You just sit and have your tea." Mother sat down with her. "I need a little rest. We'll get to know each other before you meet the rest of the gang. Then I'll put you to work." To me she said, "Go say hi to your brother."

"I'll be fine," Gisela said when I hesitated.

"How are ya, kid?" Hal said, looking up from what was always his job, hand plucking the small pinfeathers along the backbone of the pheasants after Mother had drawn and trussed the birds. He and Dot each used a pair of tweezers to pull the tiny black shafts sticking out of the birds' skin.

"One down and two to go." He took off his glasses and wiped them with a dishtowel.

Dorothy, in a navy blue serge dress with white lace at the cuffs and high collar, looked matronly even though she was only a few years older than me. The dress hung almost to her ankles, and she wore sensible black shoes with a stacked heel. Holding the tweezers with her thumb and index finger, she approached each tiny feather as if offended by the naked bird. She made a face at our uncooked supper, and lifted her cheek to me for a hello kiss.

I had affection for Dorothy even though she represented everything I didn't want to be. She made Hal happy, and that seemed to be enough for her.

"Take over for me, will you?" Hal said. "I've got some business to discuss with Dad."

"Sorry, I can't. I've got a friend here. She's in with Mother."
I could just picture Mother talking Gisela's ear off, and
wanted to be there just in case.

"Who's here?" Dorothy asked. "Someone from the sorority?"
An innocent question that made me cringe under the
circumstances.

"No. She's a new friend. We're both psychology majors
and met in class."

"Oh," she said without interest.

"Her name is Gisela. She's new to Minneapolis, just returned from abroad, where she attended boarding school."

"Maybe she'd like to learn to pluck the pin feathers off a
game bird," Hal said.

"Nice try." I stood with my hand on the doorknob. "You
two have fun."

In the kitchen Gisela, now wearing a bright yellow apron
and vigorously turning the crank of an eggbeater, was laughing over something with Mother. The aroma of roasting
chicken filled the warm room. I knew Mother had been up
at dawn, killing a chicken to serve along with the pheasants.
The chicken would have been ready for the oven, and the
game birds ready for Hal and Dorothy, before she fixed
breakfast and sat down for a cup of coffee with Dad.

"We're baking a cake. Chocolate." Gisela sounded as if she
were having the time of her life. "My first cake."

I peeled potatoes and watched them working together.
Quite a team, I smiled to myself.

"I'm learning all about Switzerland," Mother exclaimed
with a happy look on her face. "Now I've got Duke for my
adopted son and Gisela for my adopted daughter."

I felt faint. When Mother liked someone, she worked fast.
Gisela, who was concentrating on the cake batter and did
not look up, clearly was feeling welcome.

Mother filled the baking pans, and giggling like school
kids, Gisela and I used our fingers to lick every bit of the

sweet chocolate out of the mixing bowl. We washed and dried the utensils, then Mother invited Gisela to see her garden after asking me to set the table. The two of them headed to where Hal and Dot were cleaning the pheasants. I was tempted to run after them to make the introductions, but stayed inside.

Hal came into the dining room as I was reaching for the candles, about to put the finishing touches on the table.

"Dorothy and I met Gisela. Looks like Mother is adding to her brood," Hal said.

"I'm glad she likes her. She's a good friend."

"Well, she seems like a nice kid," he said. "Mother says time for sandwiches."

Uncle Edward and Aunt Margaret showed up while we were sitting on the front steps eating our lunch, and Gisela quickly endeared herself to both of them. Shaking Uncle Edward's hand she said, "I've envied Ruth ever since I met Satin Dancer."

Aunt Margaret, who noticed Gisela's accent right away, asked "What's it called when the French greet each other with a kiss?"

"*Faire la bise*. It's really just touching cheeks and kissing the air." Gisela demonstrated, and the two of them smiled together like old friends.

Edward and Margaret went inside, leaving us to enjoy the sun filtering through the pines that sparkled on the lake. Gisela, with a touch of longing in her voice, sighed as she said, "I love your family. I think you grew up in paradise." She stretched out her legs and leaned back, looking up at the tops of the trees. "Although I do think your brother's a bit conservative, dressed just like your dad; and he and Dorothy seemed a bit disappointed that I don't belong to a sorority. I wonder if the two of them know how to relax."

"Hal has traditional ideas about a woman's place being in the home, and Dorothy fits that role perfectly."

We walked for about half an hour along the shore. There wasn't a cloud in the sky. By the time we returned, Mother had barded the pheasants, covering the breasts with bacon slices. The whole house was filled with aromas from the oven. Gisela and I joined the others in the living room and Uncle Edward told her about the few times I fell off Satin Dancer. He laughed when he said, "She was so determined that she always brushed herself off, climbed on again, and never cried."

"Even when I wiped the blood off her chin or her knees," Aunt Margaret chimed in.

"Guess you could say I was a tomboy," I said to Gisela.

Then Hal told the story about how he had tricked me into doing half his chores for him when we had our old mare, Cloud.

"She loved horses so much, she mucked out Cloud's stall for me as soon as she could lift a shovel—just for the fun of it."

Everyone laughed and kidded me about falling for his ruse.

"I'm too comfortable to move," Mother said. She was in her favorite chair, her feet resting on an ottoman. I went to the kitchen to check on the birds in the oven.

"Ten more minutes," I called from the kitchen, leaning against the counter. No wonder Mother needed to rest. I felt tired just thinking about all the work she had already done that day.

From the kitchen I listened to Hal and Gisela discussing politics while Mother rested her eyes.

"My father says conflict in Europe is inevitable," Gisela said. "Hitler and his Nazi Party instigated a national boycott of Jewish businesses and professionals a few months ago."

"I'm sure your father knows what he's talking about. My point is, why would the US get involved?" Hal said. "Our security isn't threatened."

Gisela didn't back down. "People in this country need to open their eyes. Who knows who will be next on his list?"

"You can't blame us for not wanting to interfere in Germany. The economic depression still gives us a pretty grim picture here," Hal said.

"What do you think, Peter?" Gisela asked Dad.

"I think Hal is right. I'm confident that Roosevelt can fulfill his promise of economic recovery. I don't think our security is threatened," Dad answered. He tapped his pipe on the ashtray, knocking out the tobacco and refilling it. Mother sat up.

"Don't light that, Peter. We're going to eat soon." Interrupting the war talk, she turned to Gisela. "I like hearing your perspective. It gives us something more to think about."

"I thought you were sound asleep," Hal said to Mother, offering her a hand to help her get out of the chair.

We all moved to the dining room. Dad carved, arranging the pheasants and the whole chicken on two platters. There were bowls filled with green beans and mashed potatoes, and Aunt Margaret had brought canned fruit cocktail ambrosia sprinkled with dried coconut, a family favorite. Hal sliced Dorothy's homemade bread, and Gisela's cake sat on the buffet alongside an apple pie Mother had baked before we arrived.

Just as we started to eat, Hal cut into our usual dinnertime banter and asked me what I thought about Hitler's anti-Semitism.

"I just read that Albert Einstein has moved to the US and will teach at Princeton," I said.

"It's Germany's loss," Gisela said. "He's brilliant, and a pacifist."

"Tell us about Paris, Gisela," Mother said. She changed the subject a second time, not giving Hal the chance to disagree with, or challenge, Gisela or me.

"I love Paris," Gisela said with nostalgia in her voice. "I could walk around the city all day."

"What is it you love most?" Dorothy asked.

"If I had to sum it up, I'd say light and laughter. The cafés and shops are vibrant, the fruits and vegetables in the outdoor markets so fresh. And the architecture. Everywhere you look, it captures your eye," Gisela said. "Oh. I forgot the flowers. Flowers in every tiny window balcony and for sale in the food markets."

"I'd love to go someday," Dorothy said to Hal.

"You'll have to learn to speak French first."

We settled into the easy rhythm of chatting and eating. I relaxed and forgot about Dad's announcement until we'd finished dessert.

He clapped his hands to get our attention and lifted his glass of port.

"A superb dinner. Almost everyone is here who is important to our family." His smile included Gisela. "But Duke is missing. Where is he today, Ruth?"

I gulped and swallowed wrong. My choking stopped Dad's speech. When I'd calmed down, I said, "He's studying for a big exam." Gisela looked across the table at me with a raised eyebrow.

"Well, we miss him," Dad continued. "Today is a big day for Mother and me." He looked over at Mother, who dabbed at her eyes with her hanky. "Now, Rose, let me at least tell them first." He got up and stood behind her with his hands on her shoulders.

He had our full attention. Hal and I exchanged a worried look. The clock clicked as the little doors opened and the cuckoo called out six times, startling all of us.

Uncle Edward burped and excused himself, looking sheepish. Hal laughed nervously, an old habit from childhood when things got difficult.

Dad waited for a few seconds. "Mother and I have decided to leave the lake and move to Minneapolis. With Ruth and Hal away from home, it doesn't make sense to keep this old place. It's a long trip for me to the office, and way too much work for Rose." He kept his hands on Mother's shoulders.

Dad's news met stunned silence. Then we all started talking at once, asking questions. Mother plastered a big smile on her face while she answered our concerns.

"Really, I want to move. I'm alone all day long with Peter at work."

Eventually we all quieted down, and Dorothy and Aunt Margaret began to clear the table. Uncle Edward scraped the leftovers from our plates to take home for his hogs, and Gisela joined the cleanup in the kitchen. The four of us listened to their voices rising and falling interspersed with laughter, running water, and the clatter of dishes.

We moved closer together at one end of the cleared table with Mother and Dad facing Hal and me. Hal, seeming at a loss for words, picked at a spot of candle wax that had hardened on the tablecloth.

"I thought maybe Mother had hinted to you, Ruthie," Dad said. "When we drove in this morning you told Gisela that Grandpa had built the house, and you said Mother never lived anywhere else."

"Did you?" Mother asked me. She stood up and put her arms around my neck, resting her chin on my head.

"It shouldn't surprise you, Peter. Ruth has always worried about me. Remember how she used to stay with me during my all-day sleeping bouts years ago?"

"I remember, Rose." He had a tender look on his face "Those days weren't easy for any of us."

"I know. All I'm trying to say is that a mother and daughter have a special bond." She put her hands on my shoulders and gave me a squeeze. "Why don't you and Hal help in the kitchen? I want to talk with Ruth for a minute."

Taking my hand, she led me into the living room where we sat together on our old maroon sofa with its saggy cushions.

"What's the matter?" Mother asked, holding me close against her side.

"The house—it means so much to you."

"No, it's something else. You've been jumpy today, watching every move Gisela makes—are you worried that Hal will make her uncomfortable?"

It always startled me when Mother guessed my feelings.

"I thought you were the one worried about Hal. You changed the subject twice when he seemed to disagree with Gisela about Germany."

"It seemed the right thing to do. He can be so rigid with his opinions." She took my hand. "Why did Mrs. Sullivan really call me?"

There was no hint of accusation. She looked at me with expectation in her hazel eyes, the same color as Hal's.

"I told Mrs. Sullivan a big fat lie so I could get a weekend pass. I told her that I needed to come home, that you were ill, so I could spend the weekend with Gisela. I've been anxious about school, and I haven't made close friends with any of the girls in the sorority. Gisela's the first person I feel at ease with."

"So that's all it is?" She sounded relieved. "You've always hated rules."

"I'm sorry—" I started to apologize. She interrupted.

"I want you to be independent, Ruthie. You're going to have so many more opportunities than I ever dreamed of."

She let my hand go and said, "Don't worry, everything will work out just fine for me with the move to Minneapolis. We'll be closer to each other."

Our conversation ended when Hal appeared in the doorway and announced, "The kitchen's spic and span. Gisela wants to walk down to the lake, you two want to come along?"

"You go, Ruth. I'm too tired to move," Mother said. "Come and sit with me, Dorothy. You look tired too."

The three of us walked down the well-worn trail that led through the conifers to the lakeshore, the same path my grandparents had walked. Mother and her brothers had walked it as children, and so had Hal and I.

We sat in a row at the end of the rickety old dock with me in the middle, swinging our feet as dusk swallowed the daylight. I relaxed, watching the glow of the setting sun disappear into the lake.

"I always thought one of us would end up living out here at the lake, raising our own family." Hal sounded subdued, and a little sad.

"Maybe you and Dorothy can move out here. Keep it in the family," I said. "It's hard to imagine strangers moving in, changing everything."

"Maybe."

Gisela sat so close to me that our shoulders brushed.

We all seemed content to watch an occasional loon skid in for a landing on the placid water of the cove and glide around the island.

Gisela broke the silence. "I've never seen so many loons. I wonder what they're doing."

"They're gathering to migrate. It's only this time of year you see so many in one place," Hal said. "Do you know that they winter on the ocean?"

Gisela leaned across me and shook her head. "No."

Hal had a profound respect and deep knowledge of the workings of nature. Years ago he'd taught Duke and me all he knew about the loons.

"Hal's an expert on bird life," I said. "Tell her the story."

In a hushed voice he started the story of the loon's arduous flight from freshwater to saltwater. I silently thanked Gisela's incisive instinct for details. Every cell in my body reveled in her warmth as she leaned across me to listen to Hal.

"Loons are fiercely territorial and have very few predators. There's plenty of fish in the deep freshwater lakes they inhabit. It's an idyllic life, until fall when the chicks have grown and the lakes start to freeze. Then they are off to a whole new life, unknown and dangerous. Those that survive must learn quickly to drink rainwater and eat saltwater fish."

"Why don't they just go south, down where lakes don't freeze?" Gisela said.

"That's even more dangerous. Too much competition from other freshwater birds, such as herons and grebes. The warmer lakes are shallower and have aquatic plants that make the water murky. Loons need deep, clear water to dive for fish."

"What about the saltwater of the ocean? How do they adapt?" Gisela asked.

"Loons are born with salt glands between their eyes that drip all winter, draining the excess salt. I imagine much like tears," Hal said.

We sat quietly until Gisela said, "Like crying for the safety of the life they leave behind." Her voice sounded sad.

We fell silent again. A loon wailed out on the lake as if reflecting our mood. Another answered with its ghostly *woo-ooo* traveling across the water. I shivered.

"What I want to know is how they make the decision to winter on the ocean. Is it evolution or choice?"

"Maybe necessity," Gisela answered, pushing gently against me.

I looked over at Hal, who stared straight ahead. Gisela discreetly covered my hand, resting between us, with hers. Our fingers intertwined while we watched the stars pop out and the lake gradually blend into the darkness.

I let go of Gisela's hand when Hal changed position, but was puzzled when he said, "Thanks sis" as he stood up from the dock.

"For what?" I asked.

"For suggesting that Dot and I consider moving out to the lake. While we've been sitting here, I've been thinking that with help from Dorothy's family, we might be able to work out a way to buy the house from Mom and Dad."

"I hope so. It would make Mother very happy," I said.

Hal reached down to help Gisela and me stand up, then stayed with us for a few more moments.

"Our lives certainly are changing," he said with a catch in his voice. He turned toward the house and left us alone.

Gisela waited until he disappeared into the darkness. She reached out to me and held me close without words.

Indeed, they are.

FIFTEEN

I squeaked in right at curfew, only to discover that Mrs. Sullivan was waiting for me. She started to say good night and then, on what seemed to be a second thought asked, "Where's your costume?"

My costume? The reason I had given for going home was to pick up my costume for the ball. I'd forgotten all about it. "My brother," I said as my mind raced. "Hal will bring it in Monday or Tuesday. Mother needed to make one more alteration." I cringed at another lie.

She frowned. "Well, I hope it gets here in time. The costume ball is one of the most important social events of the year."

❧

That night I dreamed about Rollie. She rode up on Hornet, looking spirited, dressed in black accented by her red boots and a red bandanna. When she leaned down to say something, I saw her face was wrinkled and pinched like an old hag.

"Follow me," she called out, waving as Hornet reared up on his hind legs. "I can't, I have an exam," my dream self said.

They galloped off and disappeared, leaving me in a cloud of dust unable to see which way they'd gone.

Still thinking about the dream upon my arrival at the stables, I wrapped my arms around Satin Dancer's long neck and rested in her warmth, ready to sort out my mixed-up feelings. She nickered "thanks" when I scratched the favorite spot on her withers, and in the relaxed comfort of our silent communication I was able to unburden my problems.

I eventually let go of Satin Dancer and turned to my chores. Deep in thought I shoveled out stalls, raking in fresh straw while replaying the dream over and over, trying to figure it out while I worked.

A clamor at the open barn door startled me. Duke stood in the doorway, a dark outline against the sunlight. He'd dropped his bicycle. "Break time," he called into the hollow of the barn, the words echoing off the rafters.

"Ruth, are you in there?"

"I'm in Satin D's stall."

"Well come on out in the sunshine, both of you. I brought lunch, salami on rye. Your favorite."

I moved slowly, gathering my thoughts. Satin Dancer followed, and we both greeted Duke who offered her a carrot pulled from his pocket. She munched contentedly while we stood together.

"Turn Satin D out to pasture so we can eat. I'm starving."

"Don't be so impatient." It irritated me that he had interrupted my thoughts.

We sat on the grass. The simple act of taking a break on the ground reminded me of how Rollie and I had done the same thing many times. I missed our conversations and her wise way of teaching me about the world of rodeo, pointing out things I needed to know without making me feel stupid.

"Hey, where are you today?" His tone jarred me. "I asked you about your costume. You didn't even hear me."

My frustration spilled out. "I don't give a hoot about that silly costume. Why is everyone so interested in it?"

"Whoa. What's wrong?"

"I'm sick and tired of everyone gabbing about the next social event, who's coming and what everyone's wearing." I wanted him to take his sandwich and leave me alone.

"Don't be cross with me."

"Well, I am cross. You always stitch me up for all the dances. You just expect me to be your date on Saturday night. I need room to breathe. I want to be left alone sometimes." My words tumbled out.

"I thought that was what you wanted. You told me you don't want to date other fellas. Besides, I haven't seen you for two Saturdays in a row."

"Never mind." My hands shook as I took a gulp of water to wash down the crusts of rye bread. Tears stung my eyes. I didn't want to cry. What a trap to be caught in, unable to confide my deepest secret with my best friend.

I tried to imagine what he would do if I were to say, "Help me, Duke. My world is upside down. I'm falling in love with a woman." Tears trickled down my cheeks.

Duke took out his handkerchief. "Here, let me catch those. You've got little rivulets in the dust on your face."

I grabbed the handkerchief with a barely audible "I can do it," then wiped away my tears.

He looked stunned. We rarely quarreled, and I hardly ever cried. I had to say something and blurted out, "Mother and Dad are leaving the lake, moving to Minneapolis."

"That's why you're so upset?" He moved closer to put his arm around me. I closed my eyes and let him hold me.

"They told us yesterday." I took a breath. "Hal's upset too. I suggested that he and Dorothy should try and buy the house. He told us, uh . . . me on the way to the train station that he and Dorothy are going to try to get the money together."

"Us?" Duke asked. He took his arm away from my shoulder.

"No one else," I said.

"You started to say us and then changed your mind," Duke said as natural as if we were discussing the weather. His voice didn't rise like it did when he was excited or anxious. He didn't sound angry. I decided to tell him.

"Gisela went home with me. We were going to have lunch and pick up my costume. There was so much going on. I forgot."

"Forgot what?" Duke's logical mind was an asset. He worked math problems and solved puzzles with ease. Why couldn't he understand?

"The costume. That's why I went home."

He looked dejected and fell silent, pulling a strand of grass, chewing on it. He thought for a moment. "Gisela? That's the girl from Europe, isn't it?"

"Yes, my new friend. I wanted to show her the lake."

"Why's she so special?"

Duke knew about my difficulty in feeling close to any of the girls in the sorority, and knew I didn't feel like I fit in.

"She has serious opinions about the world. She's independent and knows what she wants." I stood. "My lunchtime is over."

"I'll stick around till you're done. We can get some coffee."

"No. I'm too tired. I'm just going home."

"Too tired for coffee?" He knew how much I loved a cup of coffee to perk me up after work.

"Can't you tell I want to be alone?" Why was he being so stubborn?

"All right. Don't bite my head off." He turned to walk away. "I don't know why you're so sore with me."

He rode away on his bicycle.

I felt guilty, and took out my self-loathing on a bale of hay, kicking until my toe hurt inside my boot. I found it difficult to concentrate on my work and saw Rollie's face again. I'd read that Freud called dreams a peephole into the unconscious and worried about Rollie, how gruesome she'd appeared. Maybe it was some kind of warning.

Stuck in this terrible mood I finished my chores and set off to meet Gisela at the diner.

❧

The streetcar that would take me to the diner was full of passengers dressed in their Sunday best—the men in suits and women in dresses and hats. Because it was so crowded, I had to stand in the rear, which made me feel even more conspicuous in my trousers and riding boots, and I noticed several people giving me strange looks. I hadn't bothered to remove my jacket so sweat trickled down my back, and to make matters worse the leather of the overhead strap burned my palms and stretched my fingers when the car lurched forward.

As more folks boarded the car, I found it harder to breathe until I could no longer stand the crush of people. At the next stop, I jumped off several blocks early and walked as fast as I could toward the diner where Gisela and I had agreed to meet. I couldn't quiet the thoughts that tumbled like stones crashing downhill. My boots pounded the sidewalk, and I hardly felt the wind that tossed my hair. Ringlets clung to my forehead and neck, and despite the chilly temperature I continued to perspire. Worried about my appearance I ran my fingers through my hair, trying to settle it down.

I could see Gisela through the front window of the diner, bent over a book. She glanced outside and waved at me.

"Hi." I sat across from her feeling the blood pounding in my temples—anger at Duke, mixed with my confusion, cooked in a soup of conflict that threatened to boil over.

"It's really cold outside. Hot in here."

My face felt flushed and damp. I shrugged out of my jacket and wrapped it around my shoulders as if it could protect me.

The first sip of coffee stung my nose with its strong burnt smell. Adding milk only turned it a sickly brown color, and it still left a sourness in my mouth, so I stirred in four teaspoons of sugar and tried to ignore the metallic taste.

"What happened?" Gisela asked. "You don't look like yourself."

Her concern alarmed me.

"I'm a mess." I patted at my hair, but knew it wouldn't help. Jumbled curls flew out in every direction.

"I can see," she said. "It looks like you ran all the way from the stables."

"Only partway," I said. "The streetcar was stuffy and crowded. I got off early."

For some reason, the idea of running all the way from the stables struck me as funny. I began to laugh, a strange, hysterical sound. Gisela shifted in her seat and glanced around the room. Her look sobered me.

My day spilled out, my words falling over one another. I told her how I'd pushed Duke away with my anger, and how I hated myself for the insensitive way I had told him about my parents' decision to move.

"I was sadistic, blurting it out without thinking about how much my family means to him." I tossed the jacket off my shoulders in a rush of heat. "He's been my best friend forever and now I've hurt him."

"If he's really your friend, he'll forgive you." Her eyes narrowed. "That's what friends do."

I sank deeper into misery and kept on talking. I told her about my dream, how it didn't make any sense.

"I'm trapped, boxed in, caught between you and Duke . . . and my life."

I couldn't tell from her face whether or not she agreed with me. I wanted her to understand the anguish I felt. Feeling strangled by my own words I gulped my lukewarm coffee. Gisela took some money out of her pocket and laid it on the table.

"Come on, let's go," she said decisively, but not with anger.
"Where?" I asked. My throat constricted. I struggled to
hold back tears that threatened to flow for the second time
that day. I chewed my lip, willed my tears to dry, and hurried
to catch up with her.

Winter lurked around the corner as we walked toward
Gisela's room. A gust of wind picked up maple leaves that
swirled through the air and crunched under our feet. This
time I felt the cold through my jacket, pulling the hood over
my head and the fox-trimmed collar close around my neck.
The softness of the animal's fur soothed me.

I stood behind Gisela while she found her key. In the few
seconds it took her to fiddle with the lock, I changed my mind
about being there. I wanted to turn around, run home, and
get under the covers of my own bed. Then I wanted to stay.
About to change my mind again, I silently urged her to hurry.

She opened the door and the familiar scents of her room—
her perfume, candle wax, and the faint aroma of the Earl
Grey tea she drank—calmed me.

I belong here.

But I couldn't get comfortable on the window seat, and
realized I couldn't stay.

"I feel foolish saying this. I'm expected home at five thirty."

"Don't talk like that. You're not being foolish." She warmed
my shaking hands in hers and sat facing me. "This is complicated for both of us. The time constraints of the sorority
are a big part of it." She pulled me toward her, and I leaned
into her shoulder. After a while, I melted into her embrace.
Warmth flooded my body. My heartbeat slowed.

I curled up beside her, my head in her lap while she ran
her fingers through my tangles.

The radiator hissed and startled me. I sat up, like a cat
alert to danger, and felt the chill again, despite the warm
room. I reached for my jacket, pulling it like an afghan over
my chest.

I twisted my head so I could see her face. "What are we going to do?"

"It depends on what you do: stay where you are, or make changes in your life so you can discover what you really want—not what's expected of you by society or a bunch of sorority sisters."

"And my family and Duke. Don't forget them."

"That's the life you know that's familiar in every way. It's like the loons who take their flight away from all they've known in their young lives. If they stay, they'll die. If they take the chance to change, they have to adapt to a whole new way of life. It may not look ideal to outsiders, but it's what saves them from certain death."

Gisela stood, fussed with the radiator, then walked over and turned on the lamp where Madge the Flapper did her endless dance. She returned, her deep blue eyes bright as she looked down at me, and I could see that she was trying to hold back tears.

"You mean more to me than anyone I've ever met. I'm willing to wait while you make up your mind." She sounded hoarse as she sat down again and reached for me.

"I could face the danger in the arena riding next to a thousand pound steer, but I can't face losing my family," I said.

Gisela felt me tremble and held me tighter. I didn't move until I knew it was time to leave.

I fumbled with the buttons on my jacket.

"I have to hurry or I'll be late," I said, my hand on the doorknob.

Gisela reached for her coat. "I'll walk you out and wait for the tram with you."

Outside, we huddled together against the cold wind from the north. The sky seemed lower, ominous in its closeness as the street lamps blinked on and we waited in a pool of faint light. The streetcar approached just as it began to rain, and Gisela sounded sad when she said "I won't see you until Thursday in class."

I knew she would be worried about me, and did my best to reassure her by trying to sound strong and said "I'll be better by then" before boarding the trolley. On the way home, every familiar street we passed made Gisela and her cozy room seem farther away. Chilled to the bone, and feeling too frail to stand up to a scolding, I became anxious at the thought of being late for dinner and in my mind urged the driver to go faster.

The rain had picked up by the time we reached my stop and I hurried the short distance to the sorority. No one noticed me enter through the side door. I shrugged off my soaked jacket and hung it to dry. Most of the girls were downstairs for the pre-dinner social hour. Still panting, I hurried upstairs to change and freshen up.

I stripped off my damp clothes. The idea of a hot bath tempted me. Taking advantage of the upstairs quiet, I grabbed my towel and robe. Dinner would be served in a half hour so I would have to be quick. The hot water released the tension in my neck as I soaked in the deep clawfoot bathtub.

Steam rose from the water. I saw Rollie's wizened dream face on the ceiling. The bare overhead light bulb seemed to spin in the still air. I held on to the edge of the tub to stop the spinning.

The dinner bell rang. I needed to hurry and got out of the bath, sitting on the commode to dry myself.

"Ruth, are you up here?" Elena called from the hallway. I didn't have the energy to answer and reached for my robe—just before everything went dark.

The next thing I remember is looking up at Mrs. Sullivan from the bathroom floor. She held her cool hand on my forehead saying, "Well, you must have a fever." She took a thermometer out of her pocket.

"What happened?" I said.

Elena stood next to Mrs. Sullivan.

"You fainted. I heard you fall," Elena said full of excitement. "You ran the water too hot. Your face looked like it was on fire. Now you're pale as a ghost."

"Okay, Elena. That's enough," Mrs. Sullivan said. "Go out and let the others know everything is fine."

Mrs. Sullivan walked me down the hall and put me to bed.

"Open wide," she said and stuck a thermometer under my tongue. She waited a few minutes and declared, "You do have a fever. I'll call the doctor in the morning."

She brought me a cup of broth and returned later, fussing over me like a mother hen and tucking me in with extra blankets.

"You have a touch of the grippe. It will pass."

I couldn't sleep. The blankets pressed heavily on my body. With everyone downstairs or studying, my troubles returned. Thoughts rambled, and I invented prayers: *God, have mercy on me. Make everyone leave me alone.* That didn't sound right. *Please, God, let it be all right to love Gisela.* That scared me. *Shouldn't I tell the truth to God? What is the truth?* I wondered if it was a sin to love Gisela. How could it be a sin to love someone? *Let me fly like a loon. Please, please understand.* I wished it could be that easy—create a clumsy prayer and everything will be just fine. Guilt crept in. *Show me what to do about Duke.* I fell into a troubled sleep.

I awoke covered in sweat. My heart, pounding a steady rhythm like a drum, kept me awake. I watched the window, listening to Elena's breathing until dawn lightened the sky.

Every part of my body ached and in the morning I refused to get out of bed. Mrs. Sullivan called the doctor as promised, and later in the day he bustled into the room all business.

"What seems to be the problem, young lady?"

"I'm just too tired to get up," I said.

He went through his routine, asking me to open my mouth and say "ahh" as he placed a stethoscope on my chest to listen to my heart and lungs. "Your heart is as strong as a horse. You can get up and go to class tomorrow."

He quickly packed his black bag, but didn't leave the room until he had patted me on the head in a small attempt to offer some comfort. "There. There. Why the tears?"

I turned over to face the wall, my shoulders shaking. Apparently he couldn't hear anguish through his ice-cold stethoscope.

"You'll be fine," the doctor told me as he left the room, although when he spoke to Mrs. Sullivan out in the hall I overheard him say "You're right, she's got a touch of the grippe, but keep a watch on her. There might be something else."

"What do you mean, doctor?" Mrs. Sullivan asked.

"Well, it could be nervous strain. She's crying, and you know how these young girls take on too much."

"I don't understand it. She's one of our most popular girls, engaged in so many social activities and doing well in her classes. It doesn't make sense."

"Usually this sort of thing goes away. Let her rest." I heard the two of them head down the hall for the stairs.

I sobbed into the wall until I fell asleep.

That evening, Elena quietly gathered her things and moved out of our room. I pretended to be asleep.

Mrs. Sullivan poked her head in.

"I'm isolating you. The doctor says it could be contagious and that you need rest."

She closed the door firmly.

The next few days were a blur. No one except Mrs. Sullivan came into my room, and I lost touch of how much time had passed.

She had been hovering over me, telling me I needed to eat, but stopped leaving food when I barely touched my plate. She now only brought a fresh cup of broth at mealtimes, urging me to try and get it down.

"Did I miss my day at the stables?" I asked her, and then became anxious as I thought about Satin Dancer. "What about my horse?"

"Duke told them you're ill. He checked on your horse and her boarding is paid until next month." Mrs. Sullivan answered, "He's been here every day, asking about you."

Of course he would do that.

"So what should I tell him?" she asked, sounding irritated.

I didn't have an answer.

"You can't stay in bed forever."

I turned over. *Oh, yes I can.*

Seeming to have lost patience, she picked up the latest half-empty cup and scolded me, "You need your strength."

And, even though the thought of food turned my stomach, I knew she was right because she needed to steady me as I walked down the hall to the bathroom.

I drifted in and out of fitful sleep for the rest of what seemed like an endless day. While awake, I mulled over a passage from *The Well of Loneliness* where Angela asks Stephen if they could ever marry, and Stephen answers "No." Although Stephen eventually begs Angela to run away with her, it turns out that Angela is unable to give up the respectability marriage provides to be with the woman she loves, even though her husband is boring—and mistreats her.

It worried me that I might be as fearful as Angela, who was willing to give up the woman she loved to stay with a man who abused her. *Could I be that weak?*

A hard rain pounded the window, finally lulling me into a deep sleep. Sometime during the night the rain stopped, and I awoke before daylight to the sound of *tap-tap-tap* as the last bit of water dripped onto the tin roof of the veranda below. The sky cleared, and a sliver of moon showed up like a raised eyebrow scolding me. I looked for answers from the cosmos outside my window, praying for the strength I would need to get out of bed and get on with my life.

God's reply came as dawn swallowed the last of the stars: Staring at a sky brilliant with streaks of coral, I realized without a doubt that I would have to find the courage to defy all I knew, and had been taught to believe, in order to love Gisela. That morning I asked for oatmeal when Mrs. Sullivan came in to check on me.

At noon I asked for soup instead of broth.

"Then we'll see you at the dinner table tonight?" Mrs. Sullivan asked, when she brought me a hot bowl of chicken soup with large chunks of carrots.

"I'll try." I knew it was a lie, but I wanted her to leave. The aroma of the soup energized my senses and gave me hope. I devoured it as soon as she closed the door.

On Thursday, I refused to get up and bathe, and Mrs. Sullivan looked down at me in defeat. "I give up. It's time to call the doctor again, or perhaps your parents?"

"No. I'm feeling better. I'll come down for dinner tomorrow." I did feel better, but wanted more time to think about things.

But on Friday I decided it was easier to face Mrs. Sullivan's annoyance than to participate in the social hour before dinner. She relented and sent up my food, but later when she checked on me she issued a warning, "It's been five days. If you can't get up tomorrow, I *will* call your parents."

❧

Saturday morning the house filled with the exuberant voices of the other girls. "What's going on?" I asked when Mrs. Sullivan opened my door to wake me.

"Everyone's excited about the Masquers ball tonight and getting ready for the big football game this afternoon against Nebraska."

I'd forgotten all about the big day. Duke and I had planned to attend the game and, of course, the dance, before I took to my bed. Now it didn't matter.

"Shall I tell Duke that you'll go?" she asked before she left to get my breakfast.

"No," I answered, aware I'd tried her patience to the limit. "Tell him I'm sorry."

"You'll have to get out of bed and tell him that yourself." She closed the door on the gaiety in the hallway.

She returned a short time later with a poached egg on toast and a glass of milk. "Your temperature is normal, but you've hardly said anything for a week, and I just don't know what to do with you. At least you've started eating." She hadn't bothered to hide her annoyance, and quickly turned away, leaving me alone again.

Eventually the house quieted, everyone had left for the game. Half awake, I heard Mrs. Sullivan talking with someone in the hall outside my room.

"I've been calling here the last two days. No one will put me through to Ruth."

All of a sudden I was wide awake, and recognized Gisela's voice.

"I'm so sorry, dear. I couldn't place you since you don't belong to a sorority. I didn't know you were her friend when you called, the one she spent the weekend with," Mrs. Sullivan said. "Perhaps you can shed some light on what's going on with her."

"I'll try. I saw Ruth last Sunday. She was feverish then, and I've been concerned about her. We have a class together, and this Thursday is the first one she's missed. It's a demanding class. Maybe she's been studying too hard."

"She's hardly been up all week. Try and persuade her to bathe."

The door opened. "You have a visitor," Mrs. Sullivan said without entering the room.

Sixteen

Gisela stood at the foot of my bed. "She says you refuse to get up." The cool breeze of her voice soothed my warm skin, bringing blue sky and sunshine into my stuffy room.

"Something didn't seem right," she continued, sitting down on the bed with me.

"How did you get past her?"

"I finally mentioned that I was worried enough about you to call your parents or have your brother stop by if I couldn't see you." The words flew out of her mouth like a flock of waxwings startled into flight.

"You were going to call Hal?"

She took my hand in hers. "I didn't have a choice. She wouldn't let me talk to you."

Gisela fetched a washcloth and basin from the bathroom. The cool compresses on my forehead, along with her tender touch, were balm for my agitated spirit.

She dipped the washcloth in the water and wrung it out. "Do you think she's peeking through the keyhole?"

"She wouldn't dare."

"I'm kidding. Anyway, I hope I'm kidding." Gisela smiled

in a way that made me laugh for the first time in a week. It felt good. I sat up and stretched.

Vaguely remembering my hot bath on Sunday, I realized how grimy I felt, worse than after a full day mucking out a horse barn.

"Phew. I need a bath."

She insisted on carrying my clothes and held out her arm to steady me as we walked down the hall to the bathroom.

"Really I'm fine. A little wobbly from all that sleeping."

The silent house gave us a sense of privacy.

"Where is everyone?" Gisela started the bathwater.

I told her about the football game and the Masquers ball. She had trouble believing everyone had gone to the game.

"Kind of like those lemmings," she said, reminding me of our first conversation.

"I can manage okay by myself." I gathered my soap and shampoo and stood next to her in my robe while the tub filled with warm water.

She waited in the hallway until I called out, "I'm squeaky clean and dressed." I wore a loose cotton housedress and a towel wrapped turban-style around my hair.

Back in my room, Gisela struggled with my tangles for several minutes. "The comb keeps getting stuck," she said.

I handed her a jar of Colgate Brilliantine.

"Try a dab of this. It's the only thing that helps." She massaged the pomade into my hair until her fingers, playing through my curls, released the snarls. I stood up and checked myself in the mirror.

Not too bad.

"Mrs. Sullivan can be such a snob. I heard what she said to you about not being in a sorority."

Gisela shrugged, shook out a Pall Mall, and offered one to me.

"Oh. You can't smoke upstairs," I said, feeling self-conscious telling her what to do.

She put away her cigarettes. "You're going to drown in the rules around this place. I couldn't see you because I don't belong to a sorority. You have to be home at certain times and in bed. My god, Ruth, you were responsible for yourself on a rodeo circuit. No one told you what to do. Let's go downstairs and have a smoke."

I led the way to the cold, empty parlor. With the fire unlit, it smelled of stale ashes. We sat in two overstuffed armchairs with a round side table between us, and it seemed like Gisela was a mile away. I took the lighted cigarette she offered, but it made me feel lightheaded. My mind wandered to the haven of my bed, and Gisela's voice seemed to come from far off in the distance, as if my ears were filled with cotton.

"I asked, have you thought about moving home for a while?" Gisela said, bending closer to me.

I hesitated, my mind on not being able to bear the thought of facing my sorority sisters enthusiastically rehashing the football game, cheeks rosy from the fresh air, when they flooded in later to dress for the ball. But Gisela's question struck a nerve—how would I make it through the rest of the term? And what would I tell my parents and Mrs. Sullivan if I chose to leave the sorority house?

"There would be so much explaining."

"The term is almost over, and the commute isn't that bad. You could ride in with your dad. Think about it."

It made sense. *If I went home, I could help Mother pack up the house for their move.* "I'll think about it later. Right now, I'm too tired to think," I said.

Gisela decided to leave. I wanted her to stay, but she wouldn't. "You need to rest and decide what to do." I was too tired to be reasonable, and we said our goodbyes without touching.

Alone in the parlor I sat back and closed my eyes, but was suddenly startled by Mrs. Sullivan, who had quietly entered the room and was now sitting in the chair next to me—most likely still warm from Gisela's body.

"So that's your friend. I'm still trying to figure out why you lied to me to spend the weekend with *her.*" The sarcasm in her voice made me cringe, and although she'd insulted Gisela, what could I say? *I think I love her, and thought you wouldn't understand.*

The old house creaked in a chasm of silence awaiting an answer, but my only reply was a simple "I'm tired," and the moment I stood up and turned away from Mrs. Sullivan I knew I needed to leave the sorority in order to sort out my life.

Later that afternoon, loud laughter and chatter drove me under the covers, where I muffled the spirited noise of the girls returning from the football game by pulling the pillow over my ears and curling up in a ball. A soft knock on my door brought me to the surface.

"It's me," Elena said through a crack in the door. "Mrs. Sullivan said you were up and dressed." She looked puzzled when she saw me peeking over the edge of the blankets, my clothes thrown over the chair. "I thought you might want to come down. There's a whole gang coming over."

"Oh," I said and sat up, patting down my hair.

"Duke went to the game with us and is staying for dinner. He's hoping you'll come to the Masquers ball."

"I don't think so. I had a dizzy spell earlier."

"Well okay, then. What should I tell him?"

"You can tell him I miss him." Hating myself for sending a message I knew would have a different meaning for him than it did for me, I wasn't ready to level with him and selfishly wanted him to stay my best friend. I missed his company and his sense of humor.

Elena stood in the doorway, seeming reluctant to leave.

"And tell him I'll be better soon."

"I will." She didn't close the door and didn't leave as I thought she would. "Umm . . ." She hesitated. "Would you . . . I mean do you think it would be all right if I go with Duke?"

I thought for a moment. "What would you wear?"

"Maybe I could borrow your cowboy hat."

"Take it. Have a good time." I slid under my blankets and wondered if I should be furious or grateful.

The next day I called Mother and burst into tears, unable to find the words to tell her what was wrong with me.

"I'm exhausted," I managed to say through my sobs, trying to compose myself. One of the girls from down the hall stood watching me with her arms folded.

"Tell me what happened? You sound too upset to just be exhausted."

"I can't. There's a five minute limit on calls, and someone is waiting to use the phone."

"Whatever it is, I want you home as soon as possible. Your father and Hal will be there Monday to discuss it with Mrs. Sullivan."

❧

On Monday morning I attended all my classes, picked up my missed assignments, and then cleaned my room while waiting for Hal and Dad, who arrived right on time. When I met them in the parlor, Hal gripped my arm as if he thought I might collapse. "You're so thin," he said instead of greeting me.

I couldn't tell if he was concerned about me or embarrassed to have to show up and rescue me.

The three of us sat down with Mrs. Sullivan in her office. Dad spoke first. "Mrs. Thompson and I have decided that Ruth should move home for the rest of the term. I can drop her off at her classes on my way to the office."

Dad and Mrs. Sullivan looked at me, waiting for my reaction, while Hal seemed to be examining the books over Mrs. Sullivan's shoulder.

"I do want to move home Dad, but I've got midterm exams." My week's absence had made me realize just how far behind I'd fallen, and the ride in from the lake would take precious time that I needed for my studies. "I should probably stay a few more days so I can catch up."

Hal shifted uncomfortably in his chair.

Ignoring what Dad had said, Mrs. Sullivan spoke to him as if I weren't present. "I've been worried about Ruth ever since she spent a weekend with that friend of hers, Gisela."

"What does that have to do with her exhaustion?" Dad asked.

"She lied to me," Mrs. Sullivan said, still talking about me as if I weren't in the room. "I need to be able to trust my girls, and Ruth has given me doubts about her character."

Hal's face reddened and I held my breath, but Dad cut in before he could say anything.

"We know Gisela, and think very highly of her. Ruth told her mother about the lie. It doesn't concern us. Right now, the most important thing is her health."

"Of course, I'm also worried about her exhaustion. The doctor has been here and declared her well. I think it has been hard for her to adjust to our rules." She looked at me. "Isn't that the explanation you gave me?" Her tone accused me of a crime.

I nodded.

"I'm sorry I lied. I knew you'd say no if I asked for permission to spend the night with a girlfriend who didn't belong to a sorority."

Mrs. Sullivan pursed her lips, her eyes narrowed.

"I worry about my girls," she said to Dad and Hal without looking at me. "Whatever is bothering Ruth is my concern while she's under my roof. I haven't been able to reach her. I agree she probably will do better at home."

My skin crawled with resentment. Mrs. Sullivan had no right to be so condescending to my father.

Finally, she turned to me. "I accept your apology, dear."

I forgot all about wanting to stay another week to finish the term and wanted to leave right then with Dad and Hal.

Dad didn't forget.

"Can she stay the rest of the week and sit her midterm exams?" Dad asked with authority. He sat up straight and looked Mrs. Sullivan in the eye, taking control as if he were tired of her nonsense. He used to do the same thing to Hal and me when we were small. He would put up with a lot, until he'd had enough of our shenanigans.

"Of course she can," Mrs. Sullivan said, all business now. "Her dues are paid until the end of the term. After all, Ruth is still a part of this sorority. She doesn't have to leave unless she wants to. Although she will still have to follow our rules."

"Then it's all settled," Dad said. "We'll see you next Saturday." He shook Mrs. Sullivan's hand and walked out of her office.

"Say hello to Dorothy for me, Hal dear," Mrs. Sullivan said to him as we followed Dad out.

"Yes, of course. She'll be delighted you remembered her."

In the hallway, Dad turned to Hal.

"I'll get the car, it's starting to freeze out there." He hugged me, then held me at arms length and looked into my eyes. "Chin up. Mother and I are behind you, whatever you need to do. See you Saturday."

Then he left Hal and me alone at the door.

"Take it easy, kid. Dorothy will be relieved to hear there's no scandal, that you just hit a rough patch and got sick. Study hard and don't make it any worse on us." He patted me on the shoulder and walked out into the cold.

~✿~

I spoke with Gisela only briefly on Thursday, confirming that I would be moving back home. We parted, knowing we would not see each other for another week.

In a phone conversation, I also put off seeing Duke, convincing him I needed every free minute to study. The Friday we finished our exams, we met outside the library on the steps where I had first seen Gisela two months earlier.

He raised his arms over his head and shouted, "Yahoo! We're free!" His words reverberated in the gray mist that surrounded us. "Midterms are over, and you're well again."

He released me from a giant bear hug. "I sure did miss you."

We walked toward the park, our first time together since our conversation at the stables two weeks ago. All alone, we took shelter in the bandstand. Who else would be out on what was the coldest day of the year so far?

"I lost my job at the stables," I said as a soft rain started to fall, "and Uncle Edward has taken Satin Dancer to his barn for the winter."

Duke pulled his usual small picnic out of his knapsack and set out sandwiches and coffee without looking at me.

He knows something is up. I've got to tell him soon.

"Sit down," he said, handing me a sandwich.

"I resigned from the drama club."

He listened with a quizzical expression.

I kept talking fast so he wouldn't ask questions. "You know how much I loved acting."

"What's really wrong? Mrs. Sullivan wouldn't tell me anything, and Elena said she'd barely seen you since she moved out of your room."

He pushed the hair off his forehead and waited. I looked into his clear eyes. I'd imagined and dreaded this moment. I could no longer postpone it.

"I can't see you anymore."

"What do you mean can't see me?"

"I can't go on dates or to parties, or on picnics like this."

"Why? This doesn't make sense. You've just been sick."

He was right. It didn't make any sense. I wanted to stuff the words back down my throat and start over. "I'm confused, too confused to explain."

"You owe me more than that. Please try. I can take it."

"I'm moving home. I'm going to help Mother pack in my spare time."

"Is that all? I can drive out and pick you up." He paused for a moment. "I'll bet you could spend the night at the sorority house." He sounded enthusiastic again, problem solved.

"No. That's not it," I said, annoyed at him for making me answer so many questions.

I saw dread on his face and knew it would have been easier if he'd gotten angry with me. I took a gulp of air, a sip of coffee, and plunged.

"I haven't only been sick. I've been panic stricken and confused. I've wanted to die, dreamed about dying. I wanted to stay in bed forever."

I simply couldn't say the words: "I've fallen in love with Gisela."

I blurted out, "It's me. You haven't done anything wrong. It's not fair to you. It's not what I want."

"Whoa. If it's not what you want—?"

I didn't let him finish his question. "It's what I want," I said in almost a whisper. "I can't explain it."

Duke reached for me. "Why not?" I let him pull me close. "Is it because I took Elena to that stupid dance?"

"No. I told her to go with you. It's way more than that." I buried my head in his shoulder so I wouldn't have to see his disappointment. "I'm sorry I don't have an answer for you."

We held on to each other, not saying anything. After a while, he let me go.

"What will I do?"

He'd turned pale and I could hear the alarm in his voice. His fear stabbed at my heart. We'd leaned on each other for so long, living in our own world that we rarely socialized without being together. I knew how nervous he felt in social situations, and tried to say something that would make him feel better.

"You'll be fine. There are lots of girls who will want to go to the parties with you." I thought of Elena and how every time she mentioned Duke, her face lit up.

"I don't care about that," he said. "I'll miss you. I always thought that someday—"

"What?"

"I played handball with Hal the other day, and he asked me for the umpteenth time if you and I were ever going to get engaged."

"Oh, Duke . . ." I wanted to apologize to him, but couldn't find the right words. I'd forgotten that he and Hal played handball at the St. Paul Athletic Club at least once a month. *Why couldn't Hal keep his mitts off my life?*

"Hal has asked me the same question, but you and I never talked about it."

"It's my fault. I've taken everything for granted. I love your family, and the two of us always have such a good time together. I just thought the time wasn't right."

"You know Mother and Dad will always welcome you. You're like a second son to them. You'll always be like another brother to me."

"I don't want to be your brother." Tears clouded his eyes.

I held him, afraid of what I had done, knowing I held his broken heart while my own moved toward beating a little freer.

"We should make a run for it; it's getting dark," I said, shivering in the cold as I pulled away from him.

❦

The next day I sorted out my clothes and emptied drawers as rain ran down the window like giant tears.

Elena watched me pack my things. She seemed astonished I would leave the safety and camaraderie of the sorority just because I was exhausted.

"There must be something else. What about Duke? What about all the Christmas parties? You can't drive in from the lake every weekend."

"I'm not planning to drive in. I need to rest." I sat down to emphasize my point.

"Who will he take to the parties if you're not coming in?" She looked like a child eager to snatch a cookie.

I opened my closet. "I really don't know." I could imagine Elena licking her chops and slammed the closet door harder than I intended.

I must have startled her, because she grabbed her books and headed for the door. "Well, have fun at home" she said in a sarcastic tone as she headed down the hall.

Did Elena really care that little about me?

It was no wonder since I had offered so little of myself.

By two o'clock, the rain had turned to snow and was falling in huge flakes. Dad and Uncle Edward packed my belongings in Uncle Edward's brand new Packard that had the heater blasting. Gisela had agreed to come home with me for the weekend, and we stopped at her place to pick her up on the way out of town.

Seventeen

B y the time we reached home the snow had piled up higher and faster than anyone could remember. Gisela ended up staying the whole midterm break because the roads weren't clear enough for Dad to drive her home.

The two of us sorted out and packed away memories of Mother's childhood and mine. We pulled old clothes from a musty trunk and played dress-up. Our laughter brought Mother in to join us.

"You sound like you're having so much fun, I just had to check on my girls."

During the day, we were her girls, delighting in our silliness. At night in my childhood attic room, high above the rest of the house, it was different. We were each other's girls, warming our flesh with the clandestine touch and taste of love while snow poured from the sky. At first, I was Gisela's blank page. Slowly we wrote the story of my sexual awakening together. Under an avalanche of down comforters, we found the sacred places that sent waves of ecstasy through the give and take of our lovemaking.

"I had no idea it would be like this," I said in my transcendent state, our bodies entwined, naked and cozy in our cocoon.

"Nor did I," Gisela said. She kissed my ear, my neck, my lips. We fell fast asleep in each other's arms.

One morning at breakfast Dad said, "I'm glad you left the sorority. I haven't seen you this happy in a long time." Gisela and I looked at each other, barely able to contain our secret.

Time flew by, with the roads plowed much too soon to suit Gisela and me. The day Dad and I drove her home, I walked her upstairs while he waited with the motor running. Inside her room she held me and whispered in my ear, "We'll study together. You can spend the night with me . . . cousin."

Dad and I returned to find that Hal, the dutiful son, had arrived with groceries.

"I've been worried about you out here. I couldn't get a call through," he said. "I'll spend the night and drive back tomorrow morning."

"It's been a long week" Mother sighed, putting away the last dish. "Dad and I are turning in."

As soon as we were alone, Hal said "I played my last handball game with Duke this week."

I waited for him to go on.

"He's accepted a scholarship from the University of Chicago. He packed up and left a few days ago. Decided not to finish winter term."

"I know," I lied. "I'll miss him." I wiped every inch of the counters, folded the dishcloth, and hung it to dry before I moved from the kitchen to the living room. I needed to sit down.

Hal followed me.

"What's going on here? You broke off with him for no reason."

"I don't need to explain anything to you. I'm confused about a lot of things and need to try living my life without him."

"You just lied to me. I know for a fact that you did not know he was leaving for Chicago. Duke's part of our family, and you've tossed him away as if he means nothing to us. I'd like to know why."

I'd managed to forget Duke during the week with Gisela.

"Is there someone else?"

"No!" I shouted and ran upstairs.

※

Our family spent Thanksgiving and Christmas of 1932 without Duke, the first time in many years, and Gisela sat in his place at the table. Mother and Dad accepted my story that Duke and I needed to take a break from each other. On the outside I looked the same, but inside I carried my love for Gisela, so forbidden that I refused to share it even with Mother.

"Even the greatest pleasures have consequences," Gisela had said in the beginning. Two women in love would shock my family, and it terrified me to even think about breaking the taboo. Our camouflaged love was keeping me alive, but also weighed heavily on my heart.

Mother and Dad moved to their new house on West 24th Street in March, not far from the university campus. To everyone's relief, Hal and Dorothy were able to move out to the lake, keeping the property in the family.

Even though I knew that Hal and Dorothy were disappointed in me, I resigned from Kappa Rho. I found a place I could afford on Washington Avenue, across the river from the campus and closer to the stables where I was rehired. Up three flights of stairs, my new apartment had a tiny kitchen, a room with a Murphy bed, and a separate bathroom. The stairwell, lit with a bare light bulb, smelled of age and airless darkness. Light from a large window in my main room looked out on the street, giving my home life.

I cleaned and scrubbed the wood floors until the place sparkled. Dad and Hal brought over the old maroon couch from the lake.

Gisela and I played house, preferring my place to hers. My neighbors minded their own business, unlike the boarders where she lived. Inside my door, we'd kick off our shoes along with our cares. Music from the radio would fill the room while we fixed a simple supper and left the rest of the world outside.

※

Gisela socialized with a circle of friends every so often. Some of the girls spoke fluent French, like Gisela, and the others at least studied the language. They called themselves the French Club. Some of them were lovers and lived together. Outside of our rooms, I felt uncomfortable in my new role with Gisela—as well as with her friends. I often didn't join her on her nights out with them, and resented the time she spent away from me.

"We're just in a French club," she told me one night when I complained that I'd missed her. "The gals are like us. To most of them it's natural, and some are like you."

"How's that?" I asked, uneasy about how she might answer.

"New to the idea of love between women. I've always known I'm different from all those so-called normal folks out there. You're just discovering who you are."

"I am. You're right. I'm just not ready to run around in a crowd."

She held open her arms. "Come here. We definitely don't want a crowd tonight."

One of the many things I loved about Gisela was that she let me stumble through my feelings. No matter what happened, she never judged me.

❧

It didn't take long for the fun of meeting in our single rooms to wear off, and Gisela tried to convince me we should move in together.

"We'd see more of each other. No more schlepping from my place to yours."

I hesitated. We sat close together on the couch, catching up on our reading. Newspapers and magazines littered the floor. I worried out loud about two women living together. "It seems that as economic problems escalate, every magazine or newspaper has some sort of article or advertisement about a woman's place being at home with children—cooking and cleaning—so her husband can bring home a paycheck."

Gisela tried to soothe me with logic, scoffing at what she called outdated attitudes.

"No one cares about two old maids living together." She tossed aside the newspaper she'd been reading and leaned over to kiss me. "The men only want someone to greet them, martini in hand, after a hard day at the office, and the women won't miss the competition of two attractive spinsters."

We laughed at that, and then Gisela turned serious.

"It's uppity women they're afraid of. Women in the Twenties suffered and sacrificed to get us the vote. We're still struggling and lagging behind in education and jobs."

I couldn't argue with that.

"We can't let ourselves be dictated to by bigots. Besides, if we live together, most people will just think we're smart, saving a few dollars in these difficult times."

❧

A few days later, Gisela insisted I come to a meeting of the French Club. She wanted us to be together to learn the truth about a rumor she'd heard. Our hostess served drinks and there were canapés. No one spoke French that night, and there was a buzz in the room that bordered on hysteria.

A member of the club, Elizabeth, told a story about a woman down at the mill who dressed as a man in order to get work as a painter.

"Subtle hints that women who do a man's job are dykes is one more threat used to discriminate against us," she said. "One of the men found out she was a woman and started harassing her. She ended up badly beaten and left unconscious near the railroad tracks at Second Avenue."

Elizabeth worked as a secretary in the business office and heard most of the gossip about went on at the mill.

"I know a friend of the woman who was attacked. She was too intimidated to report the beating to the police, and no one ever inquired about why she didn't return to work. Her friends tended to her until she healed." Elizabeth shuddered. "The people who beat her called her an invert and other horrible names and spit on her. The men made an assumption based on her appearance that almost cost her life. They didn't know if she was lesbian, or if she dressed as a man to help support her family." She took a sip of her drink. "It's hateful discrimination, a warning about how careful we must be."

"What about you?" someone asked Elizabeth.

"I'm a secretary, so I'm invisible if I'm careful."

On the way home Gisela said "We'd be safer living together as spinsters or cousins. This spending the night together can raise suspicions, draw attention to us."

That night in bed as Gisela held me in her arms she declared, "In their ignorance they can turn their backs on us and call us names—take away our jobs or even break our bones—but they can't stop our love for each other."

"How do you stay so confident in your beliefs?"

"I love you. That's how."

❧

Gisela's determination and logic wore me down. I'd heard all her arguments by then, and finally realized how much I too wanted us to live together. I didn't want it to matter what others might say, and in a bold move, surprised her one night when we were in my room getting ready for bed.

"You're so beautiful," I said, watching her brush her long golden hair, wavy from being twisted in braids all day and then added "And I give up."

"What do you give up?"

"You win. Let's find ourselves an apartment. I don't want to spend any more nights away from you."

She threw down her hairbrush and jumped up.

"Oh my God. You're serious!" Gisela shouted and pulled me toward the bed.

"You are marvelous," she murmured in my ear as my inside world hummed.

❧

We each made a wish list for the perfect place. Noticing that mine included two bedrooms, Gisela asked "Why, Miss Marvelous?"

"Just in case someone drops in unexpectedly."

She gave me a funny look, and then it dawned on her. "Right. The family. Fine. One can be our office made to look like a bedroom."

We read the classified ads together on Sunday mornings. There were three apartments with potential the day we found what we'd been looking for, one of which was not far from the house on Sheridan Avenue where Gisela had lived with her parents. I could tell from the sound of her voice that this was the one she hoped would fit our needs.

It turned out to be just what we both wanted: An apartment in a neighborhood with trees and lawns. Mrs. Mahoney, the landlady, showed us in but then let us investigate without her.

Cream-colored crown moldings that gave the living room a feel of elegance separated the high ceilings and pale green walls. All the rooms were clean and freshly painted. The bedrooms were soft pink.

"The kitchen is rather small," I pointed out.

"We'll take turns cooking," Gisela replied from the doorway.

And, there were two bedrooms, just as I had requested.

"Perfect!" we both said at the same time.

Mrs. Mahoney invited us in for tea to discuss the lease. "My husband died three years ago and I had the house made into two units. I live downstairs and am quiet. You look like two nice girls. I don't want any children running around like little hellions over my head." She was delighted when Gisela told her she had once lived nearby with her family.

"Welcome home" she said, handing us the lease and leaving us alone for the second time.

"Yes. Welcome home indeed Miss Marvelous," Gisela laughed, looking happier than I had ever seen her.

The date was July 1, 1934.

Mother and Dad were our first visitors. Dad, always practical, wholeheartedly approved of our decision to double up to save money. Mother sewed identical curtains for each of our bedrooms. After we settled in, we often invited them for Sunday dinner. Hal and Dorothy joined us on the Sundays they drove in from the lake to attend Mass with Mother.

Most special occasions, like birthdays and holidays, were still celebrated in Mother and Dad's home. Uncle Edward and Aunt Margaret showed up for those family dinners as well. During grace, Mother blessed all members of our family, including Uncle Michael, Chloe, and Mac. Then she would add, "And bless our missing pieces; those who reside in our hearts," and I knew she was including Duke.

We celebrated Gisela's twenty-third birthday in our apartment with my family. Mother and Dad had left early, and Dorothy was helping Gisela in the kitchen.

Hal and I sat together in the living room. He had laced his after-dinner coffee with brandy, since Prohibition had ended months ago, and he could now buy legal liquor.

"Loosen up. Have some."

"No thanks. I'm loose." He seemed fidgety. I passed him a plate of ginger cookies.

"What's with you two? Why no fellas at these dinners? I'd like some younger-than-Dad male company." He chewed his cookie and took a sip of coffee. "I miss Duke."

I braced myself.

"Don't you go out to dances, places you can meet men?"

"I don't have time for that. I'm working at the stables and studying."

"Sounds pretty boring to me. You better find a new beau. Get a man in your life before you get too old. I could introduce you to a couple of my single friends from the University Club."

It didn't sound quite like innocent brotherly concern, and I wished he'd mind his own business.

"I don't need your help." The words came out more harshly than I intended. My face flushed hot. "I haven't met any friends of yours who interest me."

"Hey. Cool down. I'm just teasing. You're a good-looking gal. I just don't understand why you don't have a fella."

I stood up and walked away to end the conversation.

※

Most Saturdays we went to the movies. We had great fun debating which was the most alluring actress, Marlene Dietrich, so daring in *The Scarlett Empress,* or Katharine

Hepburn in *Spitfire,* fierce and defiant when accused of witchcraft. I favored Dietrich, and Gisela swooned over Hepburn. We both loved Fred Astaire and Ginger Rogers dancing in *The Gay Divorcee.*

"So many beautiful women, and they always fall in love with a man," Gisela laughed after we saw Claudette Colbert in *It Happened One Night.*

We took long rides with Satin Dancer and Lonnie, still Gisela's favorite horse since our first ride together.

Almost a year had passed since Gisela's article that pointed out the debris along Basset Creek had run in the *Tribune.* She'd joined a group of men and women who once a month picked up glass bottles and other trash. It became her passion. I loved that aspect of Gisela. Once she decided something needed her attention, she gave herself over to it.

I declined invitations to join them. I didn't have the stomach for garbage, preferring to help Mother in her garden and relishing the close moments we spent together.

One beautiful autumn day the two of us were pulling vegetables from the garden to store in the root cellar for the winter. Dad gathered dry leaves to pack the fat rutabagas, potatoes, carrots, and turnips in baskets and placed them in the dirt cellar under their house.

"Leave the beets in the ground," Mother said to me. "Come in and have some soup."

We left Dad to finish the gardening.

"I'm worried about Hal. He always has an excuse to miss our Sunday dinners," she said when we finished eating "You two haven't had a falling out, have you?"

"Not really, but I don't think he's ever forgiven me for not marrying Duke."

"We all miss Duke and wish it could have worked out."

"I loved him too much like a brother to marry him. It was right for him to leave," I said, hoping she believed me. I did my best to keep my voice neutral. "Hal scolded me recently for not having a new beau. He seemed angry that we don't invite men to dinner."

Mother cleared our bowls from the table and said, "Sometimes our lives don't work out as we'd planned. I'm sure Hal just wants the best for you. He's looked out for you and worried about you since the day you were born. I remember he was so excited to hold you when you were only a few hours old."

"Well I wish he would mind his own business now," I answered. "I'm old enough to take care of myself."

As Mother turned around and wiped her eyes with a wet hand, I wondered if she had brushed away a tear.

"Your dad and I just want you to be happy. We're always behind both of you, Ruthie."

EIGHTEEN

Gisela continued to try to get me more involved with her friends. In support of this effort, as soon as it was published she brought home a copy of Gertrude Stein's book *The Autobiography of Alice B. Toklas.*

"All the gals in the French Club are reading it. We'll discuss it at our next meeting," she said. "It will be grand fun and intellectual at the same time."

She suggested we read the book out loud, taking turns reading a chapter to each other, so after getting in bed and propping ourselves up with pillows that's what we would do. I enjoyed both the book and the reading aloud, until one night Gisela stopped reading and handed me the book.

"It's your turn," she said. "I can't stand to read about Paris, while sitting here stifled in Minneapolis. In Paris, Alice and Gertrude give lavish dinner parties and have the art crowd and literary elite over at all hours—that's how people live there! Can you imagine being in the same room with Picasso, or Hemingway?"

All I heard was that she felt stifled, but she didn't seem to notice.

"I read that Gertrude and Alice were invited to tea with

Mrs. Roosevelt in the White House. Imagine that, high society lesbians in the White House."

When I didn't respond she asked, "What's wrong?"

"I'm holding you back."

"No. Go ahead, read. It's your turn," she said.

"You said you were stifled here in Minneapolis. Is that how you feel about me?"

She looked startled. "No honey, I'm just homesick. I know the Boulevard Saint-Michel and rue Notre-Dame des Champs. Every place in the book makes me think of my father, my life there."

She tried to joke with me.

"Maybe Mrs. Roosevelt has a secret."

"What would that be?"

"That she's like us," she said in a stage whisper and winked at me. "In love with a woman."

"Don't be absurd." I laughed at her outrageous idea.

"Let's move to Paris. Wouldn't it be fun to live it up at their dinner parties? I'd introduce you as Miss Marvelous. Everyone would wonder about us. They'd say 'such a handsome couple.'" She took the book from me and proceeded to read Gertrude's poem, *Love Song of Alice B.*

"It all makes perfect sense. Don't you think?" She finished the poem and kissed me. I didn't agree about it making sense, but I had to admit it did make me feel romantic. We didn't read any more that night.

As soon as Gisela heard that Gertrude Stein would be appearing at the St. Paul Women's City Club, she bought tickets for us.

"Everyone's going," she said to me. "She's giving one of the lectures on English literature that she gave at the University of Chicago."

"Who's everyone?"

"Most of the gals in the French Club, and anyone else who can get a ticket."

I frowned and said, "I don't know."

"Come on, Ruth. It's no different than it would have been going out with your sorority sisters. I'll bet some of those girls are like us, too. You just don't know it."

"I doubt it." I couldn't imagine Elena or anyone else I knew from the sorority being like us.

"Everyone in literary circles knows Alice and Gertrude are like an old married couple. They don't make a show of it, or hide it either. Some will come to gawk at her. Most won't care. They care about her writing, and what she has to say about literature and modern art."

I must have looked skeptical.

"No one will be focused on us. It's like going out to the movies. It's not like the whole French Club is going to march in together, waving a flag and saying 'look at us.' We know enough to be discreet."

She sat down to the dinner I'd fixed and waited for me to join her.

"You place too much importance on what everyone thinks," Gisela declared. "Don't let me down. I already bought the tickets. She only allows five hundred people to attend each lecture and always sells out."

But my concerns continued. "I hate having to hide and separate our lives into compartments. I try to avoid situations where I might have to explain myself, like with that fella that's been pestering me at the Guidance Clinic. He asked me to dinner again yesterday. When I politely declined, he mocked me, asking if I was one of those 'spinster types.' It upset me. Maybe I should wear some kind of ring so he'll leave me alone."

"It's hard. I do it too, compartmentalize, but I don't have anyone pursuing me. Maybe I'm wearing a do not disturb sign."

In the end I agreed to attend, having read about Miss Stein's lectures in the *Tribune*. Her work certainly didn't fit neatly into any literary box, and I really did want to hear what she had to say.

※

The night of the lecture was bitter cold, even for December, and the morning newspaper had warned the event might have to be canceled due to a looming blizzard.

Apprehension rattled around my rib cage while I dressed for our night out. I was worried about running into someone from the clinic, but seeing Gisela made me forget my anxiety. She'd rolled her hair in a chignon, tucking a silk hibiscus flower behind her ear, and the light caught strands of gold in the waves left by the braids she'd let loose.

"Stunning," I said.

"Why thank you, Miss M. Shall we go?"

I'd dressed in a black skirt and high-necked white blouse with a cameo at my throat, hoping I'd blend into the crowd. But seeing how beautiful Gisela looked, I wasn't so sure. No one, man or woman, would be able to keep their eyes off her. I was glad I'd decided to go, and tried not to mind that Jean from the French Club would pick us up downstairs.

"Three's a crowd," she said. "We'll just be three friends with the hottest tickets in town."

Gisela was right, even with her gorgeous hair, we were only a speck in the crowd of men and women who all seemed to be buzzing with anticipation. I relaxed, determined to enjoy the evening.

The curtains opened without any fanfare, revealing Gertrude Stein sitting alone on the bare stage next to a table with a white cloth and a glass of water. She exuded a commanding presence, but the content of her talk baffled me at first. How could something that seemed so devoid of ideas be considered literary? Then, as her talk went on and I listened to the rhythm of her speech, she delighted me with her innovative artistry by explaining English literature through the medium of comparing the relationship of one word to the next.

Afterward, we chatted in the lobby with a couple of Gisela's friends.

"She's famous because no one can understand her," Jean said.

I disagreed.

"It wasn't so much the words, but the way they sounded. If I let them flow through my mind, it all made sense to me." The group was quiet while I spoke.

"Like what she said about narrative: 'Twenty-five years rolls around so quickly, but one hundred years do not roll around at all. They end, the century ends.'" I paused.

"Go on," Jean said.

"She cleared my confusion by concluding, 'What makes narrative difficult is a century begins and ends, but no part of a narrative begins, and no part ends.'"

"It's exhausting," Gisela said. "And fascinating."

"Well, I can't believe I paid two dollars for a ticket to hear her speak," one of the other women said. "I laughed when she called literature static and declared she'd fixed it by getting rid of punctuation."

"I'm disappointed that she didn't talk about Alice. I think I saw her hovering around offstage," another woman said. "The newspapers talk about the two of them as if they are husband and wife."

"We're lucky to live in such a progressive time and place. Things will change. I can feel it," Jean said. "They're accepted as a couple out west. And the Chicago press treats them that way, talking about Alice as the 'wife' or 'mate' who protects Gertrude."

I was relieved that Miss Stein had stuck to the topic of her lecture, but also felt a bit sorry she hadn't spoken of her relationship with Alice.

"She's so matronly looking," I said outside on the way to our car, "she could be someone's grandmother."

"I told you not to worry," Gisela said as we both shivered in the biting wind that swirled snow all around us.

❧

On Saturday I answered the doorbell and found Hal standing by himself on the stoop. It was unusual to see him without Dorothy, and uninvited. The only time I'd seen him recently was at Mother and Dad's. I asked him in. He seemed tense, his voice strained as he made small talk.

"Is everything all right?" I said, afraid he might have bad news.

"Dorothy's out Christmas shopping. Haven't seen you in a while." He leaned against the credenza and flipped the red scarf that still draped over Gisela's Madge the Flapper lamp. The gesture made me uneasy.

"I've been here, just really busy at work," I said.

"Where's Gisela?" He glanced down the hallway.

"Out working on one of her projects. Want some coffee?" I needed something to do, he was making me nervous.

He paced around the room and didn't touch the coffee I gave him, then stopped and stared out the window. The day was crisp and clear, almost too bright, with fresh snow piled high in drifts. I sat down on the couch, hoping he would join me and relax.

"I saw you at the Gertrude Stein lecture," he said, turning around.

"You were there?"

"Don't be dull. How else would I have seen you?"

"It was so packed. I didn't notice you. How did you like it?" I didn't dare challenge his rude remark.

"It was Dorothy's idea. She read the damn book about those two mannish-looking women and insisted I tag along with her. Couldn't stand the dry humor and stupid puns. Mostly rubbish if you ask me."

So that was it. I was relieved he wasn't spying on me, following me.

"I enjoyed the lecture—though it was hard to understand at times. Brilliant if you listened carefully."

"Want to know what I don't understand?" He didn't wait for an answer. "I overheard a couple of guys at the University Club the other day. One of them works at Vocational Services in the same office as Gisela. They were talking about her, about how masculine she looks wearing trousers. The boys say it's a waste. She's a good-looking gal. That French Club she belongs to is a well known charade."

He caught me off guard.

"What are you saying?"

"There are rumors about Gisela, and you're included because you live together. I can't stand it," he said, his voice quiet and restrained. "My sister, one of those . . . I should have known when you were thrown out of Kappa Rho."

"I wasn't thrown out," I managed to say.

"It doesn't help that you run around all the time in your stable clothes and brag about riding in the rodeo like a cowboy. The two of you make quite a couple. Should I call you Alice, or is it Gisela who plays that role?"

I was stunned.

"I never bragged. I ride horses."

It sounded silly, ineffective, even to me. I fought to stay calm, wanting only to be able to tell him how much I loved Gisela. How much she loved me.

And even though I wanted him to know it was he who made it sound ugly, I knew with all my heart that the truth would make things worse.

Hal towered over me as I stayed sitting on the couch, too petrified to stand.

"You watch out. You're going to break our parents' hearts." His voice drummed in my ears. "I saw you in the lobby with all those lesbians, discussing the most famous lesbians of all."

He opened and closed his fists, his face distorted with anger. I didn't want to believe my own brother would hit me, but his eyes unfeeling and hard as wet stones reminded me of the story of the woman down at the mill.

"You better leave." It was the best I could do.

"You bet I'll leave. When I'm good and ready," he said, with a snarl. "Is it true?"

Finally I stood and found my voice. "You have no right to make accusations you know nothing about." My words echoed from a deep, hollow emptiness in my stomach. "How dare you attack me in my home, or question me about my life."

"Maybe it was the rodeo that ruined you." He stormed toward the front door, slamming it on his way out.

Ashamed that I felt too threatened by my own brother to defend our relationship, I didn't tell Gisela about his tirade. If she got angry enough, she could be like a bulldog with teeth tight on a bone. What if she decided to confront him? I didn't want to have to choose between the two of them.

❧

Not long after Hal's confrontation, Gisela said, "What's wrong with that brother of yours? I stopped by to say hi to your parents and Hal was there. At first he ignored me, then he excused himself and left in a big hurry as if I might have the plague."

NINETEEN

My old sorority roommate, Elena, embraced me like a long lost friend. It was chance that, out of everyone in the class of 1936, we were seated together while waiting to receive diplomas for our B.A. degrees.

We chatted briefly and then she said, "I'm getting married in two weeks."

I prepared myself for a typical Elena conversation and plastered a smile on my face. "Congratulations."

"I can't wait to start a family." Then, as insensitive as ever, she asked "Is Duke here?"

Hearing his name revived memories of the carefree year we'd spent together during my first year at college. How different my life would have been if I had not met Gisela. I scanned the audience and found her, sitting next to Mother and Dad. Hal and Dorothy sat on their other side. Gisela waved.

"I'm going to work in the Child Guidance Clinic, an assistant to one of the psychiatrists."

"You're actually going to use your degree?" She sounded so incredulous that I had to laugh. It was unusual for a psychology major, especially a woman, to find a position doing what they wanted. Obviously Elena, like most people, assumed that after four years of college marriage was the ultimate prize.

I didn't want to disappoint her, answer her question, or rouse her suspicions. "It's a start, a step below social worker status. No plans for marriage yet. I'm planning on getting a master's degree." Elena was the first to learn about my employment, I hadn't told anyone else about the offer to work at the Guidance Clinic. I was waiting until the details were finalized to surprise Gisela, who was finishing her master's degree in industrial relations and working at Vocational Services assisting unemployed men looking for jobs.

Applause for the introduction of the valedictorian interrupted Elena's response to my reply. By the look on her face I could tell she felt sorry for me, reminding me that my hidden life hung in a precarious balance—like a spider's web in a hurricane.

I told everyone about my position at the Guidance Clinic during the lunch Mother had fixed for all of us. Even Hal seemed impressed. We had been mostly avoiding each other since his angry outburst, so his congratulations surprised me.

Later, Gisela and I splurged. We celebrated with a late supper at Mr. Charles, a small restaurant downtown near the Nicollet Hotel. Each table in the softly lit dining room had a candle burning in a red lantern, and the delicate sounds of violin and cello filled the room with one of our favorite classical pieces.

"It's very romantic," I whispered.

Gisela caressed my thigh, her hand hidden under the tablecloth. I didn't dare touch her or show any sign of affection, but was able to ignore my qualms about being the only two women in the restaurant without male escorts when she leaned in close and said, "I'm so proud of you my love." The rest of the patrons melted away, and it was just the two of us having an intimate dinner.

Sitting back she continued, "We've both had to sacrifice, but now we each have important jobs that help people less fortunate than us."

I agreed with her that it made the hard work, scrimping, and doing without for so long feel worthwhile.

"So much has changed for us since that freezing winter in your attic bedroom," she said, still resting her hand on my thigh.

We enjoyed our meal, laughing and reminiscing about how hard it had been with me interning at the clinic while finishing up my degree. Although enrolling in classes for my master's right away, as I was planning to do, meant things would continue to be challenging, the addition of my paycheck would make the situation somewhat easier.

We left the restaurant and took a taxi home. A few years ago we would have taken the streetcar, but now we avoided walking near Gateway Park where many out of work and homeless men slept. Our waiter called for the taxi, and we waited inside until it arrived. The soup lines had dispersed for the day, but a lone man stood outside the restaurant selling apples, so we bought a few before climbing into the taxi.

❧

Our lives settled into a routine. I rushed out the door to attend morning classes and spent the rest of the day working at the Guidance Clinic. The psychiatrist I worked for allowed me to be flexible with my hours, and by 1937 I'd started my master's thesis on early language development in children from impoverished families, which we saw lots of at the clinic.

On a cold day in late November, Gisela and I headed to the stables for our last ride of the year.

"If the weather keeps up like this, it's going to be another long winter," I said while we saddled up in the familiar surroundings. "Satin Dancer is off to Uncle Edward's tomorrow." She spent every winter at his farm where I knew she would be cared for with love during the bitter Minnesota cold.

"I've missed you," Gisela said while we ate lunch during a break in our ride. "It seems like forever that we've been out."

✺

We stayed in on New Year's Eve. A fierce wind drove the snow into high drifts. Branches, burdened by the heavy snow, broke and littered the sidewalks and streets. Temperatures fell below zero and stayed that way most of January. It was during this cold spell that Uncle Edward called me, worried about Satin Dancer.

"She's wheezing," he said. "But I think she's strong enough to ride out this cold. She'll be well insulated in the barn with hay and blankets. I've got a fire in the potbelly."

I asked Dad to drive me out to see for myself.

"I can't, Ruth," he said. "The roads are too slick right now. Wait till they get better."

The weather changed, giving me hope that Satin D would be fine. The ice on the roads turned to slush.

Uncle Edward called again, this time with bad news. "It's pneumonia," he said.

Gisela held me while I composed myself. "I love her too," she said. "She and Lonnie are our best friends."

Uncle Edward called the next day, his voice tense. "I'm sorry. She took a bad turn during the night. You better come out and sit with her for a day. I think it's time."

He let the news sink in. "I know it's an agonizing decision. Maybe I waited too long to call." He let out a huge sigh. "I thought she would get better. Have your dad bring you out. We can't wait any longer."

Early the next morning Gisela made oatmeal, toast, and strong coffee. We ate in silence until Dad rang the doorbell.

I grabbed my things and as I rushed out, Gisela said, her voice choked with tears, "Call me tonight. I'll try to be home from work early."

Mother and I were dressed warmly in woolen sweaters, gloves, and hats. Although we both wore trousers and boots, we covered our knees with blankets. Dad wore the same old heavy navy blue wool overcoat he wore every winter. We arrived at Uncle Edward's place just after sunrise and warmed up in the kitchen before heading out to the barn.

Uncle Edward filled us in on how the veterinarian could do nothing now to help Satin Dancer.

"It's been one of the coldest winters I can remember. She got a bug and can't shake it," he said, his eyes brimming with tears. I couldn't wait any longer and excused myself.

In the barn, Satin D looked up at me with her wise brown eyes that said, "Do something. I can't get up." I let myself into her stall and lay down next to her, resting my head on her withers. I could feel her heart racing. My own heart felt in danger of breaking loose from its roots.

I stroked her soft neck and ran my fingers through her silky mane. We spent time remembering our rodeo days, taking first place in every barrel race in the fantasy I shared with her.

"We were the best barrel racers on the San Antonio circuit—Rollie told me so," I said to her. She tried to answer with a nicker that ended in a soft hiss from deep in her lungs.

My tears dropped on her chestnut coat. Her body heaved, and she drew in jagged breaths that made a feeble sound as she exhaled through dry lips. I wiped her mouth with a damp cloth and stretched out next to her, my arm around her neck. The warmth of her body comforted me, and we both rested.

Uncle Edward came into the stall late in the afternoon and gently helped me up. He examined Satin Dancer, checking her eyes and her mouth.

"Her gums are muddy colored. She's going into shock," he said. It was already dark outside, and numbingly cold. "It's time, Ruth. Do you want to stay?" He wiped fresh tears from his eyes.

"Give us a few more minutes, please." My voice felt scratchy. I kneeled down and nuzzled her neck, ran my fingers through her mane, smoothing it for the last time. She tried to lift her head.

"Shh," I soothed her. "We were stars, you and I." Pressing my lips between her eyes I murmured, "Goodbye, Satin Dancer, beautiful friend."

I heard Uncle Edward return. I knew what he had to do.

"I can't stay" I said and ran to Mother and Dad waiting for me in the car.

Dad started the car, and we headed up the driveway to Hal and Dorothy's at the lake. When we arrived Hal seemed like the brother I loved and admired from the past. He was sympathetic, and insisted that we spend the night.

I called Gisela and told her about the day through my gulps and tears. She said, "Come home as soon as you can so we can cry together. I'll take tomorrow off." I hung up and Mother soothed me like a little girl while I cried, saying, "There, there. You'll be all right."

But this time there was nothing she could say to convince me that things would ever again be all right.

TWENTY

During the rest of the winter, Gisela and I coped the best we could.

The loss of Satin Dancer's unconditional love and equine wisdom left a huge void, as she'd been a faithful companion since her birth when at age six, with Uncle Edward's guidance, I'd cut her umbilical cord. My heart overflowed with the immense sadness of her absence.

Gisela cradled me in her arms during those times and let me sob. We took solace from the winter cold in the nest of our lovemaking, just as we had done that freezing winter so long ago at the lake. The difference now was our mature knowledge of each other's pleasure, and in the bedroom my misgivings about our relationship would fade.

We escaped into radio programs, cheered by the comedies of Jack Benny and Fibber McGee and Molly, and kept spellbound by the dramas. My favorite was *Lights Out,* with the announcer's deep voice cautioning, "It's later than you think." Stories of the supernatural thrilled me. Gisela never missed *Mr. Keene, Tracer of Lost Persons* on Thursday nights.

"I like the idea that someone would find me if I were missing," she said.

Breaking news broadcasts and commentary increased in intensity as the war overseas escalated. Gisela worried more and more about her father, whose infrequent letters had dwindled to none in the last year. Both of us listened intently to any news from France, where he still lived.

Her despair grew each day there was no word from him, and she blamed Monique. "I bet she won't let him write. She always hated me, and refused to let me live with them."

❧

March dragged into April. One night, coming home late from work, I opened the door to a dark apartment. I'd been promoted to a clinical position once I earned my master's degree, and spent long days interviewing parents, assessing test results, and making recommendations. My head was full of the nature versus nurture argument popular in the psychology department, and having seen so many impoverished children I was now convinced that not all problems sprung from genetics.

Gisela should have been home early for her favorite Thursday night program, and I looked forward to discussing my thoughts with her. I set my books and papers on the hall table and fumbled for the light. A rustle from the direction of the couch made me hesitate. I listened, then tiptoed down the hall as quietly as possible to get a closer look. I sensed someone in the room and heard what sounded like angry fingers crunching paper, then held my breath and flipped on the ceiling light switch.

Gisela squinted in the brightness. She was sitting on the couch, and I could see its pillows and afghan had been strewn around the room.

"You scared me. What happened? Why were you sitting in the dark?"

"I'm in shock." She waved a crumpled piece of paper at me. She thrust the letter into my outstretched hand and demanded, "Read it."

"What is it?"

"It's from my father." She spit out the words.

Her anger startled me. I couldn't imagine what would be so upsetting. She'd been so anxious to hear from him, and now she looked infuriated. I took the letter and looked at the date—January 15, 1940. It had taken more than three months to reach her.

She paced around the room while I read the letter. Monique had given birth to twin boys, who were now two years old, and to keep the family safe from the war that threatened everyone in Europe the four of them had moved to Argentina. She picked up the pillows from the floor and slammed them, one by one, onto the couch.

"They weren't even there. I've worried the last year for nothing. They're in Argentina. It might as well be the moon. I'll never see my father again. The twins are two years old already." She started crying, her face livid with fury rather than anguish. "They didn't even care enough about me to let me know. Now they're living in some godforsaken place I know nothing about."

She fell onto the couch, her face buried in her hands. "How could they do this to me?"

"I'm so sorry." I did my best to console her.

☙

Gisela seemed to forget about the letter from her father, but started talking about California. "Can you imagine, Ruth? Eighty degrees in Los Angeles! The streets are lined with palm trees, and movie stars are everywhere."

It made me nervous to hear her talk like that. In Minneapolis, the temperature was twenty-eight degrees. An ashen mess of snow, pushed aside by a plow weeks ago, still lined our street.

"Sweet juicy oranges, bigger than softballs, fall from the trees for the taking."

"Stop it," I cried, hoping she was teasing me. Neither of us had tasted an orange for months, and she knew it was my favorite fruit. "You're making me crazy."

"We're crazy for living here," she answered, sounding wistful. "Jean says she's going out west when she finishes school." She didn't ask me to move to California with her, or say that was what she wanted to do, but the dreamy look in her eyes made me wary.

By mid-May, Gisela seemed restless. The trees had sprouted tender green buds, the air was warmer, and no longer content to spend her time at home listening to the radio or reading a book she began to go out more often in the evening with friends.

She told me about her new group. "Some are from the Basset Creek project, a few of their friends, and some of my old French Club who are still around."

She tried to reassure me. "Even you will think it's safe. We go out with a gang of both men and women. We debate about what Roosevelt should do, talk about the world. We don't question each other about what we do in our own homes behind closed doors."

Not long after that conversation, she pleaded with me one Saturday to attend a party with her that evening. "Come along. Please. It'll be fun. I promise to introduce you as my roommate."

I wanted more than anything to make her happy and keep her close, so I agreed to go.

At the party, she kept her promise and introduced me to a few people. I stood by her side in a small group. She laughed at a joke someone told, her eyes sparkled with interest at another person's comment, and I noticed how animated she appeared.

I wandered away from Gisela and sat on a couch, listening to Glen Miller's "Moonlight Serenade" playing on a phonograph nearby. A young man with a sweet face sat down next to me

"I'm Jerry," he said over the music.

We exchanged small talk, and he asked if he could get me a drink.

"Just coffee. Three sugars." I handed him my cup.

Upon returning he said, "I added a little surprise. See if you like it."

It tasted sweet, but burned as I swallowed.

"What is it?"

"I laced it with a little brandy and left out the sugar. It won't hurt you. It'll help you unwind." He smiled.

Am I that obvious?

I liked the soothing effect and accepted his offer of a second cup.

Gisela appeared while Jerry was in the kitchen. "You look like you're enjoying yourself. Where'd Jerry go?"

I did feel more relaxed.

"He's getting me another brandied coffee. I like brandy. It sweetens coffee even better than all that sugar I usually use."

"That Jerry. He's such a scamp." She laughed. "I hope I don't have to get jealous." She patted me on the knee and said, "We should go home soon or we'll miss the last streetcar."

"You know Gisela?" Jerry asked as he handed me my coffee and sat down.

"Yes. We're roommates." It slid off my tongue easily, without any problem.

A lingering glow from the brandy warmed me on the way home. It *had* been fun.

I'd managed to make Gisela happy that night, but it got harder as 1940 moved into 1941. She began obsessing about the world news, descending into depression every time we went to the movies where the newsreels that brought moving pictures of the war to America reminded her of how close to danger her father might have been.

"We're the lemmings we talked about all those years ago," she said after we left the movie theatre one night. "First we see neutral Norway is invaded by the Germans, leaving Oslo occupied, then we hear about a French luxury liner painted a dull gray disembarking from New York, carrying metal parts and airplanes bound for our allies." She paused, looking dejected.

I knew better than to interrupt her when she was in one of her moods.

"Then the story about the World's Fair and the highway of the future twenty years from now. That's all bad enough, but that story about a rodeo in California!"

"It was a bit much," I replied, but couldn't resist saying, "It wasn't as bad as naming the debutante of the year."

That sent her into a rant the second we stepped off the streetcar. "Ostriches," she yelled at the deserted street as the trolley rolled away from us.

It seemed safer now, more than ever, to stay home—the exact opposite of what Gisela needed to tame the turmoil she was feeling about the world.

Twenty-One

On Sunday, December 7, 1941, Gisela and I were at Mother and Dad's.

We had a quiet lunch, and then Mother, Gisela, and I joined Dad in the living room, where he was listening to an NFL football game on the radio. Mother was trying to teach us how to knit, but the noise from the cheering crowd, and the announcer's loud voice calling the plays, distracted us. We were about to return to the kitchen, so we could close the door, when we heard an urgent announcement:

"We interrupt this broadcast to bring you this important bulletin from the United Press . . . Flash . . . Washington . . . The White House has just announced an attack on Pearl Harbor, Hawaii . . . details are not yet available . . . stay tuned for new developments as they are received."

Stunned, we sat waiting for more information, but the announcer cut away and returned to the football game. Since the crowd did not yet know what had happened, the cheers and the game continued. We all stared at the radio, as if the answers to our many questions would come any second. Dad finally gave up on the game, but stayed glued to the radio, dialing frantically, seeking more news.

It wasn't until much later in the day that we learned the Japanese had made a surprise and devastating airstrike on American battleships. Sketchy details trickled in between the swing and sway music of Sammy Kaye's "Sunday Serenade." Our dinner was eaten mostly in shocked silence.

"It's for sure the US will be at war now," Gisela said as we listened to the latest bulletin.

"We should have known something like this would happen," Dad dropped his fork and got up from the table. "I'm going to call Hal. See what he thinks."

None of us knew what to do with ourselves. I felt waves of terror every time I heard a new snippet of information. "Several Japanese planes down. The island of Oahu taken by surprise on a glorious Sunday morning. Many lives lost."

It was later in the evening, on her weekly radio show from the White House, that Eleanor Roosevelt provided more complete information. Finally, we understood the severity of the attack.

President Roosevelt's address to the nation the next day, in which he also asked Congress to declare a state of war, became the dividing line of life before and after Pearl Harbor for all of us. But it was Eleanor Roosevelt's words that stayed with me in the coming months as our lives turned upside down: "You cannot escape anxiety. You cannot escape a clutch of fear at your heart, and yet I hope the certainty of what we have to meet will make you rise above these fears."

❧

A week later Gisela announced she needed to travel to Buffalo, New York for a work related conference. I tried to get more details from her, but all she would say was "It's about vocational recruiting for a company called Consolidated Aircraft. I don't know any more than that."

She arrived home from the airport by taxi four days later

looking sharp in her navy blue business suit and white blouse. She kicked off her galoshes and shoes, sinking wearily onto the couch.

"Whew." She sighed. "And we complain about the severe Minneapolis winters. Buffalo was a nightmare."

At dinner, I bombarded her with questions about the conference.

"It was about recruiting women. All the men will be overseas. Consolidated makes war planes."

"Why did you go, is Social Services in Minneapolis going to be sending women to Buffalo?" I asked.

"No. They've opened a factory in California. I'm one of very few women who have experience in hiring and recruiting. They asked my opinion about adding women to the workforce. That's all."

Hesitant to ask if she was going to work for them I said, "You must be tired. Let's go to bed." She was tired. Too tired to give me any more than a quick kiss on the lips before turning over to fall fast asleep.

I didn't ask any more questions, and pretended to forget about it.

❧

The first day of February, Jean came home from California and stopped by to see Gisela. I wasn't proud of it, but I was jealous of Jean's friendship with Gisela, and had been relieved when she had accepted a job in Los Angeles shortly after earning her nursing degree.

"I wouldn't have returned to Minnesota except to say goodbye to my parents. I've joined the Red Cross and will head overseas soon. Since I speak French, I'll probably be sent somewhere in France."

"Paris?" Gisela asked.

"I don't know. There's Nazi occupation there for sure, but

not as much destruction as elsewhere. As a nurse, I'll go where I'm needed."

I admired her courage and dedication, but worried when she started to talk about what it was like living in California.

"It's been crazy since the Pearl Harbor attack. There are blackouts at night along the coast, and we've all been instructed what to do in case of an air raid."

"Other than that, what do you think about living there?" Gisela asked.

"Even with the war, it's like the pictures in magazines and what you see in the movies. Everything is so much easier. You can take a dip in the ocean all year long, and never have to worry about skidding on ice or shoveling snow. Or humidity and mosquitoes the size of bats."

Gisela refilled our coffee cups.

"I've heard talk of an attack on the California coast by the Japanese," I said.

"Their submarines have been detected offshore of Santa Barbara, but we are all going on about our business even on the coast," Jean answered. "Since the beginning of the internment of Japanese citizens in detention camps, the fear has subsided for some of the people who blame them for the attack on Pearl Harbor, but rumors and race prejudice are rampant. The majority of the Japanese people here in the US are peace loving, and contribute to our economy, and it's sickening to those of us who believe it's wrong for them to be rounded up and treated like war criminals."

Gisela frowned. "I've read about that happening in California. I can understand the fear of Japanese, but I read naval intelligence believes less than three percent might be inclined toward sabotage or spying, so it's incredible that whole families are being relocated to the camps." She paused, then asked "And what about women? I've heard the war has given us more independence and increases our opportunities to be together out west."

"True," Jean answered. "With so many women entering the workforce and the men overseas, the war has given us more independence and even increases our opportunities to be together. Also we're not easy targets for persecution like the Japanese who are perceived as a threat based on their physical characteristics."

Gisela turned to me. "What do you think, hon?"

To my surprise, Jean rescued me. "I don't want to give the wrong impression. It's still necessary to be discreet."

"I guess we have to be careful no matter where we live," I said in answer to Gisela's question.

I'd heard enough, and worried that Jean's influence over Gisela could take her away from me. I wanted to tell her to leave us alone, to keep quiet about her love of California and her assignment in France. But I didn't want to say anything stupid.

"I'm going to let you two catch up with each other. I need to wash my hair. Good to see you, Jean."

It troubled me that even after Jean left, Gisela couldn't stop talking about her plans. "I wish I had her nerve. I bet they could use more of us French speakers."

"Oh Gisela, you wouldn't. Even your father thought it safer to leave France because of the war."

"I know. I said I wish I had the nerve. I want a change of scenery. I'm sick of dreary winters. I'm sick of listening to the radio, and the news, and staying home most of the time," she answered, sounding agitated. "I want to be involved, contribute to the war effort."

"Jean's always excited about everything. It can't be that different, living in California."

"It is that different. You want everything to be easygoing and dull. You've only been out with me a few times to the picture show since we went to that party months ago."

"I had a good time that night. I liked Jerry, but didn't really fit in with your friends."

"I know. You've told me a million times."

She caught me off guard. We'd skirted around this kind of discussion for a while. I'd been complacent, expecting her home most evenings, but content to wait for her if she went out.

She apologized the next day. "What are we going to do? I'm not happy here, and you don't want to leave."

All the next week Gisela went out of her way to be nice. She offered to cook dinner on Sunday for my family.

"No thanks, I'm not in the mood for company."

"Then let's go out for a ride. I miss Lonnie and our time together. It might lift your spirits to visit the stables and be among horses again."

"You don't understand. I can't."

"You have to come up for air sometime."

I walked down the hall and shut myself in my office.

"I'm sorry" she said later, but then changed her mind. "No. I'm not sorry. I don't always want to have to be sorry for everything I do or say." She sounded more resigned than resentful.

I knew that night that she would leave. I just didn't know how long it would be before I lost her.

❧

Gisela did not wait long to confirm what I had suspected. A few days later, we sat outside our small kitchen at the round dining table upon which until the last few months Gisela had always placed a bright tablecloth and fresh flowers in a vase.

During dinner that night we struggled at conversation and ate without either of us speaking very much. Sensing something was bothering her, I asked if anything was wrong, and what she said shocked me.

"I've been offered a position with Consolidated Aircraft in San Diego."

"How?" I asked. My mind reeled. I wanted to stop her, make promises I knew I couldn't keep.

"My boss at the Vocational Center recommended me. I'll
be in personnel, both recruiting and hiring women for their
new factory. It's an opportunity I can't pass up."

"You knew all along, since you went to Buffalo." I was so
hurt I wanted to run.

"No. I only found out last week that they wanted me."

"You went for an interview, not for a conference. You
deceived me. You already knew when Jean was here."

"I didn't."

My world collapsed. She had that look on her face, stubborn to the bone.

"You can come with me. Or you could come later."

I stood.

"How can you do this to me?" I clenched my fists into
tight balls at my side.

That night in bed, she comforted me.

"I don't want us to hate each other. I love you. I just don't
love living this way. My life is on hold, waiting for you to
choose us over your fears."

There was nothing I could do or say to change her mind.
I'd convinced myself that things would work out, that I would
eventually change, but she didn't want to wait any longer.

"Love can't thrive on unhappiness," she said and turned
out the light.

❧

The day of Gisela's departure finally came. Once she had
called a taxi she sat down next to me on the couch, but I
couldn't think of anything to say except "Don't go," so we
waited in silence, neither of us seeming to have any words
left. Over the last few weeks we'd cried together, trying our
best to find a solution that would satisfy both of our needs.
We had made love for the last time the night before, and
now I watched while she traced the outline of a heart on

the back of my hand with her index finger. The room was so quiet I could hear footsteps on the sidewalk and a door slam downstairs. The sound of a horn honking, announcing the arrival of her taxi, startled both of us.

Neither of us made a move until the taxi driver honked a second time. Gisela embraced me, whispering "I love you," but I was too choked up to answer.

After kissing me tenderly, "I'd better go" was all she could say, and the feeling of her lips on mine left a bittersweet memory as I stood at the window watching the taxi's taillights disappear in the distance. Her steamer trunks had already been picked up and taken to the train station, she hadn't left very much behind, and I had no idea how I would be able to bear the emptiness.

The dreary life Gisela had so despised felt like it swallowed me, smothering any emotions I might have felt when I received a short note from her letting me know she had safely arrived and had moved in with a couple of Jean's friends in San Diego.

A month later, she sent a postcard with a breathtaking photo of the Pacific Ocean.

> There's blue sky every day, and people arriving from all parts of the country to work in the defense industry. Housing is a big problem. I'm lucky to have found a little place of my own in La Jolla on a cliff across from the ocean. I miss you. I love you. I wish you'd change your mind and come out here.
>
> Love you, G

I'd long ago lost my sense of adventure and answered her pleas for me to reconsider with vague excuses. Mother tried to console me, and on the day Gisela left had said, "I know how much you love her. I love her, too. Sometimes there are things we just don't understand, but have to accept."

Twenty-two

The first few months without Gisela were endless, and I continually blamed myself for her leaving. I coiled inward, spending most weekends sleeping all day just as Mother had done during my childhood. My social life consisted of a bridge club with colleagues from work and Dutch treat dinners with Gisela's friend Jerry, who called often until he shipped overseas. I also helped Mother with her victory garden during the good weather, taking comfort in our closeness even though I did my best to hide my grief from her. Soon to be thirty years old, I felt tired all the time and lost my focus at work.

A phone call from Dad at five o'clock on an ordinary Monday, the last day of August, collapsed my flimsy world.

"Come right away. It's Mother."

His tone frightened me.

"What happened? Is she ill?"

"Just come home. Right now."

I pictured Mother huddled in bed. *What could I do?* I called a taxi, threw on my clothes, and rushed over.

Dad ripped open the door before I reached the porch.

"She's gone, Ruthie." He broke down in tears. "I couldn't tell you on the phone."

The impact of his words caused me to stumble in shock, but he grabbed hold of my arm and helped me inside.

"A police officer pounded on the door. Got me out of bed a few hours ago. He said there had been an accident." He broke down again.

"What happened? What accident?"

"She fell out of her rowboat fishing on the lake near Annandale sometime Sunday. She must have had a heart attack. No one saw it happen. Two men saw her floating in the reeds." He held on to me, his own lifeline. "What will we do?"

My mind grappled to find the answer. We sat together on the sofa. "Where's Hal?"

"On the way over with Dorothy. I told him on the phone."

I held Dad's hand.

"It's all my fault. I've been working late hours all month. A couple of times, I slept over at the office." He bent over, hiding his face in his hands. His shoulders shook.

"Where is she, Dad?"

"Washburn Mortuary. Hal will make the arrangements. I can't do it."

He handed me a note in Mother's careful handwriting.

> *Peter Dear,*
> *I'm off to Annandale for a day of fishing. I'll rent a cabin for the night and see you Monday early evening.*
>
> *Love, Rose*

"I worked all day in my office Saturday and Sunday on a deal for a company out of Wisconsin. I found the note late Sunday afternoon. I should have been home."

"It's not your fault. You know she always found peace out on the lake in her rowboat. She loved Lake Annandale."

"We should have stayed out at Lake Minnetonka. She could just take her rowboat out from the dock." He sobbed. "I thought she'd be happier here. I didn't think she was lonely. You and Gisela stopped by so often. She has Hal and Dorothy. And her garden."

We sat together for what seemed forever. Finally, I got up and put on a pot of coffee, moving in a fog of disbelief. I'd never seen my father cry.

While I waited for the coffee to perk, I wandered around the small house and caught glimpses of Mother's life. Her plaid bathrobe was hanging on a hook behind the bathroom door—she must have worn it for twenty years. In the bedroom, sunlight filtered through the curtains onto the large bed built by my grandfather for his wedding night. I ran my fingers over the rockroses he'd carved on the headboard. Until I was six or seven years old, Mother and I spent many hours together in that bed when she suffered from her headaches.

I sat on the stool at her vanity with her fragrances surrounding me and noticed strands of silver hair jutting in all directions from her tortoiseshell brush. The face powder and special White Shoulders cologne she saved for the most important occasions reminded me of being a child and watching her get ready for holiday dinners or a trip to Minneapolis. I opened a drawer, and her daily scent of lavender greeted me.

The rumpled bedcovers were reflected in the mirror. For a moment I was a child again. Fatigue heavy as winter blankets called me to climb in. *She's there under the covers. We can cuddle together.* I shook my head. Not the time to crumble.

I sat, smelling and touching Mother's things. My fingers, without direction from me, straightened the objects of her personal life. The coolness of a glass jar of Pond's night cream comforted me. I turned it round and round in my hands with no mind, no thought.

Hal and Dorothy arrived. I heard Dorothy comforting Dad, Hal asking questions. I went out to greet them.

Hal looked horrible, his face gray and drawn. He nodded at me, cool as ever, even under these circumstances. I felt sorry for him. Nothing seemed to go right in his life. He and Dorothy didn't have the children they'd wanted, and his myopic vision had kept him from joining the army, forcing him to the sidelines.

I left them alone with Dad and busied myself in the kitchen making coffee. Returning to the others a short time later, it unnerved me to see Hal's hand shaking as he reached for a cup from the tray I brought in.

We all sat down in the familiar setting of the living room and tried to rehash the details of what had happened to Mother. We agreed she'd seemed fine. She'd been occupied with the women's guild at the church and in charge of the altar flowers. She supplied vegetables from her bountiful garden to the neighbors. We'd never gone hungry, even in the leanest of times, thanks to food from her garden and her flock of chickens.

"I just remembered something," I said. "I also got one of her notes in the mail last week. She must not have been able to reach me by phone."

"I'd like to see that note," Hal said in an officious tone. "What did it say?"

"Not much, just that she planned to go fishing on the weekend and couldn't pick up my coat at the cleaners like she'd promised." I couldn't remember any more details right then. "Dad got one too."

Hal paced with his hands in his pockets. The scowl on his face made him look older, even a little mean. "You must remember something."

I regretted mentioning the letter. It seemed to have upset him for some reason, but I couldn't imagine why.

"We need to eat," Dorothy said. "Come on, Ruth. Help me."

She fried bacon and eggs. I set the table and could hear Dad and Hal discussing what the policeman had said. The simple motion of setting out forks, knives, and spoons was all the effort I could exert right then. I walked like a zombie to the hutch and grabbed six plates. I set a place for Mother and one for Gisela—or maybe Duke—both were Mother's adopted kids. When I realized what I had done, I started to cry. Don't fall apart yet, I told myself, stopping my tears and wiping my eyes. I wanted to stay strong for Dad.

"There's no butter," Dorothy called from the kitchen. "We'll have to eat dry toast."

Fine. Eat dry toast.

"Did you hear me, Ruth?"

I'd heard her, but the words from Dad and Hal's conversation were reverberating in my head—funeral Mass, heart attack, flowers. What could I do about dry toast? What could I do about anything?

❦

Daylight woke me on Saturday, the morning of Mother's funeral Mass. Hal had taken over all the arrangements and signed the death certificate. Together, he and Dad had decided not to have an autopsy. The coroner had declared the cause of death as drowning due to a heart attack.

The reality of the coroner's conclusion finally hit me, and I ducked my head under the blanket to block out the brightness of a day I didn't want to face.

Dad insisted that Hal send telegrams to Uncle Michael and Chloe in Montana, as well as to Duke and Gisela. Even though I wanted to contact Gisela myself, I couldn't muster up the energy it would take to ask Hal to let me send her the telegram. I tried calling her, but she didn't answer.

I'll telephone later, I consoled myself. *How can I survive the loss of Mother without Gisela by my side?* I tried again several times, but there was still no answer.

Would Duke come for the funeral? Chicago wasn't that far away, but I wondered if he would show up. He had been part of our family since we both were thirteen, until I had broken off with him, and I knew how much he loved Mother.

The phone rang. I stumbled out of bed to the desk in the hallway and picked up the receiver.

"I'll pick you up at nine," Hal said, his voice flat.

"Okay," I mumbled.

"You all right?"

"I don't know. I guess."

"You know how Mother was loved by the whole congregation. We don't want to let her down," Hal said with older brother authority.

"What do you mean?" I felt a stab of resentment at our family tradition of not making a public display of emotions. "Do you think I'll embarrass you or something?"

"No." Hal let out a long sigh. "Let's just not mention those letters to anyone."

"Why not? Why would anyone care?"

"Let's just go with this, Ruth." He overflowed with impatience. "We can talk about it later. I'll honk to let you know I'm outside." He hung up the telephone. I felt a chill and reached for my bathrobe.

Why was Hal so worried about the notes? They were innocent enough, and not all that important.

❧

The interior of the church had remained unchanged my whole life, and the aroma of burning candles and incense awoke memories of my First Communion and my childhood awe for the ceremony of the Mass. By habit, I dipped my hand in the holy water and crossed myself, after which we were escorted by an usher to the front row where Dorothy, already seated, waited for us.

Again out of habit I genuflected before entering the pew, but unsure of what to say to God my mind went blank as I stared at Mother's coffin, which was covered in white lilies with a bank of flowers surrounding it. We'd held the Rosary and viewing at the mortuary on Wednesday, deciding on a closed casket for the Mass, and I looked around to see who was settling in across the aisle.

Duke!

He looked very dapper, wearing a dark linen suit and white shirt with a red bow tie. Not bright red like a fire engine, but darker, like blood. Nevertheless it was red, and, I thought, oddly out of place.

Because he wasn't in uniform I guessed he hadn't joined the military.

He nodded, and as our eyes met I felt my chest constrict. I finally let myself feel how much I'd missed his friendship.

The Mass ended, and we all filed outside. Duke stood in the line waiting to express his condolences but saved me for last, eyes veiled as if he was worried about how I would respond to him. As we hugged everyone else seemed to fade into the background, and it felt as if we were alone. His strength and the smell of his familiar aftershave melted away the years.

"I've missed you," he said. "Can we catch up with each other before I have to return to Chicago?"

"Yes" was all I managed to say just as a couple of Mother's friends from the church guild engulfed me with their murmurs of solace, which I could not ignore.

Later Duke and I stood together at Mother's open grave in St. Mary's Cemetery, the air fragrant with rich soil, freshly cut grass, and lilies. We listened to the priest say the final rites, and then graveyard assistants lowered Mother's casket into the ground. Dad tossed the first shovelful of earth, which hit the coffin with a soft thud; then he passed the shovel to Hal and me. Uncle Edward put his arm around Dad's shoulder as he led him to his car.

While the mourners dispersed to their vehicles, Duke and I stayed together at the gravesite. *Where was Gisela? Why hadn't she called?* Hal had mentioned on the way to the church that she hadn't answered his telegram, but we'd heard from Chloe, Mac, and Uncle Michael, who had sent flowers and regrets that they couldn't be with us. With two young children, Chloe and Mac really couldn't travel.

Duke held my hand, a simple gesture of comfort that needed no words. Grief like a paper sack full of nails settled in behind my breastbone. Gasping for breath I turned to look over the cemetery, now empty of the living. The perfect early autumn day irritated me. The warmth of the sun and deep blue of the sky mocked my grief. *Where's the rain, the cluster of black umbrellas?* I swallowed my tears and leaned on Duke's shoulder.

He offered to drive me to the luncheon gathering put on by the church guild at Hal and Dorothy's, our old home at the lake, the only other place Mother had ever lived.

"It's inconceivable she's gone, Ruthie. What happened? Hal didn't give me any details."

I filled him in on what we knew. "Her lungs were full of water. Another person fishing nearby found her body in the reeds and pulled her out of the lake. The coroner determined she'd been dead for about an hour."

Duke started the engine of his roadster. "I'm so sorry she was alone. I loved her kindness and acceptance of me."

"She died doing what made her happy," I said, feeling the heaviness of loss. He lit a cigarette in a long ivory holder that had turned a peculiar color of gold from the nicotine, holding out the open pack to me.

The smoke from our cigarettes filled the car and Duke rolled down his window.

As the scenery flashed by, I thought about how much Mother missed living on Lake Minnetonka. I could feel myself sinking and turned to Duke.

"You've been in Chicago a long time. What are you doing there?"

"Thanks to Roosevelt's New Deal and the WPA, I've been gainfully employed as an engineer. I've been working on the State Street subway tunnel since 1938. It's due to open in '43, but I won't be there."

"That doesn't sound fair."

"Technically, I'm in the Army Corps of Engineers. I won't be official and in uniform until I finish my part of the project, but then the army will send me where I'm needed."

"Are you happy?"

"Other than feeling conspicuous dressed like this, I'm doing well and like Chicago. I'm eager to wear the uniform and serve the country. What about you?"

"I'm good. I started working for the Child Guidance Clinic at the university as a staff assistant after my undergraduate degree, then moved up to clinical psychologist."

"I'm proud of you. Not many women can say they have such a prestigious job."

"The psychiatrist I had interned for, who later hired me as an assistant, liked my work and promoted me after I finished my master's degree." In truth, my mentor had left the clinic a couple of months ago, and I'd been struggling to fit in under the new leadership.

We stayed in safe territory. Even though I'd cut him out of my life, I selfishly missed Duke—especially his enthusiasm and easy company. I liked having him near me again, and wondered if he was in a relationship.

"Whatever happened to your friend Gisela? I thought she would be at the funeral."

I tensed.

He's curious. That's all. I willed myself to relax. "Gisela moved out west, near San Diego, about six months ago."

The sharp stabbing pain poked at my heart. I desperately missed her.

"And Satin Dancer? She must be a regal old lady by now."

Oh god. Of course, he doesn't know.

My composure, my neat package, ripped apart in a soggy mess. A loud sob escaped. Duke pulled off the road and stopped the car. He reached over to hold me.

"I didn't know."

I held my breath, tried to stop my tears. I gulped for air.

"No," he said. "Cry."

"I'm so embarrassed," I sputtered between sobs.

"Don't talk crazy, Ruth. You've always held too much in. You've got to let it out." He sounded so far away I could barely hear him.

"What?"

He handed me his handkerchief and said, "Ever since I've known you, it's been hard for you to let anyone know what's going on inside."

I sobbed until there were no tears left. Duke's kindness and his acceptance of me without judgment had broken the barrier holding back my grief. I'd been strong since Mother's death, for Dad and to please Hal. With no one to talk to, I'd turned inward since Gisela had left, my despair held close, pretending to be just fine. There was no one else like Duke in my life. He'd been my best friend, but I'd thrown him away like a used train ticket.

I remembered the last time we'd been together, so long ago. I'd told him we couldn't see each other any more. I'd been so in love with Gisela that I'd hardly noticed he'd left Minneapolis for Chicago.

"I'm sorry," I sniffled.

"For what?" he asked.

"I didn't even say goodbye. I must have really hurt you."

"Don't, Ruth. Today is bigger than that."

We were parked a few miles outside Minneapolis on the road to Wayzata. I stopped my sobbing and held up his handkerchief. I mimed wringing it out and then offered it to him. He politely smiled as he refused my offer.

"I have something for us," he said, his voice lighter.

He got out of the car and opened the trunk. He returned with a thermos and a couple of wrapped sandwiches. "For old times' sake," he said. "I still never travel without refreshments."

We drank the coffee, hot and sweet the way we both always liked it, but left the sandwiches since neither of us had an appetite. Duke packed away the uneaten food and then pulled down the soft top on the car. We continued on our journey and could have been a happy couple out for a Saturday drive on a beautiful day, but memories and heartache, mixed with regret, swirled around me and blew through my hair.

The whipping of the wind removed any possibility of conversation, and grateful to be with my own thoughts I watched the familiar countryside speed by.

What would it be like to tell Duke about Gisela? I still hadn't told anyone about my love for her, and held the secret so tightly that at times I could hardly breathe. Mother had been my only devoted ally, although she didn't know the truth that I'd longed to share with her, and now she was gone. I wrapped myself in a cloak of what I perceived to be a bleak future.

Duke slowed the car down, "We're almost there," he shouted over the roar of the engine.

For a moment I couldn't remember why we were at the lake until I realized that we'd returned to Mother's birthplace, now Hal and Dorothy's home, to mourn with family and friends.

As he parked alongside the cars that had already arrived, he said gently "There's going to be a crowd. Will you be all right?"

"Let me get my bearings." I ran my fingers through the mess the ride in the open car had made of my hair, repairing my face the best I could in the mirror of my powder compact. It would have to do.

"I'm okay. Let's go in."

He took my arm, and we walked up to the house together.

It didn't take Duke any time at all to return to his previous role of acting the part of my escort. He guided me around the crowd, making sure I greeted everyone and accepted their condolences. He sat me down when I felt faint and put food in front of me.

"Eat," he insisted.

Again, I had no appetite, and could only manage to push down a few bites.

At the end of the day, he stood at the door with Hal and Dorothy, thanking everyone for coming. Dad and I sat in the kitchen looking at each other, lost in the same fog.

The last guests finally departed and Duke and I helped Dorothy clean up. Working in silence, we washed and dried the dishes in Mother's old kitchen where Dorothy had kept things almost the same during the time she and Hal had lived in the house.

As I stacked clean dishes in the cupboard, I realized that Mother had stacked dishes in this cupboard most of her life. She had played with her brothers in the same places Hal and I discovered as children, and hiked the same trails we did. I tried to grasp what it would have been like for her to live in one place all her life, except for these last few years before her death.

Mother had treasured the times we gathered together as a family in Montana with her two brothers, Michael and Edward. Having been a child when Michael left Minnesota to homestead and never return, her words said during grace at family gatherings echoed in my head: "Bless our missing pieces, those who reside in our hearts." Now Mother was our newest missing piece.

Duke found me on the sun porch wrapped in a blanket, staring out at the lake.

"Come on, let's go. Dorothy's gone to bed. Hal and your dad are still at the kitchen table."

It took me a while to respond. I tried to shake myself out of the haze. "Go where?"

"Home. I need to get you home and me to my hotel. It's getting late."

I must have been on the porch for at least an hour. It seemed like just a few minutes. Duke led me to the kitchen.

Dad and Hal sat at the table without talking, staring into space.

"Dad, I'm leaving now," I said and gave him a kiss on the cheek. He stood and hugged me.

When Dad let me go, Hal said, "Can I take you to lunch tomorrow? We've got some stuff to clear up."

I was too tired to worry about what stuff he meant.

"Sure. Okay."

"I'll pick you up around one o'clock."

On the way to the car I turned for one last look down at the empty spot at the dock where Mother's weather beaten rowboat had always been tied during my childhood.

With her gone, we're all cut loose from our moorings.

TWENTY-THREE

I gave Duke my address and dozed on the way home, not waking until we were parked near my building. "It's too dark to see the numbers, which one's yours?" he asked.

I pointed it out, and he gave a low whistle. "Pretty nice place. It must cost a fortune."

In the light of the street lamp the stately old ivy-covered house did look elegant, with its clipped lawn and brick walk leading to the front door.

"I can afford it."

But I didn't mention that I couldn't keep the place by myself for much longer. Gisela had left me enough money to help with the rent until the lease expired in a couple of months.

Duke got out of the car and opened my door. I didn't want him to leave.

"Will you come up? I don't feel like being alone."

"I'd love to. Now I don't have to invite myself in." He smiled in a sweet way that made me glad I'd asked.

As I fumbled in my purse for the keys a crescent moon, hanging high above the trees to the west, caught my attention, it's halo spreading a soft glow behind a veil of cirrus clouds.

"I like this," Duke declared when we got inside. But as he looked around the living room and up at the high ceilings, he added, "It's kind of empty."

Gisela had taken all of her belongings—paintings, books, even the Madge the Flapper lamp that she'd brought over from her boardinghouse room. The bare top of the credenza reminded me of her every time I walked into the living room. I almost enjoyed the martyrdom the blatantly empty space suggested, as if she might walk in and notice I'd been too hurt to fill it.

While I made coffee in the kitchen, Duke stayed in the living room.

"I'm moving soon," I called to him.

"So that explains why it's so empty in here."

I returned, setting a tray on the coffee table, and we sat next to each other on the sofa. I wanted to tell him about Gisela, to come clean about why I'd rejected him.

I stalled, unsure of what to say. I handed him a cup and asked more about his life in Chicago. While I listened I noticed the changes in his face. He'd always been thin and lanky, with a boyish look; now his features were filled out and mature. His high cheekbones and closely cropped hair made him look handsome. His pale eyebrows, rising and falling as he spoke, gave his face character. But his eyes were the same, still curious and kind.

I was only half listening as he spoke.

Why not tell Duke? I had nothing to lose. He wouldn't tell Hal or Dad. With Mother gone, nothing much seemed to matter to me.

"I've been yakking too much," he said.

I took a deep breath.

"Gisela and I lived here together before she left for out west." I hoped I sounded casual, offhand, not constricted as I really felt.

He took a sip of coffee.

"That's nice. She must have been good company for you, and helped with the rent."

"It was more than that." I took another deep breath.

Just tell him. He's your only real friend.

Duke waited while I gathered my thoughts.

"I loved her. Still love her," I said for the first time to another person.

"Why did she move to California?" His gentle concern soothed me. He turned toward me with all his attention.

"She left because I was afraid if someone found out we loved each other they might hurt us, or we'd lose our jobs. But alone in this apartment it seemed right—we were just two people in love, and we were safe."

I got up and leaned on the empty credenza.

"Gisela was bolder about our relationship. She didn't flaunt it, but she hated the secrecy and isolation I imposed on us. She said people are more open in California. Maybe she's right. I don't know."

"This explains so much—why you rejected me, refused to see me. I transferred to the University of Chicago just to forget what happened between us."

I sat next to him again. He rested his elbows on his thighs and buried his face in his hands.

"I'm sorry," I said.

The radiator sighed in the silence between us. I finished one cigarette and lit another. I watched the blue smoke swirl around us, waiting for Duke to say something, anything.

"Don't be sorry." He wiped his eyes. He made a fist with one hand and slammed it into the palm of his other hand. He jumped to his feet and strode to the window and turned around.

I'd never seen Duke this agitated, and stayed riveted to the couch, not quite sure what was going on.

"See this red tie?" He yanked it loose from his throat and tossed it to me.

"It's a code—the red tie is a signal to other men that I, too, live a dual life, a concealed life. That's what makes me angry that we have to hide in the shadow of our hearts. I prefer men. I've known for a long time, but didn't admit it to myself until after I moved to Chicago.

"I didn't mean to wear the tie to Rosie's funeral. I grabbed it by mistake in my rush to pack." He gave a short laugh. "It's incredible. I realized this morning it was the only tie I'd brought with me."

Stunned into silence I waited, holding his tie and twisting it in my fingers. I could see out the window from where I was sitting, it was almost midnight and the sliver of moon had slipped away.

"I was so hurt the day you broke off with me. I couldn't understand why you were too confused to see me anymore—no more parties or dates. It never occurred to me that you were falling in love with Gisela."

He took both my hands in his. "I told myself I didn't care. I tried to hate you, to forget I'd ever known you."

It was my turn to be gentle. "I'm sorry, Duke. I was so wrapped up in myself, and so bewildered."

"It doesn't matter now. I spent my first year in Chicago so confused I didn't know which way to turn, who to hate, who to love. I couldn't put two and two together to come up with me as I am today. At first I hoped you were just depressed, and angry with me for taking our relationship for granted, that you'd get over it.

"I thought I was regular. You know, normal. That my crazy feelings for guys were just that—crazy! I even thought you and I might get married, like Hal wanted for us." He shook his head.

"I did too. I didn't think we had a choice. I always loved you," I said softly.

"The funny thing is, it all makes sense now," he continued. "Even though I never met Gisela, I was sort of jealous.

You seemed so impressed that she was from Europe, and more sophisticated than the sorority girls."

"I wish I'd had the guts to be truthful."

"Don't blame yourself, there's no rulebook for this kind of life. I tried to replace you with other women, but it took being in Chicago to open my eyes. Some friends I met the first year introduced me to bars that are just for men, and then it all started to make sense. There are also private parties, a meeting place on the beach, lots going on."

"How can it be? Both of us? How did it happen that we ended up friends that first day at school?"

"I suspected that I was different," he said. "With the two of us in a so-called normal relationship all through high school and college, I felt safe and convinced myself I was fine."

"And so did I. You were my haven." I ached for both of us. "I didn't know my own feelings until I met Gisela. I still get confused, and don't have the courage to find other women—don't even know if I'd want to."

He leaned back on the sofa, stretched his arms overhead, and let out a huge sigh.

"This is a lot for one day for both of us. You must be exhausted."

His caring broke through my façade and memories of the day engulfed me. Mother in a casket with worn rosary beads clutched in her hands, Dad at the gravesite with a shovelful of fresh earth while Hal and I waited our turn, and then the luncheon with too many kind words.

I sobbed again, inhaling and exhaling great gulps of air that racked my body. Duke didn't say anything. He handed me a clean handkerchief and anchored me with his tender friendship.

He pulled me close, and cried with me. I leaned into him.

"I'm so tired I could sleep standing up," I said, wiping my eyes and still sniffling. "But I'm too hungry to go to bed."

I went into the kitchen to put together baloney sandwiches with mayonnaise and lettuce, one of our favorites.

"Are you lonely?" Duke asked when we'd finished eating.

"Yes. I miss Gisela all the time."

"It'll take a while."

I yawned.

"Let's get you to bed. I have a room at the St. Paul Hotel, so you can kick me out."

"No. Stay. I don't want to sleep alone."

At first, we fell onto the bed without taking off our clothes. We both lay perfectly still. "This isn't going to work. I can't fall asleep in a suit," Duke said, sitting up.

"I don't mind if you sleep in your underwear. I'll get changed for bed. We'll both be more comfortable."

I undressed in the bathroom and put a robe on over a sleeveless cotton nightgown. By the time I returned his carefully folded pants hung with his shirt and jacket on a chair, and he looked so peaceful I thought he'd fallen asleep.

I took off my robe and slipped in beside him.

"Are you sure you want me to stay?"

"I want you to hold me," I answered, moving closer to him.

He cradled me in his arms, my head resting on his chest as he caressed my cheek and ran his fingers through my curls.

"I've always fancied your wild hair," he whispered in my ear.

For a while, we lay still as the quiet after midnight embraced us. I floated in the sea of his warmth, craving his tender touch.

We shifted, then kissed, our tongues speaking in the mysterious language of longing. As we drew apart Duke looked into my eyes and started to say something, but I put a finger on his lips and moved into his arms. I gave myself to him entirely, leaving the world behind—no thought, no remorse, no reality other than our lovemaking. Our bodies merged in uncharted territory. I surrendered in that unfamiliar place and afterward fell into an exhausted sleep.

※

We woke around ten o'clock Sunday morning. Duke rolled over and opened his eyes. "I don't know what to say."

The untamed passion of our lovemaking, pitted against the harsh reality of morning, had left me speechless as well, and I needed time to gather my thoughts.

He reached for me and held me close. In the safety of his arms I wondered out loud, "How could we be together and not connect deeply after being so close for so many years?"

He spoke softly, "Are you sorry?"

It seemed like an odd question, and I couldn't decide if I *was* sorry. As I tried to reconcile what we'd done with how much I missed Gisela, I guessed the combination of our sadness, loneliness, and loss must have undermined our normally reasonable behavior and controlled emotions.

Unable to come up with an answer to his question, I gently untangled myself from his arms and reached for my robe. Sitting on the edge of the bed I asked, "How can I be sorry for love?"

"I've always loved you. And can't help but wonder what it would have been like if we had lived our lives as everyone expected."

"As if we were normal?" I asked.

"At least we know what that's like now, and seem to have lived through it." He paused before adding, "I guess we could plead temporary insanity."

That made us both laugh in the way that grief shortens the distance between hysterics and weeping. Tears rolled down our cheeks, and we clung together until we regained control.

I showered first while he made coffee. His day-old beard gave him a disheveled look, even after his shower. "I did my best" he sighed, and I noticed he wasn't wearing his tie.

We drank the coffee and ate buttered toast with cinnamon and sugar, a favorite of ours that Mother used to make when we were kids.

"We could have a leisurely lunch later in the roof garden at the St. Paul Hotel," he said. "It'll cheer you up."

"I can't, I'm meeting Hal."

He looked disappointed. Then, as he was getting ready to go, he asked, "Can we have dinner tonight? I've decided to stay another day or two."

"I'm so glad you're staying!" I was limp with relief that he wasn't leaving right away. "Dinner with you will be my pleasure."

Before I could say anything more, the doorbell rang.

"Hal," I whispered, with my eye to the peephole. "He's early."

Duke opened the door and greeted Hal with a handshake.

"Ruth felt really rotten last night, and I couldn't leave her alone."

"Thanks, Duke. And thanks for coming to Mother's service," Hal said, dropping Duke's hand. "It's been good to see you." He sounded genuine. But his eyes, cold and magnified by his glasses, gave him away when they met mine over Duke's shoulder. This was the first time he'd stepped across the threshold of my home since he'd told me he disapproved of Gisela and me living together.

As Hal walked Duke to his car, I grabbed my purse and went downstairs to meet my brother like the good sister I was doing my best to be.

Twenty-four

Hal didn't take his attention from the road as he drove along Franklin Avenue toward the river. He was such a creature of habit I assumed he was heading for the University Club. I didn't bother to ask where we were going, and we rode along without saying much.

He slowed down just beyond the edge of town and pulled into the parking lot of a roadhouse on the river. The gravel crunched, grinding into the tires of his clean, polished sedan, so out of place among the other dusty vehicles parked out front.

The smell of whiskey and old cigarette smoke met us at the entrance to the tavern, where only a few booths were occupied. As we stood outlined in the harsh daylight of the open doorway, a couple of uniformed servicemen at the bar turned toward us. We must have looked like misfits—me in a dark blue dress and stylish white and navy high heels, Hal in a double-breasted tan suit, holding his leather driving gloves.

"Sit anywhere you'd like," the bartender called to us as we waited for our eyes to adjust to the poorly lit interior.

I followed Hal to a booth in the corner, away from the bar.

"I like it here," he said. "The food is good and cheap." As soon as the waitress appeared he ordered for both of us, chicken fried steak and a side salad.

"I'll have a martini, and bring me a beer with my food, sweetie," he added.

"I'll have coffee," I said, thinking how strange it was to be sitting across from Hal in a roadhouse the day after our mother's funeral.

Shouldn't we be at home with Dad and Dorothy?

"Bring that drink right away, and there'll be a tip in it for you," he called as the waitress walked away. She quickly returned with his cocktail.

"So how does Duke like Chicago?" he asked as he took a swallow of his martini.

"I think he's happy there. He's working on the State Street Tunnel and has joined the Army Corps of Engineers." I suspected Hal wanted to ask about him spending the night with me and tried to keep the conversation general, as if it were any old day.

Our food arrived, making me realize how hungry I was. "This is good," I said between bites, starting to relax a little. But without much to say to each other, I found myself sinking into sadness listening to the melancholy lyrics of Lena Horne's "Stormy Weather" playing on the jukebox, and wondered why in the world had Hal brought me to this dingy place.

He ordered another beer halfway through his meal. I asked for more coffee.

"Thanks. I feel better now," I said, pushing my plate away. "Yesterday was a long day and I forgot to eat. I made baloney sandwiches late last night for Duke and me." Right away, I regretted reminding him that Duke had stayed overnight, and I noticed that same cold look in his eyes that he'd flashed at me over Duke's shoulder earlier in the day.

"I think you should move home with Dad."

His statement took me by surprise.

"I can't. I've still got a couple of more months on my lease."

The waitress stopped by the table and he ordered another beer.

He didn't respond, but sat with his arms folded over his chest and glared at me. The waitress brought his beer, which he reached for right away, taking a big gulp.

"Your place is to help Dad." He looked comical with a foam mustache from his beer, but quickly wiped his face. "He can't live alone."

So this was why he'd invited me to lunch.

"I'll help out, but I can't take care of Dad. I don't even know if he needs to be taken care of."

"Need your own space for entertaining?" His sarcasm appalled me, but his next question felt like a slap across the face, "Who do you like better—men or women?"

"It's outrageous that you would say such a thing."

He picked up his beer and stared at me, but I refused to crumble under his accusatory look and calmly said, "I don't lead a loose life."

"I'm just saying that you owe Dad." His beer glass was empty.

"I don't get it," I said without lowering my gaze. "What do I owe Dad?"

"She knew." He got up from the table. "I've got to pee. Think about it while I'm gone."

I watched him bump a chair and excuse himself as if it were a person.

Mother knew about Gisela and me? That actually made sense, since she always seemed to instinctively know how I was feeling. Then I remembered how she'd held me and comforted me the day Gisela left. The tone of her voice, and the way she'd said "I know how much you love her. I love her too." had haunted me, causing me to wonder if she'd guessed the truth about us. But she never let on that she knew, so I had let it go.

Then it hit me, Hal must have told her! *But why?* Lava hot rage rose in my chest. I didn't give a damn why.

When he returned to the table, I began to consider how best to get away from him. Although he probably wouldn't make a public scene, I knew I didn't want to be trapped alone in the car with him while he continued to lash out at me.

"Maybe you should order some coffee," I suggested with a false sense of calm.

"Don't patronize me, Ruth. I'm not finished with our conversation."

The waitress headed our way with another beer that he must have ordered on his way to the men's room. She set the glass on the table and cleared away our plates.

"Maybe she didn't just have a heart attack and fall out of her rowboat."

"Stop it, Hal," I said under my breath. "You've had too much to drink."

"You think so? You think this is easy for me?" He curled his lip and looked at me with scorn.

"What exactly did you say to her?"

He seemed to be dumbfounded. It took him a long time to answer my question.

"Nothing," he answered almost inaudibly as he reached for his beer.

I could tell he was lying and stared at him without blinking. He turned away from me.

"Tell me."

He started to cry. It occurred to me that he must have planned to bring me to a place where he thought I couldn't get up and walk out, and where we wouldn't run into anyone he knew. I pitied Hal for having such a weak spirit, and pretentious attitudes.

"She deserved to know the truth about you. Everyone knew but her." He took out his handkerchief and blew his nose. "I had to tell her."

This was too much. My fury brought me into focus.

"You're pathetic Hal," I spit out at him. "I'm shocked that you would insinuate that Mother died because of my love for Gisela. You should be ashamed of yourself."

"I told her you and Gisela were lesbians, like Gertrude and Alice. She knew what I meant. I didn't have to explain it to her. She defended you both, saying that you were close friends, who loved each other. I told her for her own good. Before someone from her church told her."

"You went too far, Hal. I can't imagine how deeply you must have hurt her. It was vicious of you to challenge her to choose between us. Family meant more than anything to her. Mother had enough love for all of us. She would never have been able to understand why you would turn on me like that."

"Maybe you should have thought of that a long time ago, Ruth. You should have thought about how much you would hurt her if she knew about you and Gisela."

"Did you also tell Dad?"

"No. I didn't tell him." Hal crumpled like a rag doll into the corner of his seat.

"I'm leaving. I'll have the bartender call a taxi for me." I stood, placed my hands flat on the table, and looked into his watery eyes. "You should be ashamed of yourself." Then I left without another word as he sat alone with his beer.

❧

What I learned from Hal left no room in my heart for forgiveness. I wrote my brother off as one of the bigots Gisela had warned me about. The only thing that held me together on the ride home was that I would see Duke again that night.

I paid the taxi driver and ran upstairs. I didn't tear out my hair or run around in a screaming frenzy, but kicked off my shoes and crawled into bed without getting undressed. Needing to escape, I fell into a sound sleep, dreaming about walking along a narrow path high above a stormy sea. As the ground crumbled under my feet I climbed higher, slipped, and began to fall—the insistent ring of the doorbell startled me awake before I hit the water.

Confused and trying to make sense of why I was sleeping in my clothes, I heard furious knocking on the door and more frantic ringing of the bell.

Duke! I vaulted out of bed and tripped over a discarded shoe, which caused me to stumble toward the window. Pulling it open, I saw Duke standing under the street lamp looking up at the house.

"I'm here," I shouted.

I finally let him in and as he hugged me he asked, "What happened to you? Your hair stinks of booze and cigarette smoke, and you're a rumpled mess! Where have you been?"

"Lunch with Hal. I left him at a roadhouse down by the river hours ago. I fell asleep."

"I can see that. Your eyes are all puffy."

"I need a bath to wash away the stench. Make yourself at home."

"Are you sure you're all right?"

"Yes. Yes. Just sit down and wait for me." I had a raw urgency to get into the tub.

A half hour later, I reappeared dressed in comfortable slacks and a soft jersey sweater Gisela had left behind, my hair still damp.

"That's better," Duke greeted me, holding a cocktail. "I brought a bottle of scotch. Hope you don't mind."

"Of course not."

The ice cubes tinkled against the glass as he took a swallow. "Try it." He handed me the glass.

I kind of liked the smoky taste of the watered down liquor.

"I can make you a light one, it'll help relax you."

I accepted. He handed me the drink and sat down beside me.

"Now tell me what happened," he said.

My experience with Hal tumbled out. I told the whole story, ending with my shock when he insinuated that my love for Gisela had caused Mother's death.

"We both know Hal's always been narrow minded, critical about what he doesn't understand, but he has no right to suggest you are responsible for Rosie's death. That's downright evil."

"I think he wanted me to share his burden, lessen his guilt over what he thinks he did to Mother."

The more we talked, the more relaxed I felt. A calm came over me. I started to feel that with Duke's support I could move on—not immediately, but someday.

Duke suggested it was time for dinner, and thought we should eat at his hotel. I agreed, and excusing myself went to change out of my comfortable clothes into a dress suitable for a night out with a gentleman.

❧

We enjoyed a lovely dinner, neither of us making a move to end the evening until Duke finally asked, "Shall I send you home in a taxi?"

I knew immediately from the twinkle in his eyes he was teasing, and that he understood the last thing I wanted was to be alone.

"Sure" I answered trying to sound aloof. "It's been fun seeing you again." Neither of us could keep up the farce and both burst into laughter.

After we had calmed down, he agreed to stay the night with me before returning to Chicago the following morning, and I waited in the lobby while he went to collect his suitcase and pay his bill.

Later we relaxed in my apartment. With a coffee and brandy in each hand, Duke sat down beside me on the couch.

"Do you have anyone special in your life?" I asked, taking a cup from him. He'd been so kind over the last two days, listening to me go on and on about myself, and I realized I still didn't know much about his life.

He looked thoughtful, "I met someone recently—at the army recruiting office—George, he's a surgeon, and we get on well together. I've been infatuated and in love in the past, but it's never lasted."

He put his arm around me, "It's not the easiest thing in the world to find someone, but then there's also the challenge of figuring out how to live together, which you well know."

"True. I hope it works out for you and George. I can't bear to think about you without love in your life. You deserve the best."

"And so do you. You've found love, now you need to retrieve it," he said removing his arm from my shoulder and stretching. "Try calling Gisela again in the morning. From what you've told me about her, she wouldn't have ignored a telegram."

"It really is strange that I haven't heard from her. We talk every once in a while to catch up with each other, but it's been over a month now. Maybe she sent flowers and I didn't notice, or maybe they got lost in the delivery."

"Well, you need to find out what really happened," he said as he stood up and yawned. We'd finished our drinks and both of us decided we were too tired to talk anymore.

I again undressed in the bathroom, emerging in my robe and nightgown, but this time Duke had put on pajamas in the privacy of the bedroom.

"You smell sweet," he said. "Like cinnamon." He held me spoon fashion until I fell into a deep sleep.

I opened my eyes reluctantly the next morning, knowing it was the day Duke would be leaving, but not wanting him to go.

At the last minute, as if reluctant to leave, he said, "I wish you'd come home with me. I've got a nice apartment with two bedrooms. You could stay until you get settled in a job and find your own place."

"You know I can't. I have to pack up this apartment, and help Dad sort out Mother's things." Suddenly I felt the weight of what was still ahead.

Duke took both my hands while we said goodbye. Then he hugged me.

"I'm not that far away." Then, kissing me as if I were fragile, he whispered in my ear "Call her."

The air through the open window held the fragrance of another perfect fall day with the leaves beginning to turn. Duke lowered the soft top on his car and waved as he disappeared around the same corner that had gobbled up Gisela.

※

I needed time to collect myself after Duke left, and called my office requesting another day off. I planned to call Gisela in the evening, nine o'clock my time, but the day dragged by. *I should have gone to work.* Trying to calm myself, I called Dad.

"Come over," he said. "Hal and Dorothy are here."

"I can't," I lied. "I'm at work."

I took down the curtains Mother had made for our two bedrooms and washed them with Ivory Snow in the kitchen sink. While they dried on the clothesline, I tried to take a nap, but my fretful thoughts pushed away the relief of sleep. *Maybe I should wait. Let Gisela call me. By now she has the telegram.* I imagined her returning from a trip, opening the envelope, and her shock upon learning that Mother had died. *Why hasn't she called me?* Then I did my best to convince myself that it didn't matter.

I pressed and rehung the curtains, which now looked as fresh and pretty as the day we'd moved in. Then, remembering how pleased Mother had been when we asked her to help us decorate, I collapsed on the bed and cried. Feeling devastated that she had died alone, and that I hadn't been able to say goodbye, I became angry with Hal at the possibility that he had hurt her with my truth, which hardened my heart toward him even more.

Would knowing have made Mother love me any less?

I awoke in the dark around seven o'clock after a dreamless sleep, got up and tried to listen to a radio drama, but couldn't concentrate. Turning the dial, I found a classical station playing a familiar Mozart piano concerto, but the music made me heavy hearted—it was one of Gisela's favorites.

Another hour dragged on.

I couldn't wait another minute and hoped Gisela would be home. But what if she doesn't answer? *Just do it.*

With an unsteady hand, I picked up the telephone and dialed zero for the long distance operator.

"Your number please," she greeted me. I hung up without saying a word. Her officious tone increased my nervousness. I argued with myself that it was too early to call. *Come on, you're wasting precious time.* My finger hesitated over the zero. I dialed again.

This time I gave the operator my number.

"Speak directly into the receiver. I can barely hear you. Repeat the number, please."

I spoke louder, more firmly.

"And the number you're calling, will this be station-to-station or person-to-person?"

Wishing the woman behind the voice knew how I was feeling and could somehow make it easier, I pictured her sitting in front of a switchboard waiting to poke the cord into the board to connect me with Gisela, impatient to get on to the next customer. Somehow we managed to work out the details of the call, and the phone began to ring.

Gisela answered on the fifth ring, her "hello" breathless, as if she'd run to answer the phone. "Long distance calling. I have a person-to-person call from a Miss Ruth Thompson for Gisela Nilsen."

"Is that you, Ruth?" Gisela sounded excited.

"Is this Gisela Nilsen?" The anonymous operator asked.

"Yes. Yes. Put her on," Gisela said.

"One moment. I'll connect you."

The line went quiet, with an occasional ping, and it seemed to take forever for Gisela to answer.

"Gisela, I'm so glad you're home!"

She knew me too well, and must have sensed my heavy heart because right away she asked, "What's wrong? What's happened?"

It all came out in a flood. Everything, except what happened with Duke, spilled into the telephone receiver and over the wires to Gisela in California. She didn't interrupt and kept me talking, saying "uh-huh" or "go on" every once in a while. When I finished, the line crackled and scratched until she spoke into the space between us.

"Ruth, I'm so sorry. I wish I would have known about Rose. I would have come home. It's too much for you to have handled alone."

"You didn't get a telegram from Hal? He said he sent one."

"No. Nothing. And after what you've just told me about him, I'm not surprised." She paused and the line filled with static. She tried to talk over the noise. "We can't talk about all this long distance. Come out and visit."

"But—"

"No buts. No protests. I'm worried about you. We need to be together to talk things through, I'll wire you the details."

I couldn't say no and knew I needed her strength.

❧

The next day, I stopped by to see Dad and fixed dinner for both of us. While we ate, I told him that I'd talked to Gisela and explained that the reason why she wasn't at Mother's funeral was that she didn't receive the telegram Hal said he'd sent. Even though I wanted to tattle on Hal, I couldn't risk hurting Dad, or confessing about my relationship with Gisela. "She wants me to come out west for a visit."

"All the way out to California? Is it safe? The Japanese may have plans to attack the West Coast."

"Gisela's been out there six months, and she's fine. Besides I'll only be gone a couple of weeks." I didn't want to give in to my guilt for leaving him. *What if Hal was right, and it was my place to take care of Dad?*

"Well, let's get Hal and Dorothy over before you go, and tie up the loose ends around Mother's things."

I agreed to stay a while longer and called Gisela that night.

"You're falling into Hal's trap, putting what someone else wants over your own needs."

I slumped in the chair at the desk. Listening to the static on the line, I pressed the telephone receiver to my ear as if an answer to my dilemma would magically enter my head.

"Dad's grown dependent on me in the last week," I said. "Maybe I should wait a few weeks until he gets stronger."

"Why don't you move in with him? It would solve his problems as well as Hal's. That way you'll totally lose yourself." She paused. "And what about me? I miss you every day."

"Give me some time, I'll figure it out and call you in a couple of days." And before hanging up, made sure to tell her I missed her too.

At work it became apparent that I'd forgotten how to organize my thoughts, and the clinic director suggested I take a leave of absence, telling me he'd been concerned about my performance even before Mother died.

"Take as long as you need" he said, dismissing me by picking up the phone and waving me out the door.

I left without stopping by the office to process the paperwork. How could I know how long I'd be gone? Later at home, I sat and stared out the window, unable to move. The ringing telephone woke me from my apathy. I considered not answering, then thought it might be Dad needing something so I got up and walked over to the desk.

Duke's friendly voice greeted me. "Hello, Ruth. Did you call her?"

"I did call her, but now I'm even more confused." I spelled out all that had happened over the last few days and my inability to make a decision.

As soon as he heard my description of the past few days he said "Hold on," then paused for a moment before asking "How much time remains on your apartment lease?"

"A month, maybe two."

"Okay. You need a plan. There's not much left for you in Minneapolis. And from what you've told me, your job may be in jeopardy."

He was right. My boss at the Guidance Clinic hadn't assured me that he would hold my job for me, but I had not considered the possibility that I might actually lose my position—even after his curt dismissal.

"The war has created lots of jobs for women. You can find work elsewhere if you need to, so let's not worry about that."

Duke outlined a plan so simple that I couldn't argue with it: Pay the remaining rent on the apartment, cancel the lease, move my things to Dad's, buy a train ticket to California.

"You can stay in Minneapolis wallowing in your father's grief, allowing Hal to demand more and more from you, or you can think about what you really want" is how it translated in my head. But Duke's words were kinder than that, and very convincing.

Before hanging up he said, "The best thing you've done for both of us is to throw me over and follow your heart with Gisela."

"I thought my love for her would solve everything, but I didn't realize how wrong that was."

"That's true, also. My point is that even though your decision was hard on me, I've landed on my feet without you. Your dad can also survive without you to take care of him. And right now I can't think of anything you owe Hal."

Duke hadn't minced words, and it struck me that I really didn't have much left to lose. I took the trolley over to see Dad, explaining as gently as I could why I now planned to leave in early October, much sooner than I'd thought.

"Maybe Dorothy can help me out while you're gone," he said.

"I've been thinking, it might be a good idea to hire someone to help you around the house."

"We'll see," he replied doubtfully.

❧

Dad insisted on having Hal move my packed things. With both of us feeling ill at ease on the day we'd arranged for him to come by, we acted like complete strangers, and Hal only spoke in order to ask what to take and where to put it at Dad's house.

"Take all the boxes and leave the furniture. It belongs to the landlady. Dad will know where to store everything."

I turned the key in the lock for the last time, walked down the steps to ring Mrs. Mahoney's bell, and handed her the key.

"I'm sorry about your mother," she said. "Won't you come in for some tea?"

"I can't, I have to catch the trolley. My dad's waiting for me."

"I sure will miss you girls. You always put a smile on my

face with your sunny dispositions." Her words left a little nick on my heart.

By the time I got to Dad's, Hal was gone. Whether or not he thought he'd won the battle with me made no difference, I'd pushed him to the darkest recesses of my mind to protect myself from caring.

※

The next day I tackled Mother and Dad's house. A musty smell, along with a mishmash of clutter and sorrow, seemed to have settled in all the rooms. There was bacon grease splattered on the kitchen stove, and a frying pan in the sink with remnants of something once edible floating in filmy gray water.

I gathered the daily newspapers that were scattered throughout the house, giving Dad the job of hauling them out to the burn barrel and setting them on fire along with the other trash. I cleaned and scrubbed until I recognized the homey bones of the house that had been covered over since Mother's death. Only then did I feel strong enough to tackle the job of going through her belongings.

As I folded Mother's clothing and packed them into boxes to give to the church, memories of the fun Gisela and I had going through her old dresses and hats at the house on Lake Minnetonka held me up like puppet strings and kept me moving forward.

Dad watched while I finished packing. "Maybe one of the ladies from the church can come over and do some house-cleaning for you," I suggested after I'd taped the last box for pickup by the women of the church guild. "This floor could use a good scrubbing."

As usual, Dad hemmed and hawed at any mention of a housekeeper. I knew that he wanted my help, not that of a stranger, so it didn't surprise me when he said "I'll ask Dorothy at dinner tomorrow. She'll help me."

He didn't seem to realize that Hal and I were barely speaking to each other, and he had invited them to dinner the night before I was scheduled to leave.

"I forgot to tell you, Hal has to work late so they can't come. And you know, Dorothy may be too busy with her charity projects to be of much help. Plus, she's got Hal to take care of. I imagine that's a big job." Noticing his disappointment, I wanted to make him laugh to help soften my words, but my heart still weighed heavy with guilt for leaving him without any resolution of who would help him around the house.

Two days later, on Thursday, the eighth of October, Dad dropped me at the Great Northern Station, and I insisted he not come in to see me off. I watched as he walked to his car, shoulders drooping, and had to turn away to keep from changing my mind.

Once inside the station, I worked my way through the chaos to the boarding area, finally reaching the platform outside. I stood alone amidst a pandemonium alive with the shouts of joyful recognition and tearful goodbyes of men and women in uniform and their loved ones, then boarded the train.

I found a window seat, and a young soldier sat down next to me. Both lost in our thoughts, we crossed the Mississippi in silence.

I ate in the dining car the first night, exchanging small talk with men and women my age who were serving our country. It had never occurred to me to enlist, and now I questioned whether or not serving the families of Minneapolis through the Guidance Clinic was enough.

Avoiding the company of my fellow passengers for the rest of the trip, I couldn't help thinking how we were like the loons Hal had told Gisela about that night so long ago during her first visit to the lake, hoping we would all survive as the train carried us west toward the ocean and an unknown future.

Twenty-five

We changed trains in Kansas City before heading west. A couple of days later we passed Los Angeles, and when the ocean finally came into view I reveled at seeing it for the first time. While we traveled south along the coast, the sun sparkling on the water like glitter tossed from a giant hand, my spirits rose as I watched the beauty of sand and sea flash by.

And I finally allowed myself to feel excited about seeing Gisela.

"I'll be waiting in the second arch from the left," she'd said. "You'll know what I mean when you get off the train."

The train arrived midday at Union Station in San Diego, which had been built in the Spanish style of architecture with open arches lining the covered platform, and I saw exactly what Gisela had meant. I clutched the small suitcase I'd kept on board, weaving my way through the throng of porters pushing luggage carts and people waiting to greet us. I spotted Gisela scanning the crowd and ducked through one of the arches. I stood behind her before she noticed me.

Dressed neatly in a sundress with a cardigan over her shoulders, she stood out as the most beautiful woman there.

I lightly touched her bare arm and she turned toward me. The look on her face told me I'd done the right thing by coming out west. Neither of us moved for a few seconds, then I dropped my suitcase and fell into her arms. With so many people hugging, crying, and laughing we were simply part of the scene.

Neither of us spoke until Gisela held me at arm's length, saying so quietly that only I could hear: "Finally my love, you are here." Letting out a long sigh, she pulled me close again.

I didn't know whether to laugh or cry—or do both—and let my emotions run wild until wiping my tears, I launched into an apology.

Releasing me, she looked into my eyes. "There's no need to go into that now. Or ever, if I have my way."

"I'm so glad to be here. It's heaven, exactly as you described."

We made our way to where the porters had lined up the luggage so I could claim my other suitcase; then I waited outside the station while Gisela went to get her car. Palm fronds rustled in a breeze, caressing my skin like the finest silk, and I noticed the tiled dome of the train station was outlined against the deepest blue sky I'd ever seen. Turning around, I was awestruck by the unobstructed view of San Diego Bay, and finally understood why Jean had raved about California and its beauty.

Gisela loaded my luggage into the trunk of her black and white Studebaker coupe. A green gas ration decal with the letter "B" was pasted on the right side of the windshield.

"My work at Consolidated is considered essential to the war effort. The B-mileage ration sticker entitles me to eight gallons of gas a week," she said when she noticed me looking at it.

As we drove along the coastline, I asked about the chicken wire netting with fake trees and rooftops attached to it that covered stretches of the Pacific Coast Highway.

"It's camouflage to confuse the Japanese if they try to bomb San Diego," Gisela explained.

In Minnesota, young men disappeared every day, joining the armed services. The posters with Uncle Sam, pointing his finger and saying "I Want You for the US Army," were everywhere. We considered it our patriotic duty to turn our used kitchen fat over to the local butcher; and to collect scrap metal, tin cans, and rubber to produce armaments. Supposedly, one pound of fat could produce one pound of glycerin used to make explosives. It had all seemed so abstract, but seeing the camouflage here made the war seem more real to me.

With the windows rolled down, I inhaled the smell of the fresh salt air. "It feels like paradise, and looks so peaceful" I said, swallowing a moment of panic. *What if Dad had been right about the Japanese?*

"I agree. It's so calm and beautiful, it's hard to grasp that anything horrific happened out there" she replied, waving toward the ocean.

We entered La Jolla, still driving along the Coast Highway with the ocean on our left. Up ahead was a building that looked like a castle.

"That's the Grande Colonial Hotel," Gisela said as she made a right turn away from the ocean onto Eads Avenue. "We're almost home."

The Studebaker chugged up Eads to Prospect Street, where we turned left and parked in front of a small bungalow halfway down the block. The house, painted pale pink with the front yard surrounded by a low stucco wall of the same color, faced west with a panoramic view of the ocean.

"Welcome home" Gisela said, opening the wooden gate. There was nothing across the road except a grassy knoll with a path that led to the edge of the bluff. "We can watch the surf crash against the rocks from the porch swing."

The street was quiet with no traffic, and the only sound was the distant push and pull of the waves. I waited on the porch, its lattice laden with sweet-scented honeysuckle, and forgot my panic until we went inside the house together. Heavy drapes covered the windows in the front room, which Gisela shoved aside to let the sunlight in. "Blackout curtains. Everyone has them to use at night. It makes for spectacular stargazing. No lights anywhere."

We sat side by side on a long sofa the color of mourning doves that was full of throw pillows in shades of saffron and citron. A glass coffee table was strewn with the October 11, 1942 copy of the *La Jolla Light* newspaper and the latest issue of *Life* magazine.

Right away, I noticed Madge the Flapper was on a table across from us next to a plush chair that matched the sofa. Through an archway, I saw a vase of bright yellow sunflowers sitting on a red cloth in the center of the table in the dining room. No matter where she lived, Gisela always added her own touch.

"There's only one bedroom. We'll have to sleep together." She paused. "Or you can sleep on the couch if you want." The look on my face was answer enough, and she led me down the hallway. Instead of opening the curtains, Gisela lit a candle in the darkness whispering, "I was afraid I'd never see you again," as she reached for me.

The feel of her lips and hands woke my body from the nightmare of her absence, and in our deep desire we wildly undressed each other. On an oasis of cool white sheets—famished for the touch, taste, and familiar scents we both craved—we feasted in our passion and pleasure. Coming together with no fear, no boundary, no sense of loss, expressing our mutual hunger was all that mattered.

Afterward, I fell asleep with Gisela's arms around me.

"You can't understand how lonely I've been," I told her when we were both awake and still lying in bed.

"I've been lonely too. Every day since I left Minneapolis."
Her words tickled my ear. "Sometimes the choices we make
aren't always the best thing for us."

"I know," I sighed, resting in her embrace.

She ran her hands over my face and body like a curious
blind person. "I'm trying to convince myself you're really
here. I can't keep my hands off you."

"It's my turn," I laughed. "Let me see if you're real." I was
whole again, and where I wanted to be.

Gisela cooked a simple dinner, chicken grilled over char-
coal, on the small patio at the rear of the house. Allowing her
to wait on me, I relaxed on a blue and yellow striped recliner.
Flowers filled both sides of the yard, and two tall trees grew
along the far stucco wall that surrounded the garden.

"Torrey pines," she informed me. "Native to this area."

The trees had cinnamon-colored bark with furrowed
ridges and leaned toward each other, their crooked branches
touching like lovers.

We finished dinner and nestled close on the front porch
swing, her arm around my shoulder. "I can see why you love
it out here. All this beauty, and no mosquitoes." We didn't
move until the stars appeared, one by one, and formed a bowl
overhead. The only sounds were the grind of an occasional
car shifting gears, and the ever-present splash of the waves
against the cliffs.

Gisela noticed me shiver. "Let's get you to bed," she
said. "We'll sleep in. I'm a woman of leisure with the whole
week off."

Indeed she was. The next morning she fixed flapjacks,
reminding me of our early days together in the apartment on
Sheridan Avenue. We washed and dried our dishes in front
of a sunny window in the small kitchen, a well equipped
and cheerful room complete with gas stove, Frigidaire, and a
shiny chrome Kenmore wringer washing machine standing
by a door opening to the backyard.

Later that afternoon we walked down Prospect Street to the Grande Colonial Hotel. Inside, sunlight splashed over the lobby through the semicircular domed windows of leaded glass that looked out on the ocean. Admiring the marbled fireplaces and elegant chandeliers, I followed as Gisela led the way to the ice cream parlor. I scanned the menu, craving something sweet, and ordered a banana split with a glass of Coca-Cola, while Gisela just had black coffee. We sat outside overlooking the water.

"What about Rose's funeral?" she asked.

"Hal took care of Dad. My friend Duke showed up and gave me the support I needed to get through the service and burial. Thank God he was still there after my lunch with Hal."

"Duke? You mean the man you were dating when we first met? The one your family expected you to marry?" She lit a cigarette and looked out to sea.

"I could just shoot Hal. I should have been the one by your side," she said. Her eyes had turned storm gray as she took a deep draw on her cigarette, then jabbed it several times in the ashtray.

I knew she was waiting for me to say something. It seemed to upset her that I'd mentioned Duke.

"I found out something really surprising about Duke." That got her attention, and her eyes softened while she listened.

"He's the only person I've trusted enough to be honest with about my love for you. I was desperate to tell someone, but he shocked me by getting angry. He said he regretted not knowing that my loving you was the reason I broke off with him. In that moment I hated myself for hurting him."

Gisela waited while I swallowed the last bite of my ice cream and took a sip of soda. Gathering my thoughts, I finished all in one breath, "He's attracted to men. Like I'm attracted to you. He didn't even admit it to himself until he moved to Chicago."

She held up her hand to interrupt me. "Are you saying he's gay?" she asked in a low voice.

"Yes, I am. He explained it all to me, how he didn't understand until he moved away from me to Chicago."

"That is so incredible, and dangerous." She continued, her brow furrowed with concern, "Men are more often rounded up and arrested."

"We were so close all those years, but in the dark about each other's true feelings."

"Of course you were." I expected her to pound her fist on the table, but she didn't, even though she spit out the words. "It makes me so angry."

Again she softened. "And at the same time it makes me sad how you both had to hide your truth from each other—and from yourselves." She paused as a couple of servicemen and their dates took a table near us, their lively chatter and laughter seemed to distract her. "Not that you really had a choice. How would you have told each other?"

Hesitating again until a waiter who was hovering nearby moved away she added, "And no wonder Duke was so angry."

"He said that it made him furious that we have to hide in the shadow of our hearts."

"I agree. It's outrageous that so many of us live in that shadow."

Gisela put on dark glasses with rhinestones on the black rims and tied a white headscarf over her hair.

I could no longer see her eyes, but she sounded lighter and happier. "Now I don't have to be jealous of him, thinking he might steal you away from me."

"Duke convinced me to call you. My hurt feelings were holding me back. Crazy with grief, I thought you might not want to come to Mother's funeral because of me." I finished my drink and said, "If it weren't for Duke, I would have sunk further into depression."

"I might even like him if I ever get to meet him," she laughed. "My paper tiger rival."

I could feel my face flush. *If she only knew.*

"Come on let's walk," Gisela said, and we strolled along the promenade listening to the mad chatter of gulls as we watched them glide over the waves.

"I can't forgive Hal for how he treated Mother and me. And I can't forgive him for lying about sending you a telegram. Sometimes I think I hate my own brother."

The gulls scolded one another with their high-pitched cries. Gisela linked her arm through mine and stared straight ahead at the horizon.

"I don't believe in God, but I have faith in forgiveness. We free ourselves from having to carry the other person's guilty burden when we can let go of hurts caused by their spitefulness. Holding on to these injuries causes bitterness to coil in our heart like a poisonous snake."

"I don't know, I'm so angry at him. It's a lot to think about."

❧

The week flew by. I didn't forget about Hal or Mother. Gisela's love and care helped to keep most of my grief in the background. If I fell into despondency, we swam in the ocean or walked on the beach to cheer me up, making love whenever we felt like it in her cozy bungalow.

The Sunday before Gisela returned to work our walk took us past the Grande Colonial as we headed toward the village. Stopping at the entrance to La Valencia she asked, "Want to have lunch on the veranda and hobnob with the rich and famous?"

"Let's sit a minute," I said, picking a bench in the small courtyard outside the hotel entrance.

"You look pale. Are you sick?"

"I'm not sure. I got kind of dizzy and feel nauseated."

"Let me feel your forehead." I thought she might kiss me, her face was so near mine, and our thighs touched on the bench, but the people strolling by on the sidewalk took no notice of us.

Maybe she's right about California. No one has even glanced at us.

"I think you're fine. You don't have a fever."

"I'm just so tired. I could fall asleep right here."

"I shouldn't be dragging you all over the place after all you've been through. In my excitement to have you here I forgot my hospitality manners."

"Your manners are perfect. I've loved every minute."

We skipped the lunch. By the time we walked home, I was exhausted. Gisela closed the curtains in the bedroom, and encouraged me to take a nap.

I woke up hungry, but the cooking smells drifting in from the kitchen made me feel queasy. I washed my face and joined Gisela.

"You must be starving. You haven't eaten anything since breakfast."

"I'm a little dizzy again," I said, eyeing the lamb chops sizzling in an iron skillet on the stove. Gisela offered me a glass of fizzy mineral water with a lemon slice.

"Take some of these crackers with cheddar cheese and sit outside. I'll finish up the dinner."

By the time she called me in for dinner, I'd eaten some of the crackers and felt better, so I managed to enjoy the lamb and the rest of the food on my plate.

Later we moved outside to the porch and sat with our feet up on the railing, inhaling the aroma of the honeysuckle. I felt fine again, and very contented.

But when we were getting ready for bed, I complained to Gisela about my breasts being very tender.

"Are you late with your period? We always used to have them at the same time. Mine was ten days ago," Gisela said as she went out to the front room to open the curtains so we wouldn't have to wake in the dark.

While she was gone, a shock shot through me: I hadn't paid much attention to my body for the last couple of months, having been more focused on holding onto my sanity at all costs. Counting back the days to my time with Duke, it now became apparent that I'd missed a cycle.

"It's late. Maybe too much stress," was all I managed to say after she came back into the bedroom.

Pretending to fall asleep right away, my mind raced with panic until Gisela released me and rolled over as she drifted off. I quietly got up, tiptoeing into the kitchen where a full moon was shining in through the window, and put the kettle on the stove without turning on the lights. Trying to remember what I knew about pregnancy, which wasn't much, I finally realized it was essential to see a doctor as soon as possible.

I finished my tea and slipped into bed again, falling into a restless slumber before being awakened in the morning by the sweet sensation of Gisela kissing me goodbye.

"I'll be home around five o'clock, six at the latest," she whispered.

I got up as soon as I heard her car start, but it was seven in the morning, too early to phone anyone. I showered and dressed before calling the local hospital, and told the person who answered the telephone I was new in town and thought I might be pregnant. She referred me to a nearby doctor.

"I can squeeze you in at three," the receptionist said. "There's nothing earlier. You'll have to wait until next week if you want a different time." I couldn't spend another week without knowing, and accepted the appointment.

The house as always was tidy, but I swept the floors and dusted just to keep busy. My mind, my whole body, felt numb. *It can't be true!* I scolded myself for worrying, and thought it must take more than one time to get pregnant. Look at Hal and Dorothy—they'd been trying for years and still didn't have a child.

I called a taxi and arrived early for the appointment. Taking a seat in the crowded waiting room with women who were in various stages of pregnancy, I stuck my nose in a magazine with a fat-cheeked toddler on the cover. My name wasn't called until three thirty.

A nurse took my temperature and pulse before leaving me alone in an exam room. Fifteen minutes later a knock on the door announced the arrival of the doctor, who stuck a thermometer under my tongue as if he didn't believe the nurse's results.

"So Mrs. Thompson, you say you're tired all the time and nauseated, especially in the morning. Any breast tenderness?"

I nodded. He pulled the thermometer from my mouth.

"Your temperature is normal. You don't have the flu. Missed any menstrual periods?"

"Well, I've been under a lot of strain lately." Too befuddled to count, I continued, "I guess I have. One. Maybe two. I'm about ten days late this month."

"Is there a chance you might be pregnant?"

"Well, yes, maybe," I said, feeling panicked. *Oh my god this can't be true.*

"Do you know the date you might have conceived?"

I knew precisely—six days after Mother's death. "September fifth" I said, my face burning.

"Then I'd say you are. All the signs are there. Notice any thickening of your waistline?"

"A little." I'd loosened the belt on my shirtwaist dress one notch that morning. When I didn't feel nauseated I'd been hungrier than usual, and was eating more.

He thought for a moment. "By my calculations, you should deliver late May, early June."

"How can you be so sure I'm pregnant?"

"We can do the rabbit test, but it's expensive and in my experience with your symptoms and your good health, it's not necessary. The rabbit can take two to three weeks to confirm, but by then you'll know for sure anyway."

I slid off the table and stood, feeling too woozy to walk. The doctor held out his hand to steady me. "Let us know if you're still wondering at the end of the month." But I didn't hear any more of what he said because I fainted. Fell right into his arms, and came to with the nurse holding smelling salts under my nose.

"Congratulations, Mrs. Thompson. You'll be feeling fine in another few months," she said with a smile. "The doctor says you're going to have a baby."

"But I'm thirty. Isn't that too old?"

"Is that what's wrong? There can be complications, but not always. Let us know if you have any problems. And don't eat too much, you don't want to gain a lot of weight."

She offered me a glass of water and suggested I should be thrilled to be having a child. "Try to relax. Motherhood is what defines us as women." She seemed unable to reign in her enthusiasm for the joys of motherhood, but the end of the world best described what I thought about the subject.

❧

Gisela had left a thin piece of beefsteak in the fridge, which I took out and salted. I tossed a salad and scrubbed a couple of potatoes for baking, and realized she must have used all her ration coupons to buy food for my visit. I snacked on a cheese sandwich and a glass of milk while waiting outside on the porch, my head a mass of live wires.

Some of the tension in my shoulders released as I listened to the waves and basked in the ever-present perfume of the honeysuckle. Brightly colored hummingbirds the size of my thumb drank nectar from the scarlet hibiscus flowers out in the yard.

At five thirty, seeing the Studebaker heading toward the house, I went inside to brush my hair and check my face in the mirror. Normal. Nothing showed on the outside. I greeted Gisela with a hug as soon as she stepped into the front room.

She looked tired, and rested while I fried the steak and put the food on the table.

"I had a grueling day sorting out problems from last week. Men are still enlisting in droves, and creating lots of job openings for women. I bet you could easily find a teaching job at the University of San Diego. It's nearby."

I split my mind, listening to her while trying to push away thoughts of babies, motherhood, and the nurse's definition of a real woman. I didn't want to think about it, didn't want to talk about it, but couldn't focus on anything else.

"I'm a little out of touch," she continued, "but I bet psychology is even more progressive out here than in the Midwest. You might be able to get into research."

I missed having dinner discussions with Gisela, and was tempted to give my opinion on the direction of the field of psychology. But more importantly, I heard that she wanted me to stay.

"Please just consider it," she said. "I love you. I love having you out here. My personal life has been a mess since leaving you."

"I will. I'm happy here too," I replied leaning over to kiss her, then quickly changed the subject. "Tell me more about your day."

❧

Two days later, I got up early and put on coffee. Instead of eating toast and her usual bowl of corn flakes, Gisela fried herself an egg and offered to fix one for me.

"No thanks," I said and barely made it to the bathroom.

I returned feeling a little shaky, and Gisela said, "If I didn't know better, I would swear you were pregnant. You haven't met Amelia, Jean's friend."

She'd finished her eggs while I was gone and sat down with me at the table. "Anyway, Amelia's sister just had a baby, and she couldn't stand the smell of eggs."

"I think I might have the flu. Maybe even a fever now. I'm going to lie down." I didn't want to faint again and scare Gisela.

Fussing over me, she took my temperature to be sure it was okay to leave me alone, then after we kissed goodbye said "I'll be getting off work early today. When I get home, we'll change your ticket. You can't leave feeling like this."

For two days I'd managed to keep my condition from Gisela as my mind continuously raced through my options, but I knew I'd need to tell her I was pregnant soon.

The one choice that made most sense was staying with Gisela. I really couldn't bear the thought of living without her now that we were together again. But we had never discussed having children, and I couldn't shake my belief that in the eyes of society childbirth out of wedlock was as shameful as two women in love.

If Gisela would agree to help me, I might be able to hide here with her and give the child up for adoption. We wouldn't need Duke. Anyway, Gisela seemed to have forgotten about her paper tiger rival, so why bring him up? I argued with myself all morning. But how could I explain a pregnancy without bringing up Duke? I had to tell her.

Gisela came home early as planned, full of concern. When I saw the Studebaker parked at the curb, I hurried to meet her at the door, and it took only a second for her to exclaim, "I've been worried all day and couldn't concentrate."

I moved into the kitchen, away from her loving gaze.

"You look worse. Maybe you need a doctor."

"I do?"

I should have freshened up, but she'd come home much earlier than expected. Running hot water into the dishpan, I started to wash the dishes.

"I don't want you to leave on Sunday," she said, putting her arms around my waist from behind. "Come and sit with me. The dishes can wait."

I sat down at the table, staring at the black and white squares of the linoleum floor.

Gisela busied herself in the kitchen and brought us each a glass of iced tea.

"Can you at least stay at least another week?" she asked, sitting across from me.

I buried my face in my hands. "I am."

"Staying or leaving?" she asked.

"Neither one." I opened my hands, pressing my fingers on my temples. "It's what you said this morning. I'm pregnant."

"What?" She stood. "But how?"

It tumbled out.

"Duke. He was so kind and loving. No one held me after you left. My grief and longing blurred the boundaries between us. It just happened. We didn't plan it. Only once."

"Slow down. Here, drink this." She handed me my tea.

"I don't know what to do. I wasn't going to tell you, and now I have. I'll leave on Sunday and figure things out later."

"No. I don't want you to go. We can work it out together. If you leave, I will lose the love of my life."

Our eyes met and I knew she meant what she said. And I did want to stay. She pulled me up and took me in her arms.

"I can talk to a priest at that church, Mary Star of the Sea on Girard Avenue. Maybe I can arrange for an adoption."

"Don't do that yet. We have time. This doesn't change my love for you," she murmured, holding me tight.

"Are you sure?"

"I'm sure if you love me as much as I love you."

"I do."

❦

Three days later, we sat outside the ice cream parlor at the Grande Colonial. The waves crashed against the rocks and the foam caught the reflection of the waning gibbous moon.

"You know, you are going to have to tell your dad. It's his grandchild after all."

"I can't do that. It will break his heart. And he would tell Hal."

"I've been thinking a lot about it" she said, and looked away across the expanse of ocean. "There's no way to lie, or cover this up, unless you never want to see them again."

"I wouldn't miss Hal. But I love and would miss Dad, he is so kind hearted, and so alone now." I ran my fingers through my hair, making it stick out in all directions, not wanting to tell Dad or Hal anything.

"What about Duke?" Gisela said, now giving her full attention.

"Do you think I should tell him?"

"What if he wants to marry you?"

"I don't think that would happen."

"People do it, you know. A marriage of convenience with each partner living their own life on the side."

"I guess they do," I said, not wanting to talk about it.

We walked up the hill toward home, each of us lost in our own thoughts.

I called Dad the next morning, and told him I was going to stay for another couple of weeks. When he protested, I told him I was having a great time, and still had three weeks left of my leave of absence.

He cleared his throat. "I was hoping you'd come home. I've decided to retire, let the young guys take over the company. They're giving me a party."

"What will you do with your time?" I asked, concerned that he would sink into loneliness without Mother.

"I'll figure something out."

Gisela gently chided me for not telling him about the baby, and that I'd already decided not to go home at all.

"How could I with his news?"

During the next week, our relationship deepened with everything out in the open. "No more surprises," she kidded me. "My heart can't take it."

"I promise."

At her insistence I wrote a letter of resignation to the Guidance Clinic, citing family problems that necessitated my presence in California, requesting and receiving a letter of recommendation. I knew that until recently the clinic had respected my work, but also suspected the director was relieved to see me go.

Two weeks later, I still hadn't found a way to tell Dad. "You've got to," Gisela urged me. Instead, I sent him a note telling him I'd resigned and was staying even longer than planned.

"It's not going away," Gisela said. "Call your father today, or I'll do it for you."

"You wouldn't dare."

One week and then another went by before I got up the courage to call Dad. Then it seemed to take him forever to answer the telephone.

"Ruthie, I'm so glad you called. Please come home. I'm sick with worry."

I hated myself for what I was going to tell him.

"Are you all right, sweetheart?" he asked in the way he used to when I skinned my knee and needed comfort. But he couldn't make things better for me now, and I plunged right in.

"Dad, I'm in a pickle. Something happened with Duke, and I'm going to have a baby."

"You're pregnant! Oh my. Are you okay?"

"I'm fine, Dad."

"Well this is a wonderful surprise. I'm going to be a grand-dad! I wish Mother were here to help you out."

"Me too. I miss her every day."

"I don't understand. What happened? Are you two married?"

"No. Duke's in Chicago."

"Why'd you go out west? Come home. You've been gone too long. Get married in Mother's church. She'd be so happy to be a grandmother. She always hoped for Dorothy and Hal, but no luck there."

I took a deep breath. "Duke doesn't know yet." My voice caught in my throat. "He's going overseas soon. There's no time to get married." I twisted the truth to keep from answering more questions.

Dad coughed a few times.

"I might talk to a priest about adoption."

"Don't do that, Ruthie. I don't like the idea of adoption. And I don't like you being alone in this."

"I've got Gisela to help me. I'm staying out here with her. I'm not coming home."

"I'll let Hal know. He'll want to help if he can."

"You don't have to do that, Dad. I don't need anything." I wanted to say, "Don't tell Hal," but knew it wouldn't do any good.

"I'll drop you a note and let you know what he wants to do about this."

I didn't argue, and Dad's letter arrived shortly after our conversation:

November 23, 1942

Dearest Ruthie,

I told Hal about your situation. He's thin as a rail, been sick off and on ever since Mother's funeral. I know he misses her, and you too. He works for the Draft Board now and likes it. They rejected him for regular army because of his eyes.

He's worried about you. You know how bad he and Dot wanted a baby. It's too late now for them. She's thirty-six. They are excited to be aunt and uncle, and want you to bring the baby home.

I'm old, can't fix anything. I don't know what happened between you and Hal, but you two need to stick together. Maybe you can make them god-parents. Whatever you do, don't let part of our family go to adoption.

I'm excited to be a granddad. I want to be a part of your baby's life! I miss your mother every day. I'm doing okay, but this old house has too many memories. Now that I'm retired, I'm thinking of moving. I'm glad Gisela is there to help you through this. I forgot to tell Hal you're living together again. Let him know. It'll ease his mind.

Lots of Love, Dad

I showed the letter to Gisela.

"I'm proud of you," she said. "We're going to get through this."

I longed for her confidence, and was still uncertain about telling Duke, who I noticed Gisela did not seem to be encouraging me to call.

Twenty-six

Hal's letter arrived a couple of weeks after Dad's. Unwilling to open it while alone, I propped it up against the vase of flowers on the table and lay down for a nap.

I didn't hear Gisela come in. She woke me, calling my name in a low voice, then handed me the letter, saying firmly "You've got to open it."

"Let's just tear it up."

Gisela shook her head. "You can't do that, besides we've come this far. We have to know what he's thinking."

It gave me the jitters to hold the unopened envelope. "Here, you read it first." I thrust it at her.

She slit open the envelope and shook out the single page. We slowly rocked on the porch swing while she read the letter to herself.

"Typical Hal. Want me to read it out loud?" The look on her face didn't leave me much choice.

"Not really but go ahead," I said without conviction, resigned to listen to my brother's ranting.

"It's not *that* bad," Gisela said.

Dec. 9, '42

Dear Ruth,

Dot and I are tickled pink at the prospect of being an aunt and uncle. I don't understand why you went out west on this deal and waited so long to call Dad. He's a broken man without Mother.

As far as adoption is concerned, don't let it happen. If you could only realize how badly we want a child. Dad let me know last week that you're with Gisela again. At least let Dot and me have the baby. We can hold the christening at the Church of the Incarnation. Think about how happy Mother would be about that. We'll raise the child as our own.

Dot and I are with you 100 percent. I mean that. The lone wolf stuff can get tough. You belong here, not where you are. Write me and let me know what you decide to do.

Hal

Gisela held out the letter. I grabbed it and balled it up in my fist.

"How dare he ask for my child? Does he think I'm so stupid, that I can't read between the lines? He acts like he wants to help. All he wants is the baby and me away from you." I tossed the letter into a flowerbed where the hummingbirds and bumblebees were hard at work, moving through the rainbow of flowers still blooming in early December.

"He makes it sound like nothing happened between us, that he didn't break my heart."

Almost losing my balance, I pushed myself off the porch swing and rushed away from Gisela, heading for the back-yard as if I could leave my fury crumpled in the dirt of the garden. Flopping onto the lounge chair I stared at the sky, hands instinctively folded over my unborn child, deep sobs drowning out the afternoon birdsong. My heart longed for the low skies of Minnesota that fit my frame of mind better than the cloudless, never-ending blue of California.

I felt Gisela's hands on my shoulders. "He's not worth it."

I relaxed into her gentle massage and wiped my eyes with the tissues she handed me.

"Come inside. I've made iced tea."

She held out a hand to help me up and led me to the couch. We pushed the magazines aside and put our feet up on the glass coffee table. She'd put a big dollop of honey in the tea, and the sweetness soothed me.

I noticed that Gisela had smoothed the letter out on the dining table.

"That last bit about being with you one hundred percent puzzles me. I wanted to reread it." She thought for a while. "It's not an apology. You're right; he wants you to leave me, and he does want your child."

I set my glass down and stared at the wall across the room.

"He'll never be able to get me home. Even though he thinks our love is wrong, he has no right to separate me from my child."

"It won't happen. If we have to, we can move with no forwarding address and start over."

The thought of having to hide from my own brother made me shudder.

※

I carried both letters on my daily walk to the beach below Coast Boulevard. Kicking off my shoes and digging my toes in the sand, I reread Dad's letter then folded it and put it in my pocket. He seemed to be more worried about Hal than me. Still, the letter was full of his sweetness.

As was happening a lot lately, I started to cry, and a deep sense of missing Dad and Mother washed over me.

I read Hal's letter again, almost hearing his voice, rich and deep, dripping with feigned concern.

Let you care for my baby? Not on your life, dear brother.

"I'd rather bundle the little one up and give him to the nuns," I shouted out to sea.

At the shoreline, I let the saltwater cleanse away the frenzy of my rage through the soles of my feet. I bent over, soaked Hal's letter, and ripped it apart. I rolled each scrap into a ball and tossed them one by one into the receding waves as the water, cool and caressing, splashed up to my ankles. I waited until all the pieces of the letter floated out to sea, carrying bits of my heart in tiny white boats.

Exhausted, I sat down on the sand, staring at the horizon. I remembered Rollie and the deep sadness she still carried so many years after losing her daughter. Would a judge side with Hal against me? With no way to protest against his right to decide, Rollie hadn't fought against her husband, but what about a brother? I trembled at the image of Hal snatching my child from my arms.

I heard Gisela calling and looked up to see her striding toward me, her long legs moving with purpose. I'd known she would soon find me here in my favorite place. She looked good these days—tan and happy, tall and slim, her tawny hair lightened by the La Jolla sun. I couldn't imagine being without her.

She'd changed from the business suit she wore to work into a striped tee shirt and wide-legged trousers. She carried her canvas flats and looked so California, as if she'd lived here all her life.

"What is it? What happened?"

The look on her face and her concern reminded me of the responsibility I'd added to her life, and knew she worried about me, even though she tried to hide it.

"I'm fine. I've just fed the last bit of Hal's letter to the sharks."

She offered me a hand.

"Come on, get up. We'll talk about it at home. You can't just ignore your own brother."

"Yes I can, and maybe I will." I felt stronger, and decided then and there that I would never again talk to Hal.

"That's my girl." She handed me a white cardigan she'd brought for me. "We're in this together, no matter what happens."

I pulled the sweater on over my sleeveless blouse. We held hands as we walked, although I'd looked around to make sure we were alone before doing so. Gisela noticed and said, "It's okay. Sometimes pregnant ladies need a helping hand."

"Funny. I'm not quite there yet."

"I know, sweetie, but soon, just you wait." She gave me a friendly nudge. "I picked up some chopped meat and six eggs. We'll make a meat loaf with those Ritz crackers that went stale and lots of ketchup. It seems to be your favorite these days."

She was right. Nothing else tasted good to me. She'd tried to interest me in other foods, like lamb chops and beefsteak.

"Too greasy," I'd told her.

"And I've got a surprise for you."

"What is it?" My heart swelled with love and gratitude for this woman who could have turned away from me so many times. But, here she was, teasing me with a surprise. I knew it would be something sweet.

"Not until you eat some spinach. I got four cans for fifty cents at Iller's Market. Some kind of a closeout or something."

I wrinkled my nose at the thought of so many cans of spinach, but made no comment. We stood side by side, watching the setting sun light the clouds on fire. I took one last deep refreshing breath of the salt air and followed Gisela, but halfway up the steep climb toward home I needed to rest, so we sat on a bench while I caught my breath for the second time.

"Maybe you shouldn't go down to the beach by yourself."

"No, I'm fine." I didn't want her to worry about me. "It's normal to be a little winded and fatigued near the end of my first trimester." I'd read an article in *Redbook* magazine about the stages I'd be going through.

We reached the gate, but before going in I said, "All the way home I've been thinking about Hal and how I let him bully me for so long. Maybe if I'd been able to stand up to him, I wouldn't have lost him."

❧

Later I stood in the archway between the dining room and the kitchen, watching Gisela work. "Everything still seems to make me weepy."

She turned from the counter, her hands covered with the goop of the chopped meat, eggs, and crackers. Ketchup oozed between her fingers.

"Come here." She folded me into her arms without wiping her hands. I sobbed a few times while she held me.

"Everything's upside down for you." Her eyes were soft and full of love. "You better change that sweater. It's covered with ketchup."

"It's a bloody mess." We both laughed at the handprints that smeared the sweater.

I smiled and blew my nose.

"I'm fine, really I am. I'll set the table."

We settled on the porch swing later that evening with Gisela's surprise—bowls of chocolate chip ice cream. Fog swallowed the ocean except for an occasional light blinking in the distance, a buoy guiding a warship in the dark on its way to homeport in nearby San Diego.

※

We spent Christmas quietly with just the two of us, and I soon began to take my daily walks around the neighborhood instead of alone on the beach. I enjoyed looking at the gardens and Spanish style cottages that lined the streets, usually pausing in front of one not far from our bungalow with a covered walkway crowned in wisteria—its purple blooms hanging low, their perfume still faint in the air. Then I would walk up Eads to take in the panoramic view.

At Pearl, I turned north and down the hill past Mary Star of the Sea Catholic Church. Once a week I stopped in to light a candle for Mother, but had long ago given up on the idea of talking with a priest.

Soon after New Year's 1943, while out on one of my walks, footsteps coming from behind interrupted my thoughts. Turning around, I saw a woman pushing a baby buggy hurrying toward me.

She quickly caught up, and her cheery greeting surprised me. "Hi, I'm Penny. When's your due date?"

"Early June."

She stepped in front of me, looking me up and down. I was wearing a simple cotton dress without a belt.

"Yup, looks like you're right on schedule," she said with upbeat authority. "I'd say it's a boy from the way you're carrying."

Then she pulled back a blue blanket to show me her baby. He was so precious and helpless it brought tears to my eyes, suddenly reminding me of how I'd been putting off calling Duke—unsure of what I really wanted from him, and feeling vulnerable for not having the gumption to decide, I had been avoiding the topic entirely. Now, seeing a baby for the first time since becoming pregnant, I began to feel awful for my failure to act.

I composed myself the best I could, and wanting to be polite said quietly, "He's very sweet. What's his name?"

"Cal. We named him that because he was born in California. We moved here from Texas, then he came along, and a month later my hubby shipped overseas, so now it's just the two of us."

She noticed me wiping my eyes, and started to fawn over me.

"Aw, honey. Don't feel bad. Are you far away from your family?" And without waiting for an answer, she went on. "My mama and daddy haven't even had a chance to meet little Cal. They'll be out next month."

By the time she'd finished, I'd pulled myself together. Embarrassed, I excused myself and hurried home without telling her my name. Meeting her brought up how much I hated the idea of giving birth to a child who wouldn't have a family. What right did I have to keep this child, depriving him or her of a loving mother and father, aunts and uncles?

At home I lay down on the couch and napped until Gisela's key in the lock woke me. She dumped a bag of groceries and several books onto the table.

"Are you all right?" she asked, sitting down on the edge of the couch.

"I'm okay, it's just that my neck hurts and I can't get comfortable."

"I'll put away the food and rub it for you."

Returning with two cups of Earl Grey tea she mentioned in an offhand way, as if it were just an innocent comment, "Jean is finally home safely from France and has invited us to a cookout."

Still feeling threatened by what I felt was Jean's influence over Gisela, I responded with a question that didn't have an easy answer—and which could have consequences for both of us.

"What would you tell everyone about me, about my being pregnant?" I asked, the words almost sticking in my throat.

"That's something we have to decide together. Think about it while I rub your shoulders. We can't hide forever." She grabbed a chair from the dining table, set it down on the porch, and waited for me to come outside.

"It's going to rain," she said. Dark clouds gathered on the horizon. "Southern California's idea of winter."

I wrapped myself in sorrow and thought about how I missed the change of seasons.

While our tea cooled, Gisela rubbed my neck and shoulders. If I didn't join her at the cookout, I risked hurting her. If I agreed to go, I'd have to pull myself together and be prepared for questions. We drank our tea without saying much until she brought up the cookout again.

"It would do us good to get out."

"I'm too big to go out." I hated my puffy face, imagining I looked quite unattractive at the moment, and out of habit patted down my hair that was in need of a trim.

"You're too harsh on yourself." Her eyes matched the clouds that moved closer. "Are you sure you're all right? You seem distracted."

"I wasn't going to say anything. I met a woman today on my walk. She upset me. That's all."

"Tell me about her."

"It was nothing really." Then I told her about Penny.

"I don't get it. She sounds a little overly friendly, but wouldn't you like to have another new mother for a friend?"

"I want to be able to talk about my love in the casual way she talked about her hubby. She's got a whole family." I imagined loving brothers and sisters, along with aunts and uncles, who had been delighted to welcome Cal into the clan.

"We are a family, and we're going to have a new addition."

"It's not the same. What am I going to say to people when they ask about you, that you're my sister or my cousin? I've lost everyone—my mother, my father, my brother."

She didn't respond for a while, and then in almost a whisper said, "I'm trying as hard as I can to make this easier on you. I've lost my family, too. No matter what upsets you, you seem to always find a way to bring up what people will think of us." She turned toward the ocean and watched the waves slam the rocks. "You don't know how much it hurts me."

She left me alone on the porch and I could hear her starting dinner. Going inside a few minutes later I could see she'd set the table and was stirring something on the stove that smelled like chicken soup, and noticed an empty Campbell's can in the sink.

"I'm sorry," I said from the doorway. "I don't want to ruin us again."

She turned around, and I could see she'd been crying. "Must be the onions in the soup." She tried to make a joke, but it came out flat.

"I don't want to be like this. I just don't know how to change."

"How can anything change for us if you don't change? I know we'll always have to hide our truth from our workplace and most of society," she sighed and turned off the stove burner, "but I thought it would be different out here. You'd be more relaxed. But I guess neither of us thought about a baby." She filled our bowls and handed them to me. Sandwiches from leftover meat loaf along with a salad rounded out our meal.

"We're both weary," she said when she sat down. "I'm strong enough to get us through to the birth of your baby, and I want us to be together—but I want you to want us to be together too."

"I do." I hated the cowardly part of me, and *had* been content with our lives, until meeting Penny reminded me of what I didn't have. And I had felt comfortable because we didn't socialize, and my family wasn't around to be hurt by my choice. I tried to explain all this to Gisela.

"It can't always be just the two of us, soon to be three. I have some close women friends here that I've met through Jean's friend Amelia. They'd love to meet you too, and would be thrilled about the baby."

"Do they know?"

"I told Jean. I had to confide in someone. I hope you understand that."

"I know I'm a burden. I'm sorry."

"You're not a burden. Our love for each other is a gift to be cherished."

❧

Even though the next day was Saturday, Gisela left for a meeting before I got up. She kissed me goodbye and said, "Get some more sleep. I'll be home early."

I stayed in bed listening to the rain and thinking about our conversation at dinner. By the time I got up, I knew it was time to call Duke. The threat of losing Gisela again finally overcame my waffling over taking charge of my life. Telling Duke the truth would be my first change.

As I drank a cup of coffee at the dining room table, I could see the telephone staring at me from the corner of Gisela's desk. Finally mustering up the nerve to move across the room to pick up the receiver, I quickly dialed the operator, then waited for the call to go through.

Duke answered on the first ring.

"Duke. It's me."

"Ruth. It's so good to hear from you."

I explained I was living with Gisela in California. "Where in California? I'll be out west in San Diego near the navy base in a month or so. The Army Corps of Engineers is sending me out. I've been through the basic training. I'm a second lieutenant."

I hesitated before responding. I wasn't sure what I had expected, but it wasn't that he too would soon be out here.

"That is, if you want to see me. If not, I'll understand."

I tried to gather my thoughts. Even though what he said had taken me by surprise, it also calmed me, reminding me of how much we meant to each other.

"No. I want to see you. I called because I have some news."

"Are you all right? I've been going on about coming out, and am so excited to hear from you, but I haven't asked how you are?"

I took a deep breath and swallowed my fear. "I'm sorry I didn't call sooner." Then exclaimed without pausing, "I'm pregnant."

"You're pregnant? Are you sure?"

"I'm sure. I've been to a doctor. I'm five months pregnant. There's no mistake about it."

I could hear him sigh.

"Let me think a minute. I'm knocked over with this."

I worried while I waited and finally asked, "Are you mad at me?"

"No. I'm so flabbergasted I can't think. What does Gisela say about it?"

"She's doing much better than I am with it. We love each other and want to keep our child. I'm calling you because it doesn't seem fair that you don't get to have a say in what happens."

"I'm glad you did. Do you remember me telling you about George? I'd just met him before coming to Rose's funeral. We're living together. I finally found that special person."

"That's wonderful, Duke. I don't want to complicate your life, I don't know what I want from you. I'm sorry I didn't tell you sooner."

"Ruth, don't apologize. We're in this together. I know you well enough to know how hard this has been on you. Hard enough that you waited five months to call me. It will all work out."

"Promise?"

"Promise. I won't let you down. I'll call you as soon as the army decides when they're sending me out west. Wait till George hears I'm going to be a father! I'm so excited."

"You're going to tell him?"

"Of course. He knows how much I love you, and what happened between us. We tell each other everything."

"Will he come out with you?"

"He flies out tomorrow to Fort Dix, and then goes overseas. It'll do me good to see you. Just what Doctor George would order, he's been worried about me."

"What will he think about the baby?"

"He'll be thrilled. We both thought it out of the question that we'd ever have a child in our lives. I'm not a religious man, but I think God stuck his hand in this one."

"I'm so glad I told you." It felt like a burden had been lifted from my shoulders. "And I'm grateful you want to be involved, that we'll be able to see each other. I love you."

"I love you too. I'll call next week to check up on you."

For the first time since finding out about the baby, I felt capable of handling it. Now I had both Gisela and Duke for support.

The sun came out in late afternoon, and the rain freshened air boosted my spirits. I met Gisela at the door, kissed her on the cheek, and held my breath.

She looked surprised.

"I thought we'd have an omelet," I said. "And the leftover salad."

"I do look forward to the day you crave something other than bland." She hugged me.

"I called Duke today" I said quietly into her ear, thinking she'd be proud of me, but I felt her stiffen while she waited for me to go on.

"It was hard for me at first. Then he made it easier by wanting to be involved. The army is sending him out to the navy base in San Diego in a month or so. You can meet him."

"What do you mean involved?"

"I thought he might be angry with me, or wonder if he really was the father, but he seemed delighted with the news."

"Did he offer to marry you?"

"We didn't talk about it. He's fallen in love with a man named George, a surgeon."

"I'm relieved to hear that. Now you'll just have to make some decisions about his role as a father."

But then she didn't want to talk about it any more, and went to bed earlier than usual.

TWENTY-SEVEN

Hopeful that Duke's calming presence would soon help me straighten out my life, I urged Gisela to go to the cookout at Jean's house without me.

"It has nothing to do with us," I said. "I'm uncomfortable, my hair is a mess, and I don't want this to be the first impression your friends have of me."

We both agreed it was best.

As she was about to go out the door she kissed me, then paused for a moment before asking, "Are you sure you'll be all right?"

"Don't worry. I'll be fine."

I made my monthly call to Dad after Gisela left and told him about my conversation with Duke.

"Does this mean you'll be getting married?"

"Not yet. He's on his way overseas soon." Someday I would have to tell Dad the truth.

"We'll talk about it when he gets out here. Right now we're both worried about where the army will send him."

"I wish Mother were here. She'd be a lot of comfort to you. We were both scared when she had Hal. By the time you came along, she seemed to have it all under control."

"What about you, Dad?"

"I tried to act strong. I did my best. Mostly a man is useless."

We shared a few more thoughts about Mother, and he ended our conversation with "Hal and Dorothy send their love."

Gisela called around ten o'clock, the time I'd been expecting her home by, but I could barely hear her there was so much laughter and music in the background.

"The party is just getting started," she said over the din. "I'm going to sleep here at Jean's tonight."

I tossed and turned, but couldn't get comfortable all night. Gisela got home about noon the next day and said, "It's a good thing you didn't come. It was raucous until all hours. I had a great time."

I felt hurt she'd stayed out all night, but what could I say? I'd encouraged her to go.

For the next couple of weeks, Gisela often came home late. One night I accused her of ignoring me.

"It's just bad timing," she said. "I know you're not feeling great. Unfortunately, I'm working late most nights for a while, training a group of new hires."

I hated to complain, but snapped one night, exclaiming "You're never home!" Then, realizing how my outburst must have sounded, tried to soften it. "I miss you, and you're always so tired."

"It won't last much longer. I'm getting things solved."

Still feeling hurt, I said "It's every night. I'm lonely." Then I went to the kitchen to heat up the tuna casserole I'd made, but at that point Gisela said, "Oh, sweetie. I've already eaten dinner. I'm so tired I'm going to bed."

❧

The next morning when I awoke Gisela's side of the bed was empty. She must have wanted to let me sleep and was very quiet while getting ready for work. I moped around most of the day, but by late afternoon had bathed and put on a loose cotton dress.

A timid knock on the front door got my attention. I'd been in the kitchen making cornbread muffins to go with canned pork and beans. Gisela had an occasional craving herself, and knowing this was one of them I had convinced myself she would be home early since she'd left without saying goodbye.

A woman holding a baby and wearing flowered pedal pushers with a bright pink blouse peeked through the screen. She could see me standing in the arch between the kitchen and the open door, so I couldn't hide.

"Hellooo," she called. "It's me. Penny."

What on earth is she doing here? How did she find me?

"Little Cal and I brought you some of his old things you can use for your baby. He's growing like a weed."

I invited her into the living room.

"How did you find me?"

"I watched you the other day when you were so upset. I pushed Cal real slow and we followed you here to make sure you got home okay. I thought I'd run into you again, but haven't seen you for days."

I found my manners. "Thank you for thinking of me. I'm Ruth, by the way. I don't think I mentioned that the first time we met."

Penny stepped into the living room and said, "The things are in the buggy. Hold Cal, and I'll go get them." She thrust her son into my arms and turned to go outside.

Half-awake, Cal made a little cooing noise. Spittle burbled through his lips and ran down his chin. He smelled sweet, like talcum powder. I ran my finger over his soft cheek. Feeling a little weak, I sat down at the table.

How can I be expected to know what to do? What if I botch the whole thing up?

"Here you go." She plopped two bags on the table. "My mama and daddy sent so many things that he's outgrown some of the clothes without ever getting to wear them." She reached for Cal. "I'll be so surprised it'll knock me out if you don't have a boy."

I thanked her again and went into the kitchen to put on the coffeepot.

She looked grateful and sat down on the couch.

"I was disappointed I didn't see you again. This neighborhood is too quiet, so few people. Sometimes it seems Cal and I are here by ourselves."

I brought out two cups of coffee.

"I don't have much time."

"I know. I smell dinner. Your hubby coming home soon?"

"No. I'm staying with a friend. My husband's not here."

"Well no wonder you were teary the other day. We're both two lonely peas in a pod. Ray won't be home for months. I might as well not be married." Cal started to fuss and she reached in her bag and pulled out a baby bottle.

"He's formula fed. Ray didn't want to share," she laughed.

I was shocked, and couldn't imagine being so open about sexual intimacy.

She must have noticed my discomfort.

"I'm kidding. It's easier, and it's too old-fashioned to breast-feed. Nobody does it anymore."

I relaxed, watching as Cal took the bottle and looked up at her face with his wide blue eyes.

"Was it hard giving birth?"

"I won't lie. It was no picnic. Soon as I got to hold him though I forgot all the pain. That is after I counted all his fingers and toes." She laughed again, a light cheerful sound. "Bet you're feeling some kicking from your guy, and having trouble sleeping."

I agreed both were happening.

She nodded. "The fun's about to begin."

Penny didn't stay too long. When she turned and waved to me from the gate, I felt a stab of loneliness. Her openness and genuine exuberance was hard to resist.

It might be good to have a friend. I have so much to learn.

I unpacked the clean, neatly folded baby clothes Penny had left. Each outfit looked almost brand new. I couldn't wait for Gisela to get home to ooh and ahh with me over how cute they were.

The oven buzzer went off. I took the muffins out to cool, cleaned the kitchen, and set the table. Gisela would relax over dinner, and later before going to bed I would show her the clothes. Looking forward to things being right between us again, I sat on the couch with my feet up on the pillows and dozed off. By the time I awoke, the sun had set and the sky had melted into the sea, so I got up and pulled the curtains closed.

She'll be here anytime now.

I freshened up and combed my hair, then I lit a low fire under the beans and waited.

Gisela didn't make it home for dinner. I sat alone at nine o'clock and ate the overcooked beans out of the pan, then tossed it in the sink and tried to make excuses for her.

She works so hard. This is tough on her, watching me get heavier and heavier, and I must be so difficult to live with.

But by ten o'clock I was angry. *She should call me and let me know what time she'll be home. How dare she treat me like this?*

Then my anger turned to panic. *I don't know what I'll do without her. What if she's been in a car accident?*

The second she walked in the door I rose off the couch like a madwoman.

"Where were you?"

"It's okay. I'm home now." She tried to console me, but it was too late, I'd lost all reason.

Standing across from her with the table between us, my voice came from a deep empty place that not even

I recognized. It rose and fell as if I were beside myself. My pent-up feelings spilled out irrationally.

"You don't love me anymore. I hate seeing you get dressed every morning and leave. You're just pretending to want us to be a family."

Very much in control, Gisela interrupted me, pulling out a chair and saying with authority "Sit down. This isn't good for the baby."

"Not good for the baby? What about me?" I had no idea I was capable of growling.

"I said sit down. This isn't good for anyone."

"I'm leaving as soon as the baby is born," I said and lowered myself into the chair. "I'll get a job and be out of your hair." I thought I sounded more reasonable. *At least now I'm making sense.*

Gisela shook her head. She studied her fingernails and took a deep breath. She went into the kitchen and got us each a glass of water.

"I'm worn out, Ruth. I can't seem to do anything that makes it okay for us. I can't please you. It's always all about you. Don't you think I have feelings, too?"

That stunned me.

"I just fixed dinner and you didn't show up to eat it," I said. "I've been worried about how hard you work and why you're never home."

"I didn't want to show up for dinner. I didn't know you'd made something. I've stayed away as much as possible to give you time to think about the things I said to you after you ran into that woman on your walk."

"What things?"

"About us being a family and waiting for our third member. About wanting us to be together."

"You're never here."

"It's too painful. You say you've lost your family. So have I. I'll never get to Argentina to see my father and my

half-brothers. I thought I was your family." She looked at
me with sad eyes.

All of a sudden I wanted to apologize, and listened while
she continued.

"I've been working, yes. I've also been spending time
with friends. At first I didn't invite anyone over, because
I didn't want to make you uncomfortable. Now it's me who
is uncomfortable, so I stay out."

"What do you mean?"

She stared at me, maybe wondering what I didn't understand. Or maybe the blank look on her face was indifference.
What she said next shocked me.

"I need someone to be there for me in case Duke wants
to marry you."

"That's not what I want. He's—" She didn't let me finish.

"Why not? It would make your life so much easier. You
wouldn't have to be ashamed of me, of us. I was foolish.
I thought we'd make our own family, in our own way. Now
you have a choice."

I wanted to explain how wrong she was to think I wanted
to marry Duke, but she abruptly left the table. I didn't move
and listened to her undress, use the bathroom, and get into
bed. How could I have made such a mess of things? I'd dis-
graced myself. The indignity of my words fed my despair,
and I didn't want to face her.

We slept that night without touching each other, the gap
between us far greater than the expanse of the sheets.

❧

The next morning I'd gotten up early to fix breakfast, but
Gisela said she wasn't hungry as she poured a cup of coffee
and sat down at the table.

I wanted to make amends for my behavior. "I'm sorry, I
didn't mean to get so hysterical" I said, sitting across from her.

"We both said hurtful things last night," she replied. "I think we should take a break to figure out what we need from each other." She got up, leaving her half-empty cup on the table.

Her calm demeanor terrified me, and dashed any hope I had of making everything all right by apologizing.

I watched silently as she wrote Jean's number on a pad by the telephone and handed it to me.

"How long?" I stammered.

"I'm not sure. I need to sort out my feelings and can't do it here." She looked at the floor, not at me. "Call if you need anything."

She closed the door and left me alone. I couldn't find the energy to do anything but sit on the porch. The day was too bright and too sunny—the sky too vivid. I closed my eyes.

I couldn't think straight. I couldn't comprehend why she was gone. For a long while, I sat outside in a numb stupor, waiting for her to come home. The spray from the waves, smashing the rocks, rose and disappeared over and over again, mesmerizing me. She didn't return.

I finally got up and went inside, but the deathly quiet unnerved me. I tried to remember Jean, and her relationship with Gisela.

Were they lovers? Was I so unlovable that she could throw me away like this?

For two days my anguish kept me agitated. I slept to forget, and the same feverish confusion from my sorority days overtook me.

What if I never see her again?

As my temperature rose, my dreams filled with house fires and firemen holding hoses containing only a dribble of water. Buildings turned to ash. I worried about the baby, and took cool baths in between naps.

With no appetite, I forced myself to eat what I could, mostly a few bites of oatmeal and some canned soup.

More than anything I missed Gisela.

Why doesn't she call? Maybe she feels too horrible to call me.

My fever broke the day Duke's telegram arrived stating he'd soon be in San Diego. I wanted to get my life in order and opened all the windows to air out the house, but without the energy to do any household chores I spent hours in a blur of despair mixed with a desire to make things right.

Gisela had been gone four days and by early evening, unable to stand the torture any longer, I called her.

Jean answered, then handed Gisela the phone.

"I miss you," I said. "I've ruined everything."

"We're not ruined." Her tone was normal, not angry. "You can't keep your heart in a cage forever, and I didn't help by running away."

"Will you come home?"

Gisela arrived within an hour. "This time it's me who was petrified. Afraid you will never believe how much I love you." Holding me tight, she added, "I was jealous that maybe you would want Duke and the baby, and not me—that I'd lose you for good."

We held on to each other until a sharp jab in my side made us laugh. "I think he wants to join the party," I said.

I woke the next morning to the sound of Gisela bustling around the bedroom. "I'm glad you called. I needed a change of underwear," she teased me.

"So that's why you got here so soon. And I thought it was all about me."

Ruffling my hair, she said "Silly you," and lay down beside me. The caress of her hands on my bare skin and her sweet kisses made me feel whole again.

That night while we sat outside waiting for the stars to appear, Gisela wanted to know more about Duke.

As I thought for a moment, not knowing exactly how to answer, a car backfired, startling us both. Its dimmed headlights briefly lit up the yard, and then left us in darkness.

What I did know was that I wanted to honor the love I had for both Duke and Gisela without creating any more misunderstandings.

"We were two thirteen-year-old misfits, deep friends from the beginning, as if we'd each found our other half. Duke was the artist who drew fierce horses in an effort to tame his insecurities and quell his loneliness. And me, I rode Satin Dancer, pushed her to her limits, as if I could outrun the constraints of my life."

Gisela listened without interrupting me.

"We grew up together and were inseparable. Mother adopted him just like she did you. My family loved him. Hal tormented him like a younger brother, and they rivaled each other for attention."

"You weren't romantic?"

"We loved each other and always will. My family loved him too, and hinted that they expected us to marry."

"What about you two?"

"Maybe we both thought it was inevitable, but I never pictured myself in a white dress at the altar."

"But that doesn't answer my question: Were you romantic, like Annabelle and me?"

I watched the stars wander across the sky. The moon had not yet risen.

"No. We were affectionate, kissing and petting. He never pushed me. Not much more than that—until this." I folded my hands over my belly.

Gisela put her arm around me, and pulled me close. "I felt secure in our life until you said he was coming out here. I thought maybe you would want what he can give and I can't—marriage and legitimacy for your baby."

"Duke and I were a convenience for each other, a cover-up for living an inauthentic life even though neither of us was conscious of it. But neither of us wants that now. Everything was quite tidy until I met you."

"Oh. Thanks." This time the poke in my ribs came from her elbow.

"Well, you know how I am—flotsam on a river, wondering how I got to the ocean."

She didn't answer right away.

"I'm not going to let you get away with that. You're not haphazard rubbish floating down a river. You're an intelligent woman who got overwhelmed by our love for each other." She squeezed my hand. "Let's go to bed."

※

Duke called a few days later from Lindbergh Field. "I'll be over soon as I get settled here. I've got three days leave, and then I start a project that will take a month, maybe longer."

"Ask if we should pick him up?" Gisela mouthed. I read her lips and asked.

"No. I'm an officer entitled to wheels. You'll see when I get there."

Handsome in his uniform, he did a double take. "Oh my God. You *are* having a baby. Wow. I didn't know what to expect. You better sit down."

The look on his face made me laugh. "I'm pregnant, not injured. Is that any way to say hello to an old friend?"

He put down the gifts and gave me an awkward hug and a kiss on the cheek.

"I brought some things you might need from the commissary on the base. Milk, eggs, butter, whisky. Stuff like that." He unloaded the bag. "Oh, and some silk stockings one of the guys got on the black market."

"Gisela will like those. She's at work, and won't be home until six."

"Let me look at you." He held me at arm's length. "Beautiful."

"Here, feel." I guided his hand to my swollen belly. "Did you feel that?"

"Oh boy! Did I." He said with a huge grin. "That's him?"

"He's an active fella. Everyone seems to think I'm carrying a boy. Whoa, feel this." I moved one of his hands to each side and the baby seemed to wave and kick at the same time.

"Are you okay? I don't know anything about all of this. I wish George were out here with me. He'd know what to do."

"You must miss him. I wish he were here too."

"I do miss him. I know he would want us to have fun, enjoy this beautiful part of the country despite the war raging overseas. I can just hear him saying, 'You'll be here soon enough. Get to know that baby. Take care of Ruth.' It was a big part of our last conversation together."

It was such a beautiful day, we decided to go for a ride, driving north along the Coast Highway until Duke pulled over and parked on a bluff. We got out and sat on a park bench, watching the high tide roll in at the bottom of a steep cliff.

I took off the scarf I had tied over my head and ran a comb through my hair.

"If I have a boy, I want to name him Daniel after your father."

"I'd like that. We could name him Daniel Peter after both our fathers."

"I'm not sure what last name to use. Gisela's friend Jean offered to introduce me to a doctor who will alter the birth certificate to show I'm married. I guess we'll use my name."

"Daniel Peter Thompson sounds strong and important."

We were interrupted by a car pulling in next to the jeep. A man in military uniform got out and opened the door for a woman. The two walked to the edge of the bluff near our bench, then the man turned to us.

Duke stood, took off his dark glasses, and saluted.

"Good afternoon, captain."

"At ease, lieutenant. Army Corps?"

"Yes sir. Part of the infrastructure project out at Lindbergh. Just got here yesterday."

"You two have a good day. Take care of your pretty wife." The captain looked at me and winked.

Duke hesitated for a moment. "My friend, sir. She lost her husband in Italy."

The captain removed his hat before addressing me. "An honor to meet you, my dear. Please accept my condolences."

"We're so sorry," his companion added. "And you having a baby, poor thing. This war is leaving too many fatherless children."

I had no problem looking sad and too confused to say anything other than "Thank you."

The men saluted again and the couple turned to leave.

"That was horrible to lie like that. So many women really have lost their husbands," I said when we were finally alone.

"Knowing the truth is not the same as telling the truth. Sometimes a lie is safer, and sometimes not saying anything is the safest."

"I don't know. It feels like we're taking advantage of the grief of a family we don't even know. The newsreels are full of such horrific images of the war."

"That's a whole different subject. I protected myself. You can call it selfish if you want." He picked up a handful of stones.

"There's risk everywhere to be known as homosexual, but in the armed service the threat is more imminent. To be accused can lead to arrest, court martial, and dishonorable discharge. There are rumors and jokes about queers being subjected to humiliating interrogation—stripped to their skivvies and forced to answer low-down, scandalous questions for hours."

He walked to the edge of the cliff and pitched a few stones, watching them fall. Turning around he said, "A snitch can be anyone."

Appearing defenseless pitted against the ocean he bent to toss the last stone as if he were still an adolescent skipping a rock on Lake Minnetonka.

It struck fear in my heart to think that Duke might be exposed to abuse from his superiors. He'd been so professional and formal with the captain that it was hard to even begin to imagine.

"How do you manage to cope with all that, and still keep your sanity?" I asked when he returned to the bench and sat down beside me.

"What I've learned about being in the army is that if I do my job and keep my private life private, I won't be harassed. George and I were careful. We socialized openly with friends we trusted, and only in safe places. With casual acquaintances and at work we were just a couple of bachelors sharing an apartment, but it's not as easy as it sounds." Then he broke the somber mood, sounding more like his usual mischievous self. "Two handsome guys like us had to beat away the ladies."

That earned him a punch in the ribs.

"Hey, cut it out. I can't fight back in your condition. Anyway, I'm starving. Let's get something to eat."

We drove farther up the coast to the small town of Laguna Beach, deciding to eat at a restaurant called the Open Door that was across the road from the ocean. As the waiter brought a platter piled high with French fries and fried fish I could hear Gisela say, "It's called fish and chips in England," and really hoped she and Duke would like each other.

❧

Duke and I arrived home in the early evening and ended up sitting on the porch watching a glorious golden sunset, the perfect ending to a lovely day. As darkness fell we decided to go inside, and I went through the nightly ritual of closing curtains. Comfortable on the couch with my feet up on the coffee table, I listened while Duke continued his earlier thoughts.

"It's not a carefree life. It's choices, like with the captain. There was probably no harm in letting him think you're my wife, but I might see him again on the base, so I told him a spur of the moment lie."

"Knowing that, it does make sense."

"If I'd introduced you as my wife, he'd expect us to live in married housing. What if he wanted to invite us to the officers' club for drinks? I'd have to pile on more lies. It's always a dilemma."

What he said made me sad. "It was easier when you and I didn't know any better and drifted along with our college lives, dancing and listening to jazz. Before I met Gisela."

He looked surprised.

"What do you mean?"

"It was easier stepping out on the arm of a man."

"Exactly. I can see now that I used you for a shield too. Even though I didn't know it at the time, the two of us together made it easier for me. I didn't have to figure out my attraction to guys until we were apart."

I heard Gisela at the door and got up to greet her, finally getting to introduce my two favorite people to each other.

"So you're Duke" she said, shaking his hand. "Very glad to meet you, and sorry I'm late. I brought fresh vegetables from the local market to make up for it."

I left them alone while I took a meat loaf out of the oven and made a salad from the iceberg lettuce and tomato Gisela had just brought. Duke poured her a drink and I could tell they were sizing each other up.

I called them to the table, saying with a nervous laugh, "Here we are, a convention of Minnesotans out in California."

Before she sat down, Gisela kissed me on the cheek and whispered in my ear, "Relax. I approve."

"So do I," Duke said.

A short time after eating, unable to keep my eyes open any longer, I excused myself and went to bed.

As I listened to the murmur of the two people I loved talking and getting to know each other, I finally drifting off to sleep.

In my dreams I swam far out, deep down in the water of a clear, calm turquoise ocean. When I came up for air, I saw tiny footprints on the surface, and dove down to see who had made them just as an infant floated toward me, his face full of pure love.

Twenty-eight

Anytime Duke had an overnight pass he slept on our couch. Listening to him explain how he and George navigated their private and public lives, I began to be more comfortable with the idea that I too could learn to live the kind of dual reality he talked about.

One day Duke announced we should have a dinner party. "We need to do something to liven up this place. I make a great beef stew. Why don't we invite those friends of yours Gisela, Jean and Amelia? I'll get the beef at the commissary, and a bottle of wine. It will be tons of fun. I love to cook."

"I can make hors d'oeuvres," I said.

"I'll see when Jean and Amelia are available," Gisela responded, looking over with a tenderness in her eyes that bathed me in love. I felt a movement under my heart, and imagined tiny hands clasping in joy.

The night of the party, Gisela watched while I unwrapped the bouquet of red gladiolus that Duke had brought.

"How beautiful," I said, arranging the long stems in a vase. "How did you get so many?" I wondered if Gisela remembered that she'd placed three stems of red gladiolus on the coffee table the first time I visited her boardinghouse room.

"It wasn't easy. Let's just say with the right connections and some cash, you can get just about anything on a military base. The flowers represent strength of character, my dears. They are special for both of you."

"And I just thought they were pretty." Gisela put her arm around me, and I knew that she did remember.

"I love seeing a man in the kitchen, we smelled your cooking as soon as we got out of the car. The neighbors must be envious," Jean said after Gisela had made the introductions.

My one job, making snacks with crackers and cream cheese, had tired me. Leaving the three of them to help Duke in the kitchen, I took a quiet moment alone on the porch swing. With my swollen feet up on a low stool, I breathed the salt air, the laughter from inside the house making me smile as I relaxed.

Jean opened the screen door.

"Can I join you? Duke's putting on the finishing touches and shooed us all out of the kitchen."

She sat down next to me, and I had to gather the nerve to speak. "Thank you for helping us with the doctor and the birth certificate. It makes all of this so much easier."

"Dr. Rutledge is a good man. I met him in France where we triaged injured victims with the Red Cross. He's seen so much suffering and death that he likes to help. He doesn't ask questions, and only takes money to pay for the normal filing fees."

Neither of us spoke until the sun disappeared, leaving a deep violet and orange blush that blended sky and water.

Jean broke the silence. "Amelia and I were so happy to be invited tonight. Gisela is very special to both of us. I love seeing her having such a good time."

"I've been unable to fully commit to our relationship for far too long. Experiencing how all of you accept me has been a tremendous boost."

"No one blames you for anything. You've jumped over some pretty high hurdles." The ocean below the bluffs was calm, and the only sound was the gentle whoosh of the waves at low tide.

As darkness fell, Gisela came out and lit a few votive candles in ruby-red glass holders she'd placed on the porch earlier.

"Lovely, isn't it?" she said, gazing out at the last bit of disappearing light before leaving us alone again.

"You're brave to let us in, and we're glad you did. It will be wonderful to have a baby in our growing family."

Grateful for the shadowy light of the candles I said quietly, "Thank you. That means a lot to me."

At that moment we heard Duke call from the kitchen, "Dinner's ready."

"Come on. We're being far too serious. Let's join the party." Jean extended her hand to help me out of the porch swing.

"Hold it steady, and I'll push myself up." My growing body was getting harder and harder to move every day.

At the table I enjoyed the conversation, and all the compliments for Duke. "Real butter? You mean it's not Oleo? Pass it please," Amelia said.

"I haven't eaten anything this good forever," Jean said.

Duke beamed. His made-from-scratch buttermilk biscuits, and every bit of the stew, had completely disappeared.

My thoughts returned to the evening, and I had a realization as I drifted into sleep: *It's true, we are a family of sorts.*

※

Penny and I now walked together almost every day. She'd worn me down with her open and infectious enthusiasm. Her husband had been gone for months, and despite her loneliness, she never made a fuss. Since she was from Texas, I told her I'd been a hazer in a rodeo near Abilene.

"I've been to the rodeo outside Abilene many times," she said. "I'd a remembered if I saw you hazing. A woman would've stuck out mighty plain."

"You'd be surprised at the things we can hide."

"Well I guess that's true. I guess there are some things spectators just don't need to know."

She answered all my questions about childbirth, but her biggest contribution was her acceptance of Duke, Gisela, and me.

I had recently decided to risk telling Penny the truth because she'd been so kind and helpful, and I wanted her to be part of our family. When I told her Duke was the father of my baby her jaw dropped, and I held my breath waiting for her response.

"Well I'll be. And you're not planning on getting married. But you're living with Gisela, and he's got a boyfriend. You all have me so confused. If I couldn't see it with my own eyes—" She looked at my bulky body. "I wouldn't know who was having the baby."

She made me laugh with her Texas way of thinking.

"They warned me things are different out here."

"How can you be so accepting of all this?"

"Shoot. That's not hard. You all are the nicest people I've met. Without you I might have died of loneliness." She hugged me, got up to open a bottle of beer, and poured me a small glass. "This'll do you good. Get the gas bubbles popping."

Penny lived above Prospect Street on Drury Lane, in a two-bedroom cottage with lots of space, and felt like she just rattled around in it.

"Daddy bought it for us. He's a rich oilman out in Texas. I'm still waiting for him and my mama to come visit. They've promised to come in late May for Cal's first birthday."

She looked sad for about half a second. "Hey wouldn't that be something if your little guy and Cal ended up born on the same day?"

"I doubt it. I'm not due until the first week in June."

❧

Dad's latest letter sounded sad, and I told Gisela, "I sure don't miss snow in March, but I do miss Dad. He said in his letter there was a huge storm last week, and he hardly ever sees Hal anymore."

Gisela wore her old dungarees from our horse riding days and was planting petunias in pots for the front porch. She wiped a smudge of dirt from her cheek.

"Why don't you invite him out?"

Why not indeed?

Of course I should. California would be a wonderful vacation from the cold weather, but I knew I'd have to explain my life to him, and wasn't sure it was fair not to prepare him somehow.

I asked Duke what he thought about inviting Dad.

"Remember Ruth, there is no rule book. Your dad loves you and needs you now that he is alone. You have to take the chance."

"Even though he took the news about our baby pretty well, I know he still expects us to get married. He knows you're here and might try to persuade you to do the right thing."

"It'll be okay, we can handle it." Duke reassured me and gave me the courage to call Dad.

He was thrilled. "It will be almost like old times, with you and Duke and Gisela. I'll ask Hal if he and Dorothy want to come out too."

I couldn't say no, and when he called the next day and said Hal couldn't make it I breathed a sigh of relief.

❦

Dad arrived in mid April. Duke drove me to the San Diego train station to meet him, remaining with the jeep while I waited on the platform.

As soon as Dad saw me his tired expression perked up, and with a big smile he said, "Oh my Ruthie, looks like I got here just in time."

The scrutiny no longer bothered me, and I twirled around so he could have the full view. "I've still got about two months to go."

"So you think it's going to be a boy?"

"I do. I have it on good authority—a friend of mine, Penny."

Dad took off his overcoat, and as he handed it to me I noticed he wore a wrinkled shirt. Loosening his tie he said, "It sure is hot out here."

"You'll cool off on the ride to La Jolla, Duke's driving an army jeep with no roof."

Duke met us halfway and took Dad's suitcase from him. They shook hands, then embraced with genuine affection. Dad rode up front with Duke and they chatted the best they could over the noise of the jeep's motor.

When we arrived at the bungalow Dad looked around, stared at the view of the ocean, and whistled his joy. "Incredible, Ruthie, I've never seen anything like it."

We sat on the porch drinking iced tea until Gisela arrived home from work. Dad gave her a big hug and said with a laugh "At least I can still get my arms around you!"

"Are you nervous?" Gisela asked me when Duke had taken Dad to his hotel to wash up and rest before dinner.

"So far everything's fine."

Duke returned before too long with Dad, who was now wearing a fresh shirt without a tie. We relaxed in the backyard where hummingbirds were flitting around the flowers, their iridescent feathers catching the sun.

"You two have a lovely place. At home, the cold winters and my rheumatism don't get along. Looks like an early spring here."

"There's no real spring in Southern California. The flowers are almost always in bloom, and these little guys are with us all year round," Gisela said, pointing at the hummers.

"It's easy to get used to, Dad. And there's no old, dirty snow still on the ground in April."

"Even the summers are mild here, most of the time," added Gisela.

"And the company's great," Duke said, turning from the hamburgers he was cooking on the outdoor grill.

"Sounds like you kids are ganging up on me," Dad protested with a smile.

After Duke's terrific dinner he and I worked at cleaning up in the kitchen, leaving Gisela and Dad out on the front porch.

"You know what your dad told me?" Gisela asked later as we were getting ready for bed. "He said it was good to see you and Duke together again. Then he said that he and Rose always thought the two of you belonged together." She stopped and took a deep breath.

"I'm sorry, we should have guessed he would bring that up, but I thought I had made it clear to him that we are not getting married."

"That's not what he meant. He also said, 'But I know that it's you who means the most to Ruth, because Rose told me.'"

I suddenly felt the need to sit down.

"I asked how she knew. He guessed it was mother's intuition. He said neither of them knew how to say anything, and they didn't understand exactly what it meant, but they loved us both."

"This is a lot to take in," I said, trying to compose myself. "I'm shocked both Dad and Mother knew. Can you imagine how different things would have been if we'd known how to talk to each other?" I couldn't help myself and dissolved into tears. Gisela held me until I finally fell asleep.

❧

The next morning, Dad made us French toast with bacon that Duke had brought from the commissary while I gathered my thoughts about what Gisela had told me the night before. We finished eating, and I finally found the nerve to say, "Gisela told me that you and Mother knew about us."

We were out on the porch, and Dad looked out toward the ocean. "Hal told your mother, but I didn't tell Gisela that. He told her you were disgracing our family. I don't agree with him. He's wrong."

"I'm sorry you heard it from Hal and not from me. I was confused and couldn't figure out how to tell you." I didn't have the heart to say anything in that moment about the accusation Hal had made after Mother's funeral.

Dad stood up, tapped his pipe on the porch rail, filled it with fresh tobacco, then clenched the stem in his teeth. The only sounds were the constant movement of the waves in the distance and the scrape of a wooden match against the sole of his shoe. He smoked for a while without saying anything.

"It must have been hard for you and Mother. You must have been hurt by what he said."

He sat down, took the pipe out of his mouth, and set it in the ashtray. "We were mixed up. Not sure what to think. Why Hal would want to tell Mother and not me. Why he would say such a thing before you decided to tell us." He picked up his pipe and struck another match to relight it. Exhaling, he said "We both loved Gisela."

"What did Mother say about Hal?"

"We didn't talk about it much. Mother and I always looked forward to the dinners at your apartment. She wanted the whole family together—it was the answer to her prayers. You know that."

He paused to light his pipe again, then continued. "Hal only mentioned it that one time. Mother worried about you, and I don't think what Hal said made any difference, although she was upset about Gisela moving out west and wanted both of you to be happy."

I couldn't help myself and started to cry. Dad patted my shoulder, sitting down beside me.

"I've seen a lot in my life," he said while I buried my head in his chest. "Lived through the Great War, and now we're at it again. Family is all I've got, and I'm including Duke and Gisela. I'm hoping this baby will make Hal realize what he is missing by holding onto his judgments." Then I noticed his eyes had also filled with tears. We sat together for a while, but after a few minutes my body felt the need to move, so I went inside to do the breakfast dishes.

Dad followed me in, and leaning against the frame of the archway said quietly, "The most important thing you have to remember is how much your mother loved you."

"I never doubted that." I tried to control my tears.

He came over and put his arm around me. "Now, now, everything will be all right," he said in the same way Mother would console me when I was upset.

I leaned on his shoulder and blubbered, asking him to stay until the baby was born.

"Of course I'll stay. I don't want to miss my grandchild's birth."

He decided to rent a room in a house nearby, and often took walks with Penny and me.

"I love your dad," she said on one of the days he didn't join us. "You're so lucky to have him out here with you."

Cal's birthday had passed, but she still hadn't heard anything from her parents about their plans to come out to visit.

❦

The morning of June third, I woke at four a.m. Too uncomfortable to stay in bed and full of energy, I quietly cleaned out all the kitchen cupboards while Gisela slept. She left for an early meeting at seven, saying "Call me if there's any news."

I'd been feeling some abdominal pressure every once in a while for a couple of days, but Penny had convinced me it was normal. "Your body's getting ready."

At eight o'clock that morning, I winced with my first contraction and called Penny to describe the housecleaning and everything I was feeling. She said "Yup. I'd say your time could be today. That burst of energy is common. Get ready to go to the hospital."

Dad had agreed to take me to the hospital if Gisela was at work when my time came. He arrived around eight thirty for our morning routine of coffee, breakfast, and a leisurely walk.

I sat at the table while he scrambled eggs, but couldn't eat any of what he served me. "I'm feeling kind of funny. I think I'll have a glass of milk instead of coffee."

"You should eat something. You're pushing your food around without taking a bite," he said.

"There's something I didn't tell you" I began, feeling the need to let Dad know about Hal's accusation so there wouldn't be anything left unsaid before giving birth.

I rocked back and forth to comfort myself, folding my arms over my stomach. *I have to ask. This might be my only chance.* I took a deep breath and let it out slowly. "Dad, do you think Mother died because of me?"

He looked startled, as if he couldn't believe what I'd said. "What makes you say that? She had a heart attack and drowned."

"The day after her funeral, Hal accused me of breaking Mother's heart. He implied that she might have taken her own life because of me." I sat up straight, my hands in what was left of my lap. "Actually, he accused me of causing her death."

"So that's what happened between you two? I would've never dreamed he'd do something like that." He filled his cup and sat beside me. "No, Ruthie, she never felt that way about it and would never have done any such thing. That's preposterous. There's no truth to it. She knew, and she loved both of you. Hal's wrong on this all the way around."

Twenty-nine

I forced down my eggs and pushed the plate away. A sharp pain doubled me over while Dad watched with concern. "I'm glad you told me about Hal. He'll have to find his own way in all this. Right now you need to take care of yourself. Tell me what I can do to help."

His acceptance calmed me and I explained, "Well it's not time quite yet. My contractions started yesterday, but they are getting stronger." Then I repeated what Penny had said about all the signs indicating that labor would soon begin.

We left for our walk, but my contractions got stronger, so we returned home. I decided to take a shower and while drying off, my water broke.

"Dad," I yelled from the bathroom. "It's time. The baby is coming."

"I'm right here, Ruthie," he said through the door. "Don't worry, we'll get you to the hospital."

"Dad, call a taxi." *Don't worry?* I put on my bathrobe.

He was dialing the phone as I came out of the bathroom, and while I dressed, the contractions returned with excruciating pain. I knew I should be timing them, but all I wanted to do was get to the hospital.

Grabbing my packed duffel bag, and frightened by the pain, I cried out "Oh my God. Did you tell him to hurry? Did you call Dr. Rutledge?"

The taxi arrived within five minutes. Dad held my hand during a ten-minute ride to the hospital that felt like an eternity, doing his best to reassure me as I nervously peppered him with questions.

"Dad, I'm afraid. What about the doctor? We have to call Dr. Rutledge. And Gisela." I'd forgotten to tell him to call her. *What if she doesn't know?* "Did you call Gisela?"

"It's all taken care of. We're here now," he said in his everything-is-all-right voice. "Gisela is on her way. She's trying to get in touch with Duke."

In the hospital, I undressed and got on the exam table. The nurse had let Dad come in the room with me, and he held my hand until she sent him away.

It hurt worse than anything. I wanted Gisela. The same nurse let her in for a few minutes, but then made her leave too.

"Relax, dear, everything is just fine," the nurse said, giving me a wet washcloth to bite down on and closing the door as she left the room.

I wailed, holding the washcloth over my mouth, wanting more than anything to scream at the top of my lungs. The nurse came back into the room, and without even attempting to console me said "The doctor's on his way, why don't you try a different position so you won't be so uncomfortable?"

"I'm trying. It's not working," I moaned as she turned to leave again.

"Is the baby all right?" I didn't want her to go. What if I'd hurt him, doing all that moving and stretching this morning? *Dear God, Please let me have a healthy baby.*

"Everything is fine" she repeated, abandoning me again. The contractions came regularly, with each one amplifying the pressure and increasing the pain. *I could die here, and no one would know.* The room closed in on me, and this time I did scream, but no one answered. *Where is everybody?* I wanted Gisela. I wanted Duke. I wanted Dad. I whimpered, then screamed again in the closed room. The nurse finally came in and sat down with me, encouraging me to breathe in order to help the baby.

Then Dr. Rutledge appeared, holding a syringe.

"I'm going to stop your pain. Everything is fine and you're doing a great job. Soon you won't feel a thing."

"Is the baby okay?"

Examining me he said, "Your baby is in perfect position and ready to make his appearance." His words were the last thing I remembered until the nurse woke me up.

"What happened?"

"It's a boy. A healthy eight pounds. Do you want to see him?"

A few minutes later she handed me little Daniel.

"Hello, Daniel Peter Thompson. Welcome to the world."

I kissed his forehead, counting while I caressed each finger and toe, and then gazed into his blue eyes. Perfect.

Gisela arrived and said, "He's beautiful." No other words were necessary. Her love surrounded us.

I removed Daniel's newborn cap to show off his mass of wavy blondish red hair, and when the nurse reappeared asked to unwrap the swaddling that encased his little body so I could touch all of his skin.

"Not now," she said. "I'm going to take him to the nursery in a few minutes. And you'll have to leave then too, miss."

Gisela scowled at the nurse's back as she left the room. "Dr. Rutledge says everything is fine with both of you. I've left a message for Duke, so you have nothing to worry about." Bending down to kiss me she added, "We'll get you home tomorrow."

While the brush of Gisela's kiss still remained on my lips, I looked into Daniel's open eyes and whispered "You have a family, my little one. I promise." I held him close, the two of us breathing quietly together, dozing on and off, until the nurse arrived to whisk him away.

Alone in the room, I felt hollow until I remembered the dream I'd had the night Duke and Gisela finally met. I closed my eyes and let the image of an infant swimming under the sea fill me. In that moment, I embraced the meaning of pure love and fell into a deep, contented sleep.

❧

During the christening party the house overflowed with people—Gisela had invited all her friends. Some knew our story, some didn't, but it didn't matter to me anymore. They all cared about Gisela, and now Daniel, Duke, and I would be included in their circle too. Gisela and I sat on the porch swing as one by one our guests met Daniel and congratulated Duke, who beamed with pride.

The proud granddad bustled around making sure everyone had refreshments, handing out Dutch Masters cigars to those who wanted them. When the cigars were all handed out, he picked up a Kodak box camera that Hal had sent him and snapped some pictures.

I noticed Penny sitting alone on a blanket watching Cal, and handed Daniel to Gisela before going down to see how she was because she had recently learned that her parents couldn't make it out from Texas for Cal's birthday as planned. "Daddy's got a bunch of new cows or something. I don't think they'll ever have time to come out here," she'd sobbed. "They're always too busy."

Now, sitting down beside her, I told her we had a surprise for Cal as I motioned to Dad to bring over the tricycle he'd found at a secondhand store, fixed up, and painted a bright shiny blue. As he brought the trike down to the lawn where we were sitting, he rang the bell on the handlebars and got Cal's attention right away.

"He'll be tearing around on it in no time," Dad said, as Penny startled him by throwing her arms around him to thank him.

"There. There." He reassured her as he'd done for me so many times.

Cal held on to the tricycle as if he had owned it forever. While I reveled in Penny's big smile and graceful acceptance of Dad's gift, I realized her friendship had taught me there would always be people that would love me no matter what. Her life had looked so perfect the first day we met and I had envied her having a husband and father for Cal, and parents in Texas longing to meet their grandchild—never dreaming it would be me who would need to bolster her.

I waved to Gisela, who blew me a kiss then leaned down, cooing to Daniel. Party chatter drifted across the lawn as Duke wandered over and sat beside us on the blanket.

"Hey, big guy. Want to try out your new wheels?" Duke picked up Cal, who squealed with delight, and placed him on the seat. Pushing him around in a circle, Duke held him to make sure he was safe.

It was only a few minutes until Cal called "Mama" and Penny took him up to the house, leaving Duke and me alone. He sat down beside me, then reached into his breast pocket and took out an envelope.

"I got a letter from George. It took more than a month to get here." He unfolded the crinkly lightweight stationery used for overseas airmail, smoothing it out carefully. We leaned on each other, shoulder to shoulder, as he read a portion of it to me:

Bougainville, Papua New Guinea
April 25, 1943

. . . My surgery room is behind front lines, an underground bunker. Such beauty surrounds

*us, the sea, clear skies, palm trees. The contrast
with the devastation is ghastly. We patch up the
wounded and lose too many.*

*Different times. Different circumstances. It
would be a paradise to share.*

"It's hard to bear," Duke said, choked up and unable to continue reading. "We can never write anything too affectionate or personal, since the overseas armed services mail is read and censored. We have to trust it's there between the lines." Duke wiped his eyes.

The early evening cast a shadow over the front yard. Gisela and most of the guests had moved inside, while Dad sat on the swing rocking Daniel with Penny beside him cuddling Cal.

Duke concentrated on tugging at a dandelion in the grass. "Got my orders late yesterday, I ship out tomorrow."

We'd known it would be any day now, since he'd finished his work at Lindbergh a week ago. A solemn silence fell between us while the enormity of his leaving sank in.

❧

The party ended, and although most of the other guests had gone home Gisela, Jean and Amelia, Dad, Penny, and I sat inside with Duke—we'd come together in our own way, this misfit family of mine.

"It's time," Duke said. "I've got to go."

I walked out with him, holding Daniel in my arms. Neither of us bothered to hide our tears as Duke promised to write and let me know where he landed.

"I love you both. All of you," he said, indicating the group on the porch. "Thank you, for letting me be a dad. Your love and Daniel, along with George, will get me through whatever happens overseas."

I held Daniel to my shoulder while Duke enfolded us in his arms. All too soon, he let go and kissed us both. "This is it," he said, touching my cheek. He turned one last time at the gate to wave, then slid into the jeep and sat for a moment staring out to sea before starting the motor. Lifting his hand in a final farewell, Duke slowly turned down Eads Avenue and vanished into the distance on the Coast Highway.

Gisela was waiting at the door to hold Daniel and me. In her embrace, I remembered what Mother had said during our first trip to Montana to meet her brother. "A family is held together by all parts of its whole, even when a part is missing." Now I wanted to add: "It's that, but it's also love and sharing truth without shame."

What if all the missing parts of my family—my uncles, Aunt Margaret, cousin Chloe and, of course, Hal and Dorothy—would join us in love and acceptance? I felt the weight of their absence, not in shame as in the past, but as a profound loss.

THIRTY

Things were pretty dreary after Duke's departure. One Monday morning, not long after he'd shipped out, I was washing diapers and feeling blue as Dad watched from his usual spot in the archway. "You look kind of down. How'd you like some good news?" he asked.

"What?" I said still running rinsed diapers through the wringer into a basket. "You offering to hang these on the line for me?"

"Better than that I hope. You know how you and Gisela are always hinting about me staying out here?"

We'd been trying to figure out the best way to convince him to stay, and as often as we could, said how happy we were that he was with us. Although he helped out almost every day, doing odd chores around the house and some light gardening, best of all was how he'd thrived in the last couple of months. He now walked with a spring in his step, wore khaki trousers with an open neck shirt instead of a suit, and told me his tan was the result of having joined a group of guys too old to go to war who swim every day in the cove.

"I'm thinking of selling the house in Minneapolis and staying out here."

"Oh, Dad!" I shouted as I let the diapers slip back into the rinse water. "That's the greatest news, I really don't know what we'd do without you! It's what we've been wishing for."

"Hal's going to help out and take care of the details on his end," he added after I'd calmed down.

"Wait until Gisela hears. She'll be thrilled." And then I began to sob. "I was so afraid you'd leave, and Daniel would never know you."

He put his arms around me and said soothingly, "I didn't mean to make you cry."

"I'm just so happy, Dad. I can't help it. This will make missing Duke easier. It will make everything easier."

Within a month he found a nearby apartment to rent and bought a 1935 Ford Coupe that he fixed up and now had running smoothly.

Not long after, I heard Dad's car working its way up the hill. He was already at the gate, struggling to hold a high chair while opening the latch with one hand, before I could get down to help him.

"I got it at a church bazaar. Sanded it and painted it red, white, and blue in honor of Duke and George's service." He'd even painted the Stars and Stripes on the tray.

"It's just precious, Dad." I gave him a hug.

"I brought something else too." He took an envelope out of his pocket and handed it to me. "It's a letter from Dorothy. You better get us both a cup of coffee and then sit down. It's full of what I've been praying for."

The letter, five pages long, written with black ink on light pink stationery, felt heavy in my hand. Dorothy's handwriting looped and sprawled on both sides of each page as if the words had spilled onto the paper rather than being carefully placed there.

Lake Minnetonka
September 3, 1943

Dearest Dad,
   Thank you for the photos of Daniel's chris-
tening. He is a beautiful child. Ruth looks happy
and healthy, and so do you and Gisela. Duke is
handsome in his uniform. It means so much to
us to be included in the joy of having a child in
the family . . . .

I stopped reading and put the letter down. "I didn't know you sent them pictures of all of us."

"I did. I went down to the drugstore and ordered prints of all the photos. I sent them to Uncle Edward and Uncle Michael too. I hope you don't mind." Dad examined his shoes.

I felt so fortunate to have Dad's full support that I couldn't get angry. I stood and looked out the window, gathering my thoughts.

"It's just that I haven't yet decided what to tell people who don't know the whole story. Now I'm concerned they'll all be wondering about me, since I'm not married," I finally said.

"Well I'm proud of you, and wanted to help. I can understand not telling the whole world about your life. Family is different. They can't just turn away from love"

"I think it was sneaky of Hal to send you the camera," I said. "I'm still trying to decide how I feel about him."

"Read the letter. I think you'll change your mind."

Daniel chose that moment to let out a wail from the bedroom where he'd been napping.

"I'll feed him. You curl up over there on the couch and read. I've got all day." He walked down the hall to fetch Daniel and I returned to the letter.

. . . Ruth's chosen an unconventional life to live,
having a child without the sacrament of marriage.

Hal and I are heartbroken that we cannot have
children and grateful that Ruth did not choose to
let Daniel go to adoption. We have prayed together
for acceptance of Ruth's choice so that we can be
allowed to embrace our flesh and blood nephew.

Dad held Daniel while he tested the heated formula on his wrist, and then settled into the overstuffed armchair with his feet up on the ottoman. Daniel, now content, quietly looked into his grandfather's eyes as he sucked on the bottle.

"Did you ever feed me like that, Dad?"

He shook his head. "No. You get your second chance with a grandchild. I let your mother do it all alone. I was too busy commuting to Minneapolis and building my business."

For the next few minutes I continued reading about the news from home, then sitting up straight when I read:

. . . I'm really writing for Hal. He's remorseful and
overflowing with guilt. He confessed everything
to me and to our priest. It tore me apart to learn
that he felt such disdain for Ruth and chose to hurt
her without considering the consequences. Now
he is repentant and wants Ruth's forgiveness. He
knows he's hurt all of us with his bad judgment.

"This is a lot to take in, and I'm still not sure how I feel." Putting down the half-read letter I watched as Daniel finished his bottle, burped loudly, and fell asleep in Dad's arms.

"We hold Hal's future in our hands," Dad said. "And whatever you decide to do will also affect this little guy." He stood up and handed Daniel to me.

I couldn't finish reading the letter right then since I was expecting Penny to come by any minute to talk about caring for Daniel. Gisela had been correct, the University of California, San Diego needed a psychology instructor for graduate level students. I'd applied for the low paying, part-time position to get reacquainted with being at work, and had been hired.

Penny arrived right on time, and Dad said "Why don't you two go out and have lunch down in the village? I'll watch the little ones."

But Penny looked worried. "You sure? Cal's a handful. He went straight from crawling to running, and hasn't slowed down yet."

"We'll be fine" Dad reassured her, and took Cal's hand.

"Come on, buddy, let's go look for worms."

I put Daniel in his playpen in the shade under the Torrey pines. Cal waved at Penny, then ducked under a hydrangea bush in full deep-purple bloom. Clutching a bright yellow plastic pail and a red shovel, he went right to work.

"This will be fun," Dad said as he bent down to Cal's level.

It felt good to get out of the house for a while. Penny and I walked down to a hut on the beach and ordered crab sandwiches.

We ordered our food and sat at a wooden table facing the ocean. "Things are changing for us too," Penny said. "Ray is coming home soon, and we're staying out here. His specialty is fixing those big bomber planes, and the army's keeping him at Lindbergh."

She could hardly contain her excitement. "I hope you'll like him."

I could tell it was hard for Penny to concentrate on making the arrangements to watch Daniel on Tuesdays and Thursdays, so we quickly agreed I'd pick him up by six or six thirty and didn't dally, returning home within an hour.

Dad watched Cal running ahead of Penny on the sidewalk as they headed home, his bucket swinging at his side.

"She's right, that one's a handful. I'm tired, think I'll go home for a nap."

After waving goodbye I picked up Dorothy's letter, settled outside on the chaise lounge, and this time read it all the way through twice, noticing how much it threw me off balance when she mentioned they wanted to come out to La Jolla.

Keeping an eye on Daniel while trying to absorb the meaning of everything Dorothy had said, I mulled over the idea of she and Hal visiting, not moving from the lounge until I heard Gisela come home from work. After greeting each other, I handed over the letter with a simple "It's from Dorothy." She took my place and began reading while I gathered Daniel and went inside.

By the time Gisela joined us in the living room, I had fed Daniel and settled him on a blanket with his favorite toy, a soft green pony with yellow mane and button eyes.

"I've read it over and over, and I'm stunned." Gisela looked thoughtful as she carefully folded the letter. "Dorothy's laid it all out. Hal seems to have had a change of heart, and now it is up to you. What do you think?"

I didn't answer right away. My heart was filled with love, sitting next to Gisela and listening to Daniel coo to his toy. I should have felt safe, but my old fear rose and caught me off guard.

"He's been working on changing, but I haven't. I've been holding my lack of forgiveness close so I won't give in and grovel, begging him to love me like a brother should."

I couldn't sit still and began pacing from the living room to the hall and back, my armpits wet with perspiration.

"I hate being afraid of my own brother," I said remembering that horrible day at the roadhouse, Hal's drunken words, and finally his tears. "What if he tries to take Daniel away from me? I know I have the birth certificate, but what if he tries to say I'm not fit to raise my own child?"

"He can't do anything like that," Gisela said. "We're all here to support you."

Daniel whimpered and I bent to pick him up. "How am I supposed to believe what Dorothy says? It could be the first step in a plot to steal Daniel. Hal needs to do more than just claim he's had a change of heart to convince me he can really accept us and our choices."

"I don't think you heard me. You're not alone this time." We sat close, our shoulders touching while I rocked Daniel in my arms.

"Maybe your dad shouldn't have taken things into his own hands and sent the photographs, but I'm glad he did. Not standing up to Hal is the main thing keeping you from taking charge of your life. Let them come. If necessary, we'll deal with Hal as a team this time."

※

A week later, I'd made sure Daniel was fast asleep and then joined Gisela on the porch. Honeysuckle, oleander, and roses perfumed the night. A gentle breeze moved the scented air and Gisela said, "If I'd been able to make friends with Monique, I might have had a chance to meet my half brothers. Now they're lost to me."

Hearing the sadness in her voice, I remembered the good times with Hal, how he'd so often been responsible for me as a child when Mother had her headaches. How he'd taken me hiking, and had taught me all about nature. That was the uncle I wanted Daniel to have. Not the critical Hal who had turned against me. No wonder I had such mixed feelings!

"Let's invite them. I'm beginning to understand what you said about forgiveness being an unloading of a burden. I want to see for myself if he is truly sorry, or if he simply eased his own conscience with his confessions."

❧

I felt a spasm of nervousness about seeing Hal for the first time in more than a year as he and Dorothy stepped off the train. I'd been both dreading and looking forward to seeing him, and now here he was. *What if he really hadn't changed?*

While Dad waved and hurried to greet them, I stayed behind. Dorothy reached me first, grasping both of my hands and kissing me on the cheek. Hal stood behind her. I'd expected him to look sickly, pale, and older, but he was almost the Hal I remembered—slightly older, yet appearing quite fit in his beige linen suit.

"Hi sis."

Neither of us seemed to know what to do next, so Dad took charge.

"Come on Hal, help me get your luggage. Ruth, you can take Dorothy to the car."

The mild fall weather complemented the splendor of the scenery along the Pacific Coast Highway. Hal and Dorothy were enchanted with the beauty of La Jolla—and by the ocean neither of them had ever seen.

We arrived home in about forty-five minutes to find Gisela and Daniel cooling off on the porch in a lazy sea breeze, he lying on his tummy in the playpen, she reading a book.

Wearing a light cotton dress bursting with flowers, hair hanging loose over her shoulders, Gisela stood and picked up Daniel as we all got out of the car. She met us at the gate and handed Daniel to me, then shook Hal's hand as she said a warm hello to both he and Dorothy.

I introduced aunt, uncle, and nephew to each other before asking Dorothy to hold Daniel so I could go inside to help Gisela. From the kitchen I could hear both Hal and Dorothy telling Dad how wonderful it was to finally meet Daniel.

Over lunch Hal wanted to know all about the different flowers, the Torrey pines, and the hummingbirds. The return of his boyish curiosity encouraged my hope that he had truly changed.

We finished eating and Dad volunteered to take the weary travelers to their hotel so they could rest. "I'll bring them back around six."

"That was painless" Gisela said after they left, sighing with relief.

❧

The next day Hal asked if he could take me out for lunch, and nothing could have surprised me more. He must have read my expression because he declared, "I'm not the same guy, you'll be safe this time."

I told Gisela about the invitation. "Have him take you to La Valencia, and listen carefully to everything he says. He seems sincere about being a proud uncle, always cooing and making Daniel laugh."

"I've also noticed he is much gentler with Dorothy, not so critical." And because I no longer felt tense in Hal's company, I began to wonder if remorse and confession really had changed him.

"Dorothy is a dear, so in love with Daniel that it makes me hurt inside for her. You'll be fine with Hal."

The bird of paradise flowers on the veranda of La Valencia kissed the sun. Palm trees in pots and umbrellas on the tables shaded the diners. Gisela had called for a reservation and booked the most desirable table in the corner just above the cliff. Below, the ocean, deep blue and dappled with sunlight, splashed on the rocky shore.

"If beauty could cure . . ." Hal didn't finish his sentence. He looked out to the horizon with awe on his face.

I suggested we order the Crab Louie salad. "It's a specialty here. You'll like it."

While we ate, we chatted about Daniel and life in California.

"I love it out here and am hoping to be offered an associate professorship at the university by next year. I wasn't sure I'd like teaching at this level, but it's both a challenge and enjoyable," I explained.

While we lingered over coffee, without warning, Hal started his apology. "I said I'm a different guy, and I mean it." He didn't flinch. "Telling Mother about you and Gisela was vindictive and evil."

He let that sink in and then continued.

"I was only thinking of myself that day at the roadhouse. All that mattered to me was how terrified I was that I might have pushed Mother over the edge." He sounded sincere.

"And I wanted it to be your fault." As he took a sip of water the sun reflected in his glasses and I couldn't see his eyes, so I braced myself for what he might say next. Putting down his water glass he shifted slightly in his chair, making the glare disappear, and I could see a softness and vulnerability in his hazel eyes. "I am sorry, and will do everything I can to make it up to you."

"What made you do it?"

He didn't sugarcoat his actions.

"I was ambitious and narrow minded. I convinced myself that what people said about you could hinder my career." His eyes were moist with unshed tears. "I thought it was wrong. You and Gisela together."

He stopped talking, and the screech of gulls filled the air as I focused on the horizon where a flock of pelicans drifted above the surface of the water in perfect formation.

"Ah hell, Ruthie, I've always envied you—your guts and your brains." He took off his glasses and wiped his eyes. "Even as a kid, you had more spunk than me. It ate me up that you were so great with Satin Dancer by the time you were eight or nine."

I didn't want to make it easy for him.

"What about Mother? Why not just hurt me if you felt that way?"

"I wasn't rational. I acted selfishly out of ignorance. I convinced myself she had to know for her own good."

"One reason your bigotry hurt so much is that I've loved Gisela with all my heart for years. It is only recently that I've been able to take true pride in our love, and have stopped letting everyone else's opinion influence how I live my life."

Hal turned sideways in his chair and crossed his legs. I could tell I'd made him uncomfortable and waited for his response.

"I've got two more weeks to convince you I've changed."

But I didn't want to wait to see if his actions would uphold his words, and needed him to know my feelings.

It took all the courage I had to speak of my worst nightmare. "There are two things I want to be clear about, so that you absolutely understand. I deeply love Gisela, and Daniel will be raised in our home as our son."

He didn't hesitate.

"I understand. I was blinded by my prejudice toward you and Gisela. Now that I'm here and see the two of you with Daniel, I can say that the only other place I've experienced such absolute love is with Mother." He wiped his eyes again. "I know now she loved us both no matter what."

I waited while Hal paid the bill, then suggested we walk home along Coast Boulevard.

"You must be curious about Duke," I said when we stopped to admire the view.

"I admit I am confused on that one, Ruth, but figure it's none of my business. I can sure see him in Daniel's face." He paused and continued. "Dot and I will be so grateful to be part of Daniel's life that nothing else matters."

I decided not to tell him about Duke and George. *What would it accomplish?*

"Duke and I have a special relationship. I will always love him, and he will always be involved in our lives" was all I said.

※

Penny's husband, Ray, called from the naval base in San Diego to let her know he'd arrived from overseas.

"He's here," she sputtered into the phone to me. "He didn't know when it would be, so he didn't bother to mention a time in his last letter."

I waited for her to calm down, and we arranged for Dad to drive her and Cal to pick him up, otherwise he would have to wait another day for army transport to La Jolla. She could barely contain herself.

"You all are so good to me. Cal was two weeks old last time Ray saw him. I don't want to wait an extra minute."

I let them settle in for a few days and then invited Penny to bring Ray over for a cookout.

"We'll be there," she said. "When I told him about you and Gisela, he said he couldn't wait to meet you. Maybe he thinks you might have two heads or something, but I set him real straight. He knows you are the only people I'd met out here that I can call friends."

"We're all learning how to accept our lives as they are. I'm glad you're coming." I knew it was a gamble inviting Ray, but didn't want to alienate Penny by not including him.

"He's got some of that Texas attitude, but he's a good learner." I admired her honesty, and had hoped he wouldn't forbid her to associate with us. The last thing I wanted was to risk losing her friendship.

On the day of the cookout, Dad brought the grill to the front lawn and lit it as if he'd been in California all his life. We could hear Cal saying "bugs, bugs" and Dad suggesting that Hal and Ray help him to look around under the bushes. The next thing we knew the two of them were on their hands and knees with Cal, who squealed each time he found an earwig or an earthworm.

"It's my fault," Dad laughed when Gisela brought beers down to rescue the bug patrol. "I showed Cal how to dig for earthworms, and now he prefers chasing the crawly critters to playing with his toys."

Dad finished grilling the hamburgers while the sunset lit glowing embers across the sky. The clouds blazed in varying hues of orange and red that lingered until well after the sun had dropped from sight and the sky faded to deep lavender.

We gathered inside to eat. Ray turned out to be a quiet man, reluctant to talk about his experience overseas.

"I'm lucky to be a mechanic. It kept me behind the scenes and not too close to the front" was all he would say. "It's good to be home. This is the best barbecue I've had since Texas."

"Don't you just throw the whole cow on the spit?" Hal teased.

"Naw, we just do that with the pigs. We cut up the cows into thick steaks and grill 'em just till the blood stops running."

Then Ray asked Hal about his service, and Hal blushed. "It's my eyes," he explained, touching his glasses. "My left eye's almost blind. But at least the deferment landed me a job with the Draft Board."

Cal turned cranky around seven o'clock, and Penny said, "He's adjusting to having his daddy home, we better get going."

Whatever Ray thought of us he kept to himself, but while saying good night to me he added, "Thank you for taking care of Penny. She was mighty lonesome until she met you."

Hal and Dorothy stayed until the dishes were done and Dorothy had a chance to give Daniel his bottle, rocking him until he fell fast asleep. As she handed him to me she kissed his forehead then whispered, "Thanks sis. It's such a blessing to be able to hold him."

Gisela and I stood out on the porch, watching Hal and Dorothy hold hands as they walked together behind Dad, the three of them heading down the hill to their hotel.

"I couldn't be happier than I am right this minute," Gisela said. "You certainly made the right decision inviting them out."

"Thanks to you," I answered. "And Ray thanked me for our friendship with Penny." Letting out a big sigh, I was filled with gratitude for having found the courage to include all of them in our lives. "Now we have your friends and my friends."

"That equals our friends," Gisela laughed. "Come on funny girl, let's go to bed."

❧

The following morning Dad was pruning roses in the front yard, and I was washing the breakfast dishes, when I heard a vehicle stop at the curb. Looking out the window, I saw an army jeep and a man in uniform who got out, looked around, then walked toward the gate before hesitating.

"Howdy," I heard Dad say. "Can I help you?"

"I'm looking for Ruth Thompson."

My heart stopped—*Duke! Something must have happened to him.* I dried my hands and hung my apron in its place in the pantry. The clock read ten forty-five as Hal bounced Daniel on his knee and Dorothy sat next to them on the sofa.

"Ruth," Dad called.

I steadied myself before walking outside on the porch. The man, tall and handsome, was chatting with Dad. As I got closer to them, I didn't see a telegram in his hand, and must have looked puzzled.

"I'm George, Duke told me to look you up. I didn't know how to contact you, so I thought I'd just come to the house." When he noticed me leaning in relief against Dad, he asked "Is this a bad time?"

"No, this is perfect. Come in." I opened the gate and did my best to collect my thoughts. "I'm so glad to meet you, and to see you are safely home." I introduced Dad, then continued, "Duke has told me so much about you."

I could see Dorothy watching us from the open doorway. *How am I going to introduce him to Hal and Dorothy?* Wishing I'd told them the whole truth about Duke, I needed a moment to calm down. "My brother and his wife are inside with Daniel. We can chat out here for a minute before we go in."

"I'm honored that you and Gisela are willing to accept me into your family. With things as tough as they were over there, the thought of all of you kept me going and gave me something to look forward to."

George took a photo out of his wallet—Duke had his arm around me, cradling Daniel in his free arm, and Gisela stood close on my other side. The snapshot, obviously handled many times, was frayed at the edges. He turned it over and showed us the words, *Absolute Love*, written in Duke's careful handwriting.

"It's the only safe way he dared to profess his love for me," George said as he put the picture away. Dad listened without comment.

As George spoke, my fears about introducing him to Hal and Dorothy disappeared. I invited him inside, and without noticing I was taking a step backward by keeping his relationship with Duke a secret, I introduced him with the simple explanation that he was Duke's friend from Chicago.

Dad shot me a look I hadn't seen in years, a look that told me he'd caught me in a lie. *What could I do?* There didn't seem to be any way to right the situation, so I just said "And this is Daniel" as I put him in George's arms.

"I've got to sit down," George said. And, like most of us in the last few months, couldn't hide his tears as Daniel nestled into his embrace and gave him a wet, bubbly smile.

Later in the day, Gisela insisted that George stay for dinner and offered him a drink. Hal served the cocktails and the men sat in the living room while we prepared the food.

Dorothy said grace before the meal as always.

"The only person missing is Duke," George said.

We all agreed, and began to pass the food around the table. Gisela had cooked the lamb chops George brought from the commissary, searing both sides golden brown, and served them with fried potatoes and sliced tomatoes.

George looked down at his plate, and said quietly "It's like part of me is still overseas." Then he began to talk openly about his relationship with Duke, and how much he missed him. "It feels so good to be among friends and not have to hide."

Hal turned pale as a clean white sheet, excusing himself as he left the table, with Dorothy following after him saying "I'm going to make sure he is all right."

"I didn't tell him about you and Duke," I admitted as I turned to George.

Dad, who had been unusually quiet, took my hand. "Remember Ruthie, Hal has changed. You need to trust him—and to trust yourself too."

"Amen" Gisela said, as if Dad had offered a second grace.

"I'm so sorry, I should have been more careful. It's me who should apologize. I've ruined a beautiful dinner. I should leave." But as George stood up to go, Hal returned from the other room.

"No. Sit down, please. It's me who needs to apologize."

"Wait a minute," Gisela said. "No one has done anything wrong." Then, turning to Hal and Dorothy, added, "We want to have you as part of our family, and hope you can embrace each of us as we are. Just as we embrace both of you."

Hal shook his head as he took it all in. "Well, I'm still confused, but who cares?"

As we all settled down and finished eating, Hal told George that Duke had been like a little brother to him. "I used to beat the pants off him in handball. Do you play?"

"You're on buddy," George said. "I'll pick you up around ten tomorrow morning."

George and Hal spent the next five days playing handball, then meeting Dad for a swim in the cove. And, George took over Duke's place on the couch, sharing meals and spending as much time as he could with us.

The day George left to join the rest of his regiment at Lindbergh Field, he vowed to convince Duke that when the war was over, the two of them would move to La Jolla.

"We can have our first family reunion out at the lake," Hal said. "Dorothy and I hope it will be a second home for all of you."

⚜

The day after George left we took Hal and Dorothy to the train station. Returning home to a quiet and strangely empty house, Gisela and I decided to go for a swim and asked Dad to watch Daniel.

We walked down to the same stretch of beach where I'd sworn I would never let Hal hold my child. Spreading our towels on the sand, we raced to the surf, diving into the smooth, translucent wall of water.

Swimming hard to catch the next wave at its crest, we tumbled head over heels as the ocean tossed us like rag dolls. Together, we fought against the power of the sea until we could swim parallel beyond the breaking waves.

In spite of the war that kept us all in an unrelenting state of worry and fear, the salty water purged the burdens of the past from my shoulders and filled me with hope. I had lived far too long in that same state of uncertainty while I allowed the opinions of others to overshadow my love for Gisela. It now seemed indefensible that I had deceived myself for so many years.

At that moment I knew that though the risks of living my authentic truth were great, the permanence of love, like the primal pull of the ocean waves, is a stronger force. In my heart, I also knew that even with the challenge of being raised in our unconventional family, Daniel would always be loved and protected.

Returning to the sand, we stretched out on our towels in the warmth of the resplendent last rays of the sun. Mesmerized by the constant splash of waves, I dozed until squabbling gulls woke me just as the sun appeared to sink into the sea, leaving the sky streaked with blazing shades of crimson and gold.

Rising on my elbows and squinting toward the horizon, my attention was drawn to the silhouette of a seabird bobbing on water that shimmered with the afterglow of the setting sun. It dived and disappeared.

"Did you see that?" I asked Gisela, who was pulling on a shirt over her swimsuit.

She shielded her eyes with her hand, gazing out in the direction I was pointing and together we watched the bird reappear in the distance. She waited a moment before she answered.

"I see a loon who made an arduous journey all the way to the ocean, and survived."

ACKNOWLEDGMENTS

Writing suits my introverted nature, but completing a novel cannot be accomplished alone, and I would like to thank everyone who has helped me write and publish *The Winter Loon*.

First of all, special thanks goes to my critique group: Alissa Lukara, Maggie McLaughlin, and Jodine Turner, all accomplished writers, who shared invaluable feedback under the guidance of author, editor, and writing coach Shoshana Alexander.

Writing is rewriting and editing is essential. Thank you to the editors who helped me along the way: Alan Rinzler and Alissa Lukara. Special thanks to Book Savvy Studio's Deborah Mokma for the final edit of the finished manuscript, and Chris Molé who brought my vision for the book cover to life. Many thanks also to Maggie McLaughlin for book design and production.

Huge thanks to my dear friends Sandy Knapp, Suzanne Addicott, Sally Holland, Patricia Sullivan, Stephanie Wikström, Kathleen Jakse, Ted and Judith Heimer, Ellen Case, and Francine Ladd who generously gave their time to read and share opinions on at least one of the many drafts.

My deep gratitude to Pat for his loving encouragement and tolerance of the need I had to protect my writing space and time, and for his unceasing patience when asked to listen to "just one more rewrite."

Author's Note

This fictional story is inspired by my mother, who died when I was nine and who had divulged very little information about her life, refusing even to answer any questions about my biological father. Estranged from her parents, brother, and uncles, she moved across the country from the Midwest to California, ending up in a remote area of the Mojave Desert far from the nearest town. From my earliest memories, the two of us lived as a family with her woman companion until shortly before her death. Some of the things she left behind were a few photos, a newspaper clipping of her as a rodeo competitor, and her master's degree certificate from the 1930s.

When I started writing, my purpose of embarking on a healing journey gradually transformed into this novel about a young woman who struggles to define herself in a world where she does not seem to fit. As I envisioned how my mother's life might have been if she was able to live her authentic truth, I realized how much, and how little, has changed for the LGBTQ community. It is my hope that this story about the healing power of love will positively influence anyone who reads it.

About Author

Lori Henriksen is a debut author who worked as a social worker and licensed family therapist in San Francisco, California before turning to writing. She now lives in Oregon, surrounded by a forest where trails that weave through the trees follow and cross a creek with crashing waterfalls. When she isn't writing, Lori can be found hiking the forest with her rescue dogs, puttering in her garden, or out and about doing research for her next novel. More information and her blog can be found at www.lorihenriksen.com.

Loon Migration

Every year before northern lakes freeze solitary loons, dressed in the camouflage of dull winter feathers, gather in groups to start their migration to winter on the open ocean where upon arrival they must quickly adjust to a new life that is extremely different from the freshwater lakes where they hatch. Even though loons are born with dormant glands that can filter salt, for some it can take time before the glands begin functioning. A new arrival at sea eases into the unfamiliar environment by drinking rainwater that dribbles along its beak or pools like a thin skin on the ocean's surface before mixing with the saltwater. In the absence of rain, a loon is forced to drink saltwater and eat briny fish, which can end its life if the glands have not sufficiently evolved. This filtering of salt is not a learned behavior, it is innate and essential for existence, and only those who adapt in time will survive.

CPSIA information can be obtained
at www.ICGtesting.com
Printed in the USA
FSHW01n0913130718
50169FS